Ja...

Jack Hight has a doctorate in ~~...~~ ...sity of Chicago. He lives with his wife, ~~...~~ ...d dog in Washington, DC, where he is currently finishing the Saladin Trilogy. Hight is the author of two acclaimed previous novels: *Siege*, and the first part of his Saladin Trilogy, *Eagle*. Both are available from John Murray.

Praise for Jack Hight

'This is an ambitious book, written on an ambitious scale, offering a fascinating picture of momentous events' *Daily Mail*

'Action, politics and drama are the hallmarks of this excellent series which gives a fascinating and balanced insight into one of the most turbulent periods in world history. The final showdown in the last of the trilogy should be one to savour' *Lancashire Evening Post*

'Excellent ... a trip to a distant and dangerous era' Barry Forshaw

Also by Jack Hight

Siege
Eagle

Kingdom

Book Two of the Saladin Trilogy

JACK HIGHT

JOHN MURRAY

First published in Great Britain in 2012 by John Murray (Publishers)
An Hachette UK Company

First published in paperback in 2012

1

The right of Jack Hight to be identified as the Author of the Work has been asserted by him in accordance with the Copyright, Designs and Patents Act 1988.

Maps drawn by Rosie Collins

A CIP catalogue record for this title is available from the British Library

ISBN 978-1-84854-533-5
Ebook ISBN 978-1-84854-532-8

Typeset in Montotype Bembo by Servis Filmsetting Ltd, Stockport, Cheshire

Printed and bound by Clays Ltd, St Ives plc

John Murray policy is to use papers that are natural, renewable and recyclable products and made from wood grown in sustainable forests. The logging and manufacturing processes are expected to conform to the environmental regulations of the country of origin.

John Murray (Publishers)
338 Euston Road
London NW1 3BH

www.johnmurray.co.uk

For my grandparents,
Jack and Patsy, Tom and Jean

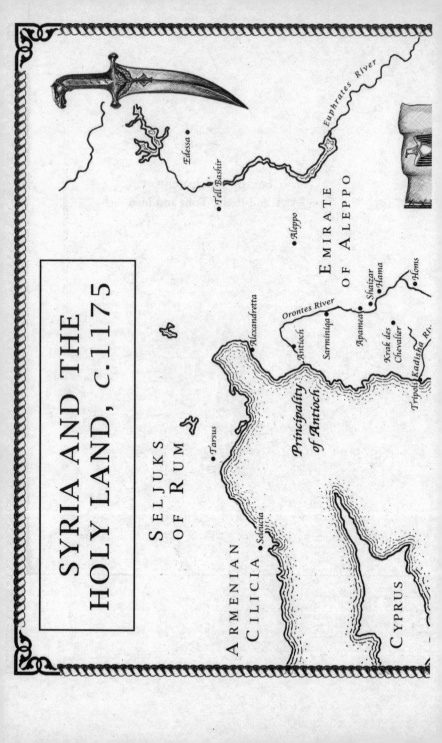

SYRIA AND THE HOLY LAND, C.1175

SELJUKS
OF RUM

ARMENIAN
CILICIA • Seleucia

• Tarsus

• Alexandretta

• Antioch

Orontes River

Principality
of Antioch

CYPRUS

• Edessa

• Tell Bashir

Euphrates River

• Aleppo

EMIRATE
OF ALEPPO

Sarminiqa

• Apamea

• Shaizar

• Hama

• Homs

Krak des
Chevalier

Tripoli Kadisha Riv

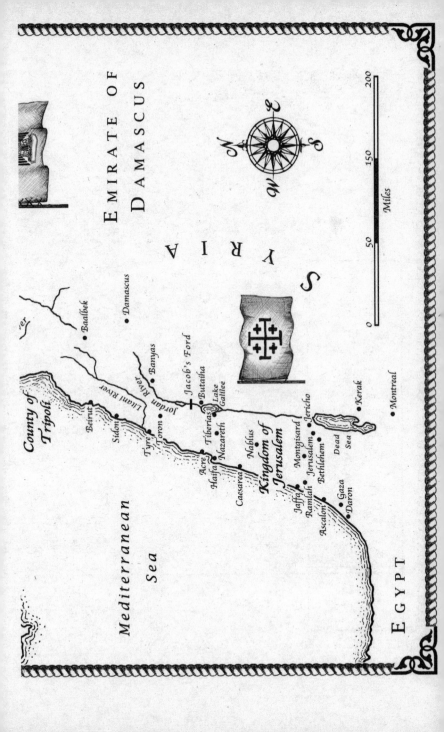

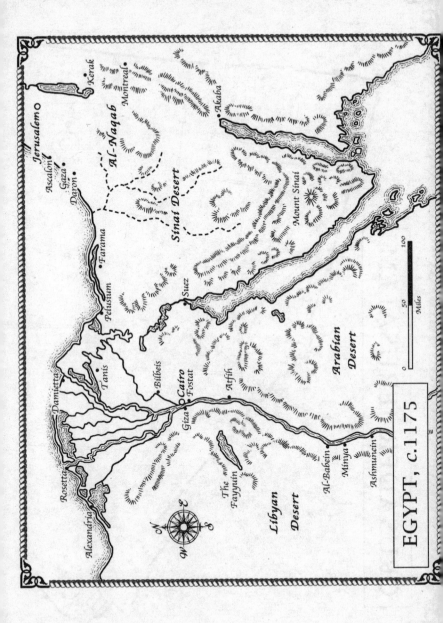

EGYPT, c.1175

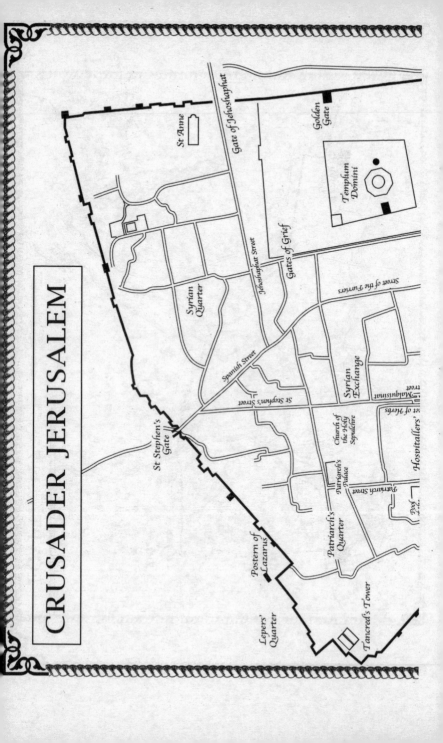

CRUSADER JERUSALEM

St Anne

Gate of Jehoshaphat

Golden Gate

Templum Domini

Syrian Quarter

Jehoshaphat Street

Gates of Grief

Spanish Street

Street of the Furriers

St Stephen's Street

Syrian Exchange

Malquisinat Street

St Stephen's Gate

Church of the Holy Sepulchre

Street of Herbs

Patriarch's Palace

Hospitallers'

Patriarch Street

Postern of Lazarus

Patriarch's Quarter

Prof ...

Lepers' Quarter

Tancred's Tower

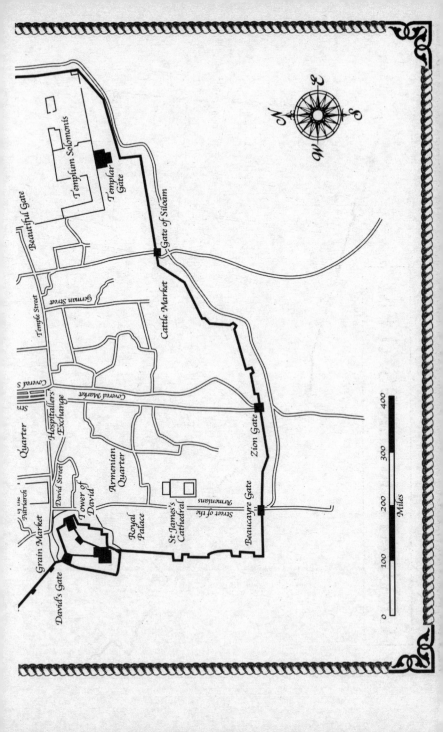

Part I
Kingdom of the Nile

Egypt, garden of the Nile. In those days it was weak after years of misrule – viziers betraying one another for power while the caliphs withdrew into luxurious seclusion. Egypt was weak but still rich. The Nile brought trade from the heart of Africa and nourished abundant crops, all of which fed the coffers of the caliph in Cairo. The Kingdom of the Nile was a fruit ripe for the plucking, and Crusader and Saracen alike longed to take it. Whoever controlled Egypt would eventually control the Holy Land. King Amalric in Jerusalem knew this. So did Nur ad-Din, the King of Syria. And so did Saladin . . .

The Chronicle of Yahya al-Dimashqi

Chapter 1

John's head jerked to the side as he was slapped. He blinked awake to the taste of blood in his mouth and looked about trying to orient himself, then groaned as the excruciating pain in his shoulders washed over him. He was still stretched out on the rack, his feet tied down at one end, his bound hands stretched too far above his head. He looked to the crank on his right. Its every turn stretched his hands and feet a little further apart. He must have fainted after the last turn. Past the crank he could see a small square window set high up in a stone wall. The light filtering through was dim. He was sure it had been day just a moment ago. How long had he been unconscious? As he watched, a hand grabbed and turned the crank. John howled as he felt his shoulders starting to dislocate. His vision dimmed and then someone slapped him again. His eyes blinked open to see Heraclius leaning over him.

The priest had an almost feminine beauty, with high cheek-bones, a thin nose and full lips. His deep-set eyes – as blue as the turquoise waters of Acre Harbour on the day years ago when John had first arrived in the Holy Land – narrowed slightly as they studied his victim. The priest smiled, betraying a grim satisfaction at the suffering he had wrought. 'Stay with me, Saxon,' he purred in heavily accented Latin. Heraclius was a half-educated country priest from the wild Auvergne in France, and he had a peasant's love of cruelty. He leaned forward to whisper

3

in John's ear. 'Tell me, why did you fight for the Saracens? Why did you betray the Cross?'

'I never betrayed the Faith,' John growled through gritted teeth.

'Liar!' Heraclius hissed. 'You killed your fellow Christians. You served the infidel, the forces of Satan.' Heraclius placed his hand on the crank. John flinched. But the priest did not turn the crank; he made a show of studying it, running his finger lightly over its handle. 'The rack is a dreadful thing. A few more turns and your arms will be pulled from their sockets. You will be crippled, unable to lift a sword ever again.' He bent over so that his breath was hot on John's face. Their eyes met. 'You spent many years in Aleppo, Saxon. You know its fortifications, its weaknesses. Tell me: how can we take the city?'

'I have told you. It will take a siege of many months. You will have to starve the people out.'

'No! There must be a secret entrance, a weak point.' John shook his head. 'I see.' Heraclius sighed and then straightened. When he spoke again it was in a louder voice, as if he were delivering a homily in church. 'All that happens is part of God's plan, Saxon, even your faithlessness. It was He who determined that the infidels would capture you; that you would betray Him by serving them. And it was God who delivered you into my hands. Do you know why? Because you have come to know our enemy, their cities, their people, their walls. You have been sent to us by God as the key to their destruction.'

'You are wasting your time. I know no secrets.'

'We shall see. Perhaps we simply need to find new ways to motivate you. Pepin! Bring the coals.'

John twisted his head to the side and saw a brawny, square-faced guard approaching, his hands wrapped in cloth. He carried a shallow bronze dish containing a layer of smouldering coals. He set the dish on the table beside the rack. Heraclius took a pair of pincers and selected a chestnut-sized coal. He held it just

4

inches from John's bare stomach and then moved it up past John's chest towards his face. John tried to twist his head away, but Pepin grabbed hold of his ears, holding him still. Heraclius held the coal just above the bridge of John's nose. The heat was intense – like the blast from an oven – and within moments John felt as if his forehead were on fire. An acrid smell filled the room as his eyebrows began to singe. Heraclius bent close so that his face was lit red by the glowing coal. 'Tell me about your master, this Yusuf.'

John swallowed. 'He is Emir of Tell Bashir. His father is the governor of Damascus and his uncle, Shirkuh, commands the armies of the Saracen king.'

'And how did you come to be in his service?'

'I came to the Holy Land with the Second Crusade. I was captured at Damascus and purchased by Yusuf as a slave. He was only a boy then.'

'You saved his life at the battle of Butaiha. Why?'

John hesitated, his eyes fixed on the burning coal. 'Yusuf is my friend.'

'He is an infidel!'

John looked away from the coal and met Heraclius's eyes. 'He is the best man I have ever known.'

'I see.' Heraclius turned away and dropped the coal back into the dish. John exhaled. 'Oh, I am not done with you,' the priest said. 'Not yet.' He nodded to Pepin, who placed the coals on a shelf just beneath John's feet. At first the warmth was almost pleasant, but then John's feet grew uncomfortably hot, as if he had set them too long beside a fire. He twitched, trying to jerk himself away, but his arms were still stretched to breaking point, and the motion caused a spasm of pain in his left shoulder. He lay still and squeezed his eyes shut, his teeth grinding as he fought against the burning in his feet. He thought he could feel blisters starting to form on his heels. And then the heat was gone. Pepin had removed the dish of coals. A moment later Heraclius's face reappeared above him.

'What of Nur ad-Din, the Saracen king? You met him, yes?' John nodded. 'How is he protected? Could an assassin reach him?'

'In camp he is surrounded by the mamluks of his private guard. In Aleppo he rarely leaves the citadel. No assassin could reach him alive.'

'Do you swear it?'

John nodded. 'By Christ's blood.'

'We shall see.' Heraclius gestured to Pepin, who replaced the dish of coals.

The pain came more quickly this time. John's entire body tensed and he began to squirm despite the pain in his shoulders. To keep from shouting, he bit his tongue so hard that it began to bleed. Heraclius watched impassively. John could smell burning flesh – his own. 'I speak the truth!' he shouted. 'What do you want from me, you bastard? What do you want me to say?'

'There, there. I believe you,' Heraclius soothed. He frowned. 'I was wrong. You are not the key to defeating the Saracens. Pepin, take the coals away.'

The heat vanished. Heraclius fetched a wet cloth, with which he gently dabbed John's feet. The relief was so overwhelming that John almost fainted. 'Thank God,' he murmured.

'Do not thank him yet,' Heraclius said. 'Your suffering has just begun.'

'But you said you believe me!'

'And I do.' Heraclius set the wet cloth aside. He crossed the room and paused before a table covered with instruments of torture: thumbscrews, hooks for tearing flesh, metal claws known as Spanish ticklers, and other devices whose use John hoped he would never learn. The priest picked up one of these last objects, a pear-shaped metal contraption with a wing nut at the top. 'Now that we have discovered what you know, I must see to your salvation. Your time amongst the infidels has stained your soul. We must wash it clean.' As he began to turn the wing nut the pear expanded, four separate pieces of metal spreading out. 'You must suffer for betraying the faith. It is the only way to find salvation.' The priest nodded to Pepin. 'Hold his mouth open. He shall pay the price for breaking his crusader's oath.'

John clenched his mouth shut, but Pepin grabbed his lower jaw with one hand and pulled back on his nose with the other. The second John's mouth opened, Heraclius shoved in the pear. It tasted of metal and blood. Heraclius gave the wing nut a twist and the pear expanded slightly, forcing John's mouth to open wider. John gagged and coughed. He jerked his head side to side, trying to spit the pear out, but Pepin grabbed him by the ears and held him still.

Heraclius's eyes betrayed an eager excitement as he watched John squirm. 'The pear of anguish is an ingenious piece of work, especially useful for punishing blasphemers and oath breakers. First, your jaw will dislocate.' Heraclius gave the wing nut another twist, forcing John's jaws further apart so that they began to ache. 'Then the skin of your mouth will tear, disfiguring you.' He gave another twist. John's jaw felt as if it were going to snap. His fingernails dug into his palms as he fought the pain. 'If I expand the pear all the way, then you will never lie again: you will be unable to speak.'

Heraclius reached out to give the wing nut another turn, but stopped at the sound of booted feet approaching. A dozen soldiers in mail entered the torture chamber, a tonsured priest in black robes at their head. John recognized the priest; it was William of Tyre, who John had met long ago when he first came to the Holy Land.

'Stop!' William demanded. 'Leave that man be!'

Heraclius turned. 'The Patriarch turned the Saxon over to me. You have no authority here, William.'

'I have the King's backing and the King's men. That man is a noble. If he is to suffer then he must first stand trial before his peers.'

'The Saxon killed our men. He threw his lot in with the infidel Saracens. He must be made to suffer if he is to be redeemed!' Heraclius reached again for the wing nut at the end of the pear.

'Stop him!'

Two guards grabbed Heraclius's arms and pulled him away. William went to the rack and pulled a lever, releasing the tension on the ropes that bound John's hands and feet. The guards removed the pear and began to untie John's bonds. He groaned in relief as he gingerly flexed his arms and legs, and then gasped as a stab of pain shot through his left shoulder. William helped him to sit up just in time for John to see Heraclius being dragged from the room by two soldiers. At the door Heraclius managed to shrug them off. He turned to face John and William.

'This is not the end!' Heraclius spat. 'The Saxon betrayed his oath. I will see that he goes before the High Court. And mark my words, William: he will burn!'

John awoke to the sound of a door creaking. He blinked against the bright light streaming in from a window above his bed. Yesterday, after his feet had been bandaged, he had been carried to this tiny room in the compound of the Knights Hospitaller. Overcome with exhaustion and pain, he had passed out as soon as they laid him in his bed.

Now he stretched out and rolled over, away from the wall. The door to the room was open and a lean young man in monk's brown robes stood in the corner. The monk was clean-shaven and tonsured, and had sunken cheeks, a weak chin and protruding eyes. He reminded John of a praying mantis. He was sniffing at the contents of the bronze chamber pot. 'His black bile is weak,' the monk murmured to himself.

'Who are you?' John sat up, wincing at the pain in his left shoulder.

The monk looked up from the chamber pot. 'Ah, you are

awake. Good. My name is Deodatus, and I am a doctor. Father William has sent me to tend to you.' He approached and nodded towards John's feet. 'May I?'

John swung himself around so his feet hung off the bed. Deodatus began to unwrap the bandages. The soles of John's feet were covered in angry, red blisters that oozed a sticky, clear fluid. Deodatus touched one of the blisters, and John winced in pain. 'Your flesh is hot. Your humours are out of balance,' the doctor said gravely. 'I understand you were subjected to the rack?'

'Yes. I cannot move my left arm without pain.'

The doctor grasped John's left wrist with one hand and placed his other hand on John's shoulder. As Deodatus lifted the arm, a stabbing pain shot through John's shoulder, as if a white-hot iron had been plunged into the joint. ''Sblood!' John cursed through clenched teeth.

Deodatus shook his head and then went to a small, leather-bound trunk. He took out a handful of dried roots, a mortar and a pestle. He murmured the Pater Noster as he ground the root to powder.

'What is that?' John asked.

'Daffodil root for the burns on your feet. It will draw the heat out.' The doctor finished grinding the root and went to the chamber pot, from which he scooped out some faeces. John's eyes widened as the doctor placed the faeces in the mortar and mixed it in with the daffodil root. The doctor approached the bed with the foul-smelling mixture.

John drew back his feet. 'Keep that away from me!'

'The faeces will help to restore your black bile,' Deodatus assured him.

John's nose wrinkled in disgust. 'Do you have any aloe?'

The doctor raised his eyebrows. 'Aloe?'

'A plant. It helps to cure burns. The doctor Ibn Jumay says—'

'A Jewish doctor?' Deodatus huffed. 'His medicine will send you to the grave.'

9

'I'll take my chances with Jewish medicine. Keep that shit away from my feet.'

'Very well. But you are still too sanguine. I must bleed you to reduce your heat.'

'No,' John replied firmly. 'You will not.'

Deodatus spread his hands. 'If you will not accept my aid then I cannot be responsible for the consequences. At least allow me to treat your shoulder. I fear the damage will fester, drawing foul humours to it.' Deodatus reached into his trunk and pulled out a short saw. He tested the blade with his thumb. 'The arm must come off.' Deodatus stepped over to the bed. He gripped John's shoulder and brought the saw blade down towards the joint. 'This will hurt.'

'Yes, it will.' John grabbed the doctor's cowl, pulled him forward and head-butted him. Deodatus stumbled back, his eyes wide and his nose dripping blood.

'You're mad! You'll die if I don't take the arm.'

'Then I'll die. If you touch my arm again, you'll join me.'

'Damned fool,' Deodatus muttered as he hurriedly closed up his trunk and tucked it under his arm. 'God help you!' On the way out he bumped into William.

William watched the doctor go and then turned to John, eyebrows raised. 'What happened?'

'The man is a quack. He doesn't know the first thing about medicine.'

'But that is the court physician!'

'A quack,' John repeated. William looked as if he would pursue the matter, but then shrugged. John met his gaze. 'I owe you my thanks. Were it not for you, I would still be in that dungeon.'

'I did not do it for you. You may be of some use to us. But first we must save you from the hangman's noose. The High Court meets tomorrow to hear your case. I will defend you.'

'Why? All that Heraclius says is true. I chose to fight for the Saracens.'

'I do not share Heraclius's belief that suffering is the only road to salvation. Whatever sins you have committed, you should be given the chance to redeem them in service of the Kingdom. But if I am to defend you, I must know the truth. How did you come to be in the service of the Saracens?'

John closed his eyes, his mind racing back to his first days in the Holy Land. 'I came as a soldier with the Second Crusade. I was captured at the siege of Damascus and purchased by Najm ad-Din Ayub, now the wali – the governor – of Damascus. I served as a household slave and then as the personal servant of Ayub's son, Yusuf. After I saved his life, he freed me.'

'And why did you not return to your people?'

'Return to what? The lord I had served, Reynald, betrayed me at Damascus. It was because of him that I was captured. And the Frankish soldiers I had fought beside were brutes. Yusuf was different. He was cultured and kind. He was my friend.'

'So when you were captured at Butaiha, you were fighting for this Yusuf. He was your lord?'

'Yes.'

'Then I will argue that you merely did your duty as a liegeman.'

John's forehead creased as he thought of the men who had died at his hands. 'But I broke my crusader's oath. I killed Franks, more than one. I deserve to die.'

'We have all fallen short of the glory of God, John, but death will not wash away your sins. You can only redeem your soul through action.'

'How?' John demanded bitterly. 'It is not only Franks that I killed.' He paused, thinking back to his home in England, to the manor of his childhood. 'I killed my brother.'

'Surely you had a reason?'

'He betrayed my father to the Normans in return for land. My father was hanged, along with a dozen other local thanes.' John shook his head. The reasons seemed almost unreal now, so long had it been since John saw England. Yet the reality of his brother's death was always fresh in his mind. 'He was a bastard, but he was my brother. I killed him, and nothing I can do will bring him back. It will not bring any of them back.'

'No, but you can save others. God has sent you to us for a reason. You have lived in both worlds, East and West. You have spent years at the court in Aleppo. You can speak to the Saracens as we cannot, understand them as we cannot. You can help to bridge the gap that divides us. That is your one true chance at salvation.'

'And if I die? Will the fire not wash me clean, as Heraclius says?'

'Look into your soul. Do you believe that suffering will save you?'

John thought back on his years in the Holy Land: the brutal march to Damascus; his capture and near death; the beatings he had suffered as a slave; his torture at the hands of Heraclius. None of it had washed away his guilt. He met William's eyes. 'Show me what I must do.'

'First we must get you through this trial. You have but to answer truthfully any questions that are asked of you.'

'What are my chances?'

'God does not deal in chance. We must trust in Him. I will come for you tomorrow, when it is time.' William turned to leave.

'You did not answer my question, Father,' John called after him. 'What are my chances?'

William looked back and shook his head. 'Not good. Heraclius has stacked the court against you. And the punishment for treason is death.'

The bells of the Church of the Holy Sepulchre were ringing to call the canons to morning prayers as John hobbled after William into the audience chamber where the High Court was meeting. He was barefoot, and the thick rugs that carpeted the floor were

12

a blessed relief to his blistered feet after the hard stone pavement of the courtyard. The members of the court waited on the far side of the room. King Amalric sat on a simple wooden throne, the dome of the church visible through the window behind him. He was young, perhaps John's age, but whereas John was lean and fit, the king was heavy-set, pudgy even. He had a ruddy complexion, straight hair the colour of straw and a slightly darker beard. His piercing blue eyes met John's across the hall, and the King laughed suddenly, a clipped laugh that sounded loud against the silence of the hall. With a start John realized that he had met him before. When he first arrived in the Holy Land, John had attended a meeting of the High Court, and Amalric – only a child at the time – had been there. John had never forgotten that peculiar boy with his clear blue eyes and strange laugh. Now Amalric was king.

Two men framed the throne, and Heraclius sat beside two others on one of the benches that ran along the side walls. A single man sat on the bench opposite them. 'This is the High Court?' John whispered to William. 'The last time I attended there were hundreds of men.'

'Only four are needed for a quorum.' William gestured to John's right, where a dour, bony man dressed in gold-embroidered robes sat beside Heraclius. 'That is the Patriarch of Jerusalem. He is the one who turned you over to be tortured.' Next to the patriarch was a dark-haired man with a thick beard and unruly eyebrows that met in the middle. Over his mail armour he wore a black surcoat bearing the Knights Hospitaller's distinctive cross: four white arrowheads, all touching at the tips. 'Gilbert d'Assailly is Grand Master of the Hospitallers. He is an Englishman like you, but don't expect any mercy from that quarter. He hates the Saracens with a passion. I have more hope for that man there.' William pointed to the opposite side of the hall where a man with steel-grey hair sat straight-backed, wearing a white surcoat emblazoned with a red cross. 'Bertrand de Blanchefort is Grand Master of the Knights Templar, and he is a man of reason. As for the King, his constable Humphrey and the seneschal Guy' – he waved to the two stern, middle-aged men flanking the throne – 'I do not know where they stand.'

They stopped a dozen feet from the throne, and John and William both knelt. 'Rise,' Guy commanded in a harsh voice. Judging from his olive skin and slight build, John guessed he had Saracen blood in him. As seneschal, it was Guy's duty to preside over the court. 'Present yourselves.'

'I am Iain of Tatewic, called John.'

'Silence!' the seneschal snapped. 'You have been accused of oath breaking. You are not to speak before this court.'

John opened his mouth to reply, but William shot him a warning look. 'I am William of Tyre. I will speak for the accused.'

'Very well.' The seneschal nodded towards Heraclius. 'The accuser will present his case.'

Heraclius rose, bowed to King Amalric and then stepped to the centre of the hall. He cleared his throat. 'This Saxon, John of Tatewic, has betrayed his crusader's oath, betrayed his faith and betrayed the Kingdom. He served the Saracens of his own free will. By his own admission, he fought with them at Banyas and Butaiha, killing dozens of his fellow Christians. He has committed treason against the Kingdom and sacrilege against the Holy Church.' He paused to look each judge in the eye. 'For justice and for the salvation of his soul, he must die for his crimes.' Heraclius bowed again and returned to his seat.

The seneschal looked to William. 'What does the accused say to these charges?'

'He pleads innocent to treason and sacrilege.'

The seneschal looked to Heraclius. 'I understand you have a witness?' Heraclius nodded. Guy raised his voice to address the armed men at the far end of the hall. 'Guards! Bring the witness.' A guard stepped out and returned a moment later with a short man in a loose-fitting burnoose. He had close-set eyes and a turned-up nose that gave him a piggish appearance. A gruesome gash ran along the left side of his face from his hairline to his jaw. The wound was recent, still angry and red, oozing blood near his temple. The man passed John and bowed before the throne. 'Present yourself,' the seneschal ordered him.

'I am Harold, a sergeant and vassal of the King.' Sergeants were Frankish warriors who, in return for title to their lands in the Kingdom of Jerusalem, served as foot-soldiers in the armies of their lord.

'Do you swear by God that you will speak the truth?' the seneschal asked.

'Aye, I do.'

The seneschal nodded. 'Heraclius, you may question the witness.'

Harold did not wait to be questioned. He pointed at John. 'That whoreson killed my brother! And he did this to me.' Harold touched the wound on his face.

'Where was this?' Heraclius asked.

'Butaiha. We had routed the Saracens. My men were mopping up, taking captives for ransom, when he arrived on horseback like some demon out of hell. He rode into a company of over one hundred men to rescue a Saracen lord. They killed seven of us, and the two of them rode out again unscathed. I have never seen the like. He is a man possessed, a demon in human flesh.'

'A man possessed,' Heraclius repeated. 'A demon who kills his own. Let us consign this demon to the fires from which he sprang!'

John noticed that the patriarch and Gilbert the Hospitaller were both nodding their heads in approval. King Amalric was listening carefully, but his expression remained neutral. William addressed the King. 'John is no demon, sire. He is a warrior who fought in defence of himself and of the lord to whom he had sworn allegiance. His honour was at stake.'

Heraclius shook his head. 'It was not honour that led him

to kill his fellow Christians, but his depravity. What are the Saracens but the hand of Satan made manifest in this world? When the Saxon killed for his Saracen master, who was he killing for?'

'He fought for his lord, nothing more,' William insisted. 'How many of you here have killed your fellow Christians in France or England? Gilbert and Bertrand, you have faced one another in battle. There was nothing heretical about that.'

'Yes, but I was not under a crusader's oath,' Gilbert replied. 'I had not sworn to fight only the Saracens and to aid my fellow Christians.'

'John's crusade was long over,' William replied. 'It ended at Damascus when our army was routed and he was captured fighting for Christ. Now, at long last he has returned to the fold. Let us welcome him back. He has suffered enough.'

'He has not!' Heraclius shouted. 'His soul is at stake. Only fire can purify it!'

William's nose wrinkled in disgust. 'Torturing this man further will only stain your black soul, Heraclius. It will not save John.'

There was a moment of silence, and then the constable Humphrey stood. He was barrel-chested and had a handsome, broad face. 'This court is not fit to decide the fate of this man's soul,' he said, his voice low and rasping, like the sound of steel on a whetstone. 'That is a matter for the Church. We are here because the safety of the Kingdom is at stake. I fear that if we let this Saxon live, more men will join the enemy. We all know of the Saracens' wealth. If there are no consequences for betraying the Kingdom, what will stop them from buying the allegiance of our sergeants? We will find our own people turned against us.'

'Hear, hear!' Gilbert agreed.

'But John did not join the Saracens of his free will,' William pointed out. 'He was captured and enslaved.'

Humphrey shook his head. 'He still chose to fight for them.'

'He chose to serve his lord, who was a Saracen. John is a man of honour: he could not do otherwise.'

'I too am a man of honour,' said the grey-haired Templar, Bertrand. 'If this man fought in the service of the lord to whom he was bound, then I am inclined to be lenient.' Bertrand turned to John. 'Tell me truly, John: why did you fight our men?'

'I owed my life to Yusuf. I fought to repay that debt.'

'And if you had it to do again?'

'I would do the same.'

Bertrand looked to Amalric. 'I cannot fault him for that. If John will swear an oath to never again take up arms against the Kingdom, then I say we pardon him.'

'An oath? I do not trust the word of this Saxon,' the Hospitaller Gilbert protested.

John spoke quietly. 'I am a man of my word.'

Gilbert snorted. 'You have already betrayed us once. If we free you, how long will it be before you betray us again?'

'I am no traitor! It was Reynald who betrayed me in Damascus and left me to die.'

'Prince Reynald?' the seneschal demanded. 'The former ruler of Antioch?'

John nodded.

'You see!' Gilbert declared. 'He besmirches the honour of a brave man in order to save himself. How can we trust this deceiver?'

John's hands balled into fists. He took a step towards Gilbert.

'Do you wish to strike me, Saxon?' the Hospitaller sneered. 'Come. You need to be taught a lesson.'

'That is enough, Gilbert!' Amalric's voice was sharply authoritative. 'I have heard enough.' He looked to Heraclius. 'Do you have anything to add?' The priest shook his head. 'William?'

'I ask only for lenience. If John has done wrong, let him earn his forgiveness in service to the Kingdom.'

Amalric nodded to the seneschal Guy, who addressed them in a loud voice. 'The accused can only be found guilty by a clear majority – four or more votes. If guilty, John shall suffer the fate of a traitor. He will be crucified and hung from the Jaffa Gate for one week. At the end of that time, his body shall be burned.' The seneschal paused to allow his words to sink in. 'Patriarch, what is your verdict?'

The patriarch stood stiffly. 'Guilty.'

Gilbert rose next. 'Guilty.'

'And you, Bertrand?' the seneschal asked.

'Not guilty!' the grand master of the Templars declared firmly.

The seneschal looked to Humphrey. 'Guilty,' the constable said gravely. John felt his mouth go dry. That was three guilty verdicts. He held his breath as the seneschal cleared his throat.

'I pronounce him not guilty,' Guy said. 'King Amalric will cast the deciding vote.'

John met Amalric's blue eyes. The king hesitated for a moment before looking away. 'Guilty.'

John felt suddenly faint, and William held his arm to steady him. John stood with his head bowed as the seneschal delivered the verdict. 'John of Tatewic, you have been pronounced guilty of treason. Tomorrow, you will be crucified before the Jaffa Gate.'

The guards came forward and took hold of John's arms. They began to escort him from the room.

'Wait!' William called. He went to John and spoke in a low voice. 'There is a way to save yourself. You can challenge the judgement. Fight to prove your innocence.'

'Fight? I can barely stand.'

'God favours the innocent, John.'

'God does not play favourites,' John muttered. But if he were to die, he would rather do so with a sword in hand. He raised his voice. 'I challenge the judgement. I will fight those who think me guilty.'

The judges turned to look at him wide-eyed. 'But this is ridiculous!' Heraclius sputtered. 'The court has decided.'

'Our laws grant him the right to challenge those who condemned him,' the seneschal declared. 'But to prove his innocence, he must defeat all four of them – or their chosen champions – in a single day.' He looked to John. 'Are you certain?'

'Yes.'

'Very well. We will meet in the courtyard at noon tomorrow, and John of Tatewic will fight to prove his innocence.'

John stood in the palace courtyard and looked up at the dome of the Church of the Holy Sepulchre. Its top had disappeared into the fine, misting rain that beaded on John's mail armour. He felt William's hand on his shoulder. 'It is almost time,' the priest said. John nodded and lowered his gaze to the courtyard. The stones that paved it were slick with moisture. That would work to John's disadvantage. His feet were a mess of torn skin and burst blisters; he had almost fainted from the pain when he pulled on his boots. The slick footing would further limit his mobility.

Across the courtyard, King Amalric, Gilbert and Humphrey stood in their mail. The seneschal was there too, along with Heraclius and the patriarch, who had brought a champion to fight for him – Harold, the man with the long gash on his face. The men drew straws to see who would fight first, and the sergeant Harold selected the shortest straw. He grinned and looked to John. 'Now you will pay for what you did to my brother.'

John did not reply. He exaggerated his limp as he walked to the centre of the courtyard. Anything he could do to make Harold over-confident would help. It was the only advantage that John had.

William handed John a three-foot sword with a grip of worn leather and a wide blade of dark-grey steel. John slashed it side to side, testing its balance. The priest offered John a shield. John tried to lift it, but a blinding pain tore through his shoulder. ''Sblood,' he growled and dropped the shield. 'It's no use. Find something to bind my arm to my body. I don't want it getting in my way.' William untied the cord about his waist and looped it around John, cinching it tight to pin John's left arm to his torso. 'My helmet,' John said.

William slid the open-faced, iron helmet over John's head. John turned to face Harold. The sergeant was a squat, thick-necked man. He, too, had opted to fight without a shield. He held his sword with both hands.

The seneschal stepped between the combatants. 'The swords have been dulled to prevent serious injury. You will fight until one of you yields or cannot continue.' He stepped out of the ring. 'Touch swords and begin.'

John turned sideways to protect his vulnerable left side. They touched swords, and Harold attacked immediately, charging and hacking down with a mighty, two-handed blow. John parried and stepped to the side and knelt, raking his sword left to right and catching Harold in the shins. With a cry of pain the sergeant fell forward, losing his sword and landing hard on the stone pavement. As Harold rolled on to his back, John knelt on top of him, slamming his knee into the man's chest. He pressed the edge of his sword against Harold's neck. 'Yield!' Harold spat in John's face. John smashed his sword's hilt into the sergeant's face, splitting his lip. He hit Harold again, spattering the stones of the courtyard with blood.

'Enough! Enough!' Amalric roared. 'John is the victor.'

John used his sword to push himself up, wincing at the pain in his feet. He hobbled towards William, who was staring at him wide-eyed. 'God is surely with you, John!'

'God had nothing to do with it. Harold was angry and over-confident. That won't happen twice.'

Across the courtyard, Harold had been dragged to the side, and now sat cradling his face in his hands. The other men were again choosing straws. The constable, Humphrey, held up the short one. Without a word he pulled on his helmet and picked up the sword that Harold had dropped. Humphrey was about John's height and size, but a few years older.

'Careful of this one,' William warned. 'The constable commands the King's armies. He is a formidable warrior.'

John faced off across from Humphrey. The two men touched swords, and Humphrey began to circle around the edge of the ring, forcing John to turn in order to keep his opponent in front of him. Each step brought a sharp pain in John's feet. Humphrey kept circling, refusing to close. 'Come on, you bastard,' John growled under his breath.

Suddenly, Humphrey charged. John just managed to turn the constable's sword aside before Humphrey slammed into him, bowling him over. Humphrey landed on top of John, and the two men skidded across the slick stones of the courtyard. John managed to throw Humphrey off, but struggled to rise with his arm pinned to his side. Humphrey was already on his feet while John was still on his knees. The constable attacked with an overhead chop. John parried, and Humphrey kicked out, catching John in the chest. John fell back into a somersault and landed again on his knees. Humphrey charged with his sword held high. As he swung down, John threw himself forward under the blow, slamming into the constable's knees. Humphrey flipped forward and landed hard, giving John time to push himself to his feet. Humphrey had also risen, and the two warriors faced off.

Humphrey began to circle again. This time, John did not wait for him to attack. Gritting his teeth against the pain in his feet, he charged, thrusting for Humphrey's chest. The constable was caught off guard and just managed to sidestep the blow. John spun and slashed for his head. Humphrey jumped back out of the way but slipped on the slick pavement. His guard came down, and John swung for his head to finish the fight. Somehow, Humphrey managed to block the blow. Their blades grated against one another and locked at the hilt, bringing the two men face to face. John head-butted Humphrey, who staggered back, his blond beard matted with blood from his nose. John attacked again, putting all his strength behind a slashing back-handed blow. Humphrey parried, but John's sword glanced off the constable's blade and caught him on the side of the helmet, leaving a deep dent. Humphrey fell to lie unconscious at John's feet.

The seneschal proclaimed the obvious: 'John is the victor.'

A moment later, Humphrey's eyes blinked open and focused on John. 'Well fought.'

John dropped his sword and extended his hand to help Humphrey to his feet. 'I had more to fight for.'

'*Hmph.*' Humphrey pulled off his helmet and gingerly touched the knot forming on the side of his head. He picked up John's sword and handed it to him. 'I like you, Saxon. I hope you live.'

Amalric and the patriarch had already drawn straws. The king held the short one. He had begun to put on his helmet when the seneschal placed a hand on his arm. 'Sire, do you not wish to choose a champion?'

Amalric shrugged off the seneschal's hand and pulled on his helmet. 'I will fight for myself.'

'But sire!' the patriarch protested. 'You could be injured, or worse.'

'How can I condemn this man to death if I am not willing to risk my own life?'

Amalric stepped into the ring and picked up the dulled sword. He rolled his broad shoulders to loosen them. The king was a large man, fleshy but strong looking, and he was fresh. At least the pain in John's feet had dulled, although he dreaded what he would find when he removed his boots. He turned sideways to the king and raised his sword.

'God save you,' Amalric said. He touched his sword to John's, then attacked straight off, grunting as he hacked down at

John's head. John parried, but the force of the blow almost knocked his sword from his hand. He gave ground as Amalric hammered at him, chopping down again and again. John managed to spin away, but Amalric was on him immediately, slashing for John's chest. John jumped backwards to avoid the blow. Amalric stepped forward and reversed the direction of his blade, sweeping it up towards John's head. John ducked and then slipped away to the centre of the ring. He went on the attack, thrusting at Amalric's chest. The king knocked the blow aside, and John spun, bringing his sword in a wide arc towards his opponent's head. His blade was met by the king's steel. John attacked again with a flurry of thrusts, but Amalric easily turned aside each blow. John was breathing hard and his arm was tiring. He had to end this fight soon, and there was only one way to get close enough to strike.

He began to retreat, letting Amalric come to him. The king gripped his sword with both hands and levelled a wicked blow at John's side. John did not even attempt to block it. He raised his sword over his head and took the blow with a grunt, feeling a sharp stab of pain as a rib snapped. Before Amalric could recover, John stepped inside his guard and brought his sword down, slamming it into the crown of the king's helmet and leaving a deep dent. The king stumbled back, a trickle of blood running down his forehead. John attacked, but Amalric recovered in time to parry his thrust. Their swords locked together, and the king shoved John, who went reeling back across the ring.

John stood bent over and gasping, each breath an agony. Across from him, Amalric pulled off his ruined helmet and cast it aside. His blond hair was matted with blood. 'My lord!' the seneschal gasped as he stepped forward.

Amalric waved him back. 'Let me finish this,' he growled and raised his sword.

John did likewise. He straightened and forced himself to smile. He would show no weakness, nothing that might give Amalric an advantage. 'I am waiting, sire.'

Amalric charged with a roar. At the last second, John threw himself at the king's legs, but Amalric was ready: he leapt over John and landed on his feet. John rolled and had begun to push himself to his feet when the king's sword slammed into his back, knocking him flat. Amalric stepped on John's sword hand and then kicked his sword away. John rolled on to his back and found himself looking up at the point of Amalric's blade. 'Well fought, John. But the fight is over. Do you yield?'

John tried to rise, but Amalric stomped on his chest, forcing him back down. John looked past the king's blade to his blue eyes, and then to the grey sky beyond. So this was how it ended. John closed his eyes. 'I yield.'

John sat hunched over, his head between his knees, staring at the damp dirt floor of his cell. Today was the day that he would die. From somewhere close by came the sound of dripping water. How many more drops, he wondered, until they came for him? How many more before he was crucified?

The dripping was swallowed up by the sound of approaching footsteps. John shivered, despite himself. The time had come. The footsteps stopped outside his cell. He looked up and was surprised to see William on the other side of the steel bars. 'I have brought someone to see you,' the priest said.

William moved aside, and Amalric stepped into the pool of torchlight before the cell. John tried to stand, but the pain from his blistered feet was too great. He sank back down. 'Forgive me if I do not rise, sire.' Amalric waved away the apology. 'Why have you come?' John asked wearily. 'Do you wish to see what a dead man looks like?'

'You are not dead yet, John of Tatewic.' Amalric produced a key and unlocked the cell. He pulled the door open. 'I have come to free you.'

John blinked stupidly. 'What?'

'I have pardoned you,' Amalric explained as he stepped into

the cell. 'I have need of men like you, John. You are a man of courage. You almost beat me yesterday fighting with one arm, after having defeated two great warriors.'

'You are wasting your time, sire. I will not fight the Saracens.'

'I do not want you to fight. I want you to serve at my court. I am surrounded by spies and intriguers. I could use someone from the outside, someone who is loyal to me alone. And I want you to tutor my young son in the ways of our enemy. You know the Saracens better than any of us. I want Prince Baldwin to speak their tongue, to know their ways. Who better to teach him? Will you serve me, John?'

'I already have a lord. I cannot serve two masters.'

Amalric frowned. 'If you will not serve me, then you will die, John.'

'We are not asking you to betray your Saracen lord,' William added, 'but to help bring about peace between our peoples. This is a chance to redeem yourself, John. A chance to earn your salvation.'

John hesitated a moment longer. He nodded. 'Very well.'

'There is one condition,' Amalric warned. 'You must swear never again to take up arms against the Kingdom or your fellow Christians.'

'I swear it.'

'Good!' Amalric began to laugh his strange, manic laugh. The outburst passed as quickly as it came. He extended his hand. John winced at the pain in his feet as Amalric pulled him upright. 'You are my man,' the king said and embraced John. 'Now, we shall have to see you married.'

'Pardon?'

'Life at court is not cheap, John. You need a wife with lands of her own.' Amalric paused. 'Why, John, you look as if you had swallowed a camel turd!'

'I do not wish for a bride, sire.'

Amalric frowned. 'It is either that or enter the priesthood.'

'I am no priest. I have loved women, killed men, betrayed vows.'

William smiled. 'That hardly disqualifies you. The Patriarch of Jerusalem is a brave warrior and a notorious womanizer.'

'Priests!' Amalric snorted. 'Do not bother with them, John. Let me find you a wife.'

'I—that is—' John took a deep breath. 'There is a woman.'

'You are married?' Amalric asked. John shook his head, and the king clapped him on the back. 'Then what is the difficulty? I will find you a local beauty, one of the Syrian Christians, with ample – assets.' He winked. 'You will forget all about this other woman.'

'No, sire. I would prefer to enter the priesthood.'

Amalric's joviality vanished. 'I cannot say I understand your choice, but very well. William will see to it. I will see you tomorrow morning at the palace.' Amalric stepped out of the cell.

'If I am free, what is to prevent me from leaving the city?' John called after him. 'From going back to the Saracens?'

Amalric turned and met his gaze. 'Your word. That is enough for me.'

The king left, and William entered the cell. 'Come, John. Let's get you to your quarters. You will stay at the Hospital of Saint John until you are ordained.' John put his arm over the priest's shoulder and leaned into him as they left the cell. 'After a suitable period as an acolyte, you will be made a canon in the Church of the Holy Sepulchre,' the priest told him. 'You will receive a monthly prebend, from which you can pay a vicar to perform your duties. You will spend most of your time at court.'

They climbed a flight of narrow stairs and stepped out into the palace courtyard. It was a brilliant autumn morning, the sky a deep blue. William helped John across the courtyard and through a wide gate that led out into the city. They paused on the far side of the gate. Straight ahead stood the vaulted halls and churches of the Hospitaller complex. John looked down the road to his right, to where a church loomed over a pig market. In the distance to his left, a rocky outcrop rose above the city: the Temple Mount. He could make out the mighty Dome of the Rock, its gilded roof glinting in the morning sun. William noticed his wide-eyed expression and smiled. 'A pretty sight, is she not? Welcome to Jerusalem, the Holy City.'

Chapter 2

Yusuf awoke with a start. The sheets of his bed were damp with sweat. In his dreams he had been on the field of battle. He had run for his life and then turned to watch as John was struck down from behind. The same nightmare had haunted him ever since the defeat at Butaiha six months ago. He rose and crossed the room to throw open the shutters. Soft morning light flooded in, along with the wavering call of the muezzins beckoning the faithful to morning prayers.

From the window of his modest home he could see the citadel, its white stone walls rising sheer from the tall hill on which it stood. Yusuf had told the king, Nur ad-Din, that he was purchasing quarters outside the palace to provide a home for his widowed sister Zimat and her son Ubadah. But that was only part of the reason. The truth was that he wished to be as far away as possible from the palace. At Butaiha, Yusuf had saved the life of the king and earned himself a new name: Saladin, 'righteous in faith'. He had become one of the king's most trusted advisers, and yet the more Nur ad-Din confided in him, the more Yusuf was wracked by guilt. For he had betrayed his lord in the worst way imaginable. He had slept with Nur ad-Din's wife, Asimat. Yusuf broke the relationship off, but not before Asimat became pregnant. She would deliver any day now, and the child was not Nur ad-Din's. It was his.

'Uncle!'

Yusuf turned to see his nephew standing in the doorway. Ubadah had the dark eyes of his mother. The arch of his brow, his straight nose and firm jaw, and his sandy brown hair all came from his father, John. But Ubadah would never know that. He thought his father was Khaldun, Zimat's deceased husband. Now, Yusuf was raising the child as his own.

'May I accompany you to prayers?' the boy asked. Ubadah was almost six years old, still too young to attend prayers, but he enjoyed playing outside the mosque while Yusuf prayed. Yusuf guessed that he was simply eager to be away from home. Zimat had been short-tempered and melancholic since John's death.

'Very well,' Yusuf said. 'Allow me to dress, and I will meet you in the courtyard.'

They walked together to Al-Jami al-Kabir, Aleppo's great mosque, and entered the courtyard. The sun had not yet risen, and the soot-covered stone of the broken walls was cast in soft pink light. Yusuf washed himself in the fountain at the centre of the courtyard and left Ubadah with strict instructions not to stray beyond the walls. He then entered the mosque, where he remained kneeling in silent prayer long after the other men had rolled up their prayer mats and left. His life had been defined by war with the Franks and service to Nur ad-Din, but now he could not think of battle without remembering John's death. He could not confront Nur ad-Din without being flooded with shame. He had failed his friend and his lord. 'Please, Allah,' he whispered. 'Grant me a chance at redemption.'

Yusuf rolled his prayer mat and rose. In the courtyard he found Ubadah playing at mock swordplay with the former vizier of Egypt. Shawar had been betrayed by his chamberlain Dhirgam and had fled Cairo with an army at his heels. He had arrived in Aleppo months ago, seeking help to retake his kingdom. He was a tall, thin man with a striking face – glittering eyes and sharp features that looked as if they had been chiselled out of stone. His hair and beard were shaved in mourning. He had vowed to not let them grow until he was once again ruling from Cairo. Ubadah mimicked a lunging blow, and Shawar clasped his hands over his chest as if he had been struck. He staggered backwards, swayed for a moment and toppled to the ground.

Yusuf clapped. 'Well done, Ubadah!' The boy grinned.

'Ah, Saladin!' Shawar rose and flashed a dazzling smile. Yusuf could not help but smile back. Shawar was a man of unfailing optimism, and Yusuf found his good humour contagious. He was one of the few who could lift Yusuf from his dark moods, and the two had become close friends. They hunted together and often dined at one another's homes.

'It is Friday. Why were you not at prayers?' Yusuf asked Shawar with mock severity. 'What is your excuse this time?'

'I longed to come, as Allah is my witness,' Shawar replied. 'But I am a Shia, and your mosques are filled with Sunnis. I fear I would not be welcome.' The Shia and the Sunni Muslims had split over who should lead Islam after the death of Mohammed. Over the centuries these differences had hardened into a mutual animosity that sometimes erupted into war. 'If you have not breakfasted,' Shawar continued, 'then I would like to offer you the pleasure of my company.'

Yusuf laughed. 'I am sure it is my sister's company that you seek, but no matter. You are welcome in my home.'

With Ubadah in tow, the two men set out across the broad square at the heart of Aleppo, walking in the shadow of the citadel. Yusuf wove around local merchants and farmers, who were setting up their carts. He stopped at one and paid four fals for two melons, which he gave to Ubadah to carry. They left the square and walked through the narrow lanes to Yusuf's new home, a two-storey structure with a courtyard that opened on to the street. Zimat was sitting at the courtyard fountain chatting with Faridah, Yusuf's concubine. Ubadah ran to his mother and began excitedly describing his mock battle with Shawar.

'I fear he dealt me a mortal blow,' Shawar proclaimed with a

30

smile. He bowed low. 'My ladies,' he said, although he looked only at Zimat. 'As-salaamu 'alaykum. It is an unexpected pleasure to see you today.'

'Ahlan wa-Sahlan,' Zimat murmured and managed a small smile. She liked Shawar, that much was clear. The occasions when Yusuf had invited the former vizier to dinner were some of the few times in the last months that Yusuf had seen his sister smile. He had even considered offering her to Shawar in marriage.

'Wa 'alaykum as-salaam,' Faridah said.

Shawar nodded at her and turned back to Zimat. 'Your brother has invited me to breakfast. I hope my presence will not be too burdensome.'

'Brother! You should have consulted me!' Zimat complained. Faridah rolled her eyes. It was obvious that Zimat was not truly angry. 'I have nothing prepared that is fit for a guest.'

'I purchased melons.' Yusuf nodded to the fruits Ubadah carried.

'I will see what can be done. Come, Faridah.' Zimat took the fruits, and the two women headed for the kitchen. Ubadah followed.

Yusuf led Shawar inside. They sat amidst cushions and Yusuf poured tea. Shawar sipped at it before clearing his throat. 'When do you think Nur ad-Din will respond to my request for aid?'

Yusuf shrugged. 'I have presented your case to him many times. He gives no answer.'

Shawar sighed. 'As much as I enjoy your hospitality, friend, I long to return to Egypt. It is a paradise. The fields are green. The air is warm.' He winked. 'The women are beautiful. You would like it. Faridah is a beauty, but she grows old. You could use another woman.'

Yusuf thought of Asimat and frowned.

'I did not mean to offend, Yusuf,' Shawar hurried to assure him. 'But I can see that you are unhappy here. You need a fresh start. Help me to retake Egypt, and I will offer you a place at my court. I could use a man of your vision and experience.'

'I would gladly follow you to Egypt, friend, but the choice is not mine to make. I serve at Nur ad-Din's pleasure. I will go if he commands me.'

'Surely he will!' Shawar declared and launched into a speech that Yusuf had heard many times. 'I will make Nur ad-Din the overlord of Egypt and give him a third of the kingdom's revenue, if only he helps me retake Cairo. He must act. Every day he waits, the traitor Dhirgam grows stronger, and his allies the Franks with him. I ask only—'

He fell silent as Zimat entered, followed by two servants carrying trays loaded with dishes of sliced melon, steaming flat-bread, olives, dates, soft cheeses, broad beans in garlic, boiled eggs and apricot jam. Zimat sat while the servants placed the dishes on the ground before Yusuf and Shawar.

'Such a feast!' Shawar exclaimed. 'You have outdone yourself, Zimat.'

'It is nothing.'

'You are too modest. Such a meal would put to shame the chefs of the Egyptian caliph himself.'

Zimat blushed and busied herself pouring more tea. Yusuf could see that his sister was pleased. Perhaps if Yusuf went to Egypt, she could come with him and marry Shawar. She would like that.

'Tell my sister what you told me about the pyramids,' Yusuf suggested to Shawar.

'They are a marvel!' Shawar described the incredible struc-tures while they breakfasted. Yusuf was sure he was exaggerating, but Zimat listened wide-eyed.

They were finishing breakfast when one of Nur ad-Din's mamluks arrived. 'You are wanted at the palace, Emir,' he told Saladin. 'Asimat has given birth to a son.'

'A son?' Yusuf murmured. His son. He suddenly felt dizzy and placed a hand on the floor to steady himself.

'Are you well, friend?' Shawar asked.

'Of course.' Yusuf forced a smile. 'The kingdom has an heir, Allah be praised.'

'Perhaps now that Allah has blessed him, Nur ad-Din will listen to my request.'

'I will ask him.'

'*Shukran*,' Shawar said and bowed, a hand over his heart. 'You are a true friend, Saladin.'

Yusuf entered the antechamber to Nur ad-Din's apartments to find that his uncle Shirkuh and the eunuch Gumushtagin had arrived before him. Shirkuh was handing his sword and dagger over to the guards who protected the king. Gumushtagin saw Yusuf first.

'As-salaamu 'alaykum, Saladin,' he said. Yusuf nodded curtly.

'Young eagle!' Shirkuh cried. He embraced Yusuf and kissed him three times, the appropriate greeting between male relatives. 'Have you heard the news? An heir to the kingdom! Perhaps this will finally dispel the dark cloud our lord has been living under.'

'Inshallah, Uncle.'

Yusuf removed the belt that held his sword and handed it to one of the guards. Another guard pushed the door open and waved them inside. 'The Malik is in his study.'

They found Nur ad-Din bent over his broad desk, lost in thought as he studied an architect's rendering. The king had changed much in the six months since his defeat at Butaiha. His black hair was now peppered with grey, his once tanned face was sallow and he had dark circles under his eyes. Deep lines of worry creased his forehead. Nur ad-Din was not yet fifty, but he looked like an old man.

'Malik,' Gumushtagin said. 'We have come at your bidding.'

Nur ad-Din straightened. 'Friends!' Yusuf saw that the fire had returned to his bright, golden eyes. The king grinned, and his tired face seemed suddenly youthful again. He rounded the

33

table and embraced first Shirkuh and then Yusuf. 'I have a son! I have named him Al-Salih. Allah has blessed me! From this day, I shall redouble my efforts to serve Him. The great mosque shall be rebuilt, and I shall establish a madras in Aleppo, a school of learning greater than any the world has ever known.'

'What of the war against the Franks?' Shirkuh asked.

Nur ad-Din's expression darkened. 'I have a score to settle with King Amalric. Come summer, I will strike the Kingdom of Jerusalem in the north.'

'And Egypt?' Yusuf asked. 'What of Shawar's offer?'

'Egypt is not my concern. I need my men with me to fight the Franks.'

'But my lord, we must do something,' Yusuf insisted. 'The Frankish king has allied with the current vizier, Dhirgam. Egypt pays Amalric tribute, money he will use to purchase mercenaries. By helping Shawar retake Egypt, you will weaken the Franks.'

'And strengthen your own position, Malik,' Gumushtagin added. Yusuf was surprised to find the eunuch on his side. 'You would be overlord of Egypt.'

Nur ad-Din's brow furrowed as he considered their arguments. 'Can this Shawar be trusted?'

'He is my friend,' Yusuf said. 'His word is true.'

'And what does the Egyptian caliph think of him, I wonder.' Nur ad-Din went to the window, where he stood looking out for a long time. 'I will let Allah decide,' he said at last. He took a bound copy of the Quran from a bookshelf that lined the back wall of the room. He handed the book to Yusuf. 'Open it.'

'Where, Malik?'

'Wherever your hand falls.'

Yusuf placed a finger in the middle of the book and flipped it open.

'Read,' Nur ad-Din told him.

Yusuf cleared his throat. '*And those who disbelieve are allies of one another, and if the faithful do not join together to make Islam*

34

victorious, there will be chaos and oppression on earth, and a great mischief and corruption.'

Shirkuh's eyes widened, and he touched his nose with his right forefinger, indicating that the answer was right in front of him. 'Allah has spoken, and his meaning is clear. He wants you to unite the faithful of Egypt and Syria. We must help Shawar.'

'There is no denying the meaning of the passage,' Gumushtagin agreed.

Nur ad-Din nodded. 'Very well. Shirkuh, you will go to Egypt and place this Shawar back on the vizier's throne.'

Shirkuh touched his palm to his chest and bowed. 'As you wish, Malik.'

'I will go, too,' Yusuf said.

'No, Saladin. I need you here to help prepare my campaign against the Franks.'

Yusuf's chest tightened at the thought of another year in Aleppo. 'I am a warrior, Malik. I best serve you on the field of battle. Once Egypt is ours, I will return for your campaign against the Franks.'

Nur ad-Din sighed. 'As you wish. At least I can count on Gumushtagin to stay and advise me.' The eunuch bowed. Nur ad-Din looked back to Shirkuh. 'You will gather your army at Damascus and ride from there to Egypt. Do not fail me. I cannot afford another defeat.'

'I will not fail, Malik. I will bring you a kingdom.'

Shirkuh left to begin gathering the army, but Yusuf remained at the palace late into the afternoon, discussing with Nur ad-Din and Gumushtagin the number of men that would be needed in Egypt and the taxes required to fund the expedition. Finally, when the sun dipped below the horizon and the muezzins began the call for evening prayers, Nur ad-Din dismissed them.

Yusuf passed through the antechamber to the dim, spiral

stairwell that led to the ground floor of the palace. He was halfway down when Gumushtagin caught up with him. 'Wait, Saladin. I wish to speak with you.'

Yusuf examined the eunuch with distaste. 'What do you want?'

'Only to help you. We are bound to one another, you and I. You saved my life, Yusuf. And I know your secret.' Gumushtagin lowered his voice to a whisper. 'Asimat's child—your child—will be king when Nur ad-Din dies.'

Yusuf felt his stomach twist. Gumushtagin was as dangerous as a snake, and he was the only one who knew the truth. 'What do you want from me?'

Gumushtagin smiled. 'I ask little. Go to Egypt with your uncle. Keep me informed. Each week, send me a report via pigeon post. When the time is right, I will let you know what to do. If you do as I ask, then you will be vizier of Egypt, and your son will be king.'

Vizier of Egypt. Yusuf had dreamed of ruling a kingdom since he was a child, and for a moment he felt a surge of his old ambition. Then he shook his head. 'Shawar is to be vizier. He is my friend.'

The eunuch's smile faded, and when he spoke again his voice had a dangerous edge. 'You have committed treason, Saladin. If you oppose me, it will cost you your life.'

Yusuf rubbed his beard, unsure what to say. It would be easy enough to keep Gumushtagin informed, but where would it end? Yusuf knew the eunuch well enough to know that the next service he demanded would not be so easy.

'It is not just your own life that is at stake, Saladin,' Gumushtagin insisted. 'Think of Asimat, of Al-Salih. They will die if Nur ad-Din learns the truth.'

'Very well,' Yusuf said reluctantly. 'I will do as you ask.'

A week later, after the supplies and men needed for the expedition had been gathered, Yusuf again strode through the halls of the palace. He had come straight from the dry plain outside the city, where the troops were preparing to depart, and his dark-grey mail was covered in a layer of dust. He stopped before the door to the harem. The two eunuch guards lowered their spears towards his chest. 'The lady Asimat has summoned me,' he told them.

One of the guards nodded. 'Follow me.' He led Yusuf down a long corridor. It was not the first time Yusuf had visited the harem. Several years ago, after Asimat miscarried, Nur ad-Din himself had encouraged Yusuf to visit her, hoping that he could cheer her. That meeting had led to others, and then to a passionate affair. But Yusuf had put an end to things months ago. He had been in bed with Asimat when the great earthquake struck, and he did not doubt that it was a sign from Allah. The last time they had met, Yusuf had lied to Asimat: he had told her that he did not love her. She had slapped him and called him a coward. He had thought he would never see her again. Why had she called for him now? Did she miss him? Did she want him? Yusuf pushed the thoughts from his mind. It did not matter. He would not betray his lord again. He had just formed this resolution when they reached the door to her apartments, and the eunuch guard pulled it open.

'My lady,' the eunuch announced in his high-pitched voice. 'Saladin.'

Asimat entered from another room, walking stiffly. This was the only sign that she had given birth only a week ago, for she was even more beautiful than Yusuf remembered. Her wavy brown hair was pinned up, revealing her long, graceful neck, the skin milky-white. She wore a white silk caftan, and as she approached, the sun struck her from behind, illuminating her form beneath the loose fabric. Yusuf felt his pulse quicken, despite his resolution to remain aloof. She nodded to the guard, who stepped outside the door. Yusuf knew that he would remain there, watching them through a spyhole.

'You wished to see me, khatun?' Yusuf searched her features

37

for some indication of why she had called for him, but her face was a frozen mask, beautiful but emotionless.

'Sit.' She gestured to cushions that lay on the floor. Then she sat across from him. 'It is not on my account that I have asked you here. It is for my son.'

Yusuf lowered his voice to a whisper. 'Our son.'

Asimat's jaw clenched and her nostrils flared. For a moment, Yusuf thought that her cold facade was about to crumble, but then her features hardened once more. 'You have spoken with Gumushtagin?' she demanded, also keeping her voice low.

Yusuf blanched. If someone had overheard his whispered conversation in the stairwell, he was as good as dead. 'How do you know?'

'It does not matter. What did he say to you?'

'He asked me to keep him informed of our progress in Egypt. He told me that he would ask more of me when the time is right.' Yusuf shrugged. 'I do not understand the game he is playing.'

'Is it not obvious? He wishes to kill Nur ad-Din and to place my son, Al-Salih, on the throne.'

'Isn't that what you want, too?' Yusuf asked, a trace of bitterness in his voice. 'You will do anything to see your son made king.'

'Not anything, Yusuf. I want Al-Salih to rule, not to serve as Gumushtagin's pawn. The eunuch would rule Nur ad-Din's kingdom as vizier until the boy comes of age. But many will oppose him. That is why Gumushtagin needs you. He will make you powerful, so that you may protect him.'

Yusuf scowled. 'I want no part in such a scheme. I will not betray my—'

'Do not be a fool, Yusuf!' Asimat hissed. 'Your honour will count for nothing if you are dead, if our child is dead.' Her dark eyes met his. 'Come, you should meet him.' She led the way to her bedroom. It had been transformed since Yusuf last visited. Heavy curtains now hung over the windows; a candelabra on a

table by the door shed a dim light. The floor was deeply carpeted and scattered with cushions. A maidservant sat amongst
them, cradling a child in her arms. Asimat took the child and
brought the babe to Yusuf, who had not moved from the
doorway.

'This is Al-Salih,' Asimat whispered as she handed him the
sleeping child. 'Careful, do not wake him.'

The babe had a thatch of brown hair and a chubby face. His
smooth, almost luminescent skin was lighter than Yusuf's olive
hue, though he was not quite so pale as Asimat. The boy
stretched in his sleep and opened his eyes. They were deep-set
and light brown, like Yusuf's, but the resemblance was not
marked. Al-Salih could easily have been another man's child.

The babe closed his eyes sleepily. Asimat took him back. She
glanced at the maidservant and then spoke in a whisper. 'He *is*
your child, Yusuf. If Gumushtagin betrays us, we will die, all
three of us. You must do anything to prevent that.'

'I will not do his bidding forever. At some point we must
stop him or else we will all become his pawns.'

'I will deal with Gumushtagin, but now is not the time. Do
as he says for now. Our son's life depends on it.'

MARCH 1164: ON THE ROAD TO EGYPT

Yusuf sat astride his horse on a high outcrop of dark-brown
stone that flaked and crumbled under his mount's stamping
hooves. Below him, mamluk troops rode four abreast into the
shadowy mouth of a wadi – a dry riverbed lined with sand and
gravel – which cut its way between the rocky hills. The long
column of troops stretched away across the sandy plain Yusuf
had just traversed, all the way to the shores of Al-Bahr al-
Mayyit, the Dead Sea, whose rainbow waters glistened under
an incandescent morning sun. Near the shore, the sea was rust-
coloured from the algae that bloomed in the salty waters.

39

Further out, the red mixed with pale whites and bright blue-greens. The army had been riding along the eastern shore for two days, keeping the sea's waters between them and the Kingdom of Jerusalem. It had been nine days since they left Damascus.

A horse nickered behind Yusuf, and he turned to see Shirkuh and Shawar approaching, their mounts picking their way across the broken ground. 'I have spoken with our Bedouin guides,' Shirkuh said as he reined in beside Yusuf. 'The land we must cross is unforgiving. The Bedouin call it Al-Naqab, the dry place. There will be no water until Beersheba. We will have to ride all day without stopping if we hope to reach it by evening.'

Shawar was looking to the sun. Now well above the horizon, it was baking the rocky soil, which radiated heat so intense that it had a physical presence. He wiped sweat from his forehead. 'Is there no easier way?'

'No. Not if we wish to stay clear of the Franks in Ascalon.'

'Very well.' Shawar straightened and flashed his winning smile. 'A kingdom is worth a little suffering.' He tapped his heels against the sides of his horse, which began to pick its way back down from the outcrop. Yusuf and Shirkuh followed.

They rode at the head of the army along the floor of the wadi. At times, the ravine was so narrow that they had to ride two abreast, the rock rising sheer on either side. At other times, it widened into washes that were broad and long enough to accommodate most of their army of seven thousand men. The trail they followed forked again and again, but always their Bedouin guides pushed on without hesitation. How they kept their bearings in this strange place, where every path looked exactly the same, Yusuf had no idea.

They rode in silence, stupefied by the heat, while the shadows that stretched across the wadi shrank to nothing and then stretched out again to cover the ravine, bringing blessed relief from the scorching sun. Finally, just as the sun was setting before them, they emerged from the hills on to a broad plain of coarse sand, which crunched under their horses' hooves. A few miles later the ruined city of Beersheba came into view. The short stretches of wall that still stood were half buried in sand. A few Bedouin tents had been erected in their lee. At the sight of the approaching army, the Bedouin quickly rolled up their tents. They were gone long before Yusuf arrived.

A well sat at the centre of the town, and Shirkuh set men to work hauling up water for the horses. Yusuf left his mount with one of his men and walked away from the camp and up a sandy hill. He knelt to pray. Since he had no water, he rubbed his hands, feet, and face with sand. Then he spread out his prayer carpet and began the isha'a, the nightly prayer. By the time he finished, the tents of the army had sprouted all across the plain. As he walked back to camp he passed a dozen men digging a latrine for the army. Just beyond, he was hailed by Shawar.

'Yusuf! I have found you at last. You must come and dine in my tent.'

'I should see to my men first,' Yusuf replied, although in truth, he had been planning to write his first report to Gumushtagin.

'Your men will survive without you for one night. I, on the other hand, am in desperate need of good company. Come. Your uncle is already in my tent.' Shawar saw that Yusuf still hesitated. The Egyptian winked. 'Food is not the only delicacy on offer.'

Yusuf raised an eyebrow. 'Very well.' Gumushtagin could wait.

Shawar's tent was impossibly luxurious. Yusuf had been sceptical when Shawar told him that he required twelve camels to transport his personal effects, but now he saw why. The low, sprawling tent was large enough to seat a hundred men. Lamps hung from the tent posts, illuminating deep carpets and shimmering screens of silk that separated off parts of the huge space. In the corner, two men were fitting together a polished wardrobe, which split in half for transport.

Shawar noticed Yusuf's wide-eyed expression. 'When I fled Egypt, I did not do so entirely empty-handed.'

Cushions had been spread in a circle, and Shirkuh was already seated and chatting with a man that Yusuf did not recognize. Yusuf sat beside his uncle, and Shawar took a seat across from him. Shawar gestured to the strange Egyptian. The man had darkly tanned skin and unexceptional features, save for his hazel eyes. 'Al-Khlata is the civilian comptroller in Cairo. He sees that taxes are collected from the populace.'

Yusuf nodded towards him. 'I am honoured to meet you.'

'Now, let us eat.' Shawar clapped his hands and veiled female servants in thin, almost transparent caftans stepped from behind one of the silk curtains. One of them came to Yusuf and placed a gold cup on the small, low table beside him. Yusuf was surprised to see it was filled with water. He had not expected Shawar to be so temperate.

Shirkuh was equally perplexed. 'No wine?' he grumbled.

'Allah forbids alcohol, and as we march in his name, it is best to obey his laws,' Shawar replied. 'And besides, in the desert, water is more precious than wine.' He raised his glass. 'To Cairo! May we see her soon!'

'To Cairo!' the men replied and drank.

The servants entered with food. One brought Yusuf a basket of steaming flatbread and a dip of mashed broad beans. Another brought a green soup with pieces of fried garlic floating in it. Yusuf poked at it with his spoon.

'It is an Egyptian speciality, made from diced jute,' Al-Khlata told him.

Shawar nodded. 'My cook came with me from Cairo. Thanks to him, I can dine as if I am in the caliph's palace, even while in the desert.' Shawar tore off a piece of flatbread, dipped it in the soup and ate, a signal for the others to begin.

Yusuf murmured, 'In the name of Allah,' and tried some of the bread. It was thicker and coarser than he was used to. The dip was creamy and rich, the soup light but savoury.

Shawar washed down the bread and soup with a swallow of water. 'Al-Khlata tells me that Beersheba was once a great city.'

The comptroller nodded. 'There was a great church here, huge buildings. It was once part of the Roman Empire.'

'And the Kingdom of the Jews before that,' Yusuf noted. All eyes turned to him. 'Their first king, Saul, built a great fort here.'

'How do you know this?' Shawar asked.

'It is written in the Franks' holy book.' John had given Yusuf a copy of the Bible years ago, and Yusuf had studied it carefully. 'It says that Abraham visited here. He made a pact with the people of the area, swearing an oath to share the wells. That is why the town is called Beersheba: "oath of the well".'

Al-Khlata snorted. 'I do not believe anything written in the books of the Franks. Superstitious nonsense!'

'Perhaps,' Yusuf said, 'but if we wish to defeat our enemies, we must know them.'

'Indeed,' Shawar agreed. 'And since we are discussing our enemies, it is time I tell you something of what awaits us in Egypt. Cairo is a nest of vipers. In my lifetime, no vizier has ruled there for more than a dozen years before being betrayed. I thought I could be the one to finally bring stability to the kingdom, but I was wrong. I was too trusting. I thought Dhirgam was my friend. As young men, we served together as scribes in the Caliph's court. We rose through the ranks together, and when I became vizier I made him my chamberlain. I did not know that the snake was in the pay of the Franks. While I was in Bilbeis inspecting the citadel, Dhirgam seized control of Cairo. His first act was to make peace with Jerusalem. His second was to send an army to kill me. I fled east to the court of your lord, Nur ad-Din. The rest you know.' Shawar shook his head, as if to dispel the painful memories. 'But enough of such sad talk! Let us enjoy ourselves.' He clapped his hands. 'Bring the girls!'

Al-Khlata took this as a sign to depart. A moment later, four serving girls entered, only now they had shed their thin caftans and wore only veils and skirts of diaphanous silk, through which Yusuf could see their toned legs and firm buttocks. They were Egyptian, brown-skinned with wide eyes lined with kohl. A man with a drum came in after the girls. He went to the corner, while the girls moved to the centre of the circle and stood absolutely still, their heads down. As the man began to beat the drum, the girls came to life, swaying their hips to the beat. The drum beat faster and they started to circle, spinning so that their skirts flared up. Yusuf sat back as they flashed past, a kaleidoscope of nubile flesh: long thin arms, finely shaped legs, tight buttocks and dark breasts with darker areoles.

The girls stopped circling. One stood just before Yusuf. She sank to her knees and arched backwards so the back of her head touched the floor. She began to rhythmically raise her hips, thrusting up with the beat of the drum. She sat straight once more, leaned forward and reached out, caressing Yusuf's cheek. She moved on to his lap and kissed him, her mouth open. Her hand moved down to caress his rock-hard zib. He ran his hands down her sides and grasped her firm buttocks. She giggled, pushed him away and stood. She took his hand and led him towards one of the screened-off rooms.

Yusuf glanced back before entering. Shirkuh was occupied with two girls. Shawar had sent the fourth girl away and sat alone. He met Yusuf's gaze and winked. 'Enjoy yourself!'

The girl was tugging on Yusuf's arm. 'Come,' she said and led him into the room.

When Yusuf awoke the next morning, he and the servant girl were still naked and tangled together. She was sleeping, her head on his chest and a half-smile on her lips. For a moment, she reminded him of Asimat. The thought made Yusuf feel sick. He dressed quickly and stepped outside. The morning air was cool after the closeness of the tent. He breathed deeply and headed for the latrine. On the way he passed Al-Khlata, leading

44

a horse. Where was he off to so early in the day, Yusuf wondered.

Yusuf reached the ditch and had begun to urinate when Shawar stepped up beside him. 'A long night?' he asked as he too began to piss. Yusuf felt himself redden. 'There is nothing to be ashamed of, friend. I am glad you enjoyed yourself. When we reach Cairo, you will have a dozen more women like her.'

'I do not wish for—'

'Think nothing of it. What is mine is yours.' Shawar finished and clapped Yusuf on the back. 'Now come. Cairo awaits!'

MARCH 1164: CAIRO

'Medinat al-Qahira!' Shawar exclaimed and gestured to the horizon. 'The greatest city in all the world!'

Yusuf squinted but could make out only a distant smudge. Nearer, feluccas and dhows glided along the Nile under triangular sails, and beyond them loomed the massive pyramids of Giza. Shawar's description had not done them justice. They dwarfed anything that Yusuf had ever seen, even the massive Roman temple in his childhood home of Baalbek.

Shirkuh pointed to a grove of palms situated along the river. 'Yusuf, have a hundred men begin building rams and siege towers.'

'That will not be necessary,' Shawar assured him. 'The people will open the gates to us. They are loyal to me. That is why they fled before us outside Bilbeis.' The day before, they had confronted an army twice their size, but the Egyptians had run almost before the battle began.

'Let us hope you are right, or we will regret letting so many escape,' Shirkuh grumbled.

'I could hardly let you butcher them,' Shawar replied. 'They are my people. Soon enough they will fight for me.'

Shirkuh grunted sceptically.

As they rode closer, the city rapidly took shape. The tall walls were studded with towers. The buildings were flat-roofed and built of the same white limestone as the walls. Beyond Cairo rose a dozen tall shapes that Yusuf initially took for minarets. Soon, he saw that they were actually massive, rectangular buildings, many storeys high.

'That is Fustat, just south of the city,' Shawar said, answering Yusuf's unasked question. 'It was founded centuries before Cairo. It is still the commercial heart of the city, famed for its pottery and crystal. It is there that the wealth of Egypt is created.'

They rode on, and soon Yusuf could see soldiers atop the walls, their armour glinting in the late afternoon sun. Shawar led the army towards an arched gate framed by two squat round towers of pale stone. Warriors with bows in hand were crowded atop the gate. Shawar seemed not to notice them.

'Perhaps we should halt beyond bow range,' Yusuf suggested.

'There is no need,' Shawar replied. He pointed to the gate where the soldiers were disappearing.

'Where are they going?' Shirkuh asked.

'The rats are abandoning the ship. I know the people of Cairo. They served Dhirgam well enough when he was strong, but now that an army is at their walls, they will turn on him. Come! The day's ride has spurred my appetite. We shall dine in the Caliph's palace.'

Shawar urged his horse to a canter, leaving Yusuf and Shirkuh behind. They exchanged a glance and then Shirkuh shrugged. 'Let us hope he knows what he is doing.' He raised his voice. 'Guards! Ride with me. The rest of the army will make camp beside the Nile.' He spurred after Shawar.

Yusuf turned back towards his younger brother Selim and the mamluk commander Qaraqush. Qaraqush was a thick-necked bull of a man. His hair had begun to grey, but he was just as fearsome a warrior as when Yusuf had first met him twelve years ago. As for Selim, he was a man now. With his dark hair and beard, wiry build and deep brown eyes, he looked like a younger, slightly taller version of Yusuf, so much so that the men had taken to calling him Al-Azrar: 'the younger'.

'If we do not return by evening prayers,' Yusuf told them, 'lay siege.'

Qaraqush nodded. 'I will not leave a stone standing.'

Yusuf spurred after Shirkuh and Shawar. As they approached the city gate, a small man in an elegant caftan of blue silk embroidered with gold came out to meet them. As he came closer, Yusuf saw that his back was crooked and hunched. His narrow face, though, was pleasant enough, with a dark beard that reached past his chest. In his hands he held a cushion upon which sat a human head.

The man stopped just short of them and bowed. 'Salaam, Shawar. I come on behalf of the Caliph to invite you to his palace. And, I bring a gift.'

'What is this?' Shirkuh demanded, gesturing to the head. It was grotesque: the face bruised and swollen, the eyes and tongue removed.

Shawar took the head and gazed at it for a moment. 'It is the head of the traitor, Dhirgam.' He looked to the man who had brought the grisly gift. 'What happened to him, Al-Fadil?'

'The people of Cairo turned on him. They tore him to pieces.'

'Such a pity,' Shawar murmured. 'I would have liked to kill him myself.' He tossed the head aside. 'Come. The Caliph awaits.'

Shawar spurred through the gate, and Yusuf and Shirkuh followed, accompanied by two-dozen mamluks from Shirkuh's private guard. A silent crowd lined the wide street. 'My people!' Shawar seemed oblivious to their lack of enthusiasm. They rode on into a broad square situated between the two halves of the palace – a dizzying collection of colonnaded porticos, domes and towers of white stone. 'The east palace is occupied by

47

courtiers,' Shawar explained. 'The Caliph lives on the west side.'

Shawar led them that way. They dismounted and climbed the broad stairs to the portico. 'Your men should wait here,' Shawar told them. Shirkuh hesitated for a moment and then nodded. Shawar led him and Yusuf inside into a high-ceilinged reception hall lined with guards. Yusuf and Shirkuh followed Shawar across the hall and through a series of luxurious rooms. The walls were hung with brightly coloured silks decorated with swirling patterns woven in gold and studded with jewels. The floors were covered in thick carpets of soft goat hair, which swallowed the sound of their footsteps. Finally, they reached the audience chamber, which was divided in the middle by a curtain of golden cloth.

'Your swords,' Shawar told them. 'It is customary to lay them before the Caliph.'

Shirkuh drew his sword and laid it on the ground before him. Yusuf did the same.

'Now kneel,' Shawar said, 'and bow three times.'

Yusuf and Shirkuh did as they were told. Shawar joined them, prostrating himself before the golden curtain. It rose to reveal the boy-caliph, sitting cross-legged on a gilt throne. Not one inch of the caliph's flesh was visible. He wore a white silk caftan, the hem and collar of which were heavy with jewels. A veil hid his face, and gloves of red silk covered his hands. On his feet were jewelled slippers. A dozen mamluk warriors stood along the wall behind the throne, and richly dressed courtiers lined the walls to the left and right.

Shawar addressed him. 'Successor of the messenger of God, God's deputy, defender of the faithful, I have returned to serve you.'

'Welcome back to Cairo, Shawar,' Al-Adid said in an adolescent warble. 'You have been missed.'

'Not as much as I have missed serving you, Caliph.'

'Then you may serve me again. I am in need of a new vizier.'

'It would be my honour, Caliph.'

'Then it is done. Rise.'

Shawar rose, and Yusuf and Shirkuh did likewise. Al-Adid gestured to one of his attendants, who stepped forward holding a red silk cushion on which lay a magnificent, gold-bladed sword with an ivory hilt encrusted with jewels. Its sheath, which lay beside it, was of gold and also covered in precious stones. 'The sword of the vizier,' the caliph said. 'It is yours.'

The courtier belted the sword about Shawar's waist. 'Shukran, great Caliph,' the vizier said and bowed.

Al-Adid waved away his thanks and turned to Shirkuh and Yusuf. 'Who are these men, Shawar?'

'Emirs from Syria. They came at the behest of Nur ad-Din to help me dispose of the traitor Dhirgam.'

'Then they have my thanks.'

Shawar cleared his throat. 'Nur ad-Din has been promised a third of our annual revenue as tribute.'

'Very well,' the caliph said in a tired voice. He seemed bored by these details. 'Is there anything else?'

Shirkuh stepped forward. 'My lord instructs me to thank you for welcoming us to Cairo. So long as I am in Egypt, I will serve you as I would serve him. To better protect you from any reprisals from Dhirgam's men, I would like to station a garrison inside the city.'

The caliph shifted on his throne. 'This is my city,' he said sharply. 'I will not turn it over to foreign troops.'

'But Shawar agreed—'

Shirkuh stopped short as Shawar shot him a warning glance. 'These are of course only suggestions, Caliph,' the vizier said in a soothing tone. 'Shirkuh is a reasonable man. He will understand that it is not possible to garrison his troops within the city.' He turned to Shirkuh and spoke in a low voice, so the caliph would not hear. 'We must not anger the caliph. If he speaks against you, I will have a riot on my hands.'

'I can put down a riot,' Shirkuh grumbled.

'Yes. But swords close markets, and dead men pay no taxes. The treasury is low, and Dhirgam will have emptied it further to pay his troops. If you want the tribute that is owed to Nur ad-Din, then your army must leave the city. They need not go far. They can stay in Giza, just across the Nile.'

Shirkuh looked as if he had just taken a sip of sour wine, but finally he nodded. 'I will move my army to Giza. But I will leave a garrison of one hundred men to take charge of the city gates.'

'Agreed.' Shawar flashed his most winning smile. 'Now come, friends. You will be guests at the Caliph's table. Let us celebrate the alliance between our two great kingdoms.'

Chapter 3

John sat with his eyes closed, submerged to his chin in the steaming waters of the bath house. A low murmur of voices surrounded him, echoing off the domed ceiling. Most spoke in French, but John also heard German, Provençal, Latin and Catalan. He ignored the sound and let his mind drift. This was his morning ritual, before he went to the church to learn to chant and lead Mass from the prayer book, and then to the palace to work for William or tutor prince Baldwin. It was a time when he could be at peace and forget that he was a man without a country, as cut off from his childhood home of England as he was from his friends in Aleppo. He belonged nowhere, and perhaps that is why he felt at home in Jerusalem. It was a city of immigrants – pilgrims from Europe and native Christians from all over Syria. A city where it was easy to leave one's past behind and fashion a new life.

John rose from the warm waters and headed for the next room, where he was scrubbed down by an attendant before being doused in cold water. He slipped into his caftan in the changing room and stepped out of the bath house into the paved courtyard of the Hospitaller complex. All around him rose tall buildings – churches, hospitals built to house sick pilgrims and barracks for the knights who served the order. The air, which would be as hot as a furnace by midday, was comfortably warm. John glanced at the sun, whose deep red rim was just rising above the tall buildings that lined the eastern side of the courtyard. There was time for a short walk and a little breakfast.

His nose wrinkled as he walked out of the complex and into a dusty street. Across the way stood the pool of the patriarch, which took up most of a city block. In the winter it was full, but now it was mostly stinking mud and refuse. In the centre of the muck, a pool of water glittered under the morning sun. A system of buckets and pulleys had been built to draw the water up to a raised channel, which crossed the street to provide water for the bath house. A beggar slept against the wall in the tiny patch of shelter underneath the channel. He stirred at the sound of John's footsteps.

'Money for a poor pilgrim far from home,' he begged in a high, plaintive whine. He had a bulbous, red nose and sunken cheeks covered with white stubble. 'Money to return to my wife and children. They need me.'

It was a story John had heard again and again from beggars all over the city. Sometimes it was even true. Plenty of men exhausted their funds during the long pilgrimage to Jerusalem and were unable to return. Plenty more had no wish to go back. Some were running away from a crime or an unwanted family. Others preferred the easy customs of the East. And others still fell in love with drink, gambling, women, or all three. From the look of him, John guessed that any money this old man got would go to drink. He tossed him a copper anyway.

He walked south and turned left on to David Street. It angled steeply uphill, and John mounted a series of steps as he passed the shops built into the southern wall of the Hospitaller complex. 'Sacred oil, my good sir?' one of the merchants called to John in French, mistaking him for a pilgrim. He held out a lead flask decorated with images of the saints on one side, and the Holy Sepulchre of Jerusalem on the other. 'It will bring you luck. No? A reliquary pendant, perhaps? It contains a splinter of the true cross! Or perhaps a pilgrim's badge to commemorate your visit to the Holy City?' John kept walking, and the merchant turned his attention to another passer-by.

Past the shops, John reached the square where David Street intersected with Zion Street. To his left, moneychangers sat before their scales, framed by imposing armed men. A few pilgrims were changing their ducats, livres, siliquae, perperi and obols for the bezants and deniers of the Kingdom. Opposite the moneychangers, labourers loitered on the southern edge of the square, hoping to be hired for some menial task. Ahead, the dome of the Templum Domini rose above the city, its gold-clad surface glinting in the morning light. The sight of it always made John smile. The priests told pilgrims that it was the Lord's Temple from the days of Christ, but Father William had confided to John that this new temple had been built by the Saracens a half-millennium ago.

John's musings were interrupted by a rumble from his hungry stomach. He walked north into the Street of Herbs, a narrow lane covered over with vaulted stonework and lined with shops selling spices and fresh fruits. The pilgrims who had spent the night asleep on the stone benches between the shops were just rising. Native Christian servants hurried from shop to shop, purchasing food for their masters' households. Robed priests and knights in armour stood out amongst them. John shouldered his way through the crowd to the stall of an olive-skinned native Christian who was busy placing out baskets of figs, apples and mangos.

'As-salaamu 'alaykum, Tiv,' he greeted him in Arabic.

The merchant smiled, showing yellowing teeth. 'Wa 'alaykum as-salaam, John. What can I do for you?'

'These mangos look good.'

'The best in all Jerusalem. Only two fals.'

John handed over the copper coins and plucked a mango from one of the baskets. He took a bite of the golden, pulpy fruit and grunted in satisfaction as the juice ran down his chin. He gestured to the overflowing baskets. 'Expecting a crowd, Tiv?'

'In four days it will be the feast of liberation, celebrating the capture of Jerusalem by the Frankish dogs.' Tiv spat to the side as he placed another basket of fruit on the table. 'The festivities, may God piss on them, always bring a crowd.'

'May you profit from them.' John moved on, eating his mango as he walked. He left the covered street and strolled through an open square filled with clucking chickens and feathers floating on the morning breeze. The powerful smell of fish filled his nose as he entered the fish market, which sat in the shade of the Church of the Holy Sepulchre. John was pushing his way through the crowd when he spotted a dark-haired woman at a stall just ahead of him. From behind, with her long hair hanging to her waist and her petite, voluptuous figure, she looked just like Zimat. She was dressed in a close-fitting white caftan and niqab, a veil which covered all her face but for her eyes. John caught a glimpse of her hands as she passed money to the merchant; they were the golden colour of the sands north of Damascus, just like Zimat's. John felt his pulse quicken. Then the woman turned and their eyes met. It was not Zimat. The woman lowered her gaze and walked away.

John cursed himself for a fool as he continued on his way. Of course it had not been Zimat. No Saracens were allowed in the city. And why would she come? She did not even know he was alive. He wondered where she was now, if she had married again, but shook the thoughts from his mind. It did not matter. He would be made a priest that very morning.

A trickle of sweat ran down John's back as he knelt on the stone floor of the sanctuary of the Church of the Holy Sepulchre and listened to the patriarch pray. The church was hot due to the dense crowd that had come to hear Sunday Mass, and the priestly garments that John wore offered no relief. His alb, a loose white tunic of linen, was belted at his waist with a cord of red silk. Over it was his chasuble, a sleeveless, suffocating garment of heavily embroidered white silk. A rectangle of linen covered his head and fell to his shoulders on either side. Over his left shoulder hung a stole of red silk with white crosses embroidered at the ends. The priest's maniple, a band of red silk embroidered with gold, was tied to his left forearm. It seemed strange, sacrilegious even, to wear the priestly vestments. Yet in only a few moments he would be a priest. More than that, he would be a canon of the Church of the Holy Sepulchre, the most sacred place in all Christendom, built on the site where Jesus had been buried and risen again.

Each canon received a monthly stipend, and in return they were to live in the dormitory, eat in common and pray the canonical hours: Matins, which took place some three hours before dawn; Lauds shortly before sunrise; Prime in the early morning hours; Terce, Sext, and None over the course of the day; Vespers at sunset; and Compline just before bed. John would live at the church, but William had told him that he would have a vicar to take his place at prayers. Most of the canons did. John would thus be free to continue his work at the palace. There were only two rules that he absolutely had to obey: he must attend the services during Advent and Lent; and he must not be absent from the church for more than three months at a time without dispensation from the patriarch.

John had met the patriarch – called Amalric, like the king – in person for the first time only a few days previously. It was the patriarch's duty to interview any candidate to become a canon. Amalric was one of the four men who had condemned John to crucifixion when he first arrived in Jerusalem, but the patriarch seemed to have no recollection of him. He had been seated at a small table in his private quarters, carving bites of meat from a roasted shoulder of pork.

'I am John of Tatewic, Your Beatitude,' John had declared.

The patriarch had not looked up from his dinner. '*Hmmm?*'

'The candidate to be named to the vacant canon's seat, Your Beatitude.'

Amalric had put down his knife and fork and squinted at John. 'Come forward.'

John had crossed the room, knelt before the patriarch and kissed his ring. Amalric waved John to his feet. After examining him for a moment, the hollow-cheeked old man had gone back to his dinner. 'How old are you?' he asked between bites.

'Thirty-three.'

'And of good blood?'

'My father was a thane – a lord – in England, as was his father and his father before him.'

'And why do you wish to be a priest?'

'To serve God, Your Beatitude.'

'*Hmmm.*' The patriarch made a sucking sound as he worked at the bits of meat stuck between his teeth. 'I owe the King a favour, and William speaks well of you. That is enough for me. I will see that the Chapter approves you, John of Tatewic.'

John had kissed the patriarch's ring and departed.

His attention returned to the cathedral. Amalric was still reading from the prayer book held open by an attendant. 'O God . . . holiness . . . pour . . . this servant of yours . . . the gift of your blessing.' He skipped entire paragraphs, reading only a word here and a phrase there. John could not tell if Amalric was simply ignorant of Latin, like so many churchmen, or if he were deliberately rushing through the service. Such things were common enough. After all, most of the congregation knew no Latin. They would not know the difference.

Amalric droned on, but John paid little attention. His scalp had begun to itch where it had been tonsured – a patch the size of a communion wafer shaved off. It was all he could do not to reach up and scratch it. He forced himself to focus on something else and found himself thinking of Zimat. Even as his hands were anointed with oil and bound, even as he stood beside the patriarch and helped him to celebrate Mass, his thoughts kept returning to her, her dark eyes and hair, the soft curve of her cheek. He had told Amalric that he was joining the priesthood to serve God, and he was. But more than that, he was joining for Zimat, so that he would not have to marry another.

When the Eucharist had been celebrated and the Creed recited, the patriarch returned to his throne, and John knelt before him. This was the key moment of the ceremony. John placed his folded hands between those of the patriarch, who spoke in a low voice: 'Do you promise me and my successors reverence and obedience?'

John hesitated. If he agreed, he would become the patriarch's man, just as he had once been Yusuf's man, and Reynald's before that. He swallowed, and said loudly, 'I promise.'

'As canon of the Church of the Holy Sepulchre, do you promise to live a life of chastity, consecrated to God and without private property?'

'I promise.'

The patriarch, still holding John's hands in his own, leaned forward and kissed John on the right cheek. 'The peace of the Lord be always with you, my son.'

'Amen.'

'My dear son, ponder well the order you have taken and the burden laid on your shoulders. Strive to lead a holy and devout life, and to please almighty God, that you may obtain His grace. May He in His kindness deign to bestow it on you.'

The patriarch released his hands. John rose and went to sit in his choir stall as a full member of the chapter of canons. He had come to the Holy Land years ago searching for redemption, and surely he had found it. His life now belonged to God.

John sat in the chancellery, a small room dominated by an oak desk covered in scrolls. He unrolled one of them. It was a list of tax revenues from the town of Ramlah. Keeping track of taxes and landholdings was not so interesting as John's work tutoring

Prince Baldwin, but he had proved adept at it. He picked up a quill with ink-stained fingers. He dipped it and began to enter numbers from the scroll into a leather-bound register. He heard the slap of sandals on the stone floor and looked up to see William enter.

John arched an eyebrow. 'I thought you were with Baldwin.'

'I have been called to audience with the King. You will tutor the Prince.'

'Shall I teach him swordplay?' John asked hopefully.

William shook his head. 'Arabic.'

John found Prince Baldwin in his quarters, playing with two wooden figures under the watchful eyes of a nurse. The prince was three, the same age John's son Ubadah had been the last time John had seen him. Like Ubadah, Baldwin was a handsome child, with fat cheeks and straight, sandy-brown hair. But Baldwin's eyes were green, not dark. Though hardly more than a babe, he had already shown himself to be a clever boy. John spent several hours a day with him, and the boy was absorbing Arabic with surprising rapidity.

'It is time for the Prince's lesson,' John said. The nurse departed, and John sat on the floor across from Baldwin. 'Arabic today. Let us begin by seeing how much you remember. Sword.'

'*Saif*,' Baldwin repeated in Arabic.

'Good. Lamp.'

'*Chiragh*.'

'Very good!' But the child had ceased paying attention. A clatter of horses' hooves had come through the open window. Baldwin flew to it, and John also rose to look down on the paved courtyard. Four knights in mail were dismounting. With them was a darker man in a white caftan.

'A Saracen?' Baldwin asked. Muslims were forbidden in the city, and this might well have been the first one the prince had ever seen.

John nodded. He watched until the men entered the palace, then returned to his place on the floor. 'Come, Prince. We should continue.'

Baldwin crossed his arms over his chest. 'No!'

'Sit!' John snapped, and Baldwin began to cry, his angelic face twisted into an ugly mask of anguish. 'Stop it. Men do not cry,' John scolded, but this only seemed to make matters worse. Baldwin began to wail. Desperate for some way to distract the child, John removed the gold cross from around his neck and set it on the floor before Baldwin. 'Look at the pretty gold.' The boy quieted instantly. He reached for the cross but froze, his eyes fixed on the door.

'Good day, young Prince.'

John turned to see a woman standing in the open doorway. She was about John's age. Her tunic fit snugly at the waist, revealing an athletic figure. Judging from the rings on her fingers and her elaborate white tunic, heavily embroidered with gold thread, she was a lady of some importance, yet John had never seen her at court.

'My lady,' he said as he replaced the cross about his neck and stood. The woman stepped into the room and pushed up her veil. She had a pleasant oval face, green eyes and full lips. A strand of hair the colour of barley escaped from her headdress to fall in curls down to her bosom. Her attention was fixed upon Baldwin, but then she noticed John staring and smiled. Her teeth were even and white.

'We have not met, Father,' the lady said in the accented French of someone who had been raised in the Holy Land. 'You are new at court?'

'Yes, my lady. My name is John of Tatewic, canon of the Church of the Holy Sepulchre and secretary to the chancellor William.' John bowed.

'Tatewic?' The lady arched a thin eyebrow. 'You are English? How do you come to be at the king's court, in the company of the king's son?'

'Amalric has instructed me to teach the boy Arabic and the ways of the Saracens.'

The lady smiled slyly. 'You only answered half my question, John of Tatewic. Never mind. I am sure you have your reasons.' She looked beyond him to Baldwin, who had wandered away to play, and suddenly it was as if John did not exist. She stepped past him and gathered her long tunic up with one hand as she sat before the boy. He ignored her, busy playing with a knight and a mamluk, both carved from wood.

'Do you recognize me, Baldwin?' she asked. The prince did not look up from his toys. 'Is that a knight? Your father perhaps?' Baldwin's only response was to turn his back to the lady.

'I am sorry,' John told her. 'He is sometimes shy around strangers.' This was a lie. Baldwin was a gregarious child, always curious and quick to smile. John had never seen him act this way.

'He shall have to overcome that. After all, he will be king one day.' The lady stood and turned towards John. For a moment she looked upset – her lips pressed together and lines radiating from the corners or her mouth. Then the lines vanished. 'Tell me, John, what do you think of King Amalric?'

'He is a good man.'

'Yes, he tries to be.'

John frowned. 'What do you mean?'

The lady did not answer. She bent down and placed a hand on Baldwin's shoulder. The boy froze. She gently kissed him on the top of his head and went to the door. She stopped and looked back. 'It was a pleasure to meet you, John of Tatewic. I hope to see you again.'

'As you wish, my lady. But tell me, what is your name?'

'Agnes.' Her eyes flicked to Baldwin and then back to John. 'Agnes de Courtenay.' And with that, she was gone.

A moment later William entered the room. 'Who was that? You are a priest now, John,' he said with mock severity. 'You are not to entertain strange women.'

'She is a lady. Agnes de Courtenay.'

'Agnes?' William's eyes opened wide.

'You know her?'

'She is the King's former wife.' William lowered his voice to a whisper. 'Baldwin's mother. What was she doing here? Did she come to see the child?' John shrugged. William's eyes narrowed. 'Be careful of her, John.'

'She seemed pleasant enough.'

'She has been forbidden from seeing Baldwin, and for good reason.'

John raised his eyebrows, but William did not elaborate.

'Now come. We have important business.' William raised his voice. 'Nurse!' The nurse entered, and William led John from the room. 'An ambassador has come from Egypt,' William said as they headed across the palace.

'What does he want?'

'That is for you to find out.'

'Me?'

'You know their ways better than any of us, John. I want you to make him feel comfortable.' William stopped before a wooden door. 'And I need to know if he can be trusted.'

William pushed the door open to reveal a small room. A single window looked out on the courtyard of the palace, and through it streamed sunlight, illuminating a broad oak table with four chairs. The Egyptian ambassador had ignored the chairs and sat cross-legged on the thick carpet. He was simply dressed, his white cotton caftan contrasting with his dark skin, the same deep-brown colour as the table. John saw at once that he was no warrior: his face was soft and his hands plump. He rose as John entered.

John inclined his head. 'As-salaamu alaykum, sayyid.'

'Wa-salaam alaykum,' the ambassador replied. His voice was soft and his Egyptian accent strange.

John placed his hand on his chest. 'My name is John—Juwan,' he added, giving it the Arabic pronunciation.

'I am Al-Khlata, secretary to Shawar, the Vizier of Egypt.'

John gestured to the chairs. 'Please sit. King Amalric has asked me to ensure that you are comfortable.'

'I have everything I need,' Al-Khlata said as he sat on the carpet.

'You shall have fruit and cool water. I insist.' John looked to William, who nodded and hurried off. John sat on the carpet across from Al-Khlata. 'You must have travelled far.'

'Across Al-Naqab,' Al-Khlata agreed. His hazel eyes narrowed as he examined John. 'How do you come to speak our language so well?'

'I spent several years at the court of Nur ad-Din.'

'And now you serve these savages?'

'We cannot all choose our masters.'

At that moment a servant boy entered with a tray upon which sat a pitcher of water, two cups and a bowl filled with cubes of mango. The boy placed the tray on the floor between them and retreated, closing the door behind him. Neither man spoke as John poured the water and handed a cup to Al-Khlata. The Egyptian took a sip and placed the water aside. John held out the bowl of mango, but Al-Khlata waved it off.

'I did not choose to serve my master, either,' the Egyptian said. 'My father was a Turcoman, born far from these lands. I do not remember him, whether he was a baker, merchant or warrior. I was bought as a child and sent to the Caliph's palace in Cairo, where I was taught to write, to recite poetry, to keep accounts.'

'Then we are not so different.'

Al-Khlata nodded. 'Tell me of your new master, the King.'

'He is a good man, honest and intelligent.'

'I have heard that he is given to drink and women.'

John shrugged. 'He is a king.'

Al-Khlata met John's eyes. 'I have heard that he is mad.'

'Far from it, but—' John's forehead creased as he hesitated.

When he spoke again, his voice was low. 'But he is odd. He sometimes laughs suddenly for no reason. You should not be offended. He is not mocking you.'

'I see.'

'And what of your vizier, Shawar?'

Al-Khlata looked amused. 'Like your king, a good man.'

John heard the door creak open behind him and looked to see the spare, straight-backed seneschal Guy standing there, with William close behind. 'Come,' Guy said in Latin. 'The King will see you now.'

William translated for Al-Khlata, who rose and followed Guy out of the door. John and William fell in behind them.

'Can he be trusted?' William whispered.

John shook his head. 'He did not eat the fruit he was offered. This is a great insult in their culture; it shows that he does not trust our hospitality. And a man who does not trust us cannot be trusted.'

William nodded. 'I was right about you, John. God did send you to us for a reason. Did you learn anything else? Why is he here?'

'I did not ask.'

'By Christ! Why not?'

John shrugged. 'You said to make him comfortable. It would not have been polite.'

'Very well,' William grumbled. 'We shall find out soon enough.'

'G-God grant you joy, Al-Khlata. Welcome to J-Jerusalem, and to my c-court,' Amalric declared in a voice too loud for the size of his private audience chamber. He sat upon a simple wooden throne, flanked by the seneschal Guy and the constable Humphrey on one side, and on the other by Gilbert and Bertrand, masters of the Hospitallers and Templars, respectively. Amalric was dressed in full regalia: the royal robe of ermine upon his shoulders, the crown of Jerusalem upon his brow, and a sceptre grasped in his right hand. He looked the part of a king, but even from the shadows at the rear of the room, John could tell that Amalric was nervous. It was not just the return of his childhood stutter; the king was also stroking his thick blond beard. John had been at court long enough to learn that this was as agitated as Amalric ever became.

Al-Khlata put his hand to his heart and bowed. 'As-salaamu alaykum, Malik,' he began in Arabic. William translated. 'I am honoured by your kind welcome. I am sure that the Caliph and Vizier Shawar will be equally pleased.'

Amalric tugged more doggedly at his beard. 'P-perhaps they will be less pleased when they hear what I have to say. If you have come to seek p-p—' The king's face reddened, he took a deep breath and started again. 'If you have come to seek our friendship, then you must know that cannot be. You have allied with Nur ad-Din. You have allowed his army into C-Cairo itself. There can be no peace between our p-peoples so long as his men remain in your lands.'

'Of course. That is precisely why Shawar has sent me. He needs your help to drive Nur ad-Din's army from Egypt.'

John could hardly believe his ears. Shawar had only just signed a treaty with Nur ad-Din. William seemed equally surprised. He stood with his mouth open, although he had not yet translated Shawar's words.

'Well?' Amalric demanded. He looked from William to John. 'What did he say?'

John cleared his throat. 'He asked us to invade Egypt, sire. Shawar wants us to drive out Nur ad-Din.'

'By Christ's wounds,' murmured the Templar, Bertrand. 'We can open the holy sites to pilgrimage: where Moses crossed the Red Sea; where Joseph and Mary rested during their flight from Bethlehem.'

William stepped closer to the throne. 'An invasion will cost money, sire.'

'The Egyptians have untold wealth,' Gilbert noted.

Amalric stroked his beard. 'Ask him what Shawar offers in return for our assistance.' William translated the request.

'Caliph al-Adid will recognize you as his overlord,' Al-Khlata replied, 'and pay you four hundred thousand dinars.'

The seneschal paled. 'That is nearly equivalent to our annual revenue, sire.'

'King of Jerusalem and lord of Egypt,' Amalric murmured. 'I could hire enough men to take Damascus. Succeed where my brother failed.' The king's forehead creased and his lips began to tremble. He burst out laughing, and Al-Khlata took a step back. The lords around the throne shifted uncomfortably. The fit subsided, and Amalric resumed his impassive expression. He looked to William. 'Offer m-my apologies to Al-Khlata. And tell him that I accept his offer.'

'Perhaps it would be wise to reflect before accepting, sire,' Guy said. 'We know nothing of this Al-Khlata. Can we trust him? Or his master? Why would Shawar turn his back on his fellow Saracens to ally with us?'

John stepped forward. 'They are Saracens, sire, but they are not the same.'

'What do you mean?' Amalric asked.

'The Egyptians are Shiites. They look to the Fatimid caliph in Cairo. Nur ad-Din and his men are Sunni, under the caliph in Baghdad.'

'They are all Mohammedans,' the seneschal said.

'Just as they consider the English and French to all be Franks,' John said, 'whereas we know that they are in fact quite different.'

'I see,' Amalric said. 'What do you say to this, William?'

'I council caution, sire. If Shawar is willing to betray Nur ad-Din, then what is to say that he will not betray us in turn?'

Bertrand nodded. 'William is right.'

'Very well,' Amalric said. 'Tell him that we need time to c-consider.'

William opened his mouth to translate, but Al-Khlata spoke

first. 'Shawar is a man of his word,' he said in accented but correct French. 'It is Nur ad-Din who has broken his oath. His general, Shirkuh, has designs on Cairo. He sits in Giza, like a hawk poised to strike. Shawar needs your aid to remove him, and he needs it now. Your answer cannot wait.'

Amalric looked to William, who frowned and shook his head. The king turned to the constable. Humphrey commanded the king's army in the field, and his word had weight. He nodded. Amalric turned back to Al-Khlata. 'You will leave tomorrow for Cairo to tell Shawar that he has my support.'

Al-Khlata bowed low. 'Thank you, Malik.'

Amalric nodded, and a servant entered to lead the Egyptian to his quarters. William frowned as he watched him go. 'I do not trust him,' he muttered.

Amalric rose from the throne and put a hand on William's shoulder. 'Nor do I, friend. But this is an opportunity we cannot ignore. Write to Bohemond of Antioch and Raymond of Tripoli. They will need to defend our northern border while I am gone.' Amalric looked to the constable. 'Gather the army, Humphrey. We leave in two weeks' time.'

APRIL 1164: GIZA

Yusuf set his quill down and rubbed his temples. He had just finished another letter to Gumushtagin, written in ghubar, the tiny Arabic script used for the pigeon post. He had told the eunuch of the consideration that Shawar had shown them, how he had kept the army well provisioned and invited Yusuf to dine with him each night. He had also written of the increasing tension between the vizier and Yusuf's uncle. Shirkuh was angry that Shawar had delivered only a fraction of the tribute that was due to Nur ad-Din. Shawar resented the presence of Shirkuh, who had informed the vizier that he planned to winter the army in Egypt. Yusuf had been forced to intervene more than once to prevent an open break between the two. All of this was information that Gumushtagin would eventually learn from Shirkuh's dispatches to Nur ad-Din. Nevertheless, each letter that he wrote left Yusuf with a nagging sense of guilt.

He rolled the scroll and slid it into a tiny tube. He wrote Gumushtagin's name on a scrap of paper and then wound it around the tube, affixing it with a dab of glue. He left his tent and strode across camp to where the *hawadi* were kept. The mail pigeons sat in their cages, cooing softly. 'For the palace in Aleppo,' Yusuf told the keeper, a stooped mamluk, too old to fight. The man nodded and went to one of the cages. He took out the pigeon and carefully tied the tube to its leg. Then he stepped outside and released the bird. It circled once and flew away, heading north-east.

'Your message will arrive tonight, Sayyid,' the keeper told him.

Yusuf was heading back to his tent when Selim hailed him. 'Brother! There you are!' Selim was breathless. He looked to have run the length of the camp.

'What is it?'

'Shirkuh needs you. It is the Franks. They are here.'

Yusuf entered Shirkuh's tent to find him speaking with a bow-legged Egyptian who smelled of fish. 'You are certain?' Shirkuh was asking him.

'I was fishing north of here, in the eastern branch of the Nile, when I saw them; maybe five thousand men. They are no more than four days' march from Cairo.'

Shirkuh handed the fisherman a sack of coins. 'Keep me informed of their movements. There is more where this came from if your information proves useful.'

'Shukran, Emir. Shukran Allah!' The fisherman bowed repeatedly as he backed from the tent.

When he had gone, Shirkuh turned to Yusuf. 'What do you make of this, young eagle?'

'The Frankish king is no fool. He knows that if Nur ad-Din

and Egypt are allied, he is in grave danger. He must be marching to drive us out.'

The lines on Shirkuh's forehead deepened. 'If he is no fool, tell me why he has come to Egypt with only five thousand men. That is not enough to face us and the Egyptians. I do not like this.'

'We should speak with Shawar,' Yusuf suggested.

'Yes, he is clever. Perhaps he will know what the Frankish king plans.'

Accompanied by a dozen members of Shirkuh's private guard, they took a barge north to Al-Maks, the port of Cairo. From there they rode to the northern gate, the Bab al-Futuh. As they approached, Yusuf saw that the gate was closed. Soldiers stood atop it with spears in hand. Atop each spear was a head. Yusuf felt a burning in his stomach as he recognized those heads. They belonged to the garrison of mamluks that Nur ad-Din had left in Cairo.

Shirkuh flushed red with anger. He reined to a stop before the gate and shouted up to the guards. 'What is the meaning of this? Open the gate immediately! I wish to speak with Shawar.'

'I am sorry, Atabeg,' one of the guards called down. 'The Vizier has ordered the city closed to you.'

'Surely there is a misunderstanding,' Yusuf said to his uncle. He raised his voice to speak to the guards. 'Inform Shawar that we will wait here until he arrives.'

They did not have to wait long before Shawar appeared atop the gate. 'Shirkuh! Yusuf! I deeply regret that we find ourselves in this awkward situation.'

'You see, it is a misunderstanding,' Yusuf told his uncle. 'Open the gate, friend,' he called up to Shawar. 'Let us in so we may talk.'

'I am afraid I cannot do that. As you can see—' he gestured to the heads '—your men are no longer welcome in Cairo.'

'I will gut you, you two-faced bastard!' Shirkuh roared.

Yusuf put a hand on his uncle's arm to calm him. 'This is no time for a falling out,' he called to Shawar. 'The Frankish army is only days away. We must discuss how we will repel them.'

'But I have no wish to repel them. It is I who invited them here.'

The burning in Yusuf's stomach grew worse. 'Why?'

'I wish to be master of Egypt,' Shawar replied. 'I never shall be, so long as your army is here.'

'But we are your allies! I am your friend.'

'Yes, we are good friends, aren't we?' Shawar smiled. 'It pains me to turn my back on a friend such as you, Yusuf, but my personal feelings do not matter. I must do what is in the best interest of Egypt.'

Yusuf could hardly believe what he was hearing. This man was nothing like the Shawar he had come to know. That smile, which Yusuf had once found so charming, now appeared false. How could Yusuf have been so blind?

'Damn your seventh grandfather, you deceitful bastard!' Shirkuh shouted. He had drawn his sword and was waving it up at Shawar. 'I will tear down the walls of Cairo stone by stone. I will cut off your head and piss down your throat!'

'You are welcome to try,' Shawar replied brightly. 'But I must warn you that if you do not leave now, my men will deal with you. I am afraid that this is the last time we will speak. Farewell, my friends.'

'Son of a donkey!' Shirkuh spluttered. 'Whore's twat!'

The men atop the walls drew back their bows. Yusuf grabbed his uncle's arm. 'Come, Uncle. We must go. We shall have our revenge later.'

APRIL 1164: CAIRO

John tugged at the rough collar of his cloak of dark brown wool. It was fastened with a brooch at the centre of the chest,

69

in the clerical style. Laymen fastened their cloaks at their right shoulder so as to leave their sword arm unencumbered. Another advantage of placing the clasp at the shoulder, John had discovered regretfully, was that it distributed the weight of the cloak in such a way that it did not chafe. He tugged at the cloak again, pulling it away from his raw neck. If it were up to him, he would have worn a simple burnoose and keffiyeh, but William had insisted that as a priest and adviser to the king he must travel in tunic and cloak, with his long stole hanging about his neck. Even in April the Egyptian heat was oppressive, and his tunic was soaked with sweat.

'What I wouldn't give to be in England right now,' he murmured.

'England?' Amalric asked as he came alongside. The two men rode near the head of a column of nearly five thousand warriors. There were just under four hundred mounted knights, each equipped with a thick mail shirt, lance, sword and shield. Surrounding the knights were three thousand sergeants; foot-soldiers who mostly wore leather jerkins and fought with spears and bows. The rearguard was composed of native cavalry, Christians who had lived in the Holy Land for generations and had more in common with the Saracens than the Franks. They wore light, padded armour and carried bamboo spears and compact, curved bows.

'I was born and raised in the Holy Land,' the king continued. 'I have never been to England, although I have heard it described often enough. The pilgrims never cease to speak of it. Fields of green, woods, water in abundance . . . I have often wondered why, if it is so lovely, so many men leave to come here.'

John was not sure how to reply. He noticed that Amalric was worriedly fingering the fragment of the true cross that he wore on a chain about his neck. He hoped that Amalric was not seeking religious consolation. John still felt uncertain in his role as a priest. He wished William were here, but the chancellor was away on a mission to the Roman court in Constantinople.

'I had to leave,' John said at last. 'I killed my brother.' Amalric did not speak, so John continued. 'He betrayed my father and several other Saxon lords to the Norman king in return for more land.'

'The Norman king?' Amalric asked. 'England has been ruled by the Angevin line for nearly a hundred years. Surely Stephen was as English as you.'

'The Normans speak French and the common people, English. And in the north we have long memories. My grandfather was a child when William the Bastard's army butchered our people. He passed the story of the Harrowing on to my father, who passed it on to me.'

'I see.' Amalric continued to finger his cross. They were riding alongside a branch of the Nile delta, making their way from Bilbeis towards Cairo. John watched a low skiff with a triangular sail gliding upstream, mirroring their progress. A man in the prow was fishing with a bamboo rod and line. He had been at it for an hour but had caught nothing. John suspected he was a spy for Shirkuh, more interested in the Frankish army than fish.

'Bernard of Clairvaux visited me last night,' Amalric said suddenly.

John's eyebrows shot up. He cleared his throat. 'Is he not dead, sire?'

The corner of Amalric's mouth twitched, then he burst into high-pitched, shrill laughter. 'In a dream, John. He came to me in a dream. He said that I am a poor Chri— a poor Chri—' The king's face was reddening as he struggled to get his words out. His stutter was always worse when he was upset. 'He said that I am not a worthy king.'

'But that is not true, sire.'

'Perhaps.' Amalric sighed. 'I have my faults, John. I divorced my wife and have since lived in sin with many women. Many women. To lie with a woman outside of marriage is a wicked sin, is it not, John?'

'It is to be expected. You are a king, sire.'

'That is hardly the appropriate answer of a man of the cloth!'

'I fear I am a poor priest.'

'*Hmph.* William tells me that a king should have a wife.' Amalric held up the piece of cross around his neck. 'Saint Bernard t-told me that I will be unw-worthy of wearing the cross unless I am a better Christian.'

'So you shall marry, sire?'

Amalric shrugged. 'Or p-perhaps I should simply cease wearing the true cross.' He took the chain from around his neck and placed it in a pouch at his waist. He grinned. 'Yes, that feels better.' The king spurred ahead, leaving John to ride alone.

The sun had reached its zenith when the ruins of ancient Heliopolis – only a few miles north-east of Cairo – appeared on the horizon. The first thing John saw was a tall column that came to a point, like a needle reaching towards the sky. As they rode closer, he could make out the remains of the city's wall of crude brick, now crumbling to dust. Beyond the wall, blocks of dark granite stood here and there, the obelisk towering over them. Its sides were decorated with strange symbols; John identified snakes, cranes and ploughs, and men in what looked to be skirts. An ornate tent of red silk stood beyond the obelisk. Surrounding the tent were ranks of Egyptian warriors holding long shields and lances.

Amalric held up a fist to signal a halt. 'Have the men take water and food,' he told the constable Humphrey. 'But be prepared for trouble.' He waved John forward.

'Yes, sire?'

'You will come with me to interpret. Fulcher and De Caesarea, you come as well,' he called to two of the nobles. Geoffrey Fulcher was an older man with greying hair and a pleasant face. He wore the dress of a Templar knight: a white surcoat with red cross and a white mantle about his shoulders.

He had returned not long ago from a mission to the court of France. Hugh de Caesarea was a hot-blooded young man, but he was reputed to have a silver tongue.

The four of them rode down an ancient street with occasional paving stones protruding from the dust. As they neared the tent the ranks of soldiers parted and a man strode out to meet them. He wore fabulous robes of red silk decorated with a swirling pattern of roses picked out in gold and silver. A jewelled sword hung from his waist. The man was tall and thin with a trimmed beard and very short black hair. He had an arresting face – sharp cheekbones and full lips that stretched back in a dazzling smile. 'God keep you, King Amalric,' the man called in Frankish. He then switched to Arabic, and John translated his next words. 'I am Shawar, vizier to the Caliph. Welcome to Heliopolis, 'Ayn Sams, as my people call it: "Well of the Sun".'

'God grant you joy,' Amalric replied as he dismounted. He clasped Shawar's arms and kissed him on the cheeks in the Saracen style.

Shawar stood rigidly, as if he were being kissed by a leper. But he recovered his composure quickly, and when the king stepped away, Shawar was smiling. 'I am so pleased that you have come! Step inside my tent, you and your men.' The tent was a grand affair, large enough to hold a hundred men. Scribes were seated cross-legged on the floor, writing desks on their laps. Shawar went to a table that held several glasses of water. He handed them to Amalric and the others. John noticed that the glass was cold, beads of moisture forming on the outside. Cold water in the desert; he wondered how the vizier had managed that. 'Drink!' Shawar said. 'You must be thirsty after your journey.'

Amalric took a gulp, then set his glass down. 'Where is Nur ad-Din's army?'

'They are camped at Giza, on the far side of the Nile.'

'Have you sought to dislodge them?'

73

'To leave the walls of Cairo to confront such a powerful foe seemed foolish.' Shawar again flashed a toothy smile. It reminded John of a cat toying with its prey. 'But now that you are here, we outnumber Nur ad-Din's forces nearly two to one. Together, we will drive his army from Egypt!'

'Together?' Amalric asked when John had translated. 'There is a matter of a treaty to sign first.'

'It is all arranged. You will be well rewarded for your assistance. Four hundred thousand dinars, as was agreed.'

'And when will we see this money?'

'Half will be paid now and half once you have driven Shirkuh from Egypt.'

John spoke for Amalric before the king could reply. 'And the Caliph will agree to this?'

Shawar blinked as if surprised. He examined John for a moment. 'Of course. I speak for the Caliph.'

Hugh spoke now. 'That is not good enough. The Caliph must witness the treaty himself. He must swear to its provisions.'

'Very well.' Shawar replied tersely. It was clear that he did not like the idea. He went to one of the scribes and held up a sheet of paper, fresh with ink. He handed it to Amalric. 'Here is the treaty. The Caliph will confirm it this very night.'

'Then it is settled.' Amalric extended his hands to embrace the vizier, but Shawar was already bowing and backing away.

'Al-Khlata will show you to your camp. I have selected a suitable location beside the Nile, just north of the city. This evening I will send a man to guide your envoys to the palace. Now, I must hurry to the city to prepare the Caliph for their arrival. Ma'a as-salaama, King Amalric.'

The vizier stepped from the tent and Al-Khlata, the messenger who had come to Jerusalem, stepped forward. He bowed to Amalric. 'If you please, great King, I will show you and your men to your camp.'

Al-Khlata led the army down a dirt track between black fields dotted by bright green sprigs of sprouting wheat. Ahead loomed the pyramids of Giza. Amalric slowed his mount to put ten paces between himself and Al-Khlata. He began to speak in a low voice to Gilbert d'Assailly, the Hospitallers' grand master. John spurred forward, just close enough to hear. 'Four hundred thousand dinars!' the king was saying. 'How many chests do you think it will take to carry such a sum?'

'But what happens once we have driven off Nur ad-Din's army?' Gilbert said darkly. 'Shawar will have no more use for us. What if he refuses to pay the rest of the gold?'

'Then we will take it.'

'And if we cannot? Cairo is not an easy nut to crack, and if we spend too much time here then Nur ad-Din will attack our lands in the Kingdom.'

'What do you suggest?'

'We leave a garrison in Cairo. Shawar will see that they are housed and fed. They will take charge of the city's gates.'

'But he will never agree to such a thing.'

'How can he not? If he refuses, we leave him to face Shirkuh alone. And besides, he can hardly haggle over the details of the treaty before the Caliph.' Amalric said nothing. He was tugging at his long blond beard. 'Just think, sire, with a garrison in Cairo we will win more than gold. We can force Shawar to do as we wish. He will be vizier, but you will be master of Egypt.'

Amalric was nodding. 'Make it so, Gilbert. Have the scribes draw up a new treaty.'

'How many men do they have?' John asked, pointing across the Nile to Shirkuh's distant camp, where hundreds of campfires blazed in the evening twilight.

'Something like six thousand, all mounted,' Al-Qadi al-Fadil said. The Egyptian official was a small, hunchbacked man with thin, ink-stained fingers. He had been sent to guide Amalric's envoys to the caliph. Amalric had again selected Geoffrey Fulcher and Hugh de Caesarea, and John as translator.

'And they have made no move to attack the city?' John asked.

'To attack across the river would be suicide. We would cut them to pieces as they emerged from their boats.'

'That means we cannot attack them either,' John pointed out.

'Not directly,' Al-Fadil agreed.

John gazed at the camp across the Nile. Yusuf would be there. John wondered what his friend would think if he saw John now. For the occasion of meeting the caliph, John had put on his full priestly regalia: the heavy, gold-embroidered chasuble over his white tunic, the long stole around his neck, the band of decorated silk tied to his left arm and the amice draped over his head. He carried copies of the treaty in a tube that hung from a leather cord around his neck. He was sure he looked impressive, but the outfit was damnably hot, even in the relative cool of the evening.

Ahead, the torch-lit walls of Cairo stood out in the gathering darkness. The path they followed led to a gate, but Al-Fadil turned away. 'Why do we not enter the city?' Hugh asked, and John translated.

'Your presence might upset the people,' Al-Fadil explained. 'We will enter directly into the palace.'

Al-Fadil led them to a narrow strip of land that ran between a canal and the city's western wall. Hugh whistled in appreciation as he gazed up at the battlements. 'How tall do you think those walls are?'

'Thirty feet, maybe,' Geoffrey replied. 'Of solid workmanship.'

A gate framed by burning torches appeared in the darkness ahead. 'Bab al-Kantara,' Al-Fadil declared. The enchanted gate. The Egyptian led the way up a ramp and across a short drawbridge to a wooden double door some ten paces wide. It swung inward and they rode into a low-ceilinged room, the walls of which were lined with guards. As John dismounted he noticed that a few of them were making the sign of the evil eye –

forming a circle with the thumb and forefinger of their right hand and shaking it at the Franks. Shawar entered at the far end of the room, and the soldiers stopped gesturing.

'As-salaamu 'alaykum, friends,' he said with a broad smile. 'The Caliph is eager to see you, but first, I must ask that you leave your weapons here.'

When John translated, Hugh frowned, but he removed his sword belt nonetheless and handed it to one of the guards. Geoffrey did the same.

'They will be returned to you when you leave,' Shawar reassured them. 'My men will polish and sharpen them, so that they are better than new. Now come, the Caliph awaits.'

The vizier led them through a second room and out into a colonnaded courtyard in which dozens of rose bushes bloomed, releasing their sweet scent into the evening air. As John entered the next courtyard, a caged panther hissed and roared at him. There were other animals that looked like something out of a dream: a horse covered in white and black stripes; a strange, deerlike creature with spindly legs and an impossibly long neck; and a huge lion with golden eyes.

From the menagerie, they passed through a series of luxurious rooms before arriving in a larger chamber, divided in the middle by a curtain of golden silk. 'You should kneel,' Shawar told them.

John dropped to one knee, but neither Geoffrey nor Hugh moved. 'It will help our cause,' John told them. 'It would be impolitic to refuse.'

Geoffrey reluctantly knelt, but Hugh remained standing. 'I kneel before my king and before God,' he grumbled, 'not this infidel.'

'It means nothing,' John assured him. Hugh looked doubtful.

'Please,' Shawar said. 'You must kneel if you are to see the Caliph.'

'Then I will not see him.'

John chose not to translate that. 'My lord,' he said to Hugh, 'as a canon of the Church of the Holy Sepulchre, I tell you that God knows the difference between a knee taken to honour and a knee taken under duress. Kneeling means nothing.'

'You are sure, priest?'

John nodded. Hugh hesitated for a moment longer and then knelt. Shawar placed his jewelled sword on the ground and prostrated himself so that his forehead touched the floor. After his third bow the curtain was raised. John's first impression of the caliph was that he was a statue or carving. He was covered from head to toe in jewelled silks and where his face should have been was a mesh veil that created the impression that his features had been erased. He reminded John of one of the statues of the saints that adorned the great portal of the Church of the Holy Sepulchre. The illusion was spoiled when the caliph's hand moved in a gesture for them to rise.

Shawar addressed the caliph. 'Successor of the messenger of God, God's deputy, defender of the faithful, may I present the Frankish envoys.' John translated quietly for Geoffrey and Hugh.

'As-salaamu 'alaykum,' the caliph said, his voice high at the beginning before breaking at the end. 'Welcome to my court.'

Geoffrey took a step forward. 'Great Caliph, I am Geoffrey Fulcher, Preceptor of the Temple in Jerusalem. God bless you and grant you joy, health and fortune.'

'And I am Hugh of Caesarea. God keep you, Caliph.'

John translated for both.

'We have brought the treaty, signed by King Amalric,' Geoffrey said.

John removed four copies of the treaty from the tube around his neck and unrolled the parchments. He stepped forward to hand them to the caliph.

'Wait!' Shawar ordered. He held out a hand, and John gave him the treaties. Shawar read quickly. His face remained expressionless, but his cheeks tinged red. 'We did not agree to your quartering troops in Cairo,' he hissed in a low voice that the caliph could not hear.

'It is for your protection, Vizier,' Geoffrey replied once John had translated.

'We can protect ourselves.'

Hugh smirked. 'In that case, we shall take our army back to Jerusalem.'

Shawar's face reddened further. The caliph leaned forward on his throne. 'Is there a problem, Vizier?'

'No, Imam,' Shawar replied. 'All is well. Al-Ifranj will help us to drive the Sunni invaders from our lands.'

'That is good. Sign the treaty.' When the boy caliph spoke again, his voice was harsh. 'We must teach the infidels a lesson.'

John knew of the rift between the Sunni and Shiites, but he was still surprised. The caliph seemed unconcerned that the Franks were Christians. He hated the Sunni Muslims much more.

Shawar turned to Geoffrey. 'The Caliph has given his consent to the treaty.' Shawar went to the table and signed all four copies. He had regained his equanimity, and he smiled as he handed two of the treaties to Geoffrey. 'There. It is done.'

'That is not enough,' Hugh said.

The vizier's smile faded. 'Pardon?'

'A treaty is only a sheet of paper. The Caliph must give me his word, man to man.'

'But—' Shawar's words ended in a gasp. Hugh was striding across the room, his hand extended to shake that of the caliph. The caliph shrank back against his throne. John heard the whisper of steel against leather as several of the mamluks standing along the back wall drew their blades. Shawar held up a hand to stop them. 'My lord!' he beseeched Hugh in Frankish. 'You cannot touch the Caliph!'

Hugh ignored him. He thrust his hand towards the caliph's

face. 'Swear that you will abide by the terms of this treaty.' He looked to John, who translated.

'What more does this man want?' the caliph asked, his voice breaking. 'I have already given my consent.'

'You are to clasp his hand.'

The caliph turned towards Shawar. 'Must I?'

John had not translated these last statements. Hugh looked to him questioningly. 'Why will he not give his word?' he demanded. 'I knew there was treachery afoot.' John chose not to translate that, either.

Shawar ignored Hugh's outburst. 'Yes, Imam. It is necessary.' The caliph extended a trembling hand.

'He must remove his glove,' Hugh insisted. 'The oath is not valid unless we clasp hands, flesh to flesh.'

Shawar went pale. 'But that is impossible!' he cried in Frankish.

'Then there will be no treaty!' Hugh declared.

Geoffrey nodded in agreement. 'We must be certain the alliance will be honoured.'

Shawar looked from one to the other, then to John. 'Make them understand,' he said in Arabic. 'The Caliph cannot take this man's hand. It is impossible.'

'Even if it means the failure of the treaty?' John asked.

'Even then.'

Hugh was standing with his hands on his hips, his jaw jutting forward belligerently. John doubted he could speak reason with the man. Instead, he looked to the caliph. He approached the throne and knelt, bowing low so that his forehead touched the floor. 'Representative of God, defender of the faithful,' he said in Arabic. 'This man is not worthy to be in your presence. He is an ifranji, a savage, an animal. He is filthy and impure, but he longs for purity. He wishes to embrace the true faith.'

The caliph leaned forward on his throne. 'Truly?'

Hugh placed a rough hand on John's shoulder. 'What are you saying, priest?'

John ignored him. He continued speaking to the caliph. 'This man has done terrible things. He has defiled his body with the flesh of swine. He has drunk alcohol. He has killed members of the faith. But he believes that if he touches your flesh with the flesh of his hand, it will purify him.'

'But that is ridiculous!' the caliph scoffed.

'It is. But the Franks are like children, Imam. They believe in mysteries and magic. You have no doubt heard that the Franks believe that in their rituals bread and wine are transformed into the very flesh and blood of their god, Jesus. They also believe that the touch of Jesus could cure the sick and raise the dead. To Franks, the touch of a holy man is a miraculous thing. They are like children, and if they embrace the faith, they can only do so as children would do.'

'Damn it!' Hugh growled. 'What are you saying, man? Will he shake my hand or will he not?'

'I am explaining the terms of the treaty in greater detail,' John replied tersely. He returned to the caliph. 'Imam, he says that it would be the great honour of his life to touch your hand, that he would count himself forever blessed.'

'And he truly wishes to embrace the one true faith?' the caliph asked in an uncertain voice.

'Yes.' John had a flash of inspiration. 'He wishes to fight against the Sunni army, against the false caliph in Baghdad, who has led so many astray. He wishes your blessing for the coming battle.'

'Very well,' the caliph consented. He removed his glove and extended his hand. John could hear the alarmed gasps and urgent whispers of the courtiers lining the walls.

Hugh grabbed the caliph's manicured hand in his own callused paw. 'We are sworn to one another, to uphold the treaty signed here today,' he said as he vigorously shook the caliph's hand. 'May God smite you if you break your word.'

'May Allah give you strength in your battle against the infidel Sunni,' the caliph replied in Arabic. Hugh released his hand,

and the caliph wiped his own on his caftan before slipping on his glove.

'Shukran,' Shawar said to John. Then he took Hugh by the arm and led him away from the throne. 'Are you satisfied now, Sir Hugh?'

'Yes, Vizier. We are allies, and we shall drive Nur ad-Din's armies from your lands.'

Chapter 4

John's horse trotted into the Nile, kicking up water that shone silver in the moonlight. He could just see the king ahead of him, urging his horse across the river, while all around he could hear the splashing of men and horses, visible only as dim shapes in the darkness. John looked upstream. A bright spot on the horizon told him where Cairo lay. His horse was swimming now, and the warm water of the Nile came up to John's waist. A moment later, his mount climbed up a sandy bank on to a low island. Knights were all around him, their horses nickering in the darkness. John was the only one amongst them not in armour. He had come in his role as a priest and translator, to offer his services after the battle.

After nearly a month of facing Shirkuh's army across the Nile, each side unable to attack, Shawar had devised a plan to surprise the enemy. He had provided one hundred members of the Egyptian army's Armenian cavalry, elite troops who fought for the caliph despite the fact that they were Christian. They had joined four hundred Frankish knights and snuck north under the cover of darkness, riding downstream while a slender crescent moon climbed across the sky. Finally, when the moon stood at its apex, their Egyptian guide had stopped at the river-bank and pointed to where an island split the river in two, making crossing on horseback possible.

John crossed the island and urged his horse into the water

again. He emerged on the far bank where the men were forming a column five riders wide. He rode to the rear. At the front, Amalric rose in his stirrups to address his troops. 'Tonight, we ride for God, to drive the Saracen scourge from these lands!' he shouted. 'Ride hard and ride fast, men, and when we reach their camp, show no mercy! Fill the Nile with the blood of these arse-faced, stone-worshipping bastards! For Christ!'

'For Christ!' the men roared back, and the army moved out at a trot. The sounds of hooves pounding on the sandy road and the jangle of tack joined the chorus of frogs along the banks of the Nile. The frogs went silent as the sky began to lighten, revealing broad green fields on either side of the river. In the distance, John could see the pyramids and the village of Giza huddled at their foot. South of the city, hundreds of cooking fires glimmered in the dawn light.

'For Christ!' Amalric roared and spurred to a gallop. The men surged after him, their horses kicking up plumes of sand. John slowed his mount to a walk, content to let the knights race ahead. They galloped into the enemy camp, and John heard screaming. But these were not cries of surprise or pain, but of disappointment. As John reached the camp, he saw why. The smouldering cooking fires were the only remaining trace of the enemy army. They had left before the Franks arrived.

John heard more shouting; cries of pain mixed with the ter-rified screams of women. He looked to see smoke rising above Giza. Finding the camp empty, the knights had moved on to sack the town. A particularly piercing wail rose above the other cries, and John winced. He thought of Zimat, of what he would do if a Frankish knight raped her.

John was riding towards Giza when he came across Humphrey, who was kicking angrily at one of the smouldering cooking fires. 'The currish maggot-ridden bastards!' the constable sputtered. 'God-cursed infidels! Onion-eyed donkey cocks!'

'Pardon, my lord,' John said, interrupting the stream of curses. 'Perhaps you should restrain the men.'

'Let them have their fun. Their blood is up, and they need some sport.'

'The Egyptians are our allies. The caliph will not look kindly on our men raping and pillaging his people.'

'The people of Giza gave shelter to the enemies of Egypt. They made their own bed.'

John frowned. The people of Giza could hardly have refused to supply and house Shirkuh's army. As he turned away in disgust, he spotted Amalric kneeling on the sandy shore, his hands clasped before him. John cantered over and dismounted. The king rose. 'The craven bastards,' he muttered and then yawned. 'I sacrificed a night's sleep for nothing.' The king noticed John's expression. 'You look as if you had lost a friend, John. What has happened?'

'The men are pillaging Giza.'

'So they are.'

'It is unholy work, sire.'

'It is the way of war, John.' Amalric began to walk away.

John bit back a choice curse. Then he had a sudden inspiration. 'This is precisely why Bernard visited you, sire!'

Amalric stopped. 'What do you mean?'

'Bernard said you are a poor Christian. He is right, but it is not because of what you do in the bedroom, much though that may displease God. No, it is because of moments like this, sire. When you let innocents perish by the sword, you make yourself unworthy to wear the true cross.'

Amalric's brow knit. 'Perhaps you are right. Humphrey! Humphrey!'

The constable strode over. 'Sire?'

'Go to Giza and bring the men to order. Tell them that any man who so much as touches a citizen of Giza will lose their head.'

'But sire—'

'Tell them!'

The king watched as Humphrey departed. Soon, the cries emanating from Giza ceased.

'You have done God's work today,' John told Amalric.

'*Hmph.*' The king took the chain with the piece of the true cross from the pouch at his belt and hung it around his neck. 'Look here, John!' he cried as he spotted a barge surging across the Nile under the power of twin banks of oars. Shawar stood in the stern. 'Come. You will translate for me.'

They met the barge where it ran ashore. Shawar stepped from the ship, a cup of wine in hand. 'God grant you good day, King Amalric! I am sure you are parched after your long ride.' He handed the king the cup.

Amalric drained it, wine dribbling from the sides of his mouth to stain his blond beard violet. 'The craven bastards escaped our trap.'

'Indeed. My lookouts say that Shirkuh's army began to leave a few hours after midnight. They headed upstream, into Upper Egypt.'

'We must follow them. How long until you can have your army across the Nile?'

'By tomorrow afternoon.'

Amalric frowned. 'Can they not move faster?'

'There is no hurry, King,' Shawar assured him with a smile. 'Shirkuh has made a fatal blunder. He is headed south into desert lands. If he leaves the Nile, his men will die of thirst. We can follow in our own good time. He cannot escape us now.'

JUNE 1164: AL-BABEIN

John wiped sweat from his brow and rewrapped the strip of cloth that kept the harsh sunlight off his head. They had been pursuing Shirkuh's army for three weeks, and summer had arrived in full force. A mile ahead, the hilltop town of Al-Babein shifted and wavered in the heat. It was mostly ruins, half-buried stones rising from the hillside like the bleached bones of some giant beast.

'A bunch of arse-faced pignuts!' Amalric cursed nearby, speaking to no one in particular. The king's face was bright red. 'Every time we get close, they flee. Why will the cowards not stand and fight!'

The reason was not hard to guess. John glanced back to the combined Frankish and Egyptian army marching behind them. Ranks of foot-soldiers four deep formed moving squares with cavalry riding in the middle. There were ten squares in all, comprising well over two thousand knights and eight thousand infantry.

'Shirkuh is no coward, sire,' John said. 'But nor is he a fool. We outnumber his forces nearly two to one.'

Amalric grunted sceptically.

'My lord!' It was the constable Humphrey, pointing upstream.

They were rounding a curve in the river, and ahead John could see that Shirkuh's army had formed a long battle line that stretched west away from the river.

A broad grin spread over Amalric's face. 'Praise God!' he roared. 'A fight at last! Constable, have the army form a line. I want my knights and infantry in the middle. Put the Armenians and Egyptian cavalry on our flanks, and hold the native cavalry in reserve.'

'Yes, sire.' Humphrey rode away and began shouting orders.

Amalric turned to John. 'What do you say, Father? Does God favour us?'

'God does not speak to me, sire.'

'But you are a priest.'

'I do not believe that God decides the battles of men, sire.'

Amalric frowned. 'We cannot be too sure, though, can we?' He kissed the fragment of the true cross that hung about his neck and then closed his eyes, his lips moving in silent prayer.

'Sire!' John shouted. 'Look!' The Saracen ranks were dissolving as first dozens, then hundreds of men turned and galloped upstream. Within seconds, Shirkuh's entire army was in flight.

'God damn them, not again!' Amalric cursed. 'The milk-livered, craven—' He stopped short and took a deep breath. 'No. They will not escape this time.' He raised his voice to a shout. 'Constable! *Constable!*'

'Yes, sire?' Humphrey called as he cantered back to join the king.

'We will leave the infantry behind and give chase.'

'Are you certain, sire? They will outnumber us.'

'One of our knights is worth three of their men. We will catch them, and we will kill them, every last one of the bastards.'

'Yes, sire.'

Amalric turned to John. 'Bless me, Father.' John hesitated. He had never blessed anyone. 'Damn it! I haven't all day. Do it, man!'

John made the sign of the cross over the king. '*In nomine patris, et filii, et spiritus Sancti.* Grant this man courage to face his enemies and strength to defeat them.' An image of Yusuf flashed into John's mind, and he added, 'And the wisdom to show mercy in victory.'

'Amen!' Amalric declared. One of the king's squires handed him his shield and long lance. The other knights had grouped around him. John made his way to the edge of the men.

'God is with us!' Amalric shouted. 'For Christ!' A trumpet began to blow and the king cantered forward, followed by his knights, the Armenians and the native cavalry. John hesitated for a moment and then he pulled a mace from his saddle and spurred after them. He would not let another slaughter happen, like at Giza.

John galloped along the river, past the fields and groves of palms that bordered the Nile's dark waters below Al-Babein. He slowed as he caught up to the native cavalry and was enveloped in a thick cloud of dust. Suddenly the riders ahead of him veered to the right, heading across green fields and leaving a wide swathe of trampled wheat. There was less dust now, and John could see the front of the charge and the Saracens beyond. They had stopped and fanned out in a battle line. Beyond them, the cultivated fields gave way to hard-baked earth and then to dunes, the sand blindingly bright under the afternoon sun.

The Frankish charge slowed and then stopped. Amalric formed his line only a hundred yards from the Saracens, close enough to see the faces of their enemy. John found himself on the right wing, with the native Christians. He spotted Yusuf's eagle standard waving over the centre of the Saracen line. A horn sounded, and the Christians surged forward.

John stayed where he was and watched as the Frankish knights slammed into the enemy's centre, which melted away under the attack, turning to flee into the desert. Amalric and his men followed, disappearing amongst the low dunes. But the rest of the Muslim army had not retreated. The left and right wings swooped down on the Armenian and native Christian cavalry, neither of whom showed much stomach for a fight now that the Frankish knights had left the field. Several hundred other Saracen warriors turned and rode into the desert after the Frankish knights, cutting off their retreat. Amalric had been too eager. He had ridden into a trap.

John did not need to stay to know how this battle would end. He turned his horse and spurred to a gallop. He sped past a farmer, weeping as he knelt amongst his trampled crops. John was on the river road now, kicking up dust as he raced towards where the infantry had been left behind. As they came into view, John was surprised to see that they were making camp.

'The Saracens!' he yelled as he rode amongst men setting up tents and starting cooking fires. 'The Saracens are coming!' Several men glanced at him, but no one stopped what they were doing. John reined in beside a Templar sergeant. 'You there! What's your name?' The man stared at John blankly. John raised his mace. 'Your name!'

'Renault, but they call me Carver, Father.'

'I am a canon of the Church of the Holy Sepulchre, your superior before God. You must do as I say. The life of every man in this army depends on it.'

The man blinked a few times and then nodded. 'Yes, Father.'

'Our army has been defeated. The Saracens will be here soon, and if we are not ready they will cut us to pieces. Do you understand?' The man nodded. 'Good. Round up the Templar sergeants and tell them what I told you. Have the men form ranks. You have my permission to kill anyone who does not do as you ask. Understood?' The man nodded again. 'Good. Now go, and God help you!'

The Templar hurried off, and soon enough Templar sergeants were roaming about the camp, yelling at the Egyptian and Christian foot-soldiers to form ranks and striking at those few poor souls who hesitated too long. You could always count on the Templars to follow orders. John looked up river and could see a cloud of dust approaching. That would be the Armenians and native cavalry, fleeing for their lives. The Saracens would be close behind. John turned back towards the infantry, who had formed a long column.

'Tighten those ranks!' he called as he rode down the line of men. 'Shield on the outside!' he yelled to an Egyptian who had put his shield on the wrong arm. He stopped beside a dozen men who remained outside the column. They were busy loading heavy chests on to wagons. 'What are you doing?'

'This is the gold the Egyptians paid us,' one of the men explained. John recognized him as one of Amalric's clerks. 'The King gave me charge of it.'

'Leave it.'

The man was aghast. 'Do you realize how much gold is in these chests?'

'Two hundred thousand dinars. And if we leave it, then the

Saracens will stop to collect spoils instead of running us down from behind and filling your arse with arrows like a pin cushion. Better to lose the gold than the lives of men.'

'Is it?' the clerk asked.

John raised his mace. 'Leave the gold, or yours will be the first life lost, friend.'

The clerk hesitated for a moment and then called for his men to join the column. It was just in time. Already, the first of the Armenians were galloping past. John could see the front ranks of the Saracen cavalry rounding a bend upstream.

He raised his voice. 'All right, men! Keep close together now! March!'

Yusuf's Arabian horse moved nimbly in the deep sand as it galloped around a dune. His men had split up after they rode into the desert, and now he rode with only Qaraqush, Al-Mashtub and ten other men. The Frankish knights had also scattered in their pursuit. Although Yusuf could not see them amidst the maze of dunes, he had heard their loud cries – 'For Christ! For the Kingdom!' – grow steadily more dispersed. Now he raised his curved bow in one hand as he reined to a halt on some flat land between the dunes. He looked over to Qaraqush. 'No more running, friend. It is time to do some hunting.'

Yusuf led them back the way they had come, following their tracks as they wove between the maze of short dunes. The scattered war cries of the Franks had ceased, replaced by cries of agony as Shirkuh's men turned to attack. The Franks' heavy horses would be clumsy in the deep, shifting sands, making them easy prey. Yusuf rounded one of the dunes and sighted seven knights a dozen yards off, their horses struggling through the sand.

'For Islam!' Yusuf cried as he nocked an arrow to his bow.

'For Christ!' the lead knight roared back. His yell was cut short as Yusuf's arrow lodged in his throat. The other knights charged, and Yusuf's men divided, riding in a circle around the

Franks and shooting arrows into their ranks. Two of the Franks' horses fell, and the other knights fled.

Yusuf shouldered his bow and then took up his shield and drew his sword. 'For Allah!' he yelled and galloped after the knights. Yusuf's horse gained quickly on the heavy Frankish chargers. He reached the rearmost knight and slashed at him. The man blocked the blow with this shield, and chopped at Yusuf, who veered away to avoid the attack. He was angling back towards the knight when he rounded a dune and rode straight into a group of twelve more knights.

Yusuf just had time to recognize the king's standard flying above them before he found himself surrounded and fighting for his life. A sword flashed towards his head, and he parried. He deflected another blow with this shield. He spurred forward, trying to escape the press of men, but before he could ride free a sword slammed into his back. His mail stopped the blade, but the force of the blow knocked him forward against his horse's neck. He straightened just in time to parry a strike that would have decapitated him. Yusuf's heart beat faster when he saw his attacker's face. It was the king. Yusuf slashed for his head, but Amalric knocked the blow aside with his shield. The king raised his sword and then froze as an arrow thudded into his chest.

Another dozen mamluks, with Shirkuh at their head, had rounded one of the dunes and were now circling the Christians and shooting arrows. Another shaft slammed into the king's chest. Yusuf saw no blood. The arrows had penetrated the king's mail, but not the leather vest beneath.

'To me!' Amalric cried. 'Retreat! Retreat!' He parried a final blow from Yusuf and spurred away, his heavy horse knocking aside the mamluks' lighter mounts. The remaining half-dozen knights galloped after him.

'It's the King! Don't let him escape!' Yusuf shouted as he spurred his horse to a gallop. He came alongside the rearmost Frank. The man hacked at him, but he turned the blow aside with his own sword before swinging backhanded and catching the man in the chin. Blood spattered the sand as the knight fell.

There were still five knights between him and the king. Yusuf spurred his mount still faster, flashing by one knight, then another and another. He knocked a blow aside with his shield as he sped past the final knight. The king was just ahead now.

And then a group of knights appeared from around the side of a dune to Yusuf's right. Yusuf just managed to raise his shield before a lance slammed into it, sending him flying. He landed in the soft sand and rolled into a ball as the Frankish horses galloped over him. He stayed huddled as he heard the clash of steel above him, the thud of hooves, then quiet. He rose slowly. The knights were gone, the king with them. Shirkuh and Yusuf's men were gone too, no doubt in pursuit. Yusuf's horse was nowhere to be seen. He whistled loudly, but it did not return. Yusuf sat down in the sand. There was no sense in trying to walk back to camp. He would only get lost amongst the dunes.

It seemed a long time later when he heard the drum of approaching hoofbeats. 'There you are, young eagle!' Shirkuh called as he rounded a dune. He slid from the saddle and embraced Yusuf. 'Thank Allah, you are alive!' He grinned. 'The Franks have fled. And we have their gold.'

'What of the King? Did he escape?'

'Escape? Ran away, more like it.'

'Should we not give chase?'

'Patience, young eagle. Their infantry is intact, and they still outnumber us, even after their losses. We will let them retreat to Cairo to lick their wounds.'

'And where shall we go?'

Shirkuh grinned his crooked-tooth smile. 'What better way to kill a snake than to cut off its head?'

'Cairo, then.'

'No, Alexandria. Cairo holds the Caliph, but it is Alexandria that furnishes the wealth of Egypt and gives them access to the sea. It is the emporium of the world, where East meets West, where the caravans end their long journey from India. And we, Yusuf, are going to take it.'

The Shining Pearl of the Mediterranean, the City of Spices, Silk City, City of Wonders – Iskandariyya. The city lay spread out below Yusuf as he stood at one of the windows high up in the lighthouse of Alexandria. The ships in the harbour looked like toys. Cleopatra's needles, the twin obelisks that stood near the harbour, seemed no larger than toothpicks.

They had arrived in Alexandria that afternoon. A delegation of citizens had met them outside the walls and presented Shirkuh with the head of the Fatimid governor. The people of Alexandria were mostly Sunni Muslims and Coptic Christians, both of whom resented the rule of the Shia caliph in Cairo. They had welcomed the army into Alexandria. While the men occupied the towers that studded the walls, the city's administrator, a Copt named Palomon, had led Yusuf and Shirkuh to the lighthouse so that they could survey the city and plan its defence.

Yusuf had heard of the lighthouse, of course. His childhood tutor, Imad ad-Din, had told him it had been constructed by the Greeks over a thousand years ago. He had described it as one of the wonders of the world, the tallest structure ever built by man, a work to rival that of God himself. None of those descriptions did the lighthouse justice. The broad base alone was taller than Alexandria's massive walls. The lighthouse rose from the base in three steps, the first of which was a huge square block at least twice as tall as the tallest tower Yusuf had ever seen. An octagonal tower rose from the block, and a circular tower rose from that, its tip touching the clouds. It was unbelievable that something so tall could stand. The secret, Palomon had told him, was that the huge blocks of white stone were soldered with lead.

The sun was setting by the time they reached the top. Shirkuh had huffed with every step, turning so red that Yusuf had worried his stout, bow-legged uncle would not survive the climb. But finally the stairs had ended and they had stepped into a circular room surrounded by arched windows. Shirkuh had staggered to a window and leaned against the embrasure. Yusuf had joined him there, and neither man had spoken a word since.

'This must be how Allah feels,' Yusuf murmured at last.

'She is spectacular, is she not?' Palomon said as he came up behind them. 'Still, Alexandria is smaller than she once was. The ruins beyond the walls mark the boundaries of the ancient city. Canals bring water from Lake Mareotis, which is used to water the public gardens, there.' He pointed to an expanse of green in the south-eastern corner of the city. 'The gardens may be used for food in the event of a siege.' He pointed to the opposite side of the city, where there stood a huge structure of white stone buildings piled one atop the other. 'That is Dar al-Sultan, the palace complex. You will stay there, Emir.'

Yusuf was only half listening. He was busy examining the city walls. They were twenty feet high and nearly as thick as they were tall. 'Four gates,' he counted, 'and twenty-one towers.'

'How many men can the city offer for the defence of the walls, if it comes to that?' Shirkuh asked Palomon.

'The Fatimid troops are all in prison or have fled. We can put maybe five thousand men in arms, but they are not soldiers.'

'We will hold them in reserve.' Shirkuh addressed Yusuf. 'We have six thousand of our own men remaining. They will guard the walls. We'll post fifty men in every tower and a hundred at each of the four gates. That leaves—' He began counting on his fingers.

'Forty-five hundred,' Yusuf supplied.

'Forty-five hundred men in reserve,' Shirkuh agreed. 'Plus the men of Alexandria. We'll position half near the palace and half in the east, near the gardens.'

Yusuf did not reply. He had thrust his head out of the window to look straight down at the base of the tower. He felt suddenly unsteady, as if he were standing on a ship at sea, the deck moving beneath him. He gripped the sides of the window embrasure, but the tower would not stop moving. He turned away and vomited.

'It happens to many on their first visit,' Palomon said. 'Come. There is a Coptic church atop the lighthouse. The priests are allowed to worship there in return for tending the fire. They will have water for you to rinse your mouth.'

He led them upstairs to a room identical to the one below, except that there was an altar along the east wall with a cross hung over it. It was surprisingly warm. There was no one in the room. 'The priests will be upstairs, tending the fire,' Palomon said, continuing up a second staircase.

When Yusuf stepped into the room above, a sudden blast of heat made it seem as if he had walked into an oven. A huge fire burned within a giant bronze brazier set in the middle of the floor. Smoke rose through a soot-covered hole in the ceiling. Two priests were throwing cords of wood on the fire. They wore nothing but loincloths, and their skin glistened in the fire-light. A third priest in a brown robe was poking at the fire with a long, bronze rod. Yusuf could only look at the fire for a moment. It was so hot in the room that even breathing was painful.

Palomon waved at the priest who was tending the fire. 'Father Josephus! Water!'

'Water!' the priest shouted back over the roar of the flames. He set the bronze rod aside and went to a barrel, from which he took a cup of water. He crossed the room and handed it to Yusuf. The water was warm. Yusuf rinsed his mouth and spat out of the window.

'*Shukran!*' he shouted and then turned away. He could not stand the heat any longer. He hurried down the stairs and stood at one of the windows, gulping the cool sea air.

Shirkuh joined him at the window and pointed to the city

below. A last ray of sunlight illuminated the city, transforming the canals into molten gold. 'Look at it,' Shirkuh whispered to Yusuf. 'The most magnificent city in the world. And it is ours!'

Yusuf stood at one of the windows of the lighthouse and looked down to where the waves crashed upon the rocks at its base. The dawn light tinged the white foam pink. Yusuf climbed to the top of the tower each morning. At first, he had come to conquer his weakness – the dizzying sensation that left him retching on the floor. After a week the sick feeling had left him, and he found that he enjoyed being so high above the world. He raised his gaze to look out to sea. The endless waves stretching to the horizon appeared motionless from this height. He closed his eyes and breathed deeply of the salty sea air.

'Pardon me, sayyid.'

Yusuf opened his eyes. It was Saqr, the boy that he had found in the desert long ago, after Reynald and his men had slaughtered his family. But Saqr was no boy now. He had been a mamluk for nearly a year. He had been posted as a lookout because of his sharp eyes. Saqr claimed that he could spot a hare sitting motionless in the desert sands at eight hundred paces.

'I think I see something,' the young mamluk said. 'In the east.'

Yusuf crossed the room and looked out, squinting against the newly risen sun. He thought he could make out a cloud of dust in the distance. 'A dust storm?'

'Look again, sayyid. You can see the reflection of sunlight off steel. There are riders in the dust.'

'*Hmm*. Yes.' In fact, Yusuf saw nothing. He was only twenty-eight and his eyes were growing feeble. He felt old for the first time in his life. Then he saw it, a flash of steel. He saw another, then dozens more, then hundreds. It was an army.

'Well done, Saqr! Hurry to the palace and inform Shirkuh. Tell him to meet me here.'

By the time Shirkuh arrived, red-faced and panting, the

Frankish and Egyptian army covered the plains east of the city, stretching from within a mile of the walls all the way to the horizon.

'How many?' Shirkuh asked as he joined Yusuf at the window.

'More than ten thousand. Too many to fight.'

Shirkuh frowned. 'They have no need to fight. They will block up the canals and then sit outside the walls while we run short of food and water. They will let hunger and thirst do their work for them.'

'What shall we do?'

Shirkuh scratched at his beard while he thought. 'We will leave,' he said at last.

'But we cannot abandon the people of Alexandria. We promised to defend the city.'

'And so we shall. You will stay with a thousand men; enough to man the walls. I will take the rest of the army south into Upper Egypt. Hopefully, my raids there will draw the Frankish army away from Alexandria.'

Yusuf looked back to the enemy troops, who were still pouring over the horizon. 'And if the Franks do not leave?'

'Then you must hold the city for as long as you can.'

Chapter 5

John took a deep breath and dunked his head beneath the cold water of Lake Mareotis. The siege was four months old. Autumn had come, but John had not given up his increasingly bracing morning bath. At first, he had come to escape the heat. Now he came seeking the calm that was impossible to find in camp. Behind him, hundreds of Muslims from the Egyptian army knelt along the shore, prostrate in prayer. They, too, came every morning. John found the gentle murmur of their voices comforting. He waited until they had finished and then waded ashore. He glanced to the east as he dressed in his linen tunic and sandals. The rim of the sun was just rising over the horizon. He would be expected at Amalric's tent soon.

John followed the Egyptian soldiers back towards camp, crossing fields long since picked clean. A range of low hills lay between him and the city. The Egyptian and Frankish armies had set up camp amongst them, with Shawar's men to the west of the southern gate and Amalric's men to its east. The level ground between the two camps was usually empty, but as he approached, John saw a crowd gathered there. A dozen Franks were headed by a stout man with small, beady eyes. He was facing a tall Egyptian soldier, backed by twenty mamluks.

'Puking, onion-eyed, stone-worshipper!' the Frank was yelling. 'You've been stealing our grain. Admit it!' He pointed a stubby finger at the Egyptian.

'*Naghil*!' the Egyptian soldier spat back. '*Kol khara!*'

'What was that, you filthy son of a whore?' one of the Frank's companions demanded.

'Eat shit,' the Egyptian enunciated carefully in Frankish.

The beady-eyed Frank swung for him. The Egyptian ducked, and one of his friends tackled the Frank from the side. A brawl ensued. John steered well clear of it. Even if he had not been expected at the king's tent, he doubted that he could do much to stop the fighting. Tensions in camp had run high ever since Shirkuh began raiding the supply caravans from Cairo. The soldiers had taken to pillaging local farms in search of food, but there was never enough. As the siege dragged on, tempers grew short. Fights between the Franks and their Egyptian allies had become an almost daily occurrence.

The guards outside Amalric's tent nodded to John as he entered. Inside, he found Amalric breakfasting on boiled wheat. 'Sire,' John said, and knelt.

Shawar entered just as John was rising. A dark-skinned Egyptian soldier entered behind the vizier.

'I have bad news,' Shawar declared cheerfully.

'Then why are you so damned happy about it?' Amalric grumbled.

'I find that good humour is the best antidote to misfortune. Nur ad-Din has invaded the principality of Antioch and scored a crushing victory. Bohemond of Antioch and Raymond of Tripoli have been captured.'

'What!' Amalric demanded, red-faced. 'Are you c-certain?'

'I am. The news reached Cairo by messenger pigeon two days ago. I learned of it this morning.'

'By his nails!' Amalric cursed. 'With Bohemond and Raymond defeated, there will be no one left to defend the Kingdom's northern border.'

'You shall have to return to protect Jerusalem,' Shawar agreed.

'Four months of siege wasted,' Amalric grumbled, then shook

his head. 'No. I'll not leave empty-handed. I'll tear down the walls of Alexandria stone by stone, if I must.'

'Perhaps that will not be necessary.' Shawar gestured to the Nubian warrior beside him. 'Jalaal, tell them what you have found.'

The Nubian spoke haltingly, in a deep voice, and John translated. 'My men and I, we were searching a nearby farmhouse for food. The farmer kept his grain out back in an old stone storeroom – older than old, Vizier, if you take my meaning. The stones were just barely holding together. He said it was empty, but we didn't believe it, him being a Copt and all. We broke the lock and had a look. The grain was gone, but we found something else. A door.'

'A door?' Amalric asked.

'A door to the catacombs,' Shawar clarified. 'Kom el-Shoqafa: the Mound of Shards.'

'What did you see?' Amalric asked Jalaal. 'How far did you go?'

'Only a few feet, Malik. We didn't dare go further. There are evil djinn below the earth. Allahu Akbar.'

'Thank you, Jalaal.' Shawar turned to Amalric. 'The catacombs are said to run beneath the city walls. If we can find the passage, then we can enter by night and overrun the defences. The people of the city will pay for their defiance.'

Amalric grinned. John did not share their enthusiasm. Yusuf might be in the city, and regardless, he had other friends amongst the Saracens. They would be slaughtered. Those who fled would be massacred before the city walls. And that would only be the beginning. For once the enemy was dead, the people of Alexandria would suffer.

'We must explore the catacombs immediately,' Amalric said.

'Yes, but quietly,' Shawar cautioned. 'I do not doubt that Shirkuh has spies in our camp. If he learns what we have discovered, then he will put his men on guard. The fewer who know of this, the better.'

'Agreed. You send Jalaal. I will choose a man that I trust. He and Jalaal will report directly to us.'

'I wish to go,' John ventured. Amalric frowned. 'I speak Arabic.' John looked to Shawar. 'The catacombs were built under the Romans, were they not?' The vizier nodded. John turned back to Amalric. 'I read Latin and Greek. I can help to find the passage into the city.' He did not add his true reason for wanting to go: if a passage were found, then he wanted to be the one to find it. He had sworn to serve Amalric, but that did not mean he would stand by and let his friends in the city die.

'Very well,' Amalric responded, 'but I will send a sergeant with you. There is no telling what dangers lie beneath the earth. The three of you will go tomorrow, at first light.'

Yusuf chewed on a small piece of flatbread as he strode down Al-Harriyah, the main street of Alexandria. He nodded at the handful of merchants who were setting out their stalls. The men were grim-faced. Food in the city was scarce, and people had little interest in the perfumes and jewels they were selling. Yusuf finished his breakfast, and his stomach grumbled in protest, demanding more. Yusuf ignored it. His men were on half-rations, and so was he. He would not eat again until that evening.

He reached the wall and climbed the stairs to the top of the eastern gate. He nodded to his men, and looked out on the enemy camp. More Franks had arrived from Jerusalem a week ago. The week before that, two hundred Egyptians had joined the army.

Yusuf walked south along the wall, nodding at his men as he passed, exchanging words with those he knew well. He walked the complete circuit of the walls each morning and evening. Seeing him helped to keep the men's spirits up. And, it allowed Yusuf to get away from the palace, where the citizens of Alexandria besieged him with an endless stream of grievances. They complained about the curfew that Yusuf had set. They complained when he took men and women from the linen and silk factories and set them to making padded armour. Most of all, they complained about the rationing system. But Yusuf had no more food to give. Most of the horses had been eaten at this point.

He was approaching one of the four towers manned by townspeople. There were a dozen men atop the tower; half as many as were required. That was typical. At first, the towns-people had been proud to strut about in their new armour, but before long they were petitioning to avoid guard duty.

'How goes it?' Yusuf asked. The Alexandrians glared resent-fully. None spoke. 'Where is your commander?'

'Inside the tower,' said an older man with close-cropped hair and a greying beard. The man pulled his cloak more tightly about him in an effort to ward off a chill brought on by hunger.

'Whipping two men,' another citizen added darkly. He was tall and must have once been fat. Now, his skin hung in folds from his neck and arms. 'What gives the bastard the right?'

Yusuf knew that putting his own men in charge of civilians created resentment, but he had no choice. He had heard too many stories of towns that had fallen when locals allowed the besiegers into the city. 'What did the men do?' he asked. The citizens shifted uneasily as they stared at the ground, refusing to meet his eye.

'They had the late watch,' a boy said at last. He was too small to wield the long, sharpened hoe that he held. 'They fell asleep on the wall.'

'But that's no reason to whip them,' the man with the baggy skin growled.

'If you do not want your friends whipped, then do not let them fall asleep,' Yusuf said. 'We must remain vigilant. Much worse is in store if the city falls.'

'Yes, sayyid,' the old man sneered and spat at Yusuf's feet.

If the man were a mamluk, Yusuf would have beaten him there on the spot. However, he could not afford to further alienate the people of Alexandria, so he mastered his anger and took the ramp down to the foot of the tower. As he approached the door to the tower's interior, he heard the crack of a whip and a muffled sob. He stopped in the doorway to watch. Some twenty townsmen were packed inside. Two were standing against the wall, stripped to the waist, angry welts across their backs. Yusuf had placed Saqr in charge of this tower. The young mamluk swung a whip, striking one of the men and eliciting a low moan. Saqr looked as if he would be sick, but he swung again. The townspeople regarded him with murderous eyes.

Saqr gave one final crack of the whip. As he coiled it, he noticed Yusuf standing in the doorway. 'My lord, Saladin,' he said and dropped to a knee.

'Step outside and catch your breath,' Yusuf told him. 'And you two—' He pointed to the whipped men. 'Find someone to look after your wounds.'

As soon as Saqr was out of the door, Yusuf was confronted with a cacophony of voices. 'All they did was fall asleep!' 'We are free people of Alexandria!' 'Bastard doesn't have any right to whip us!' 'How would he like to feel the whip's bite?'

'*Silence!*' Yusuf roared. The anger that had risen in him when the man spat at his feet now spilled out. He pointed to where the two Alexandrians had just limped from the room. 'Those men are lucky to be alive. If they were my troops, I would have had them strung up as an example.' He paused and looked about. Man after man looked away as he met their eyes. 'You are pathetic! Four months ago, you were so eager to take to the walls, to play at soldier. If you are not willing to act the part, then go back to your homes.' Yusuf's voice was rising. 'Go and huddle with the women in the dark and pray for your rescue. Pray for the real warriors who defend your homes and your families. Go, you cowards!'

'We are not cowards!' one of the Alexandrians shouted defiantly. 'And we will not be insulted!'

'You won't?' Yusuf drew his sword. 'You hate me, don't you? You hate my rules? You hate my men? If you hate me so much, then do something about it. Kill me.' He glared about him. 'Come on! Kill me! There are twenty of you and only one of me. What are you afraid of? Come on!' Not a man moved. Some hung their heads in shame. Others looked away.

'Very well.' Yusuf's voice was calm now. 'Do not question my authority again, or that of my men. I do not tell you how to weave, how to plant and harvest, how to make perfumes. Do not pretend to tell me how to defend this city.' Yusuf turned on his heel and strode out. Saqr was waiting outside.

'Thank you, sayyid.'

'Walk with me.' Yusuf led the way up the ramp, and paused atop the wall, out of earshot of the Alexandrians gathered on the tower. 'They are only common men, Saqr, but if you handle them right, they will fight like warriors. You must be firm. Do not pander to them, but listen to their complaints. Address those you can. And talk to them. You must know your men if you wish to lead them.'

'Yes, sayyid.'

'You did right to whip those men. Do not doubt yourself.' Saqr nodded. Yusuf squeezed his shoulder, and continued along the wall.

Over the last week, there had been far too many scenes like the one in the tower. The autumn rains had not yet come, and with the canal blocked, water in the city was running short. Men were always troublesome during a long siege, but thirsty, starving men were worse. Yusuf studied the mamluks he passed. Their cheekbones protruded from emaciated faces. And each day they grew thinner. At this rate, they would soon be nothing but bones. His skeleton army.

'My lord!' Qaraqush called as Yusuf approached his tower. The formerly stout mamluk's armour hung from his gaunt frame like clothes on a scarecrow. He forced a smile.

'How are the men?' Yusuf asked.

'They gripe of hunger. Who can blame them?'

'Can they fight?'

'They can hold the wall for maybe two weeks more, but if you are thinking of mounting an attack, then we had best do so now.'

Yusuf shook his head. 'We are too few.'

'We could slip out at night, as Shirkuh did.'

'And leave the people of Alexandria to suffer for our cowardice? No.'

'So we stay here to starve.'

'We stay, old friend.'

'That's it.' Jalaal pointed across a field of rich black earth to a squat structure of dirty white stone, half covered in creeping vines. It looked like any of the other half-ruined buildings that stood near the city. It was perhaps two hundred yards from the south-west corner of the walls, not far from a single column that towered over the nearby fields.

John and Jalaal headed towards the building. They carried lamps, as did the sergeant who would be exploring the catacombs with them. Adenot was a Breton with a strange accent and large eyes that made him look perpetually surprised. He had a bit of a belly, and he looked to be a practical man. He had brought a coil of rope with him.

Jalaal reached the grain shed and kicked the door open. 'In here!'

John followed the others inside. There was barely room for the three of them. On the far wall was an open doorway, no more than three feet tall. It looked as if it had been half buried. 'The farmer said he never saw it,' Jalaal explained, 'because the shed was always at least half full with grain.'

John took a flint and steel from the pouch at his waist, lit the lamps, and then got down on his hands and knees to peer into the hole. The darkness swallowed up the lamplight after only a few feet. He glanced up at his companions. The Nubian was whispering a prayer, and Adenot was clutching the medallion of the Saint-Sepulchre that hung around his neck.

John crossed himself. 'I will go first.' Pushing the lantern before him, he wormed through the hole. The ceiling was low, and he was forced to crawl on his belly along the dirt floor. Ahead, the space illuminated by the lantern slanted downward, curving to the left. As John moved forward, the ceiling grew higher. Soon he was able to crouch and then stand. Beneath him, the dirt floor gave way to widely spaced steps cut into stone. He turned and called to the others. 'The way is clear! There is a staircase leading down!'

John pulled his wool cloak about him as he waited. It was cold down here, the chill air wet with moisture. Soon, he could see the lamps of Adenot and Jalaal approaching in the darkness.

'What is this place?' Adenot asked, his eyes wide.

'That is what we are here to discover,' John replied, and led the way down. The stairs ended, and John edged forward through a stone passage and into a round chamber. On the far side of the room, a dark passage led further into the catacombs. Two other passages opened off to the left. John headed for the nearest one. It opened into an empty room. The next room was also empty, save for the bones that littered the floor and cracked underfoot. There was only one passage left to explore. The entrance was more elaborate than the others, topped by stone-work carved in the shape of a scallop shell. A broad staircase led into the darkness. John headed down, his footsteps echoing loudly. The air smelled of rock and earth. The staircase split around a dark space and then came back together. At the bottom, he found himself in a small square room with a high ceiling. To either side, passages led into darkness. Before him, two thick columns framed a doorway. The walls on either side of the columns were decorated with dragons coiled around staffs.

When Jalaal arrived behind John, he gasped. 'Signs of the devil.'

Adenot was gripping the hilt of his sword. 'This is an evil place.'

'There is nothing to fear from false idols carved in stone,'

John told Jalaal in Arabic. 'Explore that side passage.' When he had reluctantly shuffled off, John turned to Adenot and made the sign of the cross over him. 'God will protect you. Now go. See what lies in that passage.'

John went to explore the doorway framed by columns. As he entered the room his lantern illuminated a pair of horrifying figures carved into the stone on his left and right. Each was a man in armour with the head of a dog. The one on the left had the tail of a snake instead of legs. John felt the hairs on the back of his neck rise. Perhaps Adenot was right. This was an evil place. He took another step into the room, and a human form loomed in the darkness ahead.

'Christ!' John cursed. He took a deep breath and edged forward again. His lamp illuminated a life-sized female figure carved from stone. To its right was a statue of a man. Beyond them was an empty room. He left and found Jalaal and Adenot waiting for him.

'I found nothing,' Jalaal said in Arabic.

'Only bones that way,' Adenot added in French. 'You?'

'Another dead end. Let's leave this place.' He looked to Jalaal. 'Yalla.'

Adenot and the Nubian hurried up the stairs. John followed at a slower pace, but then stopped. A glimmer of light flashed in the darkness between the branches of the staircase. He held his lamp over the space and peered down. The lamplight reflected off water far below.

'Wait!' he called. 'Adenot, give me the rope.'

John tied the rope off around one of the columns that held up the ceiling. He tugged hard to make sure it held and then threw it into the hole. He heard a splash as it hit water.

Jalaal was peering into the hole. 'I am not going down there.'

John looked to Adenot. The sergeant shook his head.

'Give me your sword,' John told him. He belted the blade to his waist, took hold of the rope with both hands and positioned himself over the hole. 'Wait for me,' he told Adenot. He turned to Jalaal and spoke in Arabic. 'If you are not here when I return, I will lay a curse on you, and you will spend the afterlife haunting this place.'

'We will be here,' Jalaal assured him.

'God keep you, Father,' Adenot added.

John climbed down the rope into the darkness. He reached the water and lowered himself in. ''Sblood, that's cold.' His feet touched the bottom. The frigid water came up to his waist. He looked up to Adenot and Jalaal, some fifteen feet above. 'Pull up the rope,' he instructed them, 'then use it to lower my lantern.'

The lantern descended slowly, illuminating the space around John. He was in an octagonal room, the walls decorated with strange figures: a lion with the head of a man; human figures with the heads of dogs and crocodiles. There was only one passage from the room. John untied the lantern. 'Wait for me!' he shouted up one final time, then crossed himself and splashed from the room.

A passage opened up on his left and another on his right. John had no idea in which direction the city might lie. He whispered a silent prayer and continued straight ahead, emerging into a square room lined with rows of burial niches. He jumped as something bumped into his waist. It was a human femur, floating on the water. The lower niches in the room had been flooded, and bones floated all around. John whispered a silent prayer and pushed on.

He splashed across the room and through a series of identical square chambers. As he left the last room, he stumbled over something and pitched forward. His lantern hit the water and the flame went out, plunging him into darkness. 'Christ's wounds!' His heart was pounding now. He closed his eyes and forced himself to breathe evenly. When he opened them, he was surprised to see that the passage ahead was not completely dark. He dropped the lantern and took a cautious step ahead. There were stairs beneath his feet. He climbed a narrow staircase that led up out of the water and into a room with an altar on the far wall. A cross was carved into the stone above the altar, and it was lit by a ray of pale light. John approached and discovered a square shaft, some three feet across, cut into the ceiling above.

He climbed on to the altar, and hoisted himself up into the shaft. The walls were of rough stonework, slick with moisture. With his back against one wall and his feet against the other, he managed to work his way upwards. The mortar that held the stones in place was crumbling. Several times, he felt the stones against his back shift, but they held.

He reached the top and felt the stone ceiling. A thin beam of light filtered through a tiny crack near the edge of the shaft. John drew his sword and worked at the crack with the blade, chipping away at the crumbling mortar. The sword slipped from his hand and fell to land with a crash at the bottom of the shaft. But he had managed to expand the crack so that it was several inches long. He put an ear to it and heard distant, muffled voices.

John placed his shoulders against the stone above and found a solid purchase for his feet on the wall. He pushed and felt the stone move. Reaching out, he felt for the edge. It was no more than two inches thick. With a grunt, he managed to lift it clear of the floor and shove it to the side.

He poked his head through the hole and looked about. He was in what looked to be one of the chapels of a church. Bright light filtered through windows of stained glass. The chapel was open on one side, and the voices were coming from that direction. They were chanting in Arabic.

John pulled himself up out of the shaft. He crept to the edge of the chapel and peered around the corner to his right. Prostrate on the floor were several hundred men, their backs to him. 'Oh Allah forgive me; have mercy upon me,' they murmured as they sat back on their heels. John spotted the grizzled head of Qaraqush in the front row. Beside him was Yusuf. John ducked back around the corner. His heart was pounding in his chest. He had found a way into the city.

He slipped back inside the shaft and managed to pull the flagstone over the hole, leaving only a thin crack. He climbed down and leaned against the altar, his mind racing. It was his duty to tell Amalric. John's father had taught him that without honour, a man was little better than a beast. But what of friendship? John turned and knelt before the altar. He clasped the cross that hung from his neck in both hands. 'Guide me, Lord.' He bowed his head and squeezed his eyes shut, but no divine revelation came. He opened his eyes. The sword he had dropped lay just beside him. It was a sign.

He took the sword and then climbed atop the altar and used the blade to pry stones loose. One fell away, then another. Dirt began to shower down on him. He heard the grate of stone upon stone and scrambled off the altar just before the shaft caved in. Dust filled the room, and then it plunged into absolute darkness as the light at the top of the shaft was blocked. No one would get through that way now.

John's satisfaction was short-lived. He had sworn to serve Amalric, but he had failed him. He was an oath breaker, as Heraclius had claimed. Shame flooded through him, but it soon gave way to fear. He could not see his hand in front of his face, and he was shivering with cold. He would have to find his way back in the dark. He stumbled down the stairs and into the water. He splashed ahead, his hands held out before him. He could feel bones floating all around. He came to a wall and groped his way along it until he found the doorway leading to the next room. He had passed through three rooms when he saw light ahead. It grew in brightness as he approached. He quickened his pace, and breathed a sigh of relief when he saw the rope.

'Who's there?' a voice called from above. John looked up to see Adenot peering down into the darkness.

'It's me. Pull me up.'

John wrapped the rope around his waist, and grabbed hold of it with trembling hands. Adenot and Jalaal hauled him dripping from the water. They grabbed him by the arms and pulled him out to lie shivering on the stone stairs.

'What did you find?' Jalaal asked.

'N–nothing,' John managed through chattering teeth. 'An–n-other dead end,' he added in French.

Adenot pulled John to his feet. 'Let's go. I never want to see this place again.'

They hurried up the ramp and crawled out to find that Amalric and Shawar had come to wait for them.

'Did you find anything?' the king asked.

'Nothing but bones, sire,' Adenot replied.

'You are sure?' Shawar pressed. 'Nothing?'

'We explored every inch, Vizier,' Jalaal said.

John met Amalric's eyes. 'It is an unholy place, sire. Seal it up and forget it.'

'By the d–devil's black beard!' the king cursed.

'All is not lost,' Shawar said. 'I have been in communication with Shirkuh.'

Amalric's eyebrows shot up at this, but he said nothing.

Shawar held up a piece of paper. 'He has agreed to terms. Shirkuh will leave Egypt, if you also withdraw.'

Amalric tugged at his beard for a moment, then shook his head. 'No. A few more days in Egypt will not cost me Jerusalem, and I'll not leave this place without a fight. The defenders are few and starving. We can take the city. Shirkuh will be forced to leave then, and on my terms. Will you fight beside me, Vizier?'

Shawar grinned his cat-like smile. 'The people of Alexandria need to be taught a lesson. My men will join yours, King Amalric.'

Yusuf stood above Alexandria's southern gate and looked out on the enemy army, the front ranks of which were just visible in the dawn light. The Egyptian soldiers had gathered to the south; it was the Frankish troops who were massed on the plain before him. Thousands of foot-soldiers formed a curving line that mirrored the path of the wall. Behind them stood a row of archers. At the centre of the line was a huge battering ram constructed of several tree trunks bound together with bands of iron and capped with steel. Bronze wheels carried the ram's weight, and carpenters had built a roof over it to protect the men who would roll it to the walls. Frankish knights sat ready to charge if the ram opened a way into the city. Yusuf spotted Amalric's flag amidst the knights' standards, all flapping in a wet wind blowing in off the Mediterranean.

A piercing horn sounded, and the line of Frankish foot-soldiers surged forward, thousands of men shouting war cries: 'For Christ! For the Kingdom!' Yusuf turned towards the dozen mamluks gathered atop the gate. Their faces – lit red by a fire that simmered beneath a cauldron of hot sand – were gaunt but grimly determined. These were Yusuf's very best men, warriors like Al-Mashtub who had stood beside him for years. He had stationed them here at the gate, where he expected the fighting to be most intense. He wished he had Qaraqush and his brother Selim beside him as well, but Qaraqush was at the western wall and Selim the east. They each commanded three hundred mamluks, leaving Yusuf with four hundred trained warriors and another five hundred citizens to defend nearly a mile of wall against an army of thousands.

Yusuf addressed his men, shouting in order to be heard over the cries of the Franks. 'Our foes are many! But Allah will give us strength. Fight like lions, men! Fight to the death! *Fight for Allah!*'

'*For Allah! Allah! Allah!*' his men shouted back. They fell silent as shields went up. Yusuf turned to see that the Franks had stopped two hundred yards from the wall. Their archers loosed a cloud of arrows, which fell hissing towards the walls. Yusuf raised his shield and crouched behind the battlement just before the arrows began to rain down. Most shattered against the wall or flew over, but Yusuf heard cries of agony as a few struck home. Beside him, Al-Mashtub grunted in pain. Yusuf looked to see an arrow protruding from the mamluk's left shoulder.

'Save your speech, sayyid,' Al-Mashtub said before Yusuf even opened his mouth. The mamluk grabbed the arrow shaft and snapped it in half. 'I am not going anywhere.'

His last words were drowned out by another roar from the Franks. The foot-soldiers were rushing forward again. They carried ladders – four men to a side – with their shields held up for protection.

'Archers!' Yusuf yelled as he rose, now heedless of the arrows falling around him. 'Archers!' he cried again, pulling the man next to him to his feet. 'Let fly!' Yusuf took his own bow from his shoulder and nocked an arrow. He picked a target: one of the front men carrying a ladder. Yusuf held his breath and let fly. His arrow struck the man in the groin, just below his shield. The man fell and those behind tripped over him and dropped the ladder. They had only just picked it up when Yusuf shot again, dropping another Frank.

But most of the Franks were making it to the wall. Only a dozen yards to Yusuf's right, four Franks raised a ladder while another four spread out, firing crossbow bolts up at the defenders. The ladder made contact with the wall and a mamluk began to push it off, only to receive a crossbow bolt in the throat. Below, two men held the ladder while two more Frankish soldiers began to climb. The first carried a shield before him. The second came close behind, holding a spear. As they neared the top of the ladder, another mamluk tried to push the ladder away, but the man with the spear picked him off the wall.

'Use the rope!' Yusuf shouted as he shouldered his bow and ran to the ladder. He picked up a coil of rope that had been placed there for just this purpose, and looped it around the end of the ladder. He began to walk along the wall, dragging the top of the ladder sideways. The ladder tilted and then fell back. The Franks screamed as they hit the earth.

All along the wall, ladders were going up and being dragged down. Yusuf's mamluks shot arrows into the Franks below, while the Alexandrians hurled stones down on them. But there were too few defenders to hold off all the Franks. On the far side of the southern gate a Frank forced his way on to the wall and began to lay about with his sword, scattering Alexandrians. He was joined by another, then another. Soon half a dozen Christians were clustered atop the wall.

'Al-Mashtub! Follow me!' Without waiting for a reply, Yusuf drew his sword and sprinted towards the Franks. The wall was wide enough for four men to face Yusuf at once. They levelled their spears at his chest. At the last second, Yusuf dropped his sword and hurled himself forward on the ground, rolling beneath the spears and taking out the legs of the four men. One of them tumbled off the inside of the wall, dying instantly as he landed headfirst on the cobblestones below. The others fell across Yusuf, who found himself on his back, pinned beneath them. One of the Franks, a fat man with a thick blond beard, drew a dagger and reared back to strike. He collapsed in a spray of blood as Al-Mashtub's sword struck him in the neck. The huge mamluk impaled a second Frank and grabbed the third, hurling him from the wall. More mamluks rushed past to engage the remaining Christians. At close quarters, their swords were more effective than the Franks' spears, and the mamluks quickly cut them down.

Al-Mashtub had just helped Yusuf to his feet when there was a loud boom. The wall shook beneath them. The Franks had rolled the battering ram up to the southern gate. Yusuf's men hurled stones down on it, but they clattered off the peaked roof. A shower of burning naphtha followed the stones. The liquid engulfed the ram in flames for a moment, but the roof had been covered in wet hides. The fire burned out without catching. The ram slammed into the gate again, and Yusuf heard a loud crack as one of the three thick beams that barred the gate started to give way. The Franks manning the ram began to roll it back from the wall, so that they could build momentum before striking the gate again.

Yusuf turned to Al-Mashtub. 'We must take the ram.' He raised his voice to shout at the men at the gate, who were still hurling stones down on the ram. 'Men! Follow me!'

Yusuf led ten men down the ramp to the base of the wall. Two-dozen mamluks were gathered before the gate with spears pointing, ready to meet the Frankish assault if the ram broke through. Yusuf noticed Saqr amongst them. 'Open the gate,' he told the men.

They did not move.

'Are you mad?' Al-Mashtub demanded. 'We will be overrun!'

The ram hit the gate again. The top beam splintered in the middle. The two other beams holding the gate shut were sagging inward.

'We must do something!' Yusuf pointed to four of the men with spears. 'You four. Prepare to open the gate.' He selected another six men. 'You will take the ram and roll it inside. The rest of us will hold off the Franks.' Yusuf looked to the four men who were now standing with their shoulders braced against one of the beams barring the gate. 'Now!'

The men strained as they lifted the heavy beam from its brackets. They dropped it to the side and put their shoulders to the next beam. Yusuf raised his sword. 'Ready!' he shouted as the men removed the second beam and pulled the doors of the gate inward. 'For Islam!' He charged through the opening.

The soldiers manning the ram had their heads down as they strained against the bars protruding from its side, struggling to push it towards the wall. Yusuf impaled one and slashed across the face of another before the rest realized what was happening. They fled, and the six men Yusuf had selected went to the bars. But before they had even begun to push, dozens of Franks came rushing towards them from either side.

'Get the ram inside!' Yusuf shouted. 'Form a line, men! Stay together!'

The mamluks had just enough time to form a semicircle around the ram before the Franks struck. Yusuf sidestepped a spear thrust and plunged his sword into his enemy's gut. A sword blade slashed towards his face. He knocked the blow aside with his shield and then brought the shield up to smash the attacker's face. He spun away from another spear and lunged, dropping a fourth man. More Franks joined the attack, and they surged forward, pushing back the line of mamluks. Yusuf found himself separated from his men and surrounded by Franks on all sides. He ducked a slashing blow, but as he rose, a spear struck him in the back. The blow was turned aside by his mail, and Yusuf spun and slashed down, snapping the spear shaft in half. He impaled his attacker, but a moment later a sword rang off the back of his helmet. He staggered forward. Another Frankish foot-soldier was standing before him. The man grinned, and instinctively Yusuf stepped to the side. A spear thrust past him and impaled the grinning Frank. Yusuf spun and cut down the man with the spear.

Out of the corner of his eye, Yusuf saw a sword flashing towards his face. He ducked, but another blade was thrusting towards him. It was blocked at the last moment. Yusuf looked to see Saqr standing beside him. The young mamluk turned the sword aside and slashed across the leg of the Frank who held it. The man dropped to one knee, and Saqr drove his sword into his throat. He parried a spear, and Yusuf dispatched the attacker. Together, they fought their way back towards the line of mamluks. Saqr was quick as a snake, his sword darting through his enemies' defences and leaving them crying in agony. Yusuf blocked and lunged, parried and countered again and again, but the ranks of Franks seemed endless. Then someone grabbed Yusuf's shoulder and pulled him backwards. Yusuf spun, ready to strike.

'Easy there!' It was Al-Mashtub. He had pulled Yusuf back

behind the line of mamluks. Behind him, the ram was rolling, picking up speed.

'Fall back!' Yusuf shouted. 'Fall back!'

The ram rolled inside the gate, and Yusuf and his men began to retreat, moving backwards in step. They reached the gate and spread across the opening in a double line. Only twenty mamluks remained now, facing over a hundred Franks, with more arriving all the time. A horn began to sound, and Yusuf heard the rumble of hooves over the sound of battle. That would be the Frankish knights charging for the gate.

'Close it!' he shouted. 'Close it!'

As the mamluks began to push the gates closed, Yusuf's men fell back. The space between the two doors was small enough now that it could be defended by only three men: Yusuf, Al-Mashtub and Saqr. 'Close the gate!' Yusuf repeated as he fought desperately. But try as his men might, they could not force the gate closed against the press of Franks. As more and more Christians joined the attack, the doors of the gate began to swing wider. Now there were six men standing alongside Yusuf. And the thunder of hooves was louder. The knights were close.

Yusuf looked to Al-Mashtub. 'The sand.' Al-Mashtub nodded and left the line. Yusuf raised his voice. 'Follow me, men. One last push!'

He led his men forward. They pushed the Franks back a few feet before their charge stalled. Beyond the heads of the enemy foot-soldiers, Yusuf could see the standards of the approaching knights.

'Retreat!' he shouted. 'Inside the gate!'

His men rushed back inside. Yusuf was close behind. With a roar the Franks charged after them. But their cries of triumph turned into screams of agony as a shower of red-hot sand poured down from above. Some Franks fell to the ground, clawing at their armour, which trapped the burning grains of sand against their skin. Others ran screaming. Yusuf's men were able to push the gate closed, and the first crossbar dropped into place with a loud thump. The second followed a moment later.

Yusuf ran up the ramp to the top of the wall. The battle was still raging. Thousands of Franks swarmed the length of the walls, but his men were holding. He joined the fight and soon lost track of the number of ladders he toppled, of the number of men he killed. And all the time, Saqr stayed by his side, silent but ruthlessly efficient. Finally, as the sun began to set, a horn in the enemy camp sounded three short blasts. The attack slackened. The three blasts repeated and soon the Franks were in full retreat, carrying their wounded with them.

Yusuf slumped against the battlement. Al-Mashtub came striding along the wall towards him. 'You crazy bastard. I thought you were dead for sure when we went to seize the ram.'

'I would have been, if not for Saqr.' Yusuf looked to the young mamluk, who was still at his side. 'You saved my life.'

'I only did my duty, Emir.'

'You did well. I need a new commander for my private guard. You shall lead my khaskiya.'

'Shukran, Emir.'

Al-Mashtub spat towards the retreating Franks. 'May you rot in hell!' Then he grinned. 'Look! Three men under a flag of truce. They wish to parley.'

'Let us hope they seek peace,' Yusuf said. The excitement of the battle was fading and the gnawing hunger in his gut had returned. 'Have a list of our dead drawn up, Al-Mashtub. And have the wounded taken to the hospital. Saqr, you come with me. We shall meet with our enemy.'

John had stopped just beyond the edge of the Christian camp, behind Shawar and King Amalric. In the gathering dusk, he could just make out the southern gate of Alexandria. The gate opened enough to allow two figures to emerge.

'Here they come,' Shawar said.

'I understand their commander's name is Saladin,' Amalric said. 'What do you know of him, John?'

'I have never heard the name.'

'I am surprised at that,' Shawar said. 'He is Shirkuh's most trusted adviser.'

John shrugged. The two men had stopped halfway between the Christian camp and the wall.

'Come,' Amalric said. 'Let us meet him.'

As John approached, he saw that one of the two men was leaning on the other. John got the impression that he would have collapsed without the support. Having stopped only a few feet away, it still took John a moment to recognize the man as Yusuf. He looked terrible. His cheeks were sunken, and there were dark circles under his eyes. His mail hung loosely from his thin frame.

Amalric spoke first. 'Greetings, Saladin. Peace be upon you.'

'And upon you, King Amalric,' Yusuf replied in flawless French. 'I am honoured to meet you.'

Amalric tugged at his beard. 'You speak our tongue well.'

'Thank you, Your Majesty.' Yusuf's expression hardened as he turned to Shawar. 'As-salaamu 'alaykum, Vizier.'

'A pleasure to see you again as well, Saladin,' the Egyptian replied in Arabic.

As Yusuf turned to face John, his eyes widened and the blood drained from his cheeks. He opened his mouth to speak, but no words came.

'Are you well, Emir?' Amalric asked.

Yusuf pulled away from the young man supporting him. He stepped to John and embraced him. There were tears in his eyes as he kissed John on both cheeks. 'I cannot believe it! I saw you struck down. I thought you dead, John.'

'And I thought you were someone else: Saladin, righteous in faith.'

'Nur ad-Din gave me the name after the battle at Butaiha.'

'Amalric's forehead was creased. He had not been able to follow any of this. 'You know this man, John?'

'Saladin was called Yusuf ibn Ayub when I knew him. He was my lord amongst the Saracens.'

'Indeed?' Amalric's eyebrows rose. 'The two of you must speak, later. Now, we have important matters to discuss.' He looked to Yusuf. 'The siege is over.'

'I will not surrender,' Yusuf replied.

'You have no choice in the matter. Shirkuh has negotiated a truce.'

Yusuf looked to John. 'Is this true?'

John nodded. He produced the treaty from a pouch at his waist and handed it to Yusuf.

Yusuf frowned as he read. 'Both Shirkuh and Amalric will withdraw from Egypt,' he murmured. 'It will be left to Shawar. Why would Shirkuh agree to such a thing?'

Shawar smiled. 'Your uncle is not entirely unreasonable. I will pay him fifty thousand dinars.'

'You will pay the Franks too,' Yusuf said as he continued to scan the treaty. 'And they will be allowed to garrison troops in Cairo.'

'They are my allies,' Shawar said. 'That is why the treaty favours them.'

'You and your uncle will be given free passage to Damascus,' John said. 'That is what matters.'

'And the people of Alexandria?' Yusuf asked. 'I have sworn to protect them.'

Shawar scowled. 'They must be punished for their treachery.'

'Then this meeting is at an end. I will not surrender the city if it means their slaughter.'

'But your uncle has already signed the treaty,' Shawar protested.

Yusuf straightened and looked down his nose at the vizier. 'I have a duty to Allah greater than my duty to my uncle. I will fight if I must.'

'Saladin is right,' Amalric said. 'The people must be spared.'

Shawar's brow creased. 'But—'

'It is a small enough thing to bring this war to an end,' Amalric told him. 'There will be no reprisals, Shawar. Swear it.'

'Very well,' the vizier muttered.

'What good is his word?' Yusuf demanded.

'It will have to be good enough,' Amalric replied. 'Or you can continue to defend the city, and the people will starve. It is your choice.'

'I will honour the treaty,' Yusuf said reluctantly.

'There is one more provision,' Amalric said. 'As part of the agreement, we will take a hostage. He will stay with us until Shirkuh's army has left Egypt. Your uncle suggested that you send your brother, Selim.'

'No, I will come. I will stay with your army so that I may see the people of Alexandria are not harmed.'

'Very well. We have an agreement.' Amalric stuck out his hand.

After a moment's hesitation, Yusuf clasped it. 'My men will leave the city tomorrow,' he said. He looked to John. 'I will see you again soon, friend.'

Yusuf was the last of his men to leave the city. He rode in the dust kicked up by the long column of soldiers, most of whom walked on foot, their horses long since eaten. The people of Alexandria crowded about them on either side, shouting insults and making the sign of the evil eye. They called Yusuf *khâyin*: traitor. They had trusted him to defend their city, and he had failed. Yusuf knew that there would be little he could do once he left Egypt to prevent the vizier from punishing the citizens of Alexandria. The people knew it, too.

'You will roast in hell!' a final voice called after Yusuf. Egyptian troops lined both sides of the road outside the gate. After Yusuf's men had filed between them, they entered the city. Yusuf watched for a moment and then turned away. His men continued east, marching to join Shirkuh and the rest of the army where they waited near the city of Tell Tinnis. Yusuf rode south into the Frankish camp. He was stopped at the perimeter and led to the king's tent. Amalric and John were waiting for him. Shawar was there, too.

'Saladin!' Amalric rose to greet him. 'God grant you good day. It is a pleasure to see you again.'

Yusuf gave a short bow. 'King Amalric.' He did not greet Shawar.

'My army will begin the journey to Jerusalem tomorrow,' Amalric said. 'Until I receive news that Shirkuh has left Egypt, you will travel with us as my guest. John will show you to your quarters.'

Yusuf followed John to a nearby tent. The floor was thickly carpeted. The camp bed looked comfortable enough. There was even a lap desk with paper and ink.

'I trust you will be comfortable,' John said.

Yusuf nodded. The two friends stood in awkward silence. So much had happened since that day at Butaiha when John had saved Yusuf's life. Yusuf had hated himself for abandoning his friend to die. But John was alive.

'How did you come to be at the court of the Frankish king?' Yusuf asked at last.

'I was to be executed as a traitor, but King Amalric spared me.'

There was another silence, during which John poured them each a cup of water. He handed one to Yusuf. 'How are the men? Qaraqush? Al-Mashtub?'

'The same as ever, only thinner.'

'You look half starved yourself. I shall find you some food.'

Yusuf nodded. He had been hungry for so long that he had grown accustomed to ignoring the dull ache in his belly. But now, faced with the prospect of eating, his stomach awoke with a growl. John returned with a loaf of hot bread and some lentil stew. Yusuf tore into the bread and drank straight from the bowl.

John managed a smile. 'You eat like a wolf after a long winter.'

Yusuf finished the soup and wiped his mouth with the back of his hand. 'I eat like a starved man after a long siege.'

'Was it very hard?' John asked.

Yusuf nodded. 'I am glad to be done with Egypt. I hope I never see these lands again.' He could not keep the bitterness from his voice. It was not just the hardships he had suffered during the siege. Shawar's betrayal had wounded him. 'What of you, friend?' He gestured to John's vestments and the cross hanging from his neck. 'You are a priest now?'

'Yes.'

Yusuf shook his head in wonder. 'Why?'

'It was that or marry.'

John did not need to say more. Yusuf knew he had become a priest because of Zimat, because he would not marry another. 'I have taken Zimat and Ubadah into my household. I am raising him as my own son.'

'Thank you, brother.' John hesitated for a moment. 'How is Zimat?'

'After Butaiha, she thought you dead. She hardly spoke for months. She is better now. I have begun to look for a new husband for her.'

John's face registered not pain but rather a despairing resignation. Yusuf had seen that expression before on men he had killed, the moment they realized that they would die. 'That is good,' John managed, although his broken voice belied his words. 'She should forget me. It is for the best.'

'She will never forget you.' John winced, and Yusuf saw that his words of comfort had only hurt more. He searched for a way to change the topic. 'What is Jerusalem like?'

'A strange city. The Franks have driven out all the Jews and Muslims, and now it is half empty. Beautiful but empty.'

'I would love to see it.'

'Perhaps you shall, one day.'

'No, sooner. I do not relish the thought of riding to Damascus alone once I am freed. Do you think Amalric will allow me to accompany the Christian army as far as Jerusalem?'

'I am sure of it.' John smiled. 'It will be good to travel with you again, brother. Like old times. Do you remember our first trip to Tell Bashir, all those years ago?'

'How could I forget? You saved my life.' Yusuf met John's eyes. 'You could have come back to us at the beginning of the siege, John. I would have welcomed you.'

'I have given my word to Amalric, and to God.'

'I understand. I will not ask you to break your oath.' Yusuf shook his head. 'It is strange to see you in a priest's garb, strange that we are now enemies.'

John placed a hand on Yusuf's shoulder. 'We do not have to be. Perhaps I can best serve you here, with the Christians. I can help bring peace between our people.'

'Your king, Amalric, does not strike me as a man of peace, John. He brought his army to Egypt readily enough. And Nur ad-Din has vowed vengeance for the defeat he suffered at Butaiha.'

'Perhaps we can change their minds. If we can be friends, then who is to say all the Franks and Saracens cannot learn to share the Holy Land.'

Yusuf smiled. 'You have become a dreamer, John. Your people hate my people. Nothing can change that.'

'I pray that you are wrong.' John met his eyes. 'I have sworn an oath to Amalric, but I do not wish to be your enemy, Yusuf.'

'Nor I yours.' Yusuf forced a laugh. 'Such weighty talk! I am simply glad we are together.'

John's forehead creased. For a moment Yusuf thought he would say something more about the awkward position in which they found themselves, but then John smiled. 'Me, too, brother,' he said. 'Me, too.'

Chapter 6

'So you are forbidden to fight?' Yusuf asked. He was riding along the dried-up bed of a wadi with John at his side. Amalric and the constable Humphrey rode a few paces ahead. A hundred of the king's knights followed behind. The rest of the army had dispersed, the sergeants and lords returning to their lands.

'I am forbidden to draw blood.' John reached into his saddlebag and produced a mace – a wicked-looking club with a heavy head of grooved steel. 'I can still fight.'

'But if you smash a man's skull, will he not bleed?'

'Yes, but the mace does not draw blood, it only crushes the skull. The blood comes later. It is an after-effect.'

Yusuf laughed. 'That is ridiculous!'

'Perhaps, but if you plant a seed and later a tree appears, does that mean that you made the tree grow? No. God did that. You only planted a seed.'

'So you smash their skulls, and God makes them bleed?'

'Exactly.'

'I will never understand your faith.'

It was another version of the conversation that they had been having since leaving Alexandria. Yusuf could make no sense of the strange rules by which his friend now lived. He had marvelled at John's tonsure, his vestments, the fact that he was expected to live in a church with other religious men. He feared that the man he had known had disappeared beneath that tunic and cross.

The road left the valley floor and began to angle uphill over rocky ground. They rode past olive groves and grapevines. Here and there, goats grazed.

'All faiths have their mysteries, Yusuf,' John said. 'Is it logical that according to Islam, a man can marry five women, but a woman only one man?'

'If a woman had more than one husband, then how would we know who was the father of her children?'

'And why should that matter so?'

'Why does it matter? Surely your faith does not welcome bastards.'

'God loves all his children equally.'

'Even the ones who do not deserve His love, the murderers and the thieves?'

'Jesus forgave prostitutes and murderers alike. He teaches that all deserve to be loved.'

'And what of you, John? Do you love all men equally? The Arab and the Frank? Christian and Muslim?' He met John's eyes. 'Amalric and me?'

'Not equally. But I pray for them all.'

'And when you pray, whose victory do you ask for?'

'I pray for peace.'

'And when peace is not possible?'

'I pray for you, brother.'

'I would rather you fight for me.' Yusuf regretted the words immediately. John looked away quickly, as if he had been slapped. He spurred ahead, and Yusuf sped up to rejoin him. 'I am sorry, John. I know that you have no choice.'

'I forgive you, brother,' John murmured, his tone more irritated than forgiving.

They rode on in silence. As they crested the hill, Jerusalem came into view. 'Al-Quds Sharif,' Yusuf whispered. The Holy Sanctuary. Even at this distance he could make out the bulky

Tower of David, the dome of the Church of the Holy Sepulchre, and beyond them, the gleaming roof of the Dome of the Rock. He was surprised to find tears in his eyes.

'She is beautiful,' he said. 'More, she is a symbol of all that we have lost; not just the city but the people who died there and who have died since fighting for her. Jerusalem is where Mohammed rose into heaven before returning to write of it. She is our past, the childhood of our religion, and the Franks have taken her from us.'

'I am sure the crusaders felt the same when they first laid eyes on the city,' John observed. 'Jerusalem is where Christ died, and it was in Christian hands for hundreds of years before the Muslims took it.'

Yusuf's brow knit, but he said nothing.

'Perhaps we can learn to share the city,' John suggested.

'Perhaps.'

The road led to an arched gateway that sat in the shadow of one of the citadel's massive square towers. Merchants' carts were crowded around the gate. A tax was due on any non-edible goods that entered the city, so these men had chosen to set up shop outside. Some knelt as the king approached. Others loudly hawked their wares. 'Fine perfumes, my lord!' 'Women, sire! A slave girl for your pleasure!'

Amalric did not stop until he reached the gate, where the seneschal Guy and the patriarch waited to greet him. Yusuf and John reined in just behind the king.

'Welcome, sire!' Guy said. 'God grant you health and joy.'

'Praise God for your safe return,' the patriarch added.

'Spare me the formalities, I am tired and need a bath.' Amalric glanced back to Yusuf. 'You'll want to put your helmet on, Emir.' He spurred ahead, and Guy and the patriarch fell in beside him.

'My helmet?' Yusuf asked John.

John nodded. 'Muslims are not welcome inside the city.'

Yusuf pulled on his helmet and followed Amalric through

the gate. The road beyond was lined with men and veiled women who had come to see the return of their king. They cheered and Amalric waved.

Yusuf's helmet rang as a piece of rotten fruit slammed into it, knocking his head to the side. 'Murderer!' a veiled woman shouted. 'Go to hell, sand-demon!'

There was an angry murmur in the crowd. 'Saracen dog!' someone else yelled. A fist-sized rock sailed just in front of Yusuf's face.

'Leave him be!' Amalric roared. He had reined in his horse and was glaring at the crowd. 'The next person who throws something will lose his hand!' He looked back to Yusuf. 'I apologize, Saladin.'

'It is nothing,' Yusuf replied. He turned to John and added more quietly. 'Now I know how Reynald felt.'

'No, it is unacceptable,' Amalric was saying. 'But I shall make amends. You shall be my honoured guest tonight at the feast to celebrate my return.'

Yusuf sat beside King Amalric at the head table. John sat to Yusuf's left. Another, longer table had been set up at a right angle to the head table. It stretched the length of the barrel-vaulted hall – the first completed part of the new royal palace being built south of the Tower of David. The table was lined with an eclectic mix of men: tonsured priests beside richly dressed merchants; clean-shaven Franks next to native Christians with trimmed beards; men who ate with their hands and wiped their fingers on the fur of the dogs who milled under the table beside others who ate with fork and knife.

A servant refilled Amalric's goblet of wine and turned to Yusuf, who waved him away. The second course had yet to be served, and it was already the third time Yusuf had refused, but the first that Amalric had noticed. 'How rude of me,' the king said. 'Bring Saladin a cup of water.'

'Thank you, sire.'

Amalric nodded. 'How long will you stay with us, Emir?'

'A week, if I may. I am eager to explore the city.'

'John will serve as your guide. What do you wish to see?'

'Qubbat as-Sakhrah,' Yusuf said. 'The Dome of the Rock.'

Amalric frowned in confusion.

'The Templum Domini, sire,' John explained.

'Ah, yes, the Lord's Temple, where Christ threw out the moneychangers. The Augustinians have charge of it now.'

It was Yusuf's turn to frown. He turned to John and spoke quietly in Arabic. 'But the Dome was built after the Muslim conquest.'

'What was that?' Amalric asked.

'Saladin says that he is eager to explore the Temple,' John said.

'And the Al-Aqsa mosque,' Yusuf added. 'After Masjid al-Haram in Mecca, and the mosque of the Prophet in Medina, it is the most sacred place of worship for my people.'

'The Templum Solomonis,' John explained to Amalric. Then, to Yusuf: 'The Templars are quartered there now.'

'Be careful of them, Saladin,' the king warned. 'The Templars do not like visitors, especially Saracens.'

'Not so,' the Templar grand master, Bertrand, called from down the table. 'You will be welcome at the Temple, Saladin.'

Yusuf nodded in his direction. 'Shukran.'

The conversation paused for a moment as servants brought forth the next course: two roasted boars on platters. Yusuf blanched as one of the boars was set down before him.

'You are the guest of honour,' Amalric told him. 'You may carve.'

'I am sorry, King. The flesh of swine is forbidden to my people.'

'Ah, y-yes, s-so it is,' Amalric stuttered in embarrassment. He nodded to a servant. 'Take this a—aw—' His face contorted as words failed him. 'Remove this, and bring something more palatable.'

Heraclius, who was seated beyond John and the patriarch to Yusuf's left, leaned forward and looked towards Yusuf. 'You do not drink wine. You do not eat pork. What sort of religion is that?'

Yusuf opened his mouth to speak, but John replied first. 'Do we Christians not abstain from the flesh of animals on Fridays? And many religious orders eat no meat at all.'

The patriarch Amalric set his fork down. 'Are you comparing Christian monks to the heathen Mohammedans?'

'Yes,' John said without hesitation. 'The monks do not eat meat because they follow a rule. The Muslims follow their own rule, Your Beatitude.'

'But only one of the two rules is of God, and I have no doubt which one that is, nor should you. Christ's first miracle was to turn water into wine. God made grapes. He made swine. Why would he forbid us to enjoy them?'

'Our place is not to question Allah's designs,' Yusuf replied. 'He has commanded us to abstain from wine and pork, and so we do. It is our faith.'

'Faith?' The patriarch snorted dismissively. 'You Saracens worship a rock. What sort of faith is that?'

'We believe that Abraham placed Al-Hajaru-I-Aswad in Mecca. The black stone was sent to Adam and Eve by angels.'

'It is a rock,' Heraclius retorted.

'It is,' Yusuf agreed. 'We do not worship the stone, but rather the God who sent it. Just as you do not worship the cross, but rather the Christ who died upon it.'

'But—'

'That is enough, Heraclius,' Amalric cut across the conversation. 'A good answer, Saladin. You are as wise as you are brave. I pray that the peace between our peoples lasts for many years, and that I do not have the misfortune to meet you again in battle. To peace.' He raised his cup and drained it.

Yusuf glanced at John and then drank his water. 'To peace,' he murmured. 'Inshallah.'

John rose early the next morning and went to the baths in the Hospitaller complex. The sun was just rising as he emerged. He strolled over to the Street of Herbs and purchased two oranges from the fruit seller, Tiv. The city was quiet as he walked the short distance to the king's palace, in the shade of the Church of the Holy Sepulchre. He went to the room where Yusuf was staying and knocked. The door opened immediately. Yusuf was already dressed in a white caftan and sandals.

'I thought you would never arrive. I am eager to explore the city, John.'

John handed Yusuf an orange. 'I brought you breakfast.'

'Shukran. Now come. Let us begin.'

John led him out into the palace courtyard. They were halfway across when someone called John's name. He spotted the young Prince Baldwin playing with several companions. 'John!' the prince called again. It was the first time John had seen him in nearly seven months, and the boy was notably taller. He must be nearly four now, John calculated. The prince raced across the courtyard and wrapped his arms around John's leg.

'Who is this?' Yusuf asked.

'Prince Baldwin,' John said. 'I tutor him in Arabic.'

Yusuf crouched so that he was at the prince's height. 'Kaifa halak?'

The prince became suddenly shy. 'I am well,' he said as he peeked between John's legs.

'In Arabic,' John told him.

'Ana bekhair,' Baldwin said and then, gaining in confidence, he added, 'Motasharefon bema'refatek.'

'A pleasure to meet you as well,' Yusuf replied with a smile.

'I have never met a Saracen before,' Baldwin declared.

Yusuf's eyebrows rose. 'And what do you think?'

The prince shrugged. 'Where is your turban?'

Yusuf laughed. 'It is a cloudy day. I have no need of one.'

The prince considered this for a moment before turning to John. 'I thought the Saracens would be more . . . different.'

'As I have told you, they are men and women, just like us. Now go and play with your fellows.'

Baldwin headed back to the corner where the other children were pretending to fight with swords. Yusuf called after him: 'Ma'a as-salaama.'

'Allah yasalmak,' Baldwin replied, and ran over to join in the play.

John looked to Yusuf. 'You see. Not all Franks hate your people, Yusuf. Baldwin will be king someday. He can bring peace.'

'He is a clever child. Perhaps you are right, John.'

Later that morning John emerged from the Templum Domini with Yusuf at his side. They had been forced to leave quickly when one of the monks had taken offence at Yusuf's presence.

'Have you seen enough?' John asked hopefully.

Yusuf pointed to the Al-Aqsa mosque, which lay beyond a series of arches, the remnant of some long-vanished structure. 'I wish to visit the mosque. It is time for noon prayer.'

John's eyes widened. 'You wish to pray there?'

'How can I visit Jerusalem and not pray in Al-Aqsa, one of the holiest places in all of Islam?'

'And the Templar headquarters.'

'The Grand Master said I was welcome.'

'The other knights are not as enlightened as Bertrand.'

'I thought you said the Franks could learn to respect my people.'

'Not the Templars,' John grumbled. 'They are fanatics.'

'Please, friend. I may never return to Jerusalem again.'

'Very well,' John sighed, 'but let me do the talking.'

John led them to the Temple, which was fronted by an arcade held up by pointed arches. Two Templar sergeants with spears in hand framed the entrance that sat in the shadows of the arcade. The guards eyed Yusuf suspiciously and then looked to John.

'What is your business here, Father?' one of them asked. He was a short man with a thick, bull-like neck. From his accented French, John guessed that he was Norman, and a new arrival to the Holy Land.

John gestured to Yusuf. 'King Amalric has engaged me to show this man the city.'

'He is a Saracen?' the guard asked.

John thought about lying but decided against it. 'Yes.'

The second Templar lowered his spear so that it pointed towards Yusuf's chest. 'He is not welcome here.'

John stepped between Yusuf and the spear point. 'We will be no trouble. He only wishes to see the main hall.'

'He is a sand-devil,' the thick-necked Templar spat. 'He will not enter.'

John drew himself up straight. 'I am a canon of the Church of the Holy Sepulchre, and in the name of the Patriarch, I order you to step aside.'

'The Temple was granted to us by King Baldwin II,' the guard replied. 'The Patriarch has no power here.'

'Leave,' the other guard barked, jabbing his spear so that it stopped just inches short of John's chest.

'What is going on here?' Bertrand de Blanchefort approached from behind the guards. 'John?'

'Grand Master.'

'And Emir Saladin.' Bertrand turned to Yusuf. 'How do you find Jerusalem?'

'A beautiful city. I had wished to pray inside your Temple. It is holy to my people.'

Bertrand turned to the guards. 'Let them in.'

The bullish guard scowled and reluctantly stepped aside.

John followed Yusuf inside. They walked down a wide, high-ceilinged nave lined with columns on either side. Windows set high above shed a dim light. At the end of the nave, they found themselves standing under a dome. Yusuf pointed to a niche built into the wall of the hallway to their left. 'A mirhab; the mark on the wall indicates the direction of Mecca. I shall pray there.'

John stood just outside the niche while Yusuf began to pray, murmuring the first words of the Sura al-Fatiha. 'In the name of Allah, the Most Gracious, the Most Merciful—' Yusuf had just knelt for the first time when John noticed the bull-necked guard approaching. He held up a hand to stop him, but the man shoved him aside. He grabbed Yusuf from behind, lifted him from the ground, and set him back down facing east.

'That is the way to pray, Saracen!'

John's fists clenched. 'Leave him be, friend.'

Yusuf put a hand on John's arm. 'Easy,' he whispered. 'I do not wish to cause trouble.' He turned to the Templar. 'The Grand Master gave me permission to pray as I please.'

The Norman glared at them and then turned and stomped away. Yusuf resumed his prayers. Watching him, John could remember when he had been struck by the strangeness of Muslim prayer, the kneeling and prostrating. After seeing Yusuf pray hundreds, even thousands of times, he now realized that it was not so different from Christian prayer. He had spent more time than he wished on his knees since he became a priest. And now that he was supposed to pray seven times a day, the five daily prayers required of Muslims did not seem so odd.

His thoughts were interrupted by the Templar, who had returned without John noticing. 'East!' The man pointed as he shouted at Yusuf. 'You should face east!'

Yusuf looked to John and raised an eyebrow, as if to say: 'See. *This* is why peace between our peoples is not possible.'

John grabbed the guard by his surcoat and pulled him away. 'I said leave him be.'

The Templar knocked John's hand aside and swung at him.

John sidestepped the blow, grabbed the man's arm and pivoted, using the guard's momentum to swing him towards the wall. At the same time, he stuck out his leg. The Templar tripped over it and slammed face first into the wall. He roared in pain and began to rise. John punched him hard, catching him in the jaw, and the Norman slumped to the floor, unmoving.

A half-dozen Templars had gathered around them now and were staring at John wide-eyed. Yusuf took his arm. 'I have finished my prayers. We should go, friend.'

'Fresh bread!' a vendor cried. 'Fresh bread!' His voice was drowned out by the ring of steel upon steel. John jumped to the side to avoid the sparks flying into the street from where a blacksmith hammered down on a red-hot sword blade. He continued down the steeply sloped street, leading Yusuf through the crowd that had gathered at the shops in the shade of the Temple Mount.

'John!' It was a woman's voice. 'Here!'

John turned to find himself confronted by a veiled woman flanked by two sergeants in mail. She wore a bulky caftan that revealed nothing of the shape underneath. A single blonde curl had escaped from her headdress. 'It is I, Agnes.'

John bowed. 'God grant you joy, Lady de Courtenay.'

Agnes gestured towards Yusuf. 'And who is your friend?'

'This is Saladin, Emir of Tell Bashir.'

'My lady,' Yusuf said.

'A Saracen lord in Jerusalem . . . how intriguing.'

'He is a guest of King Amalric,' John explained.

'The lands beyond the Jordan fascinate me,' Agnes said. 'You must tell me all about them, Saladin. Come. I am not allowed at court, but I keep a home in the city not far from here.' She turned and strode through the crowd without waiting to see if they would follow. Her sergeants walked ahead of her, clearing a path.

John glanced at Yusuf, who shrugged. They followed Agnes

back towards the Mount, and down a dim passageway vaulted over with stone. Past it, Agnes turned right into the narrow streets of the Syrian quarter. The people here were mostly Jacobites, who looked to the Patriarch of Antioch rather than the Pope as their authority. They spoke Arabic, and the men wore trimmed beards and skullcaps.

Agnes's home was a nondescript building on a quiet side street. A tiled entryway opened on to an interior courtyard with a burbling fountain in the centre. 'Wait here,' she told them. She pointed to some stools in the shade of the western wall. 'I will return in a moment.'

John and Yusuf sat, and a servant brought them glasses of orange juice, so sweet that it made John's teeth ache.

Yusuf leaned close to John and whispered in Arabic. 'What do you know of this woman?'

'She is the former wife of King Amalric.'

'Why did they divorce? Was she unfaithful?'

'No. The rumour at court is that they divorced because of consanguinity. They share a great-great-grandfather.'

'Then why were they allowed to marry?'

John shrugged.

'Speaking of me?' It was Agnes, who had stepped silently back into the courtyard. She had changed into a green silk caftan, loose at the arms and tight about the waist, a plunging neckline offering a provocative glimpse of shadowy cleavage. She had removed her veil and wore her long blonde hair down around her shoulders. Both John and Yusuf rose as she approached. 'I see that you have been served refreshments,' she said and smiled. She had the sort of smile that would make men act the fool. John glanced at Yusuf, who was staring wide-eyed, enraptured.

'Please, sit,' Agnes instructed and took a seat on one of the stools. As she did so, she leaned forward, and John could not help but stare down the front of her caftan. Some very unpriestly thoughts flashed through his mind, and he decided it would be best to leave soon. He remained standing while Yusuf sat beside Agnes.

'Thank you for your courteous invitation to your home, my lady,' John said. 'But we must excuse ourselves. We are expected at the palace.'

She waved away his remark as if she were swatting a fly. 'Nonsense. The King is meeting with Chancellor William. They will be busy for some time.'

'But William is in Constantinople,' John countered.

'He returned this morning with important news. Now sit, John.'

John reluctantly did as she asked. He had heard nothing of William's return, and he was the chancellor's secretary. 'How do you know this?'

'I make it my business to stay informed. After all, Amalric is the father of my children. Tell me, how is the young prince?'

'He is well.'

'And he makes progress in his studies?'

'He has a gift for languages, and he enjoys history and sword-play. He will make a good king.' Agnes looked pleased, and John smiled, happy to have pleased her. But this was not what he wanted to discuss. He frowned as he realized how easily she had led the conversation away from William's return. 'You said that the Chancellor brings news, my lady?'

'He does. I will tell you, but first I want to hear from you, Saladin.' She turned to him and placed a hand on his knee. Yusuf blushed scarlet. 'You have recently returned from Alexandria?'

'Yes, my lady.'

'I understand that you were charged with defending the city?'

'Yes. My uncle left me with a thousand men, plus volunteers amongst the Alexandrians.'

'And how many did you face?'

'The combined Frankish and Egyptian forces numbered well over ten thousand.'

'You must have been frightened.'

'No, my lady.'

'I would have been,' Agnes said. 'I am sure of it.'

John was not so sure. The Lady de Courtenay seemed more than capable of looking after herself.

'Everyone feels fear,' Yusuf told her, 'but a warrior learns to rise above it.'

Agnes leaned towards him, revealing another glimpse of the curve of her breasts. 'And you are a great warrior, are you not?' Yusuf's eyes were locked on her bosom. John frowned. Why was she so interested in Yusuf? What could she hope to gain from him?

'Do not pout, John,' Agnes said. She winked conspiratorially at Yusuf. 'He is upset because we have ignored him.'

John forced a smile. 'I am not upset, my lady.'

'You are a poor liar. It is an endearing quality. My former husband, Amalric, is also a poor liar.' She paused, and her mouth tightened for just a moment. But when she spoke again, her tone was light. 'You must grow accustomed to women ignoring you, John. You are a priest, wedded to the Holy Church. A great loss for the women of Jerusalem. You would have been quite the catch.'

John opened his mouth to reply but could find no words. He could feel his face flushing as red as Yusuf's.

She laughed at his consternation. 'Surely you must know that women find you attractive, John. A strong jaw, eyes as blue as the summer sky, broad shoulders. Ah, but you do look ill in your priest's cloak. I would prefer you in mail, or in a simple caftan, like Saladin here.' She turned her attention back to Yusuf. 'Are you married, Emir?'

'He is not,' John said, hoping that she would turn her green eyes back towards him.

Agnes ignored him. All her attention was on Yusuf. 'Ah, but you have your eye on someone, yes?' Yusuf looked away. 'You do! What is she like? Blonde? No, of course not; she is a Saracen.

Dark hair then, and dark eyes, and golden skin like the desert sands.' Yusuf was staring speechless at his feet. 'Forgive me, Emir. I see that it pains you to speak of it. Let us talk of happier things. King Amalric is to be married. That is the news that William brings.'

'Married? Are you certain?' John thought back to his conversation with Amalric, the day they had arrived in Cairo. The king had talked of marriage. Had he known then?

'Yes, I am sure, John. He is to marry Maria Komnena, grand-niece of the Emperor Manuel.' Agnes's delicate nose wrinkled, as if she had smelled something disagreeable. 'She is a sad little thing. But she brings a large dowry, and her marriage will seal the alliance between Amalric and Manuel.'

Yusuf leaned forward, interested. 'When will this marriage take place?'

'Maria is a girl of only ten. They will wait until she is older; thirteen perhaps. Poor girl. I was no older when I was married.'

'To Amalric?' John asked.

'No, to Reynald of Marash. He was a beast of a man, but I did not have to bear with him for long. He died shortly after our marriage. After that I was engaged to Hugh of Ibelin, but he was captured in battle before we could marry. The story has a happy ending, though. After Amalric divorced me, Hugh came to court me once more. We were married last year, eight years after our first engagement.'

John winced. He had not known she had married again. He rose. 'We truly must go, Lady de Courtenay.'

'Then I bid you farewell and Godspeed on your journey, both of you.'

'Pardon, my lady? I have no plans to leave Jerusalem.'

A smile played at the corner of Agnes's mouth. 'Plans have been made for you, John. Amalric is sending you and William to Aleppo to negotiate the release of the prisoners that Nur ad-Din took at Harim.'

Agnes was very well informed indeed. John wondered who

her contacts were at court. 'Why would the King send me?' he asked.

'Amalric hopes your friendships amongst the Saracens will prove valuable in the negotiations.' She rose. 'I do not wish to keep either of you from the preparations for your journey. Thank you both for honouring me with your company.'

Yusuf bowed. 'It is we who were honoured, my lady.'

She gave him her most winning smile. 'God keep you, Saladin. My man will show you out.'

A servant stepped forward and led Yusuf towards the exit. John began to follow, but Agnes grabbed his arm. 'I have no confessor in Jerusalem, Father. I would appreciate it if you would visit from time to time to relieve me of the burden of my sins.'

John hesitated. William had warned him to be wary of the Lady de Courtenay, yet he enjoyed her easy manner, the touch of her hand on his arm, the warmth in her smile.

'Of course, my lady.'

Chapter 7

Yusuf stood at the rail of the ship and watched the coast drift past. John and William had offered to travel with him to Aleppo, and Yusuf had gladly accepted. Three days ago they had boarded a ship in Jaffa. Now, as they rounded a rocky spit of land, Yusuf could just make out the mouth of the Orontes River, a low point on the otherwise mountainous coast. The port of Saint Symeon, which served the crusader city of Antioch, lay just up the river.

'May I join you?'

Yusuf turned to see William approaching. 'Where is John?'

'Still below. I fear the sea does not agree with him.' The priest stood beside Yusuf and leaned his elbows on the rail so that the silver cross about his neck hung out over the water. 'You enjoyed your visit to Jerusalem?'

Yusuf nodded.

'I have spoken to Amalric about opening the city to Muslim settlement.'

Yusuf blinked in surprise. 'And what did Amalric say?'

'He is not opposed to the idea. The other cities of the Kingdom all have Arab residents. And half the homes in Jerusalem lie empty. Muslim settlers would mean more revenue.'

'And more taxes means that he can pay more warriors.'

'True, but that is not why I wish to open the Holy City to your people. I believe that Christians and Muslims can share

Jerusalem as they did before the Crusades. I believe that we can learn to respect one another's faiths.'

'John says the same.'

'You should listen to him.'

'Tell that to your Templars. When I visited Al-Aqsa, one of them accosted me while I prayed.'

'John told me,' William said. 'The Templar was newly arrived in the Holy Land. He may be a savage now, but the East will civilize him. Think of John. He started like that Templar and look at him now.'

'Now he is a priest,' Yusuf said with a trace of bitterness. 'He serves King Amalric.'

'Yes, but he respects your people, loves them even. He longs for peace.'

'And what of your king? Is his alliance with the Emperor Manuel meant to bring peace?'

'Amalric is no fool. He battles with Nur ad-Din because he fears him. This alliance will make the Kingdom secure. Amalric will not need to fight.'

'But he will want to. I have met your king. He is a warrior, like Nur ad-Din.'

William shrugged. 'That may be, but it is the responsibility of men like us to guide our kings, Saladin.'

'No, it is my duty to serve my king.'

'And what better way to serve him than by offering sage advice? The treaty that was signed in Egypt could be the beginning of a new age of peace. But peace is a fragile flower. We must cultivate it.'

Yusuf said nothing. Ahead, he could see a ship sailing into the mouth of the Orontes. Saint Symeon was located two miles upstream. Yusuf was curious to see it. He knew that the port would have to be taken first if an attacking army hoped to seize Antioch. That is what the Franks had done during the First Crusade. With Saint Symeon in hand, Antioch could be starved into submission. He sighed. His thoughts could not help but

143

run to war. He had been raised from birth to fight the Franks. But he had also been taught that they were savages, and John had showed him that was not true. There were brutes like the Templar guard, but there were also civilized men amongst the Franks, like William. And perhaps, in time, young Baldwin. Under John's tutelage the prince could become a man of peace, unlike Yusuf's nephew Ubadah, with his blind hatred of the Franks. Perhaps the obstacle to peace was not the Franks but Yusuf's own people. Perhaps it was he who needed to change.

Beside him, William stepped away from the rail. 'Think on what I have said, Saladin.'

As the priest walked away, John passed him to join Yusuf. John's face was pale, and there was a trace of vomit on the front of his tunic. 'What were you discussing?'

'Peace.'

John nodded but said nothing. The two friends watched as the Orontes drew closer. Finally, Yusuf spoke. 'I do not wish to be your enemy, John. Perhaps you are right. Perhaps we can live in peace.'

John smiled. 'Inshallah.'

FEBRUARY 1165: NEAR ALEPPO

John reined in beside Yusuf and William atop a rocky ridge. They had left Antioch five days ago, travelling with a caravan of Saracen merchants. Now, John could just make out the distant minaret of the citadel of Aleppo. The path leading to it crossed a desolate stretch of sun-baked ground, dotted by villages clustered around wells.

'We will arrive soon,' Yusuf said. 'I will offer the head of the caravan a dinar, as thanks for our safe journey.'

Yusuf spurred down the far side of the ridge, and John and William followed at a slower pace. The priest nodded in the direction of the city. 'You lived in Aleppo. What is it like?'

John shrugged. 'You should ask Saladin. I spent most of my time in the citadel barracks.'

'Surely you did not spend all your time at the citadel.' John flinched at the memory of his night-time visits to Zimat. William seemed not to notice. 'What are the streets like? The markets? Is it a rich town?'

'The souks bring great wealth to the city. You can buy anything you wish in them. As for the rest: the streets are broad and clean, nothing like Jerusalem. The walls and buildings are of pale stone; that is why they call it the White City.'

'What was it like to live for so long amongst the infidels?'

'Surprising. I had been told that they were monsters, but I found them cultured, intelligent, kind even to their slaves, tolerant of the beliefs of others.'

'I have always found the Saracens to be good company. I am looking forward to our visit.'

John was less eager to reach Aleppo. The closer he got to the city, the more his stomach roiled. What would Zimat think of his decision to join the priesthood? What would she say to him? He attempted to picture her face and found it dissolving into that of Agnes. He tried to drive the latter image from his thoughts, but his mind refused to obey. He could see Agnes sitting in the courtyard of her home, a slight smile on her lips, her golden hair falling down towards her breasts.

'Are you well, friend?' Yusuf asked as he rejoined them. 'You look upset.'

'Perhaps it is something I ate,' John murmured. He looked to William. 'Why did Amalric divorce the Lady de Courtenay? The real reason.'

The priest frowned. 'Politics. Agnes is the heir to Edessa, a vanished kingdom. It was a good marriage at first, but one with less and less value as it became clear that Edessa would never be recovered from Nur ad-Din. Still, so long as Amalric was only a prince, Agnes was a suitable wife. But when he became king—' William shook his head. 'He had to divorce her, even if he did not wish to.'

'He loved her?'

'You have met Agnes. What do you think?'

'She is like a desert flower,' Yusuf said.

'Amalric was smitten the moment he saw her. Agnes wanted to wait for her father's permission; but Joscelin was a prisoner in Aleppo, and Amalric did not wish to wait for a paternal blessing that might never come. He carried Agnes off by force and married her. The divorce wounded him deeply, but not as much as it hurt Agnes. She never forgave him.'

'But you say he had no choice,' John said.

'She does not see it that way,' William replied. 'Amalric tried to soften the blow. He made her a countess with income from Jaffa and Ascalon. But he could not give her what she truly wanted: access to her children.'

'Why not?'

'There were those at court who feared that she would turn them against Amalric. So the Prince Baldwin is kept in the palace. His older sister, Sibylla, has been sent to the convent of Saint Lazarus where she is being raised by her great-aunt.'

John felt a sudden wave of sympathy for Agnes. Like him, she was kept from her children and her lover by politics. No one could know the pain she felt better than him.

'You would do best to stop thinking of her, John,' William said.

'I was not—'

William held up a hand to stop him. 'I have seen the effect Agnes can have on men, but it is the allure of a siren, calling men to their doom.'

Yusuf laughed. 'You make her out to be a monster. I found her a charming woman.'

'She is that,' William agreed. 'Too charming by half.'

They rode on in silence as the pale winter sun climbed into

the sky and then began its slow descent. It was hovering just above the horizon, bathing the white stone buildings of Aleppo in rose-coloured light, when they reached the outskirts of the city. The road ran past stone houses set amidst pistachio and olive orchards. They crossed the tiny Quweq River, and the caravan that they had joined headed north to one of the cara-vanserais located outside the city wall. Yusuf led them east to the Bab Antakeya, an arched gateway framed by tall defensive towers. The gate led to an interior passage that turned sharply to the left and then back to the right. The walls of the passage were lined with men offering water, food and lodging. Yusuf ignored them, and the men paid John and William little notice. They were both dressed in caftans, and with their keffiyeh pulled down over their faces, they were indistinguishable from any of the other travellers.

They emerged from the gate on to a street so old that there were ruts in the stone paving from centuries of wagon traffic. They passed a series of souks on their left, and memories flooded back to John. He remembered walking through those markets, looking for the doctor, Ibn Jumay. He had sought a medicine to abort Zimat's child, but he had not been able to bring himself to buy it. Soon, he would see that child for the first time in years.

They emerged into Aleppo's central square. William whistled in appreciation of the citadel, which towered above them on its sheer-sided hill of white rock. At the base of the citadel, a guardhouse protected the bridge that ran across the moat. Three mamluks in chainmail stepped forth, spears extended. One, a thin young man, lowered his spear and grinned. 'Saladin! You have returned.'

Yusuf slid from the saddle and embraced the man. 'As-salaamu 'alaykum, Saqr. I have brought an old friend.' He gestured to John, who pulled his keffiyeh down to reveal his face.

'Al-ifranji?' Saqr asked, his eyes wide. 'I thought you were dead.'

'As you can see, I am alive and well. I come with this man, William of Tyre, on behalf of the Frankish king.'

'You are expected,' Saqr said. 'Come.'

They followed Saqr up the causeway and through the citadel's main gate. At the palace, servants came forth to take their horses. Gumushtagin met them in the entrance hall. 'Ahlan wa-Sahlan, Saladin,' the eunuch said with his faint lisp.

John noticed that Yusuf flinched slightly before he nodded in greeting.

Gumushtagin turned to John and William. 'Welcome, distinguished visitors. Nur ad-Din is expecting you.' He led them to a set of double doors, where the guards searched them before pulling open the doors to reveal Nur ad-Din's audience chamber. At the far side of the room, the king was seated cross-legged on a low, wide throne with a short back. Members of his court sat to either side on stools. John recognized Shirkuh and Selim amongst them. Yusuf approached and bowed low.

'Saladin!' Nur ad-Din greeted him. 'Welcome home. Your uncle told me that you volunteered to stay with the Franks as a hostage. That was noble of you.'

'King Amalric was a gracious host.'

'I am glad to hear it.' Nur ad-Din looked past Yusuf to William and John. He waved them forward. 'You are welcome at my court, William of Tyre. And I am pleased to see you again, John.' John was surprised that Nur ad-Din remembered him, but then realized that he had also greeted William by name, and the two men had never met. John reflected on what Yusuf had told him about Nur ad-Din's spies at the court in Jerusalem. Nur ad-Din had probably been informed the moment they set out for Aleppo.

'We thank you for your kind welcome,' William replied, 'and we greet you on behalf of King Amalric of Jerusalem, who desires only peace and friendship between our two kingdoms.'

Nur ad-Din nodded. 'You are no doubt weary after your

long journey. I have set aside a suite for you in my palace. Retire there and refresh yourselves. Tomorrow, you will dine at the home of Saladin, where your countrymen who are enjoying my hospitality will join you. Now, my man will take you to your rooms.' He gestured to a servant; a corpulent black man in a white caftan.

'You are most kind, Malik,' William said.

He and John bowed again and followed the servant out of the hall. 'Why did he dismiss us so quickly?' William asked John in a low voice. 'What of the negotiations?'

'They have already begun,' John said. 'Nur ad-Din wishes to show us the value of his captives. That is the purpose of tomorrow's dinner. He has selected Saladin as his chief negotiator, hence the meal at his home. We will discuss the terms of ransom there.'

'No, we will not. The Emperor Manuel's cousin Constantine has been captured, and Bohemond is Manuel's brother-in-law. Nur ad-Din will be eager to ransom them, so as to avoid any tension with Constantinople. That is to our advantage. We must show that we are willing to bide our time. We will wait for him to come to us with an offer.'

'Nur ad-Din is a patient man. I fear we will be waiting a very long time.'

The next evening Yusuf stood at the window of his room as he waited for his Frankish guests to arrive. In the courtyard below the fountain burbled in the gathering dusk and Saqr and Al-Mashtub chatted by the gate. Prayers had finished only moments before, and the city had fallen quiet as the populace headed inside for their evening meals. The silence was broken by the clip-clop of approaching horses' hooves. A moment later the gate swung open. A mamluk rode through, followed by John and the priest William. They dismounted and William headed straight for the entrance to Yusuf's home. John hesitated for a moment before following.

The newly captured Frankish prisoners arrived next. Yusuf recognized them easily enough from Nur ad-Din's descriptions. The first man was thickly set with straw-blond hair and florid cheeks covered in pale fuzz. That would be the young Prince of Antioch, Bohemond. Yusuf identified the next guest as Constantine Kalamanos, an olive-skinned young man in an elaborate caftan of blue silk. Raymond of Tripoli came next. He too was in his mid twenties, but he looked older due to his commanding presence. He was slender and straight-backed, with dark hair, a swarthy complexion and an aquiline nose that dominated his face. He reminded Yusuf of his father. Hugh of Lusignan entered last of all, followed by a mamluk with sword drawn. Hugh was an older man, his tanned face deeply lined.

The four captives had been shown inside when the final guest arrived. Yusuf had not seen Reynald de Chatillon in nearly three years. He had the same close-cropped black hair and beard, but his sharp features were now rounded. He looked to have gained a stone or two. Yusuf had not wanted to invite Reynald, but Nur ad-Din had insisted. The king was eager to see him ransomed at last. Reynald looked around the courtyard and his gaze settled on the dark window where Yusuf stood. Yusuf stepped back into his room.

There was a knock at the door, and Faridah entered. 'Your guests are waiting.' She crossed the room and straightened the belt of red silk that held his caftan.

Yusuf went downstairs and paused outside the dining-room, pressing his eye to a spyhole in order to examine his guests a final time. The Franks had been served wine and were talking amongst themselves. The half-dozen silent mamluks lining the walls were the only indication that some of the guests were also captives. Yusuf stepped away from the spyhole and entered.

'My lords and honoured guests,' he declared in Frankish, 'God keep you all and grant you health and joy. Welcome to my home. I am Saladin, Emir of Tell Bashir.' Reynald scowled, but the other men all stepped forward to greet him, telling him their names and murmuring formulaic replies of 'God keep you' or 'And may health and joy be granted you by God'. Yusuf was pleased to see that he had guessed correctly regarding their identities.

He gestured to the circle of cushions that surrounded a low, round table in the middle of the room. 'Please be seated.' Yusuf allowed his guests to sit where they wished. He ended up between William and Raymond. Bohemond and Constantine sat to Raymond's left, while John and Hugh sat to the right of William. Reynald sat directly opposite. When they were all seated, servants entered with steaming flatbread and a large bowl of badinjan muhassa, an aromatic dip of baked eggplant, ground walnuts and raw onions. Yusuf spooned a bit of the dip on to his plate and then scooped it up with a piece of bread. 'In the name of Allah, Most Gracious, Most Merciful,' he murmured, but paused with the bread halfway to his mouth. None of the Franks were eating.

'Excuse me,' William said. 'May I say grace?'

'Of course.'

William cleared his throat, and the Franks at the table bowed their heads. 'Benedicite,' the priest began in Latin as he made the sign of the cross over the food. 'The Lord, merciful and compassionate, has perpetuated the memory of His wonders. He has given food to them that fear Him.'

'Amen,' the men murmured and began to spoon the dip on to their plates.

William took a bite and sighed with satisfaction. 'You Saracens have a way with food that we Christians have not yet mastered. Thank you for having me in your home.'

'After the welcome your king gave me, it is the least I can do.'

William chuckled. 'I know the King's cooks, and I believe I have the better end of the bargain.'

'What are you saying?' Constantine called from the left side of the table. He spoke French only poorly. William translated the discussion into Greek, and he and the governor of Cilicia began to speak across the table.

Yusuf was content to ignore William. Nur ad-Din had instructed him to act as if he were in no hurry to ransom the prisoners. He turned to Raymond. 'I would love to hear about your part in the battle at Harim, if you are willing to tell the story.'

'Of course,' the Count of Tripoli replied. 'Although I fear my role in the events was none too glorious. Your king, Nur ad-Din, led us on a merry chase. Then, just when we thought we had him—' Raymond clapped his hands together '—the trap closed on us.' As the meal progressed, Raymond described the encounter in more detail. While he talked, Yusuf kept an eye on the other guests. John was quiet and kept looking to the door leading upstairs. Yusuf felt for his friend, so close to Zimat and yet unable to see her. Last night, Yusuf had told his sister that John lived and that he was here in Aleppo. She had asked to see him and then retired to her room in tears. He had not seen her since.

Beside John, William was engaged in an animated conversation with Constantine and Bohemond. Hugh and Reynald spoke quietly. Yusuf noticed that when the roasted lamb with chickpeas arrived, Hugh ate with his hands, but Reynald used a fork. He had learned some manners during his time in Aleppo.

Raymond was concluding his story as the final dish was cleared away. 'And so after nearly twenty miles of riding, I found myself stuck in that foul swamp with muck up to my horse's chest. Our cavalry was useless and our infantry even worse off. Meanwhile, the Saracens rained arrows down on us. It was a bad end to a bad day, but it could have been worse. I am alive, and the good Lord has seen fit to teach me an important lesson. The next time I face the Saracens and they retreat, I will not come rushing after them.'

On the opposite side of the table, Hugh leaned forward. 'The next time? And when might that be? We are prisoners here, if you have not forgotten, Raymond.'

'*Prisoner* is a harsh word,' Yusuf replied. 'It is true that you may not leave the city, but while you are here, you shall be treated as honoured guests.'

'Guests?' Hugh snorted. 'I would not have come to this dinner had I not been walked through the streets with a sword at my back. That is hardly the way one treats a guest.'

'And one does not invite prisoners to dinner,' Yusuf countered.

'Nur ad-Din has been most generous,' Raymond agreed in a conciliatory tone. 'We lack for nothing; neither servants nor food nor books. And we are allowed to explore the city in the company of a guard. Compared to Aleppo, I fear that Tripoli seems a provincial town.'

Yusuf appreciated Raymond's tact. 'I have never been to Tripoli.'

'It is not so busy or as prosperous as Aleppo, but it has its charms. It sits on a peninsula that curves out into the Mediterranean. That is one thing that I do miss: the smell of the sea.' Raymond looked across the table to William. 'Hopefully I will not have cause to miss it for long.'

'I pray not,' William agreed.

'You p-pray?' Bohemond slapped the table. Yusuf saw now why he was called Bohemond the Stammerer. 'You are here to do m-more than pray, priest. When—' He froze, his jaw tight and the veins in his neck bulging as he struggled to speak. 'When will I be freed?'

'Do not hold your breath,' Reynald grumbled. 'I have been here for nearly eight years.'

Constantine was sipping his wine, watching the conversation without fully understanding it. Bohemond whispered something to him, and the Roman's lip curled in a sneer as he looked towards Reynald. He turned back to Bohemond. 'Do not fear,' he said in Greek. 'We are too valuable to remain here long. Emperor Manuel will ransom us.'

'What is that?' Reynald demanded.

'He said nothing to offend you,' William said and quickly translated Constantine's words.

Reynald sat up straighter. 'And am I not valuable?' He pointed to Bohemond. 'I was Prince of Antioch before this stuttering fool stole my throne!'

William began to translate, but Constantine held up a hand to stop him. 'I understood that well enough.' He looked down his long nose at Reynald and switched to accented French. 'I am a cousin of the Roman Emperor, and Bohemond is his brother-in-law. You are a nobody.'

The bulging veins in Reynald's temples revealed his building anger. 'I had hoped to be ransomed at last,' he growled. He looked to Yusuf. 'Now I see that you have only invited me here to insult me.'

'It is not I who has insulted you, Reynald.'

'Have you not? You invite me here in the company of this usurping idiot. I know full well that Amalric will never ransom me, not so long as this boil-brained clot pole lives, and yet I must sit and watch the negotiations for his freedom.' He paused and pointed a thick finger at John. 'Worse yet, I must do so while this arse-licking Saxon, your Sodomite friend, looks on. And you say you have not insulted me!'

William's gasp was audible. Yusuf glanced at John, whose knuckles showed white around the ceramic cup he clenched. He looked back to Reynald, who was taking a long drink of wine. 'I shall have to ask you to leave, Reynald,' Yusuf said quietly.

'Why?' Reynald smirked. 'Have I offended you? Hit too close to the mark? You wouldn't want your guests to know about your ungodly doings with this—' Before Reynald could finish, John leaped to his feet, stepped straight across the table and smashed the cup into the side of his head. The cup shattered and blood ran from a cut just over Reynald's ear. The heavy-set man sat stunned for a moment, then shook his head and, with a roar, lunged for John. Two mamluks rushed forward and pulled him away.

'Get your cursed hands off me!' Reynald shouted as Yusuf's men dragged him from the room.

John had stepped down from the table. 'My apologies,' he murmured and then dropped the remains of the cup and followed Reynald into the courtyard.

'Well then,' William said, brushing crumbs from his white robe as he stood. 'Perhaps we should all depart. It grows late, and we do not wish to intrude upon your hospitality.'

Yusuf rose as well. 'I thank you all for coming. May God guide you and bring you honour and health. Ma'a as-salaama.'

'Allah yasalmak,' William replied and headed for the door. The other men added their goodbyes in a mixture of French, Greek and Arabic before also taking their leave. Yusuf followed them into the courtyard, where he found John standing in the dark shadows cast by the left-hand wall.

'I am sorry,' he said as Yusuf approached. 'I fear I have insulted your hospitality.'

'Nonsense. I wanted to hit the bastard myself.'

William walked over from the gate, where he had been seeing Reynald and the others off. 'Allow me to apologize for John. He has much to learn as a diplomat.'

'And Reynald?' Yusuf asked.

'Unfortunately, he is correct. Amalric has no desire to ransom him. The treasury in Jerusalem is low—' He let the words hang in the air.

'That is a matter to discuss another time.' Yusuf turned to John. 'Can you return tomorrow? I would like to speak with you.' He lowered his voice so that only John could hear. 'Zimat also wishes to see you.'

William spoke before John had a chance. 'He would be happy to return.'

'Tomorrow then, after morning prayers. Ma'a as-salaama.'

John examined his features in the bronze mirror in his chamber. He had woken early that day and gone to the baths, where a barber had cut his hair short and shaved him. What would Zimat think of the lines that creased his forehead and ran down either side of his mouth, of the grey hairs at his temples? There was a knock at the door, and John stepped away from the mirror and straightened his stole.

William entered. 'Morning prayers have ended, John. It is time.'

'Perhaps you should come with me. You are the King's ambassador, not I.'

'No. This is precisely why I asked Amalric to send you. My negotiations will take weeks, even months. God willing, you can move faster. Find out how much Nur ad-Din wants for Bohemond and Constantine.'

'And Raymond and Hugh? Reynald?'

'They are of no importance, but do not let Saladin know that. Show great interest in their ransom. Now go. You do not want to keep your friend waiting.'

John had no trouble retracing the path to Yusuf's home. The gate was open. John entered the courtyard to find Ibn Jumay seated at the fountain, and beside him a boy of about seven years. John recognized him instantly as Ubadah. He had John's straight, narrow nose and square chin, but he had his mother's dark-brown eyes and fine, high cheekbones. Ibn Jumay was asking him something. The boy looked about as if searching for an answer, and his eyes settled on John. Ubadah spoke to Ibn Jumay, who looked over and smiled.

'John! Welcome! As-salaamu 'alaykum!' Ibn Jumay had aged since John had last seen him. The Jewish doctor's long beard and side locks were now flecked with grey. But he stood straight and moved with a young man's ease as he approached.

The two men exchanged kisses on the cheeks. 'Wa 'alaykum as-salaam,' John said. 'It has been too long, friend. You are well?'

'Yes, God be praised. I have my practice here in town, and Yusuf has me teaching young Ubadah. But what of you? How is life amongst the Franks?'

'I miss my old friends.'

'And you are missed. Wait here. I will inform Yusuf you have arrived.' Ibn Jumay looked to the boy. 'Ubadah, greet our guest.'

Ubadah scowled, but then rose and extended his right hand, grasping John's with a firm grip. 'Welcome to my home,' he said in Frankish. 'I am Ubadah ibn Khaldun.'

Ibn Khaldun. John felt a pain in his chest. His child called another man father – Khaldun, who had died in an earthquake two years ago. That was also the last time John had seen his son. 'May God bless you and grant you joy and health,' he told Ubadah, trying to keep the sadness from his voice. He switched to Arabic. 'You speak French well.'

Ubadah shrugged. 'Uncle Yusuf makes me practise.'

'You do not like it?'

'It is a filthy language, spoken by a filthy people,' the boy said with surprising vehemence.

John took a step back, as if he had been struck. When he had recovered, he spoke in Arabic. 'There are good men amongst the Franks, Ubadah.'

The boy glared at John. 'I remember you.' He spat at John's feet and walked away.

Yusuf passed Ubadah as he entered the courtyard. 'John!' he called. 'As-salaamu 'alaykum.'

'And upon you, peace,' John replied as the friends embraced.

'I see that you have already greeted Ubadah.'

John nodded. He was still upset from the encounter.

'Good,' Yusuf said. 'Come inside.'

John followed Yusuf into the large reception room where they had dined the previous night. 'Do you wish to discuss the ransoms?' he asked. 'King Amalric is willing to pay a high price for Raymond and Hugh of Lusignan.'

'Is he? I thought that the coffers of Jerusalem were bare.' Yusuf smiled. 'I have known you long enough to see when you are lying, John. The King is not interested in Raymond or Hugh. He must ransom Bohemond and Constantine if he wishes to maintain his alliance with Constantinople.'

John's forehead creased. 'Am I that easy to read?'

'To me you are. That is no doubt why William sent you. The priest is a clever man. He hopes for direct talk between us, not diplomacy.'

'Then I shall be direct: how much for Bohemond and Constantine?'

'Three hundred thousand dinars each.' John gave a low whistle of appreciation. 'But I did not ask you here to discuss their ransom. Zimat wishes to see you.'

John's mouth went dry. 'Does she know I am a priest?'

'I told her.' Yusuf placed a hand on his shoulder. 'She is not the same woman you remember. When she thought you dead, it changed her, John. I will leave you two to talk. I am sure I can trust the honour of a priest.'

John nodded. 'Thank you, friend.'

Yusuf left the room, and a moment later, Zimat entered. Her long, lustrous black hair had not changed, nor had her slim waist, but the curves at her hips and breasts were fuller. Her face was pale, her eyes red from crying. They faced one another across the room, and neither moved. John's heart was pounding so loudly that he was sure she could hear it.

'I thought you were dead,' she said.

'I thought I would never see you again.' He approached, but she backed away.

'No—I cannot.' She took a deep breath. 'I cannot give myself to you, John. Not again. Not after what you have done.'

'But I—'

'Sit.' She gestured to the cushions on the floor. John sat, and she settled herself across from him. He could smell the sweet fragrance of her oiled hair. He had not realized how much he missed it.

'What happened to you at Butaiha?' she asked. 'Yusuf said he saw you struck down.'

'I was. But not killed. I was taken to Jerusalem, where I was to be burned as a heretic and a traitor. The King pardoned me in return for my service.'

'I see.' She met his eyes. 'Has there been anyone else? Another woman?'

'Of course not. I became a priest so that I would not have to marry another.'

'Then why did you not return?' There was a plaintive note in her voice. 'You said you would never leave me.'

'I had no choice. I gave my word to King Amalric. I owe him my life.'

'You owe me your love. You promised you would return.'

'I am here now.'

She shook her head. 'It is too late. I have asked Yusuf to find me a new husband.'

'You were promised to another before, when we first met in Baalbek.'

'We are no longer children, John. I have a son now.'

'He is my son, too.'

'He believes that Khaldun is his father. He would only despise you more if he knew the truth. Instead of the son of an emir, he would be an ifranji, the very thing he despises most. He would hate himself, and hate you the more for it.'

John's mouth set in a hard line. He was angry, but not at Zimat. It was the bitter truth of her words that stung him. 'Why did you wish to see me?' he asked.

Zimat looked away, but not before John saw the tears in her eyes. 'I thought you dead, only to have you appear in Aleppo. How could I not see you? I—I wanted to say farewell.' She rose, and he did likewise. He began to cross to her, but once again she backed away.

'Let me hold you,' he said. 'I know you still love me, Zimat.'

She shook her head. 'I cannot.' She turned and began to climb the stairs.

'Zimat!' John called, but she did not stop. She disappeared up the stairs without looking back.

Yusuf sat in the saddle and squinted against the sun as he followed the flight of his bazi. Beside him, John and Ubadah were doing the same. The hunting falcon was a magnificent creature, steel grey with a brown head and white chest. Its wingspan was more than four feet across. From this distance Yusuf could just hear the tinkle of the tiny bells attached to its ankle. On the ground below the falcon a pair of lean salukis were creeping towards a patch of brush where Ubadah had spotted a rabbit. Suddenly they lunged, and the rabbit bolted. The falcon made its sharp call – *kiy-ee, kiy-ee* – and dived, plunging from the sky at incredible speed. It pulled up at the last second, the rabbit in its claws. It flapped away a distance and settled down with its prey.

Ubadah spurred towards the falcon. Yusuf and John followed at a slower pace. When they arrived, Ubadah was holding up the rabbit. 'Look, Baba!' he called to Yusuf.

Baba. Father. The boy seemed not to have noticed the slip. Yusuf turned to John. He looked as if he had been slapped.

'Bring it here,' Yusuf told Ubadah. He tied the rabbit to his saddle alongside three others, then called the falcon. It landed on his gloved arm. He attached the jesses so that the bird would not fly off, and then slipped a hood over its head. 'Come. It is time we returned to the city.'

They rode back in silence. The negotiations had dragged on for several months. William mostly ignored Yusuf, spending his time with Raymond of Tripoli, who had taken advantage of his captivity to start a library. He had asked for William's assistance, and the two of them spent many an afternoon searching for books in the souk. John spent most of his days with Yusuf, though he had not seen Zimat again. John and Yusuf seldom mentioned the negotiations. Yusuf knew that it was a waiting game. When both sides were desperate then the talks would begin in earnest, and they would go quickly indeed.

The city gates were less than a mile off now. Yusuf took the rabbits from his saddle and handed them to Ubadah. He had hoped that spending time with John would help the boy overcome his hatred of Franks, but Ubadah had refused to even acknowledge John's presence. 'Ride ahead and give these to your mother,' Yusuf said.

When the boy had cantered off, Yusuf turned to John. 'You should put Zimat from your mind, friend.'

John started. 'How did you know I was thinking of her?'

'It is written on your face. You must try to forget her. You are a priest, and she is to be married next month.' Yusuf could see that the news pained his friend.

'Who is the husband?'

'His name is Al-Muqaddam. He is an emir. A brave warrior and a good man. It is a kindness on his part to marry Zimat. She is no longer young.'

'I still love her, Yusuf.'

Yusuf placed a hand on his friend's shoulder. 'My uncle told me once that to be great, a man must learn to rule his passions.'

'I do not wish to be great,' John murmured and spurred ahead, into the city.

'Allahu akbar! Allahu akbar!' John stood in the central square of Aleppo in the dim dawn light and listened as the strident call of the muezzins came from all parts of the city. A few men and women crossed the square on the way to the mosque. Beggars sat around the periphery, some sleeping and some requesting alms from the passers-by. Half a dozen farmers had arrived from the countryside and were setting up stalls to sell their produce. But the part of the cobbled square that John had sought out was empty. Almost ten years ago he had stood in the same place and watched as Zimat's now dead husband, Khaldun, stoned one of his wives to death for infidelity. Zimat had run that risk once to be with him. She had loved him with a passion that had surprised him.

John left the square and wandered at random through the streets, so foreign and yet so familiar. Negotiations had been concluded the previous day. Amalric would pay one hundred and fifty thousand dinars for Bohemond. Constantine was released for only a hundred and fifty silk robes. Yusuf had confided that Nur ad-Din would have let him go for free in order to win the goodwill of the Emperor Manuel, but paying no ransom would have insulted Constantine's stature. Reynald had not been ransomed, nor had Raymond or Hugh. William explained that Amalric was in no hurry for Raymond to return, because with him gone, the king would rule Tripoli as regent.

Their work done, John and William were to leave the following day. John would not go without Zimat, not again. Long ago, she had begged him to take her away with him to Frankish lands, and he had refused. He would not make the same mistake twice.

He arrived at the gate to Yusuf's home and knocked. The gate swung open, and Saqr waved him inside. 'Saladin is at the citadel,' the mamluk told him.

'I will wait for him inside.'

'Are you certain? He may not return for some time.'

'I will wait.'

John sat amidst the cushions in the dining-room and a servant brought him tea. No sooner had she left than he rose and climbed the stairs to the next floor. He opened the first door he came to, and found an otherwise empty room dominated by a loom. The next room was an empty bedchamber, as was the next. He opened the final door on the hall to find Zimat sitting on her bed.

'John!' she gasped. She stood. 'You should not be here!'

He stepped inside and closed the door behind him. 'I will not leave you, Zimat. Not again.'

'You must go!'

'Marry me instead of Al-Muqaddam. I can take you away to Frankish lands. We can be together!'

'Ubadah would have no future. What would he become? A merchant? A priest like you?' She said the word *priest* with scorn.

'We do not have to go. I will stay. I will serve Yusuf.'

She shook her head. 'It cannot be, John. Do you not understand? Al-Muqaddam is an emir. With him as his father, Ubadah can become a great lord. You could never give him that.'

'But I am his father.'

'That is why you must go,' she said, her voice beginning to break. 'You must do what is best for our son.'

'But I love you.' He crossed the room and took her face in his hands. He kissed her gently, and she kissed him back, tentatively at first and then hard. His hands slid down to her waist, and he pulled her to him.

'No.' She pushed him away, tears in her eyes. 'I must think of Ubadah. You must go, before we are discovered.' He nodded and went to the door. 'John,' she called, stopping him. 'I—I do love you.'

John could find no words to reply. His heart ached as if it were bruised. He turned and left to return to Jerusalem, to his solitary life as a priest, to a people that were more foreign to him than the Saracens.

Chapter 8

John sat beside William at one of the tables in the great hall of the Archbishop of Tyre's palace, the location that had been chosen to celebrate Amalric's marriage to Maria Komnena. John recognized several of the nobles and prelates seated around them: the grand masters of the Temple and Hospital, Humphrey of Toron, Hugh of Caesarea and Bohemond of Antioch, who John had helped to ransom two years ago to the day. John winced. Even now, it pained him to think of those days in Aleppo.

A trumpet sounded, and the guests stood. The doors to the hall swung open, and Amalric entered with his new wife on his arm. Maria looked like a frightened girl, despite her golden crown. She had no chest, and her blue-silk caftan hung from her as if she were a boy. Her wavy hair, which had been bleached blonde with lemon juice and sunlight, was held back in a tight bun that accentuated her high forehead. She had a weak chin, a pug nose and a smallish mouth with lips that seemed to be in a perpetual pout. Her eyes, ringed with black kohl, were red from crying.

The king and his new queen were followed by the seneschal, bearing the king's sceptre, and the chamberlain with his sword. Then came the Patriarch of Jerusalem, the Archbishop of Tyre, and half a dozen envoys from the emperor's court in Constantinople. The procession reached the seats at the head table, and Amalric spoke. 'Thank you for coming to celebrate this joyous day! Eat, drink, enjoy yourselves!'

The king sat, and his guests followed suit. William and John were at a side table some distance away. John nodded towards Maria. 'She looks miserable.'

'She could have done worse. Amalric is a kind man.'

'And there is more than one palace servant who has benefited from his kindness. He will not be faithful to her.'

'At least he will not beat her.'

John thanked God that he was not a woman, to be sold like chattel simply to seal an alliance. He busied himself with the duck breast on his plate.

At the head table, the emperor's chief representative stood. With his double chin, fat fingers and soft body, the duke Thoros looked like an overweight merchant, but it was said he had the ear of Emperor Manuel, and that made him a man to be reckoned with. He raised a goblet of wine. 'To King Amalric and Queen Maria; long may they reign together!' He quaffed his drink. The men in the hall followed his example.

When the goblets had been refilled, it was Amalric's turn to propose a toast. 'To Emperor Manuel, long may the friendship between our kingdoms endure!' Again, the goblets were quaffed.

'You are of Manuel's family now,' Thoros said, loudly enough that his voice reached John. 'He will stand by you whenever and wherever you have need.'

The hall quieted. The Hospitaller Gilbert, who sat at the king's table, leaned forward. 'Will he fight with us in Egypt?'

Thoros nodded. 'You are his ally.'

John looked to William and whispered, 'Did you negotiate this?'

William shook his head. 'Only the marriage.'

'Easy, Gilbert,' Amalric was saying. 'We have had peace with Egypt and Syria for two years. We should not be so eager to seek war. Let today be a day of celebration.'

'Yes, sire,' Gilbert replied. 'A day to celebrate the alliance that your marriage has sealed, an alliance that can open the Kingdom of the Nile to us. We came close last time. With a fleet to better supply our army, we could have taken Alexandria and then Egypt. Manuel can provide that fleet, and his armies will prevent Nur ad-Din from striking the Kingdom while we are gone. We will be free to take Cairo itself!'

Amalric frowned. 'I signed a treaty, Gilbert. I swore an oath.'

Heraclius spoke from his place just beyond Gilbert. 'Oaths made to an infidel mean nothing, sire.'

William cursed under his breath. 'Heraclius! I should have known he was behind this.'

John's eyes were on Amalric. 'M-my word means something,' the king said, his uncertainty manifested in the return of his childhood stutter. 'Even w-when given to an infidel.'

'Then honour your word, sire,' Heraclius said, speaking loudly so that all in the hall could hear him. 'You have taken an oath before God to protect the faithful. What better way to do so than to liberate Egypt from the infidel? There are thousands of Christians living there, and with the Land of the Nile in our power, our Kingdom will be invincible.'

The envoy Thoros nodded. 'The crown of Egypt would be a fitting present to your new wife. It will take time to plan the assault, but I am sure the Emperor's fleet could be available by the autumn of next year.'

All eyes turned to Amalric, who was tugging at his beard.

'The riches of Alexandria and Cairo, sire,' Gilbert said. 'The Kingdom of the Pharaohs. It lies waiting for you.'

Amalric took a long drink and then looked to his new wife. 'W-what do you ad-ad—What do you suggest, Maria?'

The girl shrank back into her chair in wide-eyed terror. She looked to Thoros, who nodded. 'I should like to be Queen of Egypt,' she said in a small voice.

'Then so be it!' Amalric raised his goblet. 'To Egypt!'

Yusuf stood before the door to Gumushtagin's quarters in the palace and took a deep breath to steady himself. He had not met the eunuch in private since his return from Egypt three years ago. He had hoped that Gumushtagin was done with him, but that morning a messenger had come to request a meeting. Yusuf dared not avoid the summons. He had just raised his hand to knock when the door swung open.

'Saladin!' Gumushtagin flashed his false smile. 'As-salaamu 'alaykum.'

'Salaam,' Yusuf replied curtly.

Gumushtagin affected not to notice his unfriendly tone. 'Come in. Come in.' Gumushtagin closed the door behind them and carefully latched it. 'Tell me, Saladin, would you like to be Vizier of Egypt?'

Yusuf blinked in surprise and then shook his head. 'I found nothing but hunger and suffering there. I wish to never see Egypt again.'

'That is not to be. Nur ad-Din will hold council this afternoon. This is why.' The eunuch held out three locks of dark hair.

'What is that?'

'See for yourself.' Gumushtagin handed Yusuf a roll of parchment. 'This came today via messenger pigeon from Cairo.'

Yusuf read the tiny script:

Nur ad-Din, King of Syria, defender of the faith, my land has been invaded by the ifranj. I ask for your aid to repel the infidel invader. The locks of hair are from my wives. They beseech you to come and rescue them from the outrages of the ifranj. Do not delay. If you answer my call, I promise you a third of the land of Egypt as fiefs for your emirs.

Yusuf noted the caliph's seal at the bottom. Seals, however, could be forged. 'Is it authentic?'

'We received four such messages. There can be no doubt; the Caliph himself has asked for our help.'

'What of Shawar? He rules in Egypt.'

'The Caliph appoints the Vizier. And it is Al-Adid who has called for our help.' Gumushtagin met Yusuf's eyes. 'It is an opportunity that cannot be missed.'

Yusuf frowned. 'I told you: I want nothing to do with Egypt.'

Gumushtagin stepped closer and lowered his voice. 'But you could be king!'

That gave Yusuf pause. Egypt was the greatest prize in Arabia, perhaps in all the world. 'Explain yourself,' he told Gumushtagin.

'The Caliph has invited us to Egypt. That means the Vizier is no longer in favour. When our men arrive, Shawar will be put to death.'

'I would happily do the deed. The man is a snake.'

'Shirkuh will no doubt replace Shawar as vizier,' Gumushtagin continued. 'If he should die—'

Yusuf was moving before he had time to think. He grabbed Gumushtagin by the throat and pushed him backwards until the eunuch slammed into the wall. 'Shirkuh is my uncle!' he growled.

'Unhand me,' Gumushtagin choked out.

'Why?' Yusuf leaned close. The eunuch's face was turning bright red as he struggled for air. 'I should kill you now. Asimat and my son will have nothing to fear.'

'Don't—' Gumushtagin rasped, 'throw—your life—away—'

Yusuf held the eunuch a moment longer and then released him. Gumushtagin bent over, gasping for breath. After a moment, he straightened. 'I am not asking you to betray your uncle, or Nur ad-Din. All I ask is that you do nothing. Let events unfold.'

Yusuf shook his head. 'I will not let you kill him. You may

well hold my fate in your hands, Gumushtagin, but I warn you: I am not afraid to die.'

'Do not be a fool, Yusuf. If you cross me, then I will see Asimat stoned and your son hanged.'

Yusuf's hands balled into fists. He took a step towards the eunuch, who shrank back against the wall. 'Not if I kill you first, you ball-less shit!'

Gumushtagin drew himself up straight. 'I have taken precautions. If I die, Nur ad-Din will still learn the truth. I do not fear you,' he added in a quavering voice.

'Then you are a fool.' Yusuf spat at Gumushtagin's feet and then turned and strode from the room, slamming the door behind him.

Yusuf stopped at one of the narrow windows that looked out from the spiral staircase leading up to the council chamber. Was it the last time he would see the sky? He had been a fool to let his anger get the better of him in his meeting with Gumushtagin that morning. Before the day ended, he could be dead.

He forced himself to continue to the top of the tower. The guard at the door to the council chamber waved him through. Nur ad-Din stood in the centre of the room. The king had turned fifty earlier that year, but although his black hair was now streaked with silver, he seemed a new man ever since the birth of his son and his victory at Harim. He stood straight-backed and moved with a warrior's ease. Shirkuh, Gumushtagin and Usamah were with him. Yusuf's stomach twisted with worry at the sight of Gumushtagin in whispered conversation with the king.

Nur ad-Din frowned. 'Are you well, Saladin? You look as if you have drunk donkey piss. Perhaps you have received some unpleasant news?'

Yusuf felt the blood drain from his face. The king knew. He was sure of it. Yusuf looked to the floor, unable to meet his eyes. 'I am well, Malik.'

'Good! I need you healthy for what is to come.' Nur ad-Din paused to look at each of the men present. 'The Franks are invading Egypt, and the Caliph has called on us for help. Shirkuh, you will drive the Franks back to Jerusalem.'

'Inshallah, Malik,' Shirkuh said.

'I will not make another peace with that snake Shawar. Once the Franks are defeated, you will dispose of him and have yourself declared Vizier of Egypt.'

Shirkuh grinned. 'I like the sound of that.'

Nur ad-Din clapped the rugged warrior on the back and then turned to Yusuf. 'And you, young eagle, what shall we do with you?'

Yusuf swallowed. But he straightened and met his king's eyes. He had known this day would come. He would not cower. 'I am your servant, Malik. You must use me as you see fit.'

Nur ad-Din's golden eyes studied Yusuf, and then he smiled. 'You shall serve as Shirkuh's second in command, and when Cairo falls, you shall assume the government of the city.'

Yusuf blinked in surprise. He looked from Nur ad-Din to Gumushtagin. 'It is a great honour the King bestows upon both of you,' the eunuch said. His eyes met Yusuf's. 'A reward for your incomparable loyalty.' The message was clear. Gumushtagin was giving him a second chance. Next time, he would not be so generous.

'Very well, Malik,' Yusuf murmured.

'Do not look so glum, Nephew!' Shirkuh said. He gripped Yusuf's shoulder. 'We will be rulers of Egypt! And we shall finally have our revenge on that two-faced bastard, Shawar.'

NOVEMBER 1168: BILBEIS

John stepped over dead bodies and through the splintered remains of the southern gate of Bilbeis. Acrid black smoke hung

170

in the air. Beside the gate a Saracen warrior sat moaning in pain, his bowels spilled out on the ground before him. A knight slit his throat and then yanked the gold chain from around the dead man's neck. John looked away. A line of chained women pulled along by two knights emerged from the smoky haze. One of them, a thin young woman with large brown eyes and a purplish bruise on her cheek, called out to John. 'Please, Father, help me! I am a Christian!'

One of the knights slapped her. 'Quiet, bitch!'

John's hands clenched into fists, and he glared at the man. He was one of the Duke of Nevers's men. They were newcomers to the Holy Land. Their arrival had encouraged Amalric to set out for Cairo early, before William returned from Constantinople with the emperor's fleet. The knight returned John's gaze. 'What are you looking at, priest?'

John took a step towards him, but a hand on his shoulder restrained him. It was Amalric. There was blood on the king's surcoat, and his face was pale. He smiled wanly. 'We have won the day, John. Tonight, you will celebrate a victory Mass.'

'Victory? This was a slaughter.'

'It is unfortunate, but n–necessary,' the king stuttered. 'Cairo will n–not dare to resist once they hear the f–fate of Bilbeis. The people will open the gates to us. Egy–Egy—the Kingdom of the Nile will be ours. Jerusalem will be secure for all time.'

John said nothing. He watched the line of sobbing women as they shuffled through the gate; they would be used by the men of the army before being sold at the markets in Acre or Tyre. John felt sick.

Amalric pulled on his shoulder. 'Come away, John. This is no place for a priest.'

John shrugged off the king's hand and strode into the city. Dead bodies were strewn across the main street, and the cobblestones were slick with blood. The city, only a day's march from Cairo, had fallen after a siege of three days. Once the defences were overrun, the people of Bilbeis had no hope of saving themselves from the slaughter that followed. It had started with the knights from Nevers. While the men of the city were being rounded up, a woman had spat at one of the troops and made the sign of the evil eye. The knight had cut the woman down, and the crowd of citizens panicked and ran. The men of Nevers gave chase, and once the blood started to flow, it was impossible to stop.

John heard a high-pitched cry coming from an alleyway to his right. The screaming grew louder as he turned into the narrow passage. 'No!' a woman was shouting in Arabic. 'Allah help me! No!' Then she fell silent. John quickened his pace, then stopped as he passed an open doorway. A dark-haired Egyptian woman was pinned to the floor beneath a pale-skinned Frank. The man had removed his armour and wore only a tunic, pushed up above his waist. Another Frank was just removing his mail. His surcoat was black with a white cross in the middle: the sign of the knights Hospitaller.

The woman on the floor screamed and tried to squirm free, but to no avail. The man atop cuffed her backhanded. Blood ran from her nose. She looked about in panic, and her dark eyes settled on John.

The Hospitaller who had just removed his mail looked up. 'Leave us, priest. This is not your affair.'

John did not move.

The Hospitaller raised a fist and took a step towards him. 'Are you deaf, priest?' John still did not move, and the Hospitaller's expression changed suddenly. He dropped his fists. 'You want a piece of her too, don't you, priest? A little taste of Egypt, eh?'

John removed the cross from about his neck, and the Hospitaller leered. John grasped the gold crucifix in his fist so that the top protruded between his fingers. He slammed it into the Hospitaller's grinning face. The man crumpled to the floor.

'What in God's name—!' the other man cried as he rose to his knees. Before he could stand, John grabbed him by his long hair and pulled him off the woman. She scrambled into a corner, where she drew her knees to her chest and sobbed. The man had pulled free from John's grip and now turned to face him. 'Whoreson!' he growled and stepped forward with fists raised. He swung. John caught his arm and slammed the cross into the side of his head. The man's knees buckled and he slumped to the ground. John dropped the cross and knelt on the man's chest. 'Wait—' the man murmured as he came to and saw John's fist raised above him. John punched him and felt a crunch as the man's nose broke. The man's eyes glazed over, and he fell back unconscious. John raised his fist again.

'John! What have you done?' It was Amalric.

John picked up his cross and wiped the bloody top on his tunic before hanging it about his neck. 'They were raping her.'

Amalric looked from John to the two unconscious Hospitallers. The king nodded towards the woman huddled in the corner. 'What will become of her now? Will she stay here, alone in this ruined city? How long do you think she will last before she starves to death, or someone else takes her for his own?'

'I could not stand by and do nothing.'

'It is the way of war, John.' Amalric's expression softened as he looked back to the girl. 'Ask her what her name is.'

'Halima,' the woman replied when John asked.

'Halima,' Amalric mused. 'She is pretty enough. Have her brought to my tent.' John opened his mouth to protest, but the king cut him off. 'I will treat her well, John, better than those knights would have.'

'Yes, sire.'

'Now, come. Cairo awaits.'

DECEMBER 1168: THE SINAI

Yusuf gazed into the cloudless sky as he tilted his head back to drink from his waterskin. He allowed himself only a single mouthful. He lowered the skin and replaced the stopper. He stood atop an enormous sand dune that it had taken precisely three hundred and seventeen steps to climb. Behind him, men were zigzagging up hill, the sand spilling away from their feet. The slope was too steep to ride up, so they led their horses behind them. Far away, at the bottom of the dune, those just starting to climb looked like toy figures. The column stretched along the valley between two dunes and then over another dune and another after that. There were nearly six thousand men in all. Two thousand were Nur ad-Din's own mamluks from Aleppo, Damascus and Mosul. Another thousand mamluks, including Yusuf's own contingent of two hundred men, had come with the dozen emirs who had joined the campaign. The remaining three thousand were Bedouin and Turcoman warriors – Arab and Turkish nomads who had joined the army in hope of collecting spoils. They had gathered the men in Damascus and left two weeks ago.

'A storm is coming,' their guide said from where he sat with his legs folded. Mutazz was a *badawi*, a traveller of the desert. He had a thin, weathered face, like the craggy stone floor of Al-Niqab, the rocky expanse they had crossed to reach the dune sea. While Yusuf and Shirkuh had struggled up the dunes, Mutazz strode ahead of them, never showing any sign of fatigue. Yusuf had wondered at how the badawi found his way among the towering dunes. When he asked, Mutazz had told him that the dunes spoke to him. Yusuf had smiled, thinking that Mutazz was joking, but the Bedouin was serious. 'The hiss of the sand sliding across the slopes,' he said, 'the slant of the shadows across their face, these things tell me where I am.'

Mutazz stood and pointed in the direction they were headed. Huge waves of sand stretched to the horizon. 'There. A sandstorm.'

Yusuf could just make out a brown smudge in the distance.

'When will it hit us?' Shirkuh asked.

The Bedouin shrugged. 'Hard to say. Storms are like wild

horses; they move at their own pace, sometimes a walk, sometimes a gallop.'

'Before nightfall?'

Mutazz shrugged again.

'We will press on,' Shirkuh decided. 'I'd rather face a sandstorm than spend another day among these cursed dunes without fresh water.'

'Yes, yâ sîdi.' The guide took the reins of his horse and led it down the far side of the dune. Yusuf wetted his keffiyeh – that would help to keep out the fine dust during a sandstorm – and checked his saddlebags to make certain that the tent cloth he would use as a shelter was to hand. Finally, he tugged at his horse's reins and led it down the dune, following in Mutazz's footsteps.

They continued west as noon came and went. Yusuf was walking in the shadows of a dune when he heard shouting from the men high on the hill behind them. They were pointing ahead. Yusuf noticed that the light was starting to dim, as if the sun had set.

Mutazz had stopped. 'Listen!' he said. There was a hissing sound, like steel being drawn across leather. It was growing louder. The badawi took a white tent cloth from his saddlebag. 'La-taht,' he called to his mount, which immediately lay down. He looked to Shirkuh. 'The storm is almost upon us. It is moving fast.'

The words were no sooner out of his mouth than a cloud of swirling brown sand appeared at the top of the dune before them. Yusuf pulled his keffiyeh down over his mouth and nose just before the storm hit with a shock of cold wind followed by stinging sand. Ahead, Yusuf saw that Mutazz had disappeared, drawing his tent sheet over him and his horse. A short piece of wood poked up in the middle to form a makeshift tent. Yusuf went to his saddlebag and took out his own tent cloth. Behind him, Shirkuh was shouting to the men. 'Take shelter! Take shelter!' Suddenly the full force of the storm hit them and

Shirkuh disappeared, obscured by the thick cloud of swirling sand.

Yusuf knew his uncle could take care of himself, so he busied himself with his own shelter. If he did not get it up soon, his horse would choke in the sand-thick air. Already the animal was huffing and snorting. 'La-taht,' Yusuf ordered as he pulled on the reins to make it lie down. The horse lay on the edge of the tent cloth; he would weigh it down against the wind. Yusuf drove a long pointed stick into the sand beside the horse and then crouched and pulled the sheet over them. Outside, the sand hissed and the wind howled. There was the sudden crash of thunder, and his horse's eyes rolled. 'Hudû, hudû,' Yusuf murmured and stroked the beast's neck. As the thunder faded, he thought he heard someone shouting over the fury of the storm. His horse's ears twitched. It had heard it, too.

Yusuf crawled to the edge of his shelter and looked out. He could see nothing but dust and grit, thick in the air. Then a gust of wind ripped the curtain of sand aside. He saw that his uncle had disappeared into his own tent, only a dozen feet away. Sand was already piling up on the windward side. Beyond, dozens of other shelters dotted the valley between the tall dunes. Yusuf saw two men making their way between the shelters. At first he thought that they were two of Shirkuh's men, coming to make certain that their lord had found shelter. Then he saw the mamluks lying crumpled on the ground behind them, swords in their hands. The wind shifted, and the two men disappeared in a cloud of swirling sand. Yusuf's eyes were watering, irritated by the fine dust thrown up by the wind. He blinked away the grit and peered again into the storm. He caught glimpses of the men. One wore a brown robe, the other white with dark mail showing beneath it. In their hands they held curving swords, the metal dull in the dim light. They were headed for Shirkuh's tent.

Yusuf ducked back into his shelter and blew sand from his nose. He had no doubt that the two men had come to kill

Shirkuh. The storm offered the perfect opportunity. No one would see them. No one would stop them. Yusuf thought of what Gumushtagin had told him: he only had to do nothing. If he stayed in his tent, Shirkuh would die and he would become commander of the army, then vizier of Egypt.

Yusuf forced the thought from his head. He tore two strips of linen from the tunic he wore under his chainmail and wrapped them around his hands to protect them from the stinging sand. Then he drew his blade and stepped out into the storm. He staggered against the force of the wind, which grasped at the folds of his keffiyeh, pulling it askew and exposing the back of his neck. He gritted his teeth as the sand drove into his skin. It felt as if hundreds of ants were biting at him. Yusuf had heard that if skin were left exposed for too long in a powerful sand-storm, it could be stripped from the body. He had no desire to see if the tales were true. He quickly covered his neck as he looked about. He could not see three feet in front of him. There was no sign of the two men with swords.

'*Help*!' he shouted. 'Shirkuh is in danger!' But the howling wind whipped the words away, and they were lost in the storm.

Yusuf held up a hand to shield his eyes and staggered in what he thought was the direction of Shirkuh's shelter. He took ten steps, then twenty. He stopped. Surely he had gone too far. He had begun to turn around when he saw movement out of the corner of his eye. Instinctively, he dropped to one knee and raised his sword. A blade glanced off it, and Yusuf glimpsed the man in the brown robe, a curved sword in hand and a dagger tucked into his belt. His face was hidden behind his keffiyeh. Yusuf slashed at his throat. The man jumped back to avoid the blow and disappeared into the storm.

Yusuf rose and pivoted, his sword held out before him. His heart was pounding, and he felt a hollow pain in his stomach. That was fear. Not fear of fighting, but fear of an opponent he could not see, of a knife in the back. He felt the hairs on the back of his neck rise and spun around. There was only the swirling, impenetrable sand, so thick that he could not see the tip of his sword. The whistling wind suddenly dropped and the space around cleared. Ten paces ahead and to his left stood the man in the white robe. He was only a dozen paces from Shirkuh's shelter. But where was the other man? Yusuf turned, searching for him. He saw the man in the brown robe at the same moment the man saw him. They were little more than a sword's length apart. Yusuf swung for the man's head. Their swords met with the ring of steel upon steel.

Yusuf's adversary moved fast. He kicked at Yusuf's right knee, and at the same time slashed down towards his head. Yusuf sidestepped the kick, parried the blow and then swung backhanded for the man's chest. The man brought his sword sweeping back to turn Yusuf's attack aside. Then, just as Yusuf's adversary was preparing a counterattack, the storm blew up again and Yusuf lost sight of him. He guessed where the man would strike next and dropped to one knee. He caught a glimpse of steel as his enemy's sword flashed over his head. Yusuf sprang to his feet and charged, lowering his shoulder. He slammed into the man, and Yusuf's momentum knocked them both over. He tried to rise but the man had grabbed hold of him. Together, they rolled over several times, and the man ended up on top of Yusuf. His keffiyeh obscured his face but for his glazed, blood-shot eyes. This was a Hashashin, Yusuf realized, one of the cult of trained killers who sometimes smoked hashish to increase their bravery.

The Hashashin had lost his sword in the tumble. With one hand he pinned Yusuf's sword arm to the ground, while with the other he reached to his belt and drew the curved dagger. Yusuf managed to catch the assassin's arm by the wrist, but the man leaned forward, using his body weight to press the dagger towards Yusuf's throat. The dagger inched closer, close enough that Yusuf could see the intricate Arabic script carved into the silver hilt.

In a last, desperate effort, Yusuf released his sword and jerked his hand free. He tore his attacker's keffiyeh away before the Hashashin grabbed Yusuf's arm and pinned it back down. The man grimaced as the biting sand struck his face, but he did not release Yusuf. He pressed the blade of his dagger so close that Yusuf felt it begin to cut into his skin. The Hashashin's face was growing red, showing minuscule drops of blood as if he had scraped it against a rough stone. Even drugged by hashish, the pain was too much. With a cry he released Yusuf's right hand in order to raise his keffiyeh. Yusuf found his sword and brought it up. The blade sank into the Hashashin's neck, splattering Yusuf with blood.

Yusuf shoved the man off him. He rolled over and pushed himself to his knees. He was just in time, for a sword was slicing towards his face. He managed to parry the blow, but then a booted foot caught him in the chest, knocking him sprawling on his back. The other Hashashin stood over Yusuf, his form just visible through the sand. The assassin raised his sword high. The wind howled, and his form was obscured by a cloud of sand. Yusuf was waiting for the blow when he felt hot blood spatter on his face. The wind fell, and Yusuf saw Shirkuh standing where the Hashashin had been only a moment before. He offered Yusuf a hand and pulled him to his feet.

'Uncle!' Yusuf shouted over the wind and thunder. 'You saved my life!'

'No, young eagle,' Shirkuh shouted back. 'You saved mine!'

They managed to stumble back to Shirkuh's shelter and crawled inside. Yusuf began to cough, spitting up brown phlegm.

'Do you know who they were?' Shirkuh asked.

'Hashashin.'

'I thought as much. Who do you think sent them?'

Yusuf was sure it was Gumushtagin, but if he told his uncle, then Asimat and their son might suffer for his indiscretion. He shrugged to indicate that he did not know.

'Maybe Shawar. Or Amalric,' Shirkuh speculated grimly.

'Seems like everyone wants me dead. Without you, Yusuf, they would have killed me before I even knew they were there. Shukran, young eagle.' Shirkuh kissed Yusuf on each cheek and then grinned fiercely. 'I do not care if it was Shawar or Amalric who sent the assassins. I will grind them both into the dust.'

Chapter 9

John stood beside the king and his retinue on a low rise near the walls of Cairo and looked across the dark waters of the Nile to where the sun was rising behind the pyramids of Giza. It marked the start of the seventh week of the siege. The people had not opened the city gates to them as Amalric had hoped. The massacre at Bilbeis had made them all the more determined to resist.

There was a loud clanking just behind John as the mangonel lever was released. He turned to watch the catapult in action. A basket filled with heavy stones fell, and the long arm of the device snapped upwards. The leather sling trailing from the arm swung in an arc and hurled a heavy rock – stone taken from one of the nearby pyramids. John watched as the rock crashed into the northern wall of the city, producing a shower of debris. A rock from another mangonel hit the wall a few feet away, and a chunk of stone fell loose. The wall was pitted and cracked, but it held.

The king was pulling at his beard. 'How much longer until we open a breach?'

Humphrey of Toron shrugged. 'It may be a week; less maybe.'

'Or longer,' John added.

Humphrey nodded. 'Maybe.'

'By the devil's beard!' Amalric cursed.

'We can still take the city, sire,' Grand Master Gilbert said. 'All we need is a single breach. Once Egypt is in our power, we can laugh at the armies of Nur ad-Din. No one will be able to stand against us.'

'But Egypt is not in our power, sire,' John insisted. 'And Shirkuh's army is close.'

'Do not listen to him,' Gilbert snapped. 'He cares for the infidel Saracens more than his own kind. Remember what he did to my men at Bilbeis!' Gilbert pointed a long, thin finger at John. 'He is a traitor!'

Humphrey put a hand on the Hospitaller's arm. 'Easy, Gilbert. We are all of us friends here. And the priest is right. If we are here when Shirkuh arrives, it will be a disaster.'

Amalric looked to John. 'Pray with me, Father.' They walked a few steps towards the river and knelt. Amalric held the piece of the true cross that he wore about his neck to his lips. Behind them the mangonel fired again, and another rock slammed into the wall with a loud crack. 'I have prayed for victory each night,' the king said softly. 'Sometimes I fear the Lord does not want us to succeed.'

'God does not always answer our prayers in the way we hope, sire. Perhaps leaving Egypt is for the best.'

Amalric frowned. 'Are you mad, John? If Nur ad-Din controls Egypt, then Jerusalem itself will be in danger. I will have no choice but to seek a permanent peace.'

'Maybe that is your destiny: to bring peace to the Holy Land.'

'I would rather have been a great conqueror, like my grandfather, like the first crusaders. I was so close,' Amalric sighed. 'But you are right, John. I would be a fool to stay. I will not sacrifice the lives of my men in the pursuit of my dreams.' He rose and raised his voice to address Gilbert and the others. 'I have made my decision. We will return to Jerusalem.'

'Allah will reward you!' 'Allah bless you!' 'All praise to Nur ad-Din!' The crowd of Egyptians shouted their praise as Yusuf rode beside his uncle through the Bab al-Futuh – the Gate of Conquest. And they were conquerors. The Frankish army had fled at their approach, and the gates of Cairo had opened to welcome them. It had been easy, so easy that Yusuf feared something was amiss. He rode with his hand on his sword hilt.

Shirkuh grinned at him, showing his crooked teeth. 'You look as if you have lost a friend, young eagle. Smile! Egypt is ours!' Yusuf forced a smile, but he kept his hand on his sword hilt. 'That is better,' Shirkuh said. 'Look about us.' He gestured to the cheering crowd and to the city beyond. 'All of this is now ours!'

They rode into the large square situated between the two halves of the caliph's palace. Egyptian mamluks held back the populace, creating a path to the western palace. Shawar approached along the path and flashed his brilliant smile. 'Welcome, Shirkuh! Saladin! All Cairo rejoices at your arrival.'

Yusuf and his uncle dismounted. Shirkuh walked past Shawar to the secretary Al-Fadil, who stood in the ranks of officials behind the vizier. 'Take me to the Caliph.'

Al-Fadil looked to Shawar. 'I am the Vizier,' Shawar said. 'The Caliph speaks through me.'

Shirkuh rounded on him. 'It is the Caliph who asked us to come to Egypt, not you.' He turned back to Al-Fadil. 'Take me to him.'

Al-Fadil nodded. 'Yes, yâ sîdi.'

The secretary led them to the caliph's audience chamber, where Shirkuh and Yusuf both removed their swords and knelt. Yusuf noticed Shawar enter the room behind them. He looked forward again as the curtain rose to reveal the veiled caliph. He was noticeably taller, and fatter, than when Yusuf had first met him, nearly five years ago.

Shawar stepped forward. 'Successor of the messenger of God, defender of the faithful, may I present Shirkuh and Saladin, commanders of Nur ad-Din's army.'

'As-salaamu 'alaykum,' the caliph declared. 'You are welcome in my city.' He made a motion with his hand and two fat eunuchs stepped forward carrying a chest. They placed it before the throne and opened it. Gold coins glimmered in the light from the candles that lined the walls. 'A reward for your aid.'

Shirkuh rose and bowed. 'Many thanks, Caliph. We are honoured to have been able to offer you assistance against the ifranj. I only regret that they fled before we could defeat them.'

'Yes,' Shawar said. 'You have arrived a little too late. It appears your army is no longer needed.'

Shirkuh glared at the vizier and then looked back to the caliph. 'We are here at your request, Defender of the Faithful. If you wish us to leave Egypt, then we shall go. But we are prepared to stay to protect God's deputy from his enemies—' he shot a glance at Shawar '—both within and without. There are men who would sell Egypt to the infidel in order to keep power. Men who in the past welcomed the ifranj into Egypt, who betrayed their fellow Muslims, who burned their own cities. If you wish it, I will drive these traitors from Cairo.'

Shawar's tan face had paled to a sickly yellow. 'I set fire to Fustat to keep it out of the Frank's hands,' he protested. 'And if there are traitors in the city, Caliph, I assure you that I will find them. As Vizier, I—'

The caliph raised a gloved hand. 'Enough. Shirkuh, your army will stay. But they will make camp outside the city, beside the Bab es-Sa'ada el-Luq. Water is plentiful there. You and Saladin will stay as guests in my palace. I have need of your wise council.'

Shirkuh bowed. 'I am honoured by your generous offer, Caliph, but a general should never leave his men. I will stay in camp, if it pleases you. But I shall wait on you at your pleasure. This evening perhaps, over supper?'

'Very well.'

'Alone.'

'But Caliph!' Shawar protested.

Al-Adid looked at him for a moment and then back to

Shirkuh. 'I will see you tonight, after prayers, Emir.' He waved a hand, and the golden curtain fell.

Yusuf approached his uncle and spoke in a low voice. 'Is it wise to remain outside the city?'

'I'll not stay in Cairo so long as Shawar lives. The man is a snake.'

Yusuf nodded. 'And the best way to kill a snake is to cut off its head.'

The afternoon sun shone down pitilessly as Yusuf rode down a narrow lane that wound between the tombstones, domed mausoleums and mosques of the Qarafa al-Sughra, one of the two ancient cemeteries that stood outside Cairo, just beyond the charred remains of Fustat. Shawar rode beside him. The vizier produced a silk tissue and wiped sweat from his brow. 'By Allah, it is hot,' he muttered. 'Why does your uncle insist on meeting here?'

'Shirkuh is on a pilgrimage to the tomb of Al-Shafi,' Yusuf told him.

'I am the vizier,' Shawar grumbled. 'I am not a lackey that jumps at the beck and call of an upstart Kurd.'

The vizier was clearly trying to pick a fight, but Yusuf was in no mood. They rode on in silence, surrounded by two-dozen mamluks from Shawar's private guard. Ahead, Yusuf spotted a larger structure amidst the tombs; the shrine that marked the tomb of the great Sunni jurist Al-Shafi, who had helped to create shari'a, the law by which all Muslims lived.

They dismounted outside the shrine, and Shawar again mopped his forehead. 'This had best be important.'

'Your men can wait outside,' Yusuf told him.

Shawar's eyes narrowed. 'Were we not such good friends, I would think that you meant me harm, Saladin. No, my men will accompany me.' He gestured to four mamluks, who went ahead into the shrine.

'As you wish. Shirkuh is waiting for you.'

Shawar headed for the entrance. Yusuf was close on his heels, followed by the rest of Shawar's guard. The doorway was framed by Qaraqush and Al-Mashtub. Yusuf nodded to them as he passed. The interior of the shrine was dim, and Shawar stopped while his eyes adjusted. 'Where is Shir—' he began, but the words caught in his throat. The four mamluks he had sent in were lying in their own blood. 'What is this?' he cried. 'Guards!'

But it was too late. Yusuf had fifty men stationed inside the shrine, and Shawar's mamluks were still half blind after entering from the bright sunshine. While they were being cut down, Shawar drew his sword and backed away to the centre of the shrine, where he stood in a pool of light that fell from a window above.

Yusuf drew his sword. 'It is over, Shawar.'

Shawar raised his sword to fight and then thought better of it and dropped the blade. He smiled. 'This is no way to treat a friend, Yusuf.'

'We are not friends. You betrayed me. I nearly starved to death in Alexandria.'

'It was nothing personal. That is the nature of war. Had I not joined with the Franks, how long do you think I would have lasted before your uncle eliminated me?'

'Shirkuh does not deal in murder,' Yusuf said coldly.

'Yet here you are.'

Yusuf scowled. He raised his sword, and Shawar paled. 'Do not kill me!' the vizier pleaded. Yusuf stepped closer. 'The Caliph will not stand for this!'

'Shirkuh is with the Caliph now. Al-Adid ordered your death himself.'

Something seemed to break in Shawar. His shoulders slumped. 'So this is how it ends. You and your uncle claim to be honourable men, but you are no better than I.'

'We only do the Caliph's bidding.'

'The Caliph does not piss without someone telling him

to. This is your work, Yusuf. I did not expect this of you.' Shawar knelt on the stone floor. 'I did not think you a murderer.'

'This is not murder. It is an execution.' Yusuf held the blade of his sword to the vizier's neck.

'Do what you must, but remember this: viziers in Egypt have short lives. Your uncle should think of that before he takes my post.'

The last word was still hanging in the air when Yusuf's blade struck the back of the vizier's neck, killing him instantly.

Yusuf stood in the shadows of the colonnade that fronted the caliph's palace, searching for threats in the crowd that filled the square. He saw only a mixture of curiosity and impatience as the Egyptians waited for a glimpse of the new vizier. Shirkuh was with the caliph, who was investing him with the symbols of his office: robes of scarlet silk interlaced with gold, a white turban with gold stitching at the edges, and the vizier's sword, a golden blade with the ivory hilt encrusted in precious jewels. Soon, Shirkuh would emerge to have his office proclaimed in a speech by Al-Khlata, the city's chief official now that Shawar was dead. It would be the perfect time for one of the Hashashin to strike. Yusuf had posted a line of mamluks to keep the populace back, but there were thousands of men in the square. Any one of them could hold a dagger or a crossbow.

'What do you think?'

Yusuf turned to see his uncle. Shirkuh was dressed in his new finery, and it ill-suited him. The luxurious robes were too long for his squat frame, and the tip of the ceremonial sword nearly touched the ground. Yusuf suppressed a smile as Shirkuh tugged irritably at the stiff, gold-laced collar of his tunic. 'I am told the Egyptians would be sorely disappointed if I did not wear this frippery,' he grumbled.

'You look very distinguished, Uncle.'

'*Ha*! You will never make a good courtier, Yusuf. You have

no talent for lying,' Shirkuh nodded towards the crowd. 'All is well?'

'The crowd is larger than I anticipated. We should have more men.'

'Stop fretting, Yusuf.'

'Someone has paid the Hashashin to kill you, Uncle. You know their reputation. They will not stop until you are dead.'

Shirkuh placed one of his callused hands on Yusuf's shoulder. 'We must defy our enemies, Yusuf, or they will have defeated us without even striking a blow.' A blast of trumpets drowned out his last words. He clapped Yusuf on the back. 'Come. It is time.'

The crowd cheered as Shirkuh strode down the palace steps to a platform crowded with Egyptian officials. Yusuf followed and stood at the edge of the platform as Al-Khlata began to address the crowd. Yusuf did not trust the Egyptian, who had been a confidant of Shawar, but Shirkuh had decided that he should keep his post as civilian comptroller. He knew Egypt as none of Shirkuh's men did, and could be sure that every last dinar in taxes was paid. Al-Khlata was speaking in flattering tones, telling the crowd of the new vizier's many qualities: he was the blessed of Allah, a great warrior, the father of his people, the commander of the faithful, the child of jihad, scourge of the Franks.

Yusuf was only half listening. His hand rested on the hilt of his sword as he scanned the front row of the crowd, only thirty feet away. Al-Khlata said something in a loud voice and the crowd roared, raising their hands and cheering. All except one man just behind the front row. His eyes were focused on Shirkuh. His right hand was clutching something inside his caftan. Yusuf kept his eyes on the man as he stepped down from the platform to where Qaraqush stood. 'That man,' Yusuf said and nodded. That was all that was needed. Qaraqush disappeared into the crowd, and Yusuf returned to his place.

The suspicious man had edged forward so that he was now in

the front row. He was just beside a mamluk, but the guard was paying little attention to him. The crowd cheered again, and Yusuf looked away from the man to see that his uncle was now addressing the people. Yusuf watched in alarm as Shirkuh jumped down from the platform and into the square. He stepped towards the crowd, allowing the people to reach out and touch him. Yusuf's eyes swung back as the man, now only a dozen feet from Shirkuh, removed his hand from his caftan. Yusuf saw the glint of steel. Then the man's eyes widened. Qaraqush held a knife to this throat and pulled him backwards into the crowd, just as Shirkuh passed the place where the Hashashin had stood. Yusuf breathed a sigh of relief.

Shirkuh finished greeting the crowd and mounted the steps to the platform. He was grinning, clearly pleased with the impression that he had made. As he reached Yusuf, Shirkuh slapped his nephew on the shoulder. 'See, young eagle. Nothing to fear!'

MARCH 1169: CAIRO

'You lying, camel-faced bastard! You owe me!' the Egyptian spat, showing brown teeth. Iqbal was a thickly bearded, broad-shouldered man in a homespun caftan. He had the erect bearing of an ex-soldier. He lunged towards the man he was addressing, but the courtroom guards held him back.

Shirkuh had made Yusuf the governor of Cairo, and as part of his duties Yusuf sat in judgement every Monday and Thursday. He had already heard some two-dozen cases that day and was weary of the never-ending procession of petty complaints. Nevertheless, it was his duty to provide impartial justice. Without law, a kingdom could not stand. He looked to the defendant, a merchant named Qatadah.

Qatadah spread his hands, on which he wore several gold rings. 'I told Iqbal that the investment was a risk.'

'He owes me one hundred and ten dinars!' Iqbal insisted.

'You took this money from him?' Yusuf asked.

'I am no thief, Your Excellency,' Qatadah replied. 'Iqbal gave me five silk carpets, which I told him that I would sell in Acre. I paid him twenty dinar up front, and was to pay the rest upon the return of my ship, after the carpets had been sold.'

Iqbal pointed an accusing finger at him. 'And he did not pay!'

Yusuf gestured for silence. 'Why not, Qatadah?'

'The ship was attacked by pirates. All the cargo was lost. I, too, have suffered from this, Your Excellency. I have no money with which to pay Iqbal.'

Yusuf doubted that. Besides the gold rings on his fingers, Qatadah wore a rich silk caftan with jewels at the collar. Yusuf looked from him to Al-Fadil, the Egyptian scribe who Yusuf had selected as his private secretary. Al-Fadil sat with a writing desk on his lap and the contract that Qatadah had brought held between his ink-stained fingers. Other scribes sat behind him, ready to record Yusuf's judgement.

Al-Fadil set the document aside. 'The terms of the contract are clear,' he said, speaking quietly so that the litigants could not hear. 'Qatadah has no legal obligation to pay.'

Yusuf frowned. Iqbal was an ex-soldier, probably a mamluk who had invested his meagre savings in the carpet business. For such a man, one hundred and ten dinars was the difference between a comfortable living and poverty. To Qatadah, such a sum was nothing.

Al-Fadil guessed what Yusuf was thinking. 'If you make Qatadah pay, you will see a hundred such cases daily. Worse, merchants will cease to carry cargo, afraid that if they suffer losses then they will be forced to pay the difference. Commerce will dry up. Trade will go elsewhere.'

Yusuf still hesitated.

'Tax revenues will fall, my lord. Your uncle will not like that.'

'Very well,' Yusuf muttered. Then, in a louder voice: 'This case is dismissed.'

Qatadah grinned. Iqbal spat in his direction and then stormed from the room.

Yusuf rose. 'That is enough for today.' He started to leave and then turned back to Al-Fadil. 'See that Iqbal is given a position in the palace.'

'As what, Emir?'

'He looks to be an ex-mamluk, so he will be familiar with horses. Give him a position in the stables.'

Yusuf left the chamber, but his work for the day was not yet done. There was correspondence to read in his private study. Saqr accompanied him on the short walk from the caliph's palace to that of the vizier. Yusuf entered his apartments and froze, his mouth dropping open. Standing before him were four naked women, beauties all. The one on the far right was Nubian, as black as night and with full lips and an angular face. The second was a Frank, blonde and with a voluptuous figure. The next was an Egyptian with flawless, golden skin. The last woman was a Turk with dark eyes, a narrow face and wavy chestnut hair that hung down to a pair of enormous breasts.

'What are you doing here?' Yusuf demanded.

'I bought them for you,' Faridah said as she entered from the next room. 'They do not please you, my lord?'

'I am busy.' Yusuf rubbed his temples. When he had sent his brother Selim to bring Faridah and Ibn Jumay from Aleppo, he had not expected anything like this.

'You work yourself too hard, Yusuf.' Faridah approached and put a hand on his arm. 'You need a woman.'

He reached out to push a strand of red hair back from her face. 'I have a woman.'

Faridah shook her head. 'I am old, Yusuf.'

It was true that she was no longer young. There were crow's feet at the corners of her eyes and fine wrinkles around her mouth, and Yusuf had seen her carefully plucking strands of grey from her long red hair. But he did not mind. 'You are still beautiful.'

'In only a few years I will be fifty years of age. You no longer seek my bed as you once did.' Yusuf opened his mouth to protest, but Faridah placed a finger on his lips. 'I am not angry, Yusuf. You have given me more than I could have hoped for. You saved me from a terrible life. But now you need a younger woman. You need someone who can bear you a son.' She pointed to the blonde Frankish woman. 'What about that one?' Yusuf shook his head. 'The Turk, then?'

Yusuf met the woman's dark eyes. Something in the way she met his gaze reminded him of Asimat. He felt a sudden pain in his gut as he thought of his former lover and their son. 'I do not want any of them,' he said and strode into his study.

He sat on a low divan and placed a writing desk on his lap. In the other room, he could hear Faridah addressing the women. 'You, stay. The rest of you may go.' Yusuf wondered who she had picked for him. He quickly dismissed the thought. He took up a sheaf of papers, messages from all parts of Egypt. They were all alike. A farmer or a merchant or a bath attendant claimed to have seen one of the Hashashin, but the claims invariably proved false. That was why the sect was so dangerous. The Hashashin blended in, taking up positions as merchants or soldiers, looking no different than any other man . . . until they struck.

There was a knock at the door. 'Go away, Faridah,' Yusuf said without looking up. 'I am working.'

'Excuse me, Saladin.' It was the Egyptian Al-Khlata.

'Pardon my rudeness. What is it?'

'Your uncle—'

'Does he need me?'

'He is dead.'

'*What? How?*'

But Yusuf did not wait for an answer. He sprinted across the palace to Shirkuh's apartments. In the reception room he found the huge mamluk Qadi – one of Shirkuh's most trusted men –

leaning against the wall and weeping. Yusuf continued into the bedroom, where Shirkuh lay motionless, his eyes staring sightless at the ceiling. Selim stood with the doctor Ibn Jumay. Yusuf went to his uncle and touched his hand. It was already cold. He felt tears forming and blinked them away. He looked to Ibn Jumay. 'What happened?'

'He was eating his supper and—he had a seizure. I did all I could—' The doctor's head fell.

Yusuf placed a hand on his shoulder. 'If anyone could have saved him, it was you.' He looked back to his uncle and suddenly remembered Shawar's final words: 'Viziers in Egypt have short lives.'

'The seizure,' he said to Ibn Jumay. 'Could it have been poison?'

'It is impossible to say.'

Al-Khlata had entered behind Yusuf. 'We must inform the Caliph,' he said. 'He will need to choose a new vizier.'

'Yes, of course. Selim, you will prepare our uncle for burial. I will tell the Caliph myself.'

'As for the jihad, thou art the nursling of its milk and the child of its bosom. Gird up therefore the shanks of spears to meet it and to plunge on its service into a sea of sword points.'

Yusuf stood before the caliph's palace, on the same platform where his uncle had stood not long ago, and listened as Al-Fadil presented him to the people of Cairo. They were his people now, for at the age of thirty, Yusuf was ruler of Egypt. He wore the tall white turban, the red silk robes and the jewelled sword of the vizier. Yet his mood was dark. It was only three days since his uncle had died. Yusuf had been summoned to the caliph's palace the previous day and had been told that he would succeed Shirkuh. From the dismissive way the young caliph had addressed him, Yusuf had gained the impression that he was not expected to last long in his new role.

Al-Fadil was now discussing Yusuf's exemplary righteousness.

It should have been Al-Khlata speaking, but the comptroller had excused himself, claiming an illness. Yusuf doubted that was the true reason. The comptroller had hoped to be made vizier himself, although that was hardly possible with Nur ad-Din's army still sitting a short distance outside Cairo. Yusuf would have to keep an eye on Al-Khlata. Resentful men could be dangerous.

Al-Fadil finished speaking and the crowd cheered. The applause was not quite as enthusiastic as it had been for Shirkuh. The people were still taking Yusuf's measure. He knew what was expected of him now. Shirkuh had left the platform to greet the people, and Yusuf must do the same. He jumped down, landing lightly on his feet. He started at the left edge of the crowd, walking slowly, allowing the people to greet him, to touch his robes.

'Allah guard you!' an old man with a curly, grey beard shouted.

'Bless you, King!' another man cried as he tugged at the sleeve of Yusuf's robe.

'Go back to Syria, Kurd!' a bald man spat. A mamluk shoved him back into the crowd.

Yusuf kept his face expressionless. His heart, however, was pounding. He could not shake off the suspicion that Shirkuh had been murdered. *Viziers in Egypt have short lives*. He finally allowed himself to smile when he reached the end of the row of people. He stepped back as his troops parted the crowd, creating a path to the vizier's palace. Two-dozen mamluks from Yusuf's khaskiya surrounded him and he set off, waving to the populace as he walked.

His brother Selim was waiting in the entrance hall. 'Congratulations, sayyid,' he said and bowed.

Yusuf frowned. 'I am your brother, not your lord.'

Selim bowed again. 'You are both now, Yusuf.' He held out a tightly rolled scrap of paper. 'A message has come from Aleppo.'

'From Nur ad-Din?'

'Gumushtagin.'

Yusuf's stomach twisted. He checked the message's seal. It was unbroken. 'Thank you, Brother. I will read it in my quarters.'

The dark-eyed Turkish beauty that Faridah had selected for him was waiting in his bedroom. She wore a transparent cotton shift. 'Congratulations, sayyid,' she purred. 'Do you wish to celebrate?'

Yusuf waved her away. 'Leave me.'

He went to his study and shut the door. He broke the seal and unrolled the small scrap of paper. Gumushtagin's message read: *You are Vizier, as I said you would be. The opportunity will come soon for you to aid me in turn.*

A wave of anger flooded through him. He went to the table along the back wall and swept the quills and inkstand away, splattering dark ink on the rug. The bastard! Gumushtagin was the one who had killed his uncle. Did the eunuch truly expect Yusuf to be thankful? He would kill him. He would have his head on a spear.

Yusuf's anger left as quickly as it had come. He could not touch Gumushtagin without endangering Asimat and Al-Salih. But the eunuch had made a mistake. He had made Yusuf vizier. If Gumushtagin thought he would serve as his puppet, then the eunuch was sorely mistaken. He would bide his time, and he would have his vengeance.

Yusuf held the message to one of the candles burning on his desk until it caught light. He dropped the paper on the stone floor and watched it burn to ash.

Chapter 10

John scratched at a mosquito bite on the tonsured patch atop
his head as he strode down a narrow lane in the shadow of
the Temple Mount. Usually, he would now be at the chancellery sifting though stacks of correspondence, or in council with
the king, or tutoring his son Baldwin, but this morning he had
a different task. Under his left arm he carried a small box that
contained holy water and the host. He had never before taken
confession or delivered the Sacrament of Holy Communion,
and he was nervous; doubly nervous because the woman whose
confession he was to hear was Agnes de Courtenay. It had been
over four years since John had last seen her. She had stayed at
her home in Ibelin, and John had long since forgotten about her
request that he serve as her confessor when she visited Jerusalem.
But she had not forgotten him. Yesterday she had arrived in the
city and had sent for him.

John passed a bakery that flooded the street with the rich
smell of baking bread. His stomach grumbled, and he regretted
not eating before he left the dormitory in the Church of the
Holy Sepulchre. He turned on to a sunny lane that twisted into
the heart of the Syrian quarter. After asking directions from two
Assyrian men drinking coffee in the shade of their shop, he
found Agnes's home.

He knocked, and a thin Frankish man opened the door.
'Father?'

'I am John of Tatewic. The Lady de Courtenay has sent for me.'

'You are expected.' The servant led John through the court-yard where he had met with Agnes before and into a dim room, the windows covered with intricately carved wooden screens. 'Wait here.' The floor was thickly carpeted. Cushions lay scattered around a low table set with two glasses and a bottle of wine. Beyond the table, a silk screen divided the room. Through it, John could make out the outlines of a large bed.

'John!' Agnes smiled brightly as she entered from a door to the right. She was dressed in a loose robe of green silk.

'My lady, I have come to hear your confession.'

'Sit, John.' She gestured to the cushions around the table.

'Perhaps we should go somewhere more appropriate. You have a private chapel?'

'I am more comfortable here.' She raised her chin and looked down her delicate nose at him. 'Sit.' This time, it was a command.

John placed the box with the host on the table and sat, sinking into the down-filled cushions. Agnes sat beside him, uncom-fortably close. She poured two glasses of wine and offered one to him. He hesitated.

'It is not poison, John,' Agnes said playfully.

He took a sip. The wine was uncommonly good. He set the cup aside. 'You did wish to confess, my lady?'

Agnes smiled slyly. 'I will confess this: I brought you here on false pretences. I wished to see you again, John.'

He felt his pulse quicken. He took a deep breath and forced himself to look away from Agnes's green eyes. 'I am a priest and a councillor to the King. I do not have time to wait upon your pleasure.'

He began to rise, but she placed a hand on his arm. 'Do not be upset, John. I have recently been widowed and I need to talk. You are a priest. I thought I could confide in you.'

'My apologies, Lady de Courtenay,' John said as he sat back down. 'I did not know.'

'Hugh died earlier this year while on pilgrimage to Santiago de Compostela.' Agnes shrugged. 'He wished to be closer to God, and now he is. I did not love Hugh, but I do miss him. Women are not meant to live alone, are they, Father?'

John was not sure how to respond to this.

She laughed at his discomfiture. It was a high, musical sound, like birdsong. 'But I do not wish to discuss my late husband.' She set her wine aside. 'Let us talk of you, John.'

'Of me, my lady? What is there to discuss?'

'Amalric offered you a good marriage with a large dowry, but you chose to become a priest. Why?'

John felt a pain in his chest. 'I do not wish to speak of it.'

'A woman? A Saracen?' John looked away and nodded. Agnes reached out and gently brushed a strand of hair back from his face. 'I know what it is like to be separated from the one you love, John.'

He caught her by the wrist and pulled her hand away from his hair. 'My lady, do not—' he began, but she interrupted him with a kiss. Her lips were full and soft. John closed his eyes, and an image of Zimat flashed through his mind. He shoved Agnes away with more force than he had intended, and she fell back on the cushions, her eyes wide with surprise. For the first time since John had met her, she did not look commanding or superior. She simply looked like a woman. How long had it been since he had lain with a woman? He had lost track of the years. She started to push herself up, but John put his hand on her shoulder and stopped her. He moved on top of her and kissed her hard. She kissed him back hungrily, opening her mouth to his as her arms wrapped around him. His hand ran down her side to grasp her firm buttock, pulling her tight against him.

Agnes moaned softly as he kissed her neck. He allowed her

to drag his chasuble off over his head, taking the gold cross he wore with it. He sat back and pulled off his linen alb. Agnes had untied her robe and it lay open, revealing her slim form, her skin as white as newly fallen snow. John put his arms around her back and lifted her to him, taking one of her pink nipples in his mouth. She gasped and grabbed his hair, pulling him up to kiss her mouth again. She lay back amongst the soft cushions, bringing him with her. Her hands moved down his sides to his waist.

'*Mmm*,' she purred. 'It should be a sin for a priest to be so well mounted.' She guided him inside her, and John groaned with delight. Her legs wrapped around his waist. He drove deeper, faster, grunting with pleasure. He felt a dizzying sensation, as if he were a spirit, free to float above the world. He kissed her lips, her neck. He could feel Agnes's breath hot in his ear. Then there was a sudden rush of pleasure so intense that it was almost painful. He collapsed spent and rolled off Agnes to lie panting.

She pressed herself against his side and whispered in his ear: 'Forgive me, Father, for I have sinned.'

John felt suddenly sick. He turned away and pushed himself up to sit with his head in his hands. He noticed his golden cross sitting on the wrinkled chasuble. What had he done?

He felt Agnes's hand on his back. 'I am sorry, John.'

John turned to look at her. It was the last thing he had expected her to say.

'You love her still. I can see that. I should not have seduced you.'

'I am the one to blame.' He grabbed his cross and hung it around his neck. The metal was cold against his hot skin. 'I wanted to.'

'As did I.' She pulled her robe about her and then leaned forward and kissed him gently on the cheek.

'I should go,' he said gruffly. He stood and pulled on the linen alb and the chasuble. The priestly garments had never felt so strange. He took up the box with the host. 'I will not come again.'

Agnes smiled as if she knew better. 'Farewell, then, John.'

John stood in the courtyard of the king's new palace and watched as Prince Baldwin played with several other boys. Only eight, he was already a leader. The children had been playing with wooden swords, following his commands as he organized a mock battle. Now, they cast the swords aside and began a new game. Two boys would sink their fingernails into one another's forearms. Whoever could stand the pain longer was the winner. Baldwin was facing off against a larger child, who smirked confidently as the boys gripped arms. Slowly, however, the child's smirk faded into a tight-lipped grimace. '*Enough! Enough!*' he cried. Baldwin released him, and the boy stood fighting back tears as he rubbed at the marks on his forearm. Baldwin was grinning triumphantly.

'You must not see her again, John.'

John turned towards William. The priest had been staring fixedly at the ground without speaking ever since John told him what had happened between him and Agnes.

'I told her I would not return,' John replied.

William snorted dismissively. 'You swore to remain chaste as well.' He waited a moment for a reply, but John said nothing, his eyes fixed on the playing children. 'It is not just that you broke your vow, John. Take a lover, if you must. Visit whores. God knows the Patriarch sees enough of them. But stay away from Agnes. She is only using you to gain access to Baldwin.'

'I am not a fool, William. But why shouldn't she see him? She is the boy's mother.'

'She is dangerous, John. It is not just her lack of lands that worried the High Court. She has had three husbands. Two died under mysterious circumstances.'

'Her last husband died in Spain while on pilgrimage. There is nothing mysterious about that.'

'Hugh of Ibelin was one of the healthiest men I have known—until one morning when he simply did not wake up.'

'You think she murdered him? That is preposterous!'

'I think she is a woman to be wary of.'

'I told you I would not see her again,' John grumbled. He looked back to Baldwin. The young prince had won again and raised his arms in triumph. He seemed to hardly notice the red welts that covered his forearms. John's forehead creased. 'Baldwin always wins at this game,' he noted.

'Do not change the subject, John.'

'Look. The other boy is on the verge of tears, but Baldwin hardly seems to feel the pain.'

'He is the son of a king. Royal blood flows in his veins.'

'Kings feel pain, William.'

The priest thought about this for a moment and then his tanned face paled. 'What are you saying?'

John lowered his voice to a whisper, as if he were afraid to utter the next words. 'Lepers sometimes lose feeling in their arms and legs.'

William shook his head. 'No. It is not possible.' He raised his voice. 'Baldwin! Come here!' The boy jogged over. 'Let me see your arm.'

Baldwin held out his forearm proudly. Some of the boys had dug their nails in so deep that they had broken the skin, leaving bloody, moon-shaped cuts.

'Does it hurt?' William asked.

'I am the son of a king,' the boy replied. 'I do not feel pain.'

John exchanged glances with William, and called to a guard who stood in the corner of the courtyard. 'You! Come here!' The man strode over, and John held out his hand. 'Give me your dagger.'

The guard's eyes widened in alarm. He looked to William.

'Give it to him,' the priest ordered.

John took the dagger, then grasped Baldwin's arm by the wrist, turning his palm upwards. 'Hold still,' he told the prince.

Baldwin looked on indifferently as John slowly lowered the dagger, pressing the sharp point into the boy's palm. Baldwin did not even wince as crimson blood welled up around the dagger's point.

'Enough!' William shouted.

John handed the dagger to the guard. The man crossed himself and hurried back to his post.

'May I play with the other boys now?' Baldwin asked.

'See that your cut is tended to, then you may play.' As the boy ran off towards the infirmary, William looked to John. 'The child has been cursed by God.'

'Leprosy,' Agnes repeated softly.

John was holding her hand, afraid that she might collapse. Her face was ghostly white, and she stared ahead as if not seeing him. Finally she pulled her hand away and left the room. John looked at the cushions where they had made love only three days past. It seemed so long ago now. John had come straight from the palace after discovering the horrible truth about Baldwin. Agnes was the boy's mother. She had a right to know.

'Forgive me, John,' Agnes said as she re-entered the room. Her eyes were red from crying, but she smiled brightly. 'It was rude of me to leave you standing there all alone.'

'Are you well?'

She waved aside his concern and sat amidst the cushions. 'Thank you for telling me.'

John sat beside her. 'It is terrible news.'

'It changes nothing. Baldwin will still be king. I am still his mother.' Her forehead wrinkled, and for a moment John thought she might cry.

'Is there anything I can do for you?' he asked.

She took a deep breath, and her forehead smoothed. 'No. Truly, John, I am well.' She tilted her head as if she had had a thought. 'There is one thing. You tutor Baldwin. You are often alone with him. Could you bring him here?'

'My lady, Amalric has decreed that you are not to see the boy.'

'He is my son, John, and he is sick.'

John hesitated. William had told him she would use him to see the boy. Was he right about her? He met her green eyes and saw that they were moist with tears.

'I am asking you as a mother,' Agnes said. 'Let me see my boy.'

'You ask me to go against my king.'

'You have loved before, John. You still love her, I think. Yes, I can see it in your eyes. What would you do if the woman you loved were ill? Would you not want to go to her?' John looked away, and she gripped his arm, turning him back towards her. 'If I want to see my son, I will find a way, John. This way, you can keep an eye on me. What harm can I do with you here to watch?'

'Very well,' John said. 'I will bring him to you.'

She leaned over and kissed him lightly on the lips. 'Thank you.'

John sat with his eyes closed, submerged to his chin in the steaming waters of the Hospitaller bath house. He had just come from taking Baldwin to see Agnes; it was the second such trip in the past week. The child had been shy on the first visit, but Agnes had won him over. Just before he left, Agnes had presented Baldwin with a gold bezant. The prince's eyes were wide as he held the coin. She placed it in a chest for keeping, then told him he would receive another bezant each time he came, so long as he told no one of his visits. Today, Baldwin had been eager to go and collect his coin. Agnes was certain he would continue to hold his tongue, and John prayed that she was right. There would be a price to pay if they were discovered.

But perhaps it was a price worth paying. John thought of Agnes's lithe body, the feel of her under him that morning. He knew that William would say she was only rewarding him for bringing the boy. He was probably right. John knew that he should stop seeing Agnes, yet he could not wait to be with her again. She was like a drug he could not do without.

The deep toll of bells told John that it was almost time for the noon prayer service. He dressed and hurried back to the Church of the Holy Sepulchre. Usually, he would allow his vicar to attend in his place, but today's was a Penny Mass. The canons' stipends would be distributed during prayers, and if John were not there in person, he would not be paid.

He let his mind drift during the Mass, thinking more of Agnes than of God. The service ended, and John had just received his ten gold bezants when a messenger boy arrived from the palace. 'Pardon me, Father,' he told John. 'King Amalric has asked for you.'

John paled. Had Baldwin spoken of his visits with his mother? 'What does the King want?'

The boy shrugged. 'I only know that it is urgent.'

John followed the messenger down Patriarch Street towards the slender towers and wide halls of the new palace. Amalric and his court had resided there for two years, but the royal audience chamber to which the messenger led John had been completed only a few months previously. It was a long, barrel-vaulted hall with bright light slanting in through windows set high on the walls. The king's throne had been set on a dais at the far end. Amalric sat surrounded by half a dozen courtiers.

'I told you it would be money well spent!' Heraclius was exclaiming.

'Money spent on murder is never well spent,' muttered Philippe de Milly, the new head of the Templars.

'Spare me your self-righteous prattle, Philippe,' replied the Master of the Hospital, Gilbert. 'Another Saracen is dead, and Egypt is ours for the taking. The Hospital would have paid ten times as much for that.'

John slipped in beside William. 'What is happening?'

'Shirkuh is dead,' William replied in a low voice. 'Saladin has been made vizier of Egypt. He has sent an ambassador seeking peace.'

'How did Shirkuh die?'

'Poison. Bought with our gold.'

John's jaw tightened. 'Why didn't you tell me?'

'Easy, John. I knew nothing of this.'

'Ah, John,' Amalric called, noticing his arrival. 'You know Saladin better than any of us. Tell us: what sort of ruler will he be?'

All eyes turned towards John. 'He is a great warrior and leader of men, sire. He will be a capable ruler.'

'He is a nobody!' Heraclius replied scornfully. 'Our spies say that the Caliph only made him vizier because he can be controlled.'

'Then the Caliph underestimates him.' John looked to Amalric. 'We should not do the same, sire. Remember, it was Saladin we faced at the siege of Alexandria. A thousand men against our ten thousand, and he held the city.'

'Then you would accept his offer of peace?'

'I would, sire.'

'Do not listen to him, my lord,' Gilbert snapped. 'He was Saladin's man. He is half Saracen himself! We cannot let Nur ad-Din's man hold Egypt. If we do, the Kingdom will be in a vice. The Saracens will squeeze us until we break. We must attack now, while they are weak!'

'Saladin is not weak,' John countered.

'No matter,' Heraclius said. 'Saladin will not concern us for much longer.'

'What does he mean?' William asked, looking to Amalric.

'Saladin's ambassador is not the only messenger to have come from the Saracens,' the king explained. 'We received another message from Gumushtagin.'

'The same man who helped us to eliminate Shirkuh,' Heraclius explained. 'He promises that with another payment from us, the Egyptian Al-Khlata can remove Saladin before the year is out. Cairo will be ours for the taking. Gumushtagin asks only that we support him in his bid to control Aleppo.'

John felt the blood begin to pound in his temples. So Heraclius had conspired to kill Shirkuh. And now he was going to kill Yusuf, too. John opened his mouth to speak, but William placed a hand on his shoulder and gave a shake of his head.

The Hospitaller Gilbert stepped forward. 'We must take this opportunity, sire. It will not come again.'

'And yet murder does not sit well with me,' the king muttered. He pulled at his beard and then looked to the constable. 'What say you, Humphrey?'

'Gilbert is right,' Humphrey replied in his gravelly voice. 'We must drive Nur ad-Din's men from Egypt, whatever the means.'

Amalric turned to the Master of the Templars. 'And you, Philippe?'

'Listen to the priest,' he said, nodding towards John. 'This is a fool's errand. We cannot overcome the combined might of Nur ad-Din's army and the Egyptians. They will outnumber us two to one.'

'Not after Saladin dies,' Heraclius countered. 'The Egyptians already resent his rule. When he falls, they will rise up against the remaining emirs of Nur ad-Din. Egypt will be in chaos. We need only deliver the finishing blow.'

'After Saladin is assassinated, you mean,' Philippe said. 'I want no part in murder.' He looked to Amalric. 'My commanders will not risk another adventure in Egypt. If you go, sire, you go without the Templars.'

Amalric frowned. He turned to Miles de Plancy last of all. The portly new seneschal had stood silently beside the throne throughout the audience. When he spoke, his voice was quiet. 'The Emperor Manuel has offered to send his fleet, but they will leave once again when the winter storms arrive. That does not leave us much time.' He rubbed his closely shaven chin. 'Still, I believe it is a risk worth taking.'

Every man was looking at the king in expectation. Amalric sat unmoving, his chin resting on his palm.

'Sire?' Heraclius said at last. 'What is your decision?'

'Tell Gumushtagin that we accept his offer, and pay Al-Khlata whatever is necessary. William, you write to Constantinople and ask them to send their fleet. They should arrive by October, in time for the campaign season. We will sail to Damietta and wait for news of Saladin's death. When he falls, we will strike.'

Chapter 11

'I have made my decision,' Yusuf declared to the courtroom. Even after learning that the Franks had invaded and besieged Damietta, he continued to hold his bi-weekly audience. It helped him gauge the mood of the people, and it gave the Egyptians a chance to witness his impartiality.

The two litigants looked at him expectantly. They were brothers, each with the same long face and hooded eyes. They had come to blows, then to court, over who was the rightful owner of a prized stallion named Barq. They had spent most of their time in court insulting one another, but Yusuf had finally pieced together their story. One of the brothers had won Barq at dice several years ago. He had not had the means to stable and feed the horse, so the other brother had raised it. Recently, Barq had won several races, and the brothers had fallen into bitter disagreement over how to split the winnings. Yusuf had watched the horse run. It was a magnificent beast.

'I will buy the horse for one hundred dinars,' he told the brothers. 'And you shall split the proceeds.'

The two brothers looked at one another and then embraced. It was a generous sum, twice what the horse would have fetched at market. 'Thank you, Malik,' the older brother said.

Yusuf frowned. 'I am no king. I serve at the pleasure of the Caliph.'

'Yes, Vizier.'

The younger brother was at a loss for words. He bowed repeatedly as he backed from the room.

Yusuf looked to his secretary, Al-Fadil. 'What is next?'

'Only one more case, Vizier. A woman named Shamsa.'

'What is her complaint?'

Al-Fadil examined the piece of paper before him and frowned. 'She will not say.'

Yusuf looked to the guard at the chamber entrance. 'Show her in.'

A moment later, Yusuf noticed the guards framing the doorway suck in their bellies and stand tall. He saw why when Shamsa strode into the room. She was dressed in a black caftan that revealed only her delicate hands, and a niqab that veiled all but her eyes. Still, those eyes were enough to make the scribes to either side of Yusuf sit straighter and smooth back their hair. Or perhaps it was not her eyes, but the way she moved. She did not walk so much as prowl, like a panther on the hunt. She stopped in the centre of the chamber and met Yusuf's gaze boldly. He saw both an invitation and a challenge in her dark eyes.

Yusuf cleared his throat. 'What is your case?'

She bowed low, her eyes never leaving his face. 'I wish to speak with you alone, Malik.' Her voice was surprisingly low, yet soft.

'You will address me as vizier, and you will state your case in court.'

'What I have to say is of a private nature. It concerns my lover.'

Yusuf's eyes widened.

'Your what?' Al-Fadil demanded.

'My lover,' Shamsa said matter-of-factly.

'Have you no shame, woman?' Al-Fadil asked. 'I should have you beaten. Guards!'

'Wait.' Yusuf raised a hand. Shamsa had shown no sign of fear when Al-Fadil called for the guards. 'Why tell me this?' Yusuf asked her.

'Because what I know concerns you. My lover is the one who arranged for your uncle's death.'

Yusuf waited until it became clear that she was going to say no more. 'Leave us,' he told the guards. He looked to Al-Fadil. 'All of you.'

When the last of the guards and scribes had left, Shamsa reached up and removed her niqab. She was young – not yet twenty years of age, he guessed – and she had a face that men would fight for, kill for, even. Her large eyes sat above a delicate nose and high cheekbones. Her flawless skin was creamy brown. The women that Faridah brought to him were as moths to a butterfly in comparison with her. She smiled, her full lips framing straight, white teeth. 'Thank you, Malik.'

This time, Yusuf did not think to correct her. 'Who killed Shirkuh?'

'The city administrator, Al-Khlata.'

'Guards!' Yusuf shouted. A dozen mamluks hurried into the hall. 'Bring me Al-Khlata. Now!'

'They will not find him,' Shamsa said when the men had departed. 'He has left the city.'

'Where is he?'

'I do not know, but I know something even more valuable. I know how he plans to take Cairo from you.'

Yusuf felt a burning in his gut. 'What do you mean?'

She met his gaze. 'My information comes with a price.'

'Tell me what you know first, and we shall see what reward you merit.'

'Very well. Tomorrow, the Nubian Guard will rise against you. They will drive your men from the city and Al-Khlata will take the throne as vizier.'

The Nubians – black warriors from the south of Egypt – were ten thousand men strong, and their barracks lay just outside the city. 'And the rest of the Egyptian forces?' Yusuf asked. In addition to the Nubians, the barracks near Cairo held ten thousand Egyptian infantry from northern Egypt, as well as two mamluk regiments of five thousand each and the Armenian cavalry, numbering one thousand.

'They wait to follow whoever emerges victorious.'

'How do I know that what you say is true? You say you are Al-Khlata's lover. Why betray him for me?'

'Why do rats flee a sinking ship? Al-Khlata will soon be finished. Your star is still on the rise.'

But not for long, Yusuf reflected grimly. Many of the emirs who came with him to Egypt had returned home, leaving him with only five thousand men to face twice as many Nubians. And if he barricaded himself inside Cairo, then nothing would stand in the way of the Frankish invasion. The pain in his gut suddenly increased, as if a sword had been thrust into his bowels. He hurried to the back of the chamber, where he bent over and vomited.

He felt Shamsa's hand on his back and looked up in surprise. 'You can defeat them, Malik. The Nubian barracks lie just beyond the city gates. They have families there—' She let the words hang in the air.

'I will not kill innocent women and children to save myself,' Yusuf snapped.

'The greatest of men are those who are not afraid to make the hardest decisions.'

Who was this woman? Her youthful face revealed nothing of what was clearly a ruthless intelligence. Yusuf took a deep breath. 'If what you have told me is true, then I owe you a great debt. You shall have a hundred dinars. Al-Fadil will see that you are paid.' Yusuf strode towards the doorway.

'*Wait!*' Shamsa called, and Yusuf turned back to face her. 'There is more that I must tell you, Malik. Tonight, palace servants loyal to Al-Khlata mean to murder you while you sleep. Your death is to be the signal for the Nubians' rebellion. It is expected that with you gone, your men will put up little resistance.'

'It seems I owe you my life twice over. You shall be rewarded accordingly. Tell me what you wish for. More gold? Land?'

'A greater prize by far: make me your wife.'

Yusuf blinked in surprise. 'Your reward will be worth nothing if I die in the uprising tomorrow. You should take gold instead.'

'You will not die.' Shamsa's dark eyes found his, and a smile played at the corner of her mouth. 'Tonight, you must remain vigilant . . . If you will permit me, I will ensure that you stay awake. You can determine if I am to your liking.'

Yusuf could not help but smile at the suggestion. 'I have enough worries to keep me awake for many days to come. You shall be my guest in the palace until this affair is done. I will have a servant show you to the harem, where Faridah will make you comfortable. Tomorrow evening, if I am still alive, you can claim your reward.'

The air that night was hot and still. The windows to Yusuf's bedroom had been thrown open, letting in pale moonlight that illuminated a figure lying in bed, covered with a thick blanket despite the heat. The distant sounds of the watch changing filtered in through the window, to be overlaid by the closer sound of a floorboard creaking. A moment later the door to Yusuf's chamber swung open. Four men with slippered feet crept in and stood around the bed.

'Allahu akbar,' one of them whispered. 'Egypt for the Egyptians!'

Each man raised a knife and struck. There were brief, muffled cries from the bed. The men stabbed down again and again, their knives now dark with blood. The cries ceased, and the four men left quickly, their heads down as if they were ashamed of what they had done.

Yusuf removed his eye from the spyhole that looked on to his chamber. 'It was just as Shamsa foretold,' he said to Selim and Qaraqush.

'Shall I have the assassins beheaded?' Qaraqush asked.

'Let them go. Let them think they have succeeded.'

'But Brother, the uprising—' Selim began.

'I will never see an end to rebellions if I do not deal with the Nubians now. We will let them rebel, and we will crush them.'

Yusuf entered his bedchamber and pulled back the bloody blanket. A eunuch servant – one of the men that Shamsa had named in the plot – lay tied to the bed, a gag in his mouth. He was dead, his eyes bulging wide.

'What now?' Selim asked.

'Have the body wrapped in linen, and let it be known that I am dead. Qaraqush, make certain that the men are ready.'

'What will you do?' the grizzled mamluk asked.

Yusuf pulled a fold of his keffiyeh down to hide his face, leaving only his eyes visible. 'I am dead. I shall play the part.'

Yusuf stood behind a curtain that hung over a side entrance to the caliph's audience chamber and peered through a small gap in the fabric. He had spent the previous night hidden in the gatehouse beside the Bab al-Futuh. Before the sun rose, he had dressed as a simple mamluk and left for the caliph's palace, accompanied by Saqr and Al-Mashtub. As they walked, trumpets sounded to the south, indicating that the Nubians were on the move. Yusuf had given Qaraqush orders to provide only token resistance before pretending to flee. Al-Khlata and the rebellion's ringleaders were to be allowed into the caliph's palace.

Yusuf's hand fell to his sword hilt as he saw a eunuch step into the audience chamber and address the gold curtain, behind which the caliph sat. 'Al-Adid, defender of Islam and representative of Allah, may I present Al-Mutamen al-Khlata.'

Al-Khlata strode into the chamber. He removed the jewelled sword of the vizier from his scabbard and laid it before him. The dozen Nubian commanders who accompanied him also placed their swords on the ground. They all knelt, and the gold curtain rose to reveal the veiled caliph seated on his throne. Two dozen of Yusuf's men – dressed in the uniforms of the caliph's personal guard – stood along the wall behind the throne.

'Al-Khlata,' the caliph said. 'What brings you to my court?'

'Joyous news, Al-Adid. The infidel Saladin is dead, and his Sunni troops are fleeing our city. Egypt shall soon be returned to the hands of Egyptians.'

Al-Adid gestured to Al-Khlata's sword. 'I see you carry the sword of the Vizier.'

'Forgive my presumption, Caliph. I took it from the Vizier's palace. Saladin's death was my doing. Now that he is gone, I had hoped you would allow me to serve you as vizier. But of course, you should do as you think right.'

While Al-Khlata was speaking, Al-Adid stole several glances in Yusuf's direction. Yusuf pulled back the curtain just enough so he could see the throne and nodded. The caliph looked back to Al-Khlata. 'I do not need your permission to do as I see fit,' he said. 'I declare your life forfeit for rebelling against Saladin, my appointee as the rightful ruler of Egypt.'

Al-Khlata picked up his sword. 'You are in no position to threaten me, Caliph.'

'But I am.' Yusuf stepped into the room, flanked by Saqr and Al-Mashtub.

Al-Khlata paled. 'Impossible.' He pointed his blade at Yusuf. 'You are dead!'

Yusuf's only reply was the hiss of steel against the leather of his scabbard as he drew his sword. The guards along the back wall stepped forward with swords in hand, and a dozen more of Yusuf's men arrived to block Al-Khlata's retreat from the chamber. The Nubians picked up their swords, but Yusuf could see the resignation in their faces. They were outnumbered three to one. They knew they would die.

'Caliph, stop them!' Al-Khlata begged. 'I only wished to rid Egypt of these Sunni dogs.' The caliph said nothing. Al-Khlata's pleading grew more frantic. 'I have served you faithfully for years. Please, I beg you! We had an agr—'

'Kill them!' the caliph shouted. 'Kill them all!'

Yusuf's men closed on the Nubians from all directions. Yusuf charged towards Al-Khlata, but a towering Nubian blocked his path. Yusuf parried the Nubian's curved blade before slamming his shoulder into him. He stumbled back as if he had hit a stone wall. The Nubian grinned, his teeth white against his dark skin, and hacked down at Yusuf's head. Yusuf sidestepped the blow and thrust for his opponent's chest. The Nubian brought his scimitar sweeping back to knock Yusuf's sword aside and then reversed his blade. Yusuf jumped back, but the tip of the sword grazed the mail covering his chest. The huge Nubian charged, chopping down with a mighty blow, which Yusuf parried. The Nubian kicked out, catching him in the gut and doubling him over. Yusuf's adversary grinned in triumph and swung down to decapitate him, but the sword was blocked at the last moment by Saqr's blade. Yusuf buried his sword in the Nubian's throat. The man fell, spilling blood on the white marble floor.

'You take too many risks, sayyid,' Saqr said. 'The Vizier should not—'

Al-Khlata was charging from behind Saqr. Yusuf shoved him out of the way and stepped forward to parry the Egyptian's attack. Yusuf countered with a thrust that forced Al-Khlata backwards and then pursued his foe, hacking down as Al-Khlata gave ground. The Egyptian's gold blade dented and warped under the blows from Yusuf's steel sword. Yusuf gave a final swing, and Al-Khlata's blade snapped in two. The Egyptian tossed the ruined weapon aside and sank to his knees. Beyond him, two Nubians were swarmed by Yusuf's men and taken down. Al-Mashtub cut down the last of the rebels.

'Please,' Al-Khlata begged. 'Have mercy! Spare me, and I will save your life.'

'You murdered my uncle.' Yusuf raised his sword.

'Don't be a fool! The Nubians control the palace. If you kill me, you will die!'

Yusuf brought his blade down on Al-Khlata's neck. He wiped the blade clean on the dead Egyptian's caftan. 'Al-Mashtub, once the city is in hand, have these traitors hung from the gates as a warning to those who would rebel against me.' Yusuf turned to the caliph. 'You, come with me.'

'I-I am God's deputy,' Al-Adid replied, his haughty tone undercut by the shaking in his voice. 'Do not presume to give me orders.'

'Saqr, bring him.'

Yusuf strode from the chamber, and Saqr followed with the caliph. They passed through luxurious rooms, the thick carpets now wet with blood and littered with dead Nubian warriors. A thousand of Yusuf's best men had lain in wait in the palace. They had let the Nubians enter before emerging to slaughter them. The carnage was worst in the vaulted entrance hall. Yusuf's men had sealed off the doors, trapping hundreds of Nubians before raining down arrows from the balconies above. The caliph's face paled as they passed the bodies that were now stacked three and four deep on either side of the hall. They reached the door leading outside, and Yusuf's men pulled it open. The square before the palace was packed with Nubian warriors waiting to welcome a victorious Al-Khlata.

'Go and tell the Nubians that I live,' Yusuf told the caliph. 'Tell them that if they lay down their arms, their lives will be spared.'

Al-Adid took a step outside, but then froze. 'They will not listen. Al-Khlata was right: the Nubians are too many for you to overcome. Surrender, and I will guarantee your life.'

'It is not my life you should be concerned about.' Yusuf gripped the caliph's arm and dragged him outside. His men followed and fanned out to form a line five deep atop the steps leading down to the square. 'Tell them,' Yusuf insisted, and pushed the caliph through the line.

'*The Caliph*!' someone in the square cried. '*Al-Adid*!' The cry was taken up by other Nubians. '*Al-Adid*! *Al-Adid*!'

The caliph raised his arms for silence. 'Loyal troops!' he shouted. 'I know that you are ever faithful to your caliph. I wish for no further bloodshed. Lay down your arms and accept the rule of my appointed vizier, Saladin, and your lives will be spared!'

At first there was stunned silence. Then one of the Nubians shouted, 'Saladin is a Sunni dog! Where is Al-Khlata?'

Yusuf stepped forward. 'Al-Khlata is dead, as are your commanders! If you do not wish to join them, then you will surrender now!'

'To hell with you!' one of the Nubians replied. 'Let's kill the bastard!' There was a roar of approval from the dark-skinned warriors, and they rushed up the steps. The caliph ran for the safety of the palace, while Yusuf's men surged forward. The two lines met with the clash of steel.

'You gave them a chance, sayyid,' Saqr shouted over the din of battle.

Yusuf nodded. He raised his voice and called to four mamluk archers who stood around a brazier filled with burning coals. 'It is time! Signal Qaraqush!'

The archers each took an arrow, the tips of which had been wrapped in cotton, and touched them to the coals. The arrows burst into flame, and the archers shot them high into the sky.

Yusuf looked away from the arrows and towards the Nubian barracks, which lay beyond the southern wall. A trace of smoke appeared and hung in the blue sky before the wind swept it away. There was more smoke, then more until the sky south of the city had turned black. Amongst the Nubians there were shouts of consternation. Men from the rear ranks began to slip away, heading for the southern gate. Yusuf's mamluks started to push the enemy line back down the steps as more and more Nubians fled. And then the enemy line dissolved as all the Nubians turned and ran for their barracks, desperate to save their families from the flames.

Yusuf turned to Saqr. 'Fetch the Caliph.' When Al-Adid emerged from the palace, Yusuf strode down the steps to where horses had been brought. They rode to the Bab Al-Zuwayla, and Yusuf dismounted and led Al-Adid up the stairs to the walkway above the gate. The Nubian barracks lay a quarter of a mile to the south-west. They consisted of a low wall surrounding dozens of homes, which stood amongst a few large dormitories. All of it was burning. A wind rushed at Yusuf as the fire sucked in air to feed the roaring flames.

A few hundred Nubians were fleeing south along the Nile. The rest were hurrying through the gate into the barracks, braving the terrible heat in order to save their families. Yusuf's men closed off the gates behind them. Selim had positioned a hundred men at each gate, and more mamluks surrounded the walls, ready to strike down any who scaled them. The Nubian warriors took their wives and children from their homes, only to find themselves trapped.

Yusuf felt ill, but he did not turn away. He was the ruler of Egypt now. He must show no weakness. He looked to the caliph, who had removed his veil and was retching over the side of the wall. It was the first time Yusuf had seen Al-Adid's face. He was ghostly pale, a sparse beard covering fleshy cheeks.

'Al-Khlata said you had an agreement, Caliph,' Yusuf said. 'Tell me true: did you have anything to do with this uprising?'

Al-Adid's eyes grew wide with fear. 'No,' he said, wiping traces of vomit from his mouth with the back of a gloved hand. He drew himself up, trying to recover his dignity. 'How dare you accuse me!'

'You were not contacted by Al-Khlata?'

'I told you I had nothing to do with this sordid business.'

'You swear it?' Yusuf gripped the caliph's arm and turned him towards the fire. 'Look at that. Look, damn you! This is the price of treachery. The blood of those women and children is not on my head. It is on the heads of those who betrayed me.'

The caliph looked away from the fire. 'Let me go.' His voice was small, childlike and pleading.

Yusuf released him. 'Take him back to the palace.'

A mamluk led the caliph away, and a moment later Qaraqush joined Yusuf atop the gate. Together, they watched the barracks burn. Men and women were fleeing over the walls. They were cut down by waiting mamluks as soon as their feet hit the ground. Yusuf gripped the rough stone battlements as he listened to the terrified cries of women and children. Finally, he could bear it no longer. 'That is enough. Qaraqush, tell Selim to allow the remaining Nubians to flee through the southern gate.'

'But—'

'Do you want the blood of those children on your head?'

'No, sayyid.'

'Then go, and ride fast.' Qaraqush hurried from the wall and then galloped out of the gate. Yusuf looked back to the fire and whispered: 'Allah forgive me.'

Yusuf stood at the window of his bedroom and looked out over the roofs of the city. Night had fallen, but the barracks still smouldered, turning the sky to the south red. Shamsa approached and placed a hand on his shoulder. She was naked but she walked with no shame, as if unaware that he could see her shapely legs and her small, firm breasts. They had been married that evening. Selim and Faridah had been the only witnesses. Yusuf had expected Faridah to be upset, but she seemed pleased that Yusuf had finally taken a wife. After the marriage contract had been signed, Yusuf had taken Shamsa back to his bedroom and made love to her with an urgency that surprised him. He had sought to lose himself in her, to drive the images of earlier that day from his mind.

'Come back to bed,' Shamsa told him. Yusuf did not move. 'Are you well, Malik?'

'I am your husband. You may call me Yusuf.'

She stood beside him, her head against his shoulder, and together they watched the glowing sky to the south. 'You did the right thing,' she said at last.

'Did I?'

'The Nubians will never rise against you again, and the Franks are returning to Jerusalem.'

'But the people will hate me.'

'They will forgive you. The wants of the common people are simple: low taxes, justice, security. Give them that, and they will love you. I know. I was one of them once.'

Yusuf glanced at her in surprise. He had supposed she had been raised in the home of an emir, surrounded by tutors and servants. 'Tell me.'

'My parents were farmers near Alexandria. They were killed five years ago, during the Frankish siege of the city. I had only just become a woman. I was to be married, but after the Franks—' She broke off, and when she continued her voice was harder. 'Afterwards I was not wanted for marriage.

'I came to Cairo. An attractive young woman can make her living here easily enough. I won the heart of one of my—admirers. He was a mamluk, and he offered to marry me, despite my past. We were engaged only a short while before he introduced me to his commander. The commander wanted me for his own, but he did not have me long before Al-Khlata took note of me. I became his lover.'

Yusuf frowned. 'You speak of it without shame.'

'I did not choose my fate. Men can lose their honour and win it back in battle. A disgraced woman cannot. She must make her own way. I was nothing, and now I am a queen. What do I have to be ashamed of?'

'You are no queen, Shamsa. I am not a king.'

'You will be.'

Yusuf shook his head. 'I am a Kurd and a Sunni, and hence doubly despised. Besides, viziers in Egypt do not last long, and the security and prosperity you spoke of take time.'

'You can buy time. Look at that.' She pointed across the room to an ornate table of dark wood. The top was inlaid with ivory in the shape of storks, horses and crocodiles. The sides were lined with gleaming gold. Yusuf had hardly noticed it before. 'It is worth one hundred, perhaps two hundred dinars. The palace has hundreds as fine, if not finer. Give them to the people. Let each man in Cairo carry away as much as he is able.'

'And what will I be left with?'

'Your life. Every man who takes something from the palace will have a stake in your rule. What better way to ensure their loyalty?'

Yusuf looked at her more closely. 'I begin to think that Allah sent you to me for a reason, Shamsa.'

'It was not Allah. I came to you on my own. You have greatness in you, yet you are noble, too. Al-Khlata would not have lost a moment of sleep over the fate of the Nubians. You are different.' She kissed him on the cheek and then took him by the hand and pulled him away from the window. 'Now come. Let us to bed.'

Chapter 12

The loud crack of wooden sword blades knocking together sounded in the courtyard of Agnes's home. John parried the thrust of young Baldwin, stepped inside the prince's guard, and pressed the edge of his practice sword against his opponent's neck.

'You are dead, my lord.'

'But you fought well,' Agnes called from where she watched under a canopy.

Baldwin scowled. In the two years since the debacle at Damietta, he had grown like a desert flower after the rain. He was ten now, and was tall and ungainly. He wore only breeches, and as he struggled to catch his breath, his ribs were visible under his pale skin. He showed no signs of his sickness, other than a half-dozen scars on his hands and forearms. His leprosy was slowly robbing him of feeling in his hands, and it made him prone to accidents. It also made handling a sword difficult, but Baldwin was determined to become a warrior. He and John practised several times a week. They had been meeting in Agnes's home for the past two months, ever since Amalric and William left for Constantinople. The Emperor Manuel had been furious after he sent his fleet to Damietta, only for Amalric to withdraw when the Nubian uprising failed. Amalric needed his support more than ever now that the Saracens held Egypt and Syria.

'Again,' Baldwin said.

John wiped sweat from his brow. They had been training for nearly an hour, and at almost forty years of age John found the exercise was not as easy as it once had been, particularly in the morning when his old injuries ached. He rolled his stiff shoulders. 'Perhaps you should rest, my lord.'

Baldwin's jaw clenched. John knew that the prince hated nothing more than when people made allowances for him because of his illness. The boy dealt with the many at court who shunned him because of his disease with surprising grace, but he could not abide being pitied. 'Again,' he repeated.

John nodded and raised his wooden practice sword. Baldwin attacked immediately, lunging at John's chest. John knocked the prince's blade aside, and Baldwin spun left and brought his sword arcing towards John's side. John parried and countered, swinging for the prince's head. Baldwin knelt to duck the blow and then slashed upwards. John jumped backwards, but the tip of the wooden blade caught him high on his right side.

'You are touched!' Baldwin grinned. 'I have won!'

John felt his side. There would be a wicked bruise there tomorrow. He took a deep breath and forced himself to ignore the pain. 'Your foes will be wearing mail,' he told Baldwin. 'They will hardly notice such a blow.' He resumed his fighting stance.

Baldwin's knuckles whitened where he gripped his sword. He lunged again at John's chest. This time, John sidestepped the blow and chopped at the prince's side. Baldwin just managed to parry. John reversed his sword, swinging high. Baldwin ducked, and John brought his sword down to tap the prince's head.

'You are dead again, my lord.'

Baldwin frowned as he rubbed his head. Then he grinned. 'In battle, I will be wearing a steel helmet. I will hardly notice such a blow.' The prince attacked with a series of quick lunges and John gave ground. Then Baldwin overextended himself. John sidestepped the blow and brought his wooden blade down on the back of the prince's sword hand. Baldwin jumped back and raised his blade, ready to fight. But John had lowered his sword.

'Why do you stop?' the prince demanded.

'My lord, you are bleeding.'

Baldwin looked down at his right hand. There was a red welt on the back with blood trickling from it. His brow furrowed. 'So I am,' he murmured.

Agnes hurried forward and took Baldwin's injured hand in hers. 'My dear, we must get this bandaged.'

'It is nothing.' Baldwin pulled his hand away.

Agnes gripped his arm tightly. 'It is not nothing. Bernard!' Baldwin stood impatiently while a servant rubbed his wound with a sulphurous ointment and then wrapped a strip of linen around his hand.

'You fought well today, Baldwin,' John told him.

'I lost,' the prince replied, a bit petulantly.

'Lady de Courtenay,' a man called, and John turned to see a thin fellow dressed in expensive silk step into the courtyard. John recognized him as one of the courtiers in Agnes's pay.

Baldwin gave the man a haughty stare. The prince had little patience for such men. 'What is it?' he snapped.

'It is your father, Prince. The King has returned from Constantinople.'

'How was your trip?' John asked William. They stood in the waiting-room outside the king's private audience chamber. Prince Baldwin was inside with his father.

William rolled his eyes. 'You have never seen such foolish luxury: dances in the hippodrome, luxury barges on the Bosporus, endless feasts, women whose lewd actions matched their ill-repute. It was no place for a priest.'

John smiled. 'And how do you know so much about these women's lewd actions?'

'Amalric would not stop boasting of them. He—' William

stopped short as he realized what John was implying. 'I am offended, John. I am a priest, dedicated to Christ.' He gave John a hard look. 'We are not all of us slaves to earthly passions.'

John did not want to start another argument about Agnes. 'And how did the negotiations progress?'

'The Emperor Manuel will send troops in the event that Nur ad-Din invades. And he has agreed to another joint attack on Egypt.' William nodded to the doors to the chamber. 'How is my pupil, Baldwin?'

'Stubborn, tenacious, wilful. He will make a good king.'

William met John's eyes. 'And Agnes?' John looked away, and William lowered his voice so that the guards by the door would not hear him. 'I told you to stop seeing her. She has married again, John.'

John winced. Agnes had married Reginald of Sidon last year, but it had not changed anything between them. She said it was a mere formality, and indeed, she spent little enough time in Sidon.

William sighed. 'I suppose it does not matter. Her dalliance with you will be at an end soon enough. You are leaving Jerusalem.'

Before John could question William, the doors to the audience chamber opened and the seneschal Miles stepped out. 'Father John, the King wishes to speak with you. William, your presence is also requested.'

John entered to find Amalric seated in a simple wooden chair on the far side of the room. John knelt before him. 'God grant you joy, sire.'

The king's mouth was set in a hard line. Visiting with his son always upset him. No matter how often John told the king that leprosy was a disease, Amalric persisted in seeing it as a judgement from God, a judgement against him. 'William has no doubt told you of our trip to Constantinople. Manuel has offered his fleet to support another invasion of Egypt.'

'Yes, sire.'

Amalric leaned forward. 'I want you to go to Cairo, John. I had spies in the caliph's court, but they are useless now. Saladin has dismissed all the courtiers. He depends only on his own men. I want you to be my eyes in Cairo. Tell me about Saladin's plans. Let me know how many men he has, and when they are on the move. Find out where Egypt is weak.'

John's first thought was not of Cairo or Yusuf, but of Agnes. He did not want to leave her. Or Baldwin. He had grown close to the boy. He glanced at William. Was this his doing? 'Why me, sire?'

'You speak Arabic like a Saracen. You know their ways. More importantly, you were close to Saladin. You know people at his court, people who can give you information.'

'And you are a priest,' William added. 'The Saracens respect holy men. When you travel, you will say that you are on a pilgrimage to visit the sites where the holy family stopped in Egypt. When you arrive you will join the brothers at a Coptic monastery in Mataria, just outside Cairo. The Coptic bishop in Jerusalem will prepare you a letter of introduction.'

John frowned. 'I owe Saladin my life, sire. I will not spy on him.'

Amalric was suddenly stern. 'I am your king. You will do as I command.'

'Yes, sire.'

'Do not trust your news to messenger pigeons. When you have information, ride to Ascalon and deliver it yourself.'

'We are particularly interested in Saladin's relations with Nur ad-Din,' William said. 'We want you to find ways to drive them apart.'

John shook his head. 'Saladin will never betray his lord.'

'He is vizier of Egypt now, John,' Amalric said. 'And rulers will do what they must. There is no lord above us but God.'

'When do I depart?' John asked. He was thinking of Agnes again. He would need to take his leave of her.

'Tomorrow,' William told him. 'Tonight, you and I will be busy discussing your mission in more detail.'

'And how long am I to stay in Cairo?'

'Until we send for you. And that might not be for some years.'

AUGUST 1171: CAIRO

Yusuf sat in his study, a writing desk on his lap, and blinked his tired eyes as he read a report from Selim on the army's progress in southern Egypt. Yusuf had sent his brother and Qaraqush up the Nile to deal with the remaining Nubians. The campaign was going well. The Nubians were divided amongst themselves, and Selim had been defeating scattered groups one by one. He expected the remaining warriors would soon seek peace.

Yusuf set the report aside and picked up another message. It had come by carrier pigeon from the court in Aleppo. In it, Nur ad-Din ordered Yusuf to instruct the mosques of Cairo that the khutba, a sermon delivered before Friday prayers, was to invoke Allah's blessing on the Sunni caliph in Baghdad – not the Egyptian caliph, Al-Adid. It was the eighth such letter Yusuf had received since he became vizier, two years previously. He frowned. He was only the vizier, which meant that, technically, he served at Al-Adid's pleasure. If he broke with the caliph so openly, then Al-Adid would be forced to move against him. There would be a rebellion.

Yusuf had begun to compose a response when there was a soft knock at the door. He looked up to see Shamsa standing in a tight-fitting silk caftan that accented her pregnant belly. The child would be born any day now, and unlike his child by Asimat, this one Yusuf could claim as his own.

Shamsa frowned. 'You work yourself too hard, my lord.'

'There are men in the fields who work harder.'

Shamsa crossed the room and took the quill from his hand,

placing it back in the inkwell. 'No more work for now. You have a visitor.'

'Who?'

'Your father.'

'What?' Yusuf stood. 'I thought he was in Damascus. Why was I not informed of his coming?'

'It seems he did not want you to know. He has brought your nephew Ubadah with him.'

Yusuf turned his back to her while he struggled with warring emotions: surprise, anger, joy, anxiety. It had been nearly three years since he had last seen his father, during a brief stop in Damascus on the way to Egypt. They had hardly spoken. His relations with Ayub had been frosty ever since Yusuf had refused to serve as his lieutenant in Damascus. Yusuf had been little more than a boy at the time, but he still remembered precisely what he had said when Ayub had told him that if he stayed in Damascus he might govern the city after him: *I wish for more than to govern Damascus, Father. I will be more than a mere wali.* His father had laughed.

Shamsa put a hand on his back. 'Look at your silk robes, the jewelled sword at your side. Your father will be impressed, my lord. You are the ruler of Egypt.'

'That will not matter to him,' Yusuf muttered. He passed through his bedroom and entered his private audience chamber. It was a small, thickly carpeted room, the walls hung with red silk decorated with geometric designs in silver thread. On one wall a row of open windows looked south towards the caliph's palace. Ayub and Ubadah stood near the door. Yusuf went to his nephew first and embraced him. 'Ahlan wa-Sahlan, Ubadah!' He gripped his nephew's muscular arm. Ubadah was only thirteen and lacked a beard, but he was already tall and broad-shouldered. 'You are a man now!'

'Mother sent me,' he said. 'You are to teach me the ways of a warrior.'

'You shall have a place in my army.' Yusuf gave Ubadah's

arm a final squeeze and then turned to his father. Ayub still had the angular features and piercing eyes that Yusuf remembered, but his short-cropped hair had gone completely grey. Yusuf had thought of his father as ageless, but now he realized that he was growing old, nearly sixty. Still, he stood stiff-backed, like a soldier at attention.

'Ahlan wa-Sahlan, Father.' Yusuf embraced and kissed him.

'As-salaamu 'alaykum, my son.' Ayub frowned as he gestured to Yusuf's fine robes. 'What is this frippery?'

Yusuf flinched. 'They are the robes of the Vizier of Egypt, Father. All is well in Damascus? Nur ad-Din is pleased with your governance of the city?'

'I am wali no longer. He has sent me here to counsel you. We must talk.' He glanced at Ubadah. 'In private.'

'Of course. But first you must bathe and eat. You must be tired after your long journey.'

'I am not tired. We will speak now.'

Yusuf's forehead creased. He did not appreciate being ordered about like a servant in his own palace. Still, Ayub was his father, and Yusuf was curious to know what had brought him to Cairo. 'Very well.'

When Ubadah had left, Yusuf sat on the low dais that had been set up below the windows. He found forcing his guests to look into the sun did more to establish his authority than any throne. Yusuf gestured for his father to sit on the floor before him. 'How is Mother?'

Ayub remained standing. 'I do not have time for trifles, Son. Nur ad-Din has sent me because he is displeased with you.' Yusuf blinked in surprise. 'Our lord ordered you to change the khutba to honour the Sunni Caliph in Baghdad. You have not done so.'

'Egypt is Shiite, and its people are wary of foreigners. I am a Sunni and a Kurd. My rule is far from secure. If I change the prayers, then there will be a rebellion. I have sent letters explaining this to Nur ad-Din.'

'If there is a rebellion, put it down,' Ayub said coldly. 'Nur ad-Din did not send his troops to Egypt so that they would lie idle.'

'It is not that simple, Father. Most of the emirs that came with us have returned to Syria. The loyalty of the Egyptian troops is the only thing that keeps me in power. I will not risk losing it by forcibly converting Cairo.'

'Nur ad-Din suspects that is not your only reason.'

Yusuf flushed red with anger. He stood and looked down at his father. 'What other reason could I have?' He waited for a response, but Ayub said nothing. He did not need to. Yusuf could guess well enough what his lord was thinking. A few months ago, Nur ad-Din had been confirmed as lord of Egypt by the caliph in Baghdad. But such a declaration meant little so long as the Shia caliph still ruled in Cairo. If Yusuf made Cairo Sunni, then he would be putting Egypt more firmly under Nur ad-Din's power. More to the point, he would be weakening his own position. Without the caliph in Cairo between him and Nur ad-Din, Yusuf would be expected to answer to any and all of his lord's demands. If Nur ad-Din called for Yusuf to leave Egypt, then he would have no choice but to comply – or to rebel.

'I am no traitor, Father,' Yusuf said sharply.

Ayub's expression softened. 'I believe you, Yusuf. You have always been a dutiful son. But you run a great risk. If you continue to disobey Nur ad-Din then he will come to Cairo himself with an army at his back. You will be disgraced. Our family will lose everything.'

'If I obey him, then we will lose Egypt.'

'Perhaps there is another way.' Ayub went to the window and looked out towards the caliph's palace. 'The Caliph Al-Adid has no sons. Perhaps it would make matters easier if he were to die.'

'He is a holy man, Father. I will not be party to his assassination.'

'I said nothing of assassination. He should die of—natural causes.'

Yusuf's expression hardened. 'This conversation is over, Najm ad-Din.'

'Yusuf—'

'You may call me Saladin.' Yusuf turned away and entered his apartments. Shamsa was waiting for him in the next room. He strode past her without stopping and entered his study, slamming the door behind him. He sat down to his papers, but could not concentrate. He found himself thinking of the time, years ago, when his father had used treachery to deliver Damascus to Nur ad-Din. Ayub had spread rumours about the ruler of Damascus, even paid a male prostitute to sleep with him. Yusuf wanted nothing to do with such foul tricks. He wondered if Nur ad-Din was aware of Ayub's plotting. He had thought the malik above such things.

The door swung open, and Yusuf looked up to see Shamsa. Without speaking, she moved behind him and began to rub his shoulders. Yusuf sighed. He had not realized how tense he was.

'What has upset you, my lord? It is your father?'

'He treats me as a child, Shamsa. He no sooner arrives than he begins to issue me orders.'

'He is your father. You will always be a child to him. And he does respect you. That is why he wanted to speak in private, so as not to embarrass you before your men.'

Yusuf frowned. 'Perhaps.'

'What did he say?'

'I do not wish to speak of it.'

Shamsa leaned close to his ear. 'Tell me, my lord. It is a wife's duty to relieve her husband's burdens.'

'He—he wishes for me to have Al-Adid murdered.'

Shamsa continued to massage him in silence. 'He is right,' she said at last.

Yusuf pulled away. 'No. The Caliph is my lord.'

She moved to sit across from him, lowering herself with great care. 'Your father only wants what is best for you, Yusuf.'

'My father serves Nur ad-Din first and his family second. He cares nothing for me. He never has.'

'You are wrong. Think, my lord! So long as the Caliph sits in his palace in Cairo, your rule will never be secure. He appointed you, and if you displease him, he will remove you. He has already conspired against you once. You know that he was in league with Al-Khlata.'

'He denied it.'

'You know better. The Caliph resents you. He will seek to turn the Egyptian troops against you, and eventually he will succeed. After all, they were raised to serve him.'

Yusuf frowned. He knew she was right.

Shamsa touched his arm. 'Al-Adid has no heir. If he dies you can declare yourself king. But if you wait until he has a son, it will be too late. You must act now.'

Yusuf rose and went to the window, which looked out over an interior courtyard. Rose bushes bloomed and fat bees buzzed between the flowers. Watching them, Yusuf was reminded of his youth. How many days had he spent in Baalbek under the lime trees in bloom, watching bees chart their course amongst the flowers? He scowled. He had thought then that honour was what made a ruler great. He turned from the window to face Shamsa. 'Bring me Ibn Jumay.'

The Jewish doctor was staying in the palace in order to be on hand for Shamsa's birth. He was shown in a moment later. Yusuf's childhood tutor was nearly fifty now, but his appearance was largely unchanged. He had the same kind brown eyes, the same close-cropped beard and curling sidelocks. Only his small paunch showed his advancing age.

Ibn Jumay bowed. 'Are you well, sayyid?'

'I am not the one who needs your ministrations, friend. The Caliph is unwell. I do not number long his days in this world.'

'I have heard nothing of it.'

'Nevertheless, it is so. I want you to go to him. Take away his pain. You have drugs that will ease his passage to the next life?'

Ibn Jumay opened his mouth to reply, then frowned. 'What are you asking me, sayyid?'

'I need your help, friend. Nur ad-Din will invade if I do not convert Egypt to Sunni Islam. And yet, if I do so and go against the Caliph's wishes there will be a rebellion. I would lose everything. But if the Caliph were to die a natural death—' Yusuf let the words hang in the air.

'I am no murderer, Yusuf.'

'You are a doctor, and now it is the state itself that needs your care. You would be sacrificing one life to save thousands.' Yusuf met Ibn Jumay's eyes. 'If you do not help me, then I will die.'

After a moment the doctor dropped his gaze to the floor and whispered, 'I understand, sayyid.'

'A son, my lord!'

Yusuf blinked at the midwife. Shamsa had entered labour shortly after his meeting with Ibn Jumay. The delivery had been long, stretching into the next day. Yusuf had not slept, and now he was groggy, his thoughts slow.

'You have a son. Come and greet him.'

Yusuf followed the woman into Shamsa's chamber. Her bed was surrounded by nurses and doctors, but Ibn Jumay was absent, busy at the caliph's palace. The crowd parted as Yusuf approached the bed. Shamsa was pale, her face drawn. In her arms she held a sleeping babe.

'Leave us,' she ordered. When the others had left, she patted the bed beside her. Yusuf sat and bent over to kiss her forehead. She held the babe towards him. 'Our son.' The child's face was flushed red. He had dark hair and pinched features.

'Al-Afdal,' Yusuf whispered the boy's name. 'You have given me an heir, Wife. Ask for anything you wish, and it shall be yours.'

'Send Faridah away,' Shamsa replied without hesitation.

Yusuf pulled away from her. 'Why? She welcomed you to the harem as if you were her own sister.'

'I am mother of your son now. I should reign in your harem, as you reign in Egypt. But I never will so long as Faridah is here. She rules your harem, Yusuf. She rules you, more than you know.'

'And you wish to rule me instead?'

'To help you, if you will let me.'

'If you wish to help me, then do not ask this of me.' Yusuf turned away. 'Faridah has been with me since the beginning. I cannot send her away.'

Shamsa placed a hand on his back. 'I know it is no small thing that I ask of you, my love. But it is no small thing that I have given you.' She handed him Al-Afdal.

Yusuf cradled his son awkwardly. The babe twitched and opened his eyes sleepily. Then it shut them again. Yusuf handed him back. 'Ask anything else of me, Wife. I cannot send Faridah away.'

Shamsa's face hardened. 'I wish for nothing else, Husband. If you wish to visit my bed again, you must choose: Faridah, or the mother of your son.'

Yusuf went to the window. A column of black smoke was rising over the caliph's palace. He knew what it meant. Yusuf felt suddenly nauseous. He left the room, ignoring Shamsa's calls for him to stay. He strode to his quarters, where he found Ibn Jumay waiting. The Jewish doctor's face was haggard.

'It is done, sayyid,' he said quietly. 'The Caliph died this morning of a sudden fever.'

'Did he suffer?'

Ibn Jumay closed his eyes. 'It was terrible. I am a doctor, dedicated to preserving life—'

'And you have. You have saved my life, and you have saved Egypt from civil war,' Yusuf said, although even he felt that his words were hollow.

The doctor shook his head. 'I am sorry, Yusuf, but I must resign from your service.' He headed for the door.

'Ibn Jumay, wait!' The doctor turned. 'You only did as I asked. The burden is not yours to bear.'

'I am the one who had to watch him die. Goodbye, Yusuf.'

That night Yusuf paused at the door to Faridah's room. He took a deep breath and pushed it open. She sat in bed reading by candlelight, and as Yusuf entered she looked up and smiled. She was as beautiful as ever. Older, yes, with a fuller, softer figure. But beautiful all the same. She set her book aside. 'My lord, you look as if you are walking to your execution.' She patted the bed. 'Sit.' Yusuf sat at the edge of the bed, and she began to massage his shoulders. 'Tell me.'

'The Caliph is dead. I had him killed. What have I become? Ibn Jumay has left my service. He does not wish to attend upon a murderer.'

Faridah stroked his hair. 'Ibn Jumay is a good man, but he is not a king. You wish to be great, Yusuf, and there is a price to pay for greatness.'

He shook his head. 'A great king obeys the laws of Allah. He does not slaughter women and children, as I did when I burned the Nubians' barracks. He does not commit murder.'

'A good man obeys Allah. A great king does what he must do.'

'Am I a good man, Faridah?'

'You are the best I have ever known.' She kissed him. 'Go now. There is a coronation to prepare. With the Caliph dead, you will be king.'

Yusuf looked away. 'I need your council now more than ever. Shamsa—' Yusuf faltered. He could not find the right words.

'I knew this day would come,' Faridah said. He turned back

to her, and she met his gaze. 'You are dismissing me, are you not? It is time, my lord. Shamsa is a good wife. She is all that I could have wished for you.'

'I do not love you any less, Faridah.'

'You have always been a poor liar, Yusuf.'

He saw only love in her green eyes. He longed to tell her she could stay. Instead he said, 'You will have a home wherever you wish and servants to tend to you.'

He looked away, tears in his eyes, and she gently turned his head to face her. 'You have given me more than I could have ever hoped for, Yusuf.' She kissed him and then welcomed him into her arms. They lay side by side while the candle burned low and was finally snuffed out in a pool of wax.

'You should go, sayyid,' Faridah whispered. 'You have a kingdom to rule.'

'I love you, Faridah.'

'Go.'

Yusuf rose reluctantly. He stopped in the doorway and looked back. Faridah had rolled over so that her back was to him. He could see her shoulders shaking. He turned and left, feeling as if he was leaving a part of himself behind. He feared it was the best part, too.

Yusuf stood in the shade of the portico that fronted the caliph's palace. No, not the caliph's palace, he reminded himself. It was his palace now. After the caliph had died, Yusuf had placed the rest of Al-Adid's family under lock and key. He had spent an anxious week under heavy guard in his palace, but there had been no rebellion. His father and Shamsa had been right. He was king of Egypt, and the people who had braved the summer heat to flood the square between the two palaces were his people. Yusuf tugged at his collar. The silk robes of the vizier were no longer appropriate, and he was now dressed in a caftan woven almost entirely of gold thread. It was heavy and hot, and the collar chafed.

Al-Fadil approached from the direction of the steps that led down to the square. 'It is time, Malik.'

There was a murmur in the crowd when Yusuf came in sight. He walked to the edge of the steps and stopped, his father and Al-Fadil flanking him. His guard spread out behind.

Al-Fadil began to speak in a loud voice. 'People of Cairo, welcome your new king, ruler of Upper and Lower Egypt, defender of the faith, the Malik Saladin!'

The mamluks who surrounded the square roared their approval. The people were not quite so enthusiastic, although many did cry out 'Allah protect you!' or 'Allah bless our king!' When the crowd had quieted, Al-Fadil unrolled a scroll of parchment and began to read, listing Yusuf's many accomplishments and encouraging him to protect the people, to ensure that the lands thrived, to defend Islam and to act as the scourge of the Franks.

Yusuf's gaze moved over the crowd but stopped suddenly. There was something familiar about one of the men standing in the second row. Perhaps it was the way he stood, or the set of his shoulders.

'*Malik!*' Al-Fadil had finished his speech and was whispering urgently to get Yusuf's attention.

Yusuf straightened and took a deep breath as he prepared to address the crowd. 'My people, I was not born a king,' he began. 'Allah has blessed me, but he has also given me a charge, to watch over his lands and his people as the shepherd watches over his flock. I will dispense justice. I will help the lands to thrive. And I will defend Egypt from its enemies. I was not born a king, but I shall rule as one!' He paused to allow the crowd to cheer but received only quiet applause. They would cheer soon enough.

Yusuf gestured to the palace behind him. 'A king does not need a home such as this. A king should live a simple life and devote every last fal to the good of the people. That is why I shall remain in the Vizier's palace. For the palace of the Caliph

– Allah grant him peace – does not belong to me. It belongs to you, the people of Cairo, who built it, who paid for its riches with the taxes taken from you. And so I give it back to you; the palace, and all that it contains!'

This time the roar of the crowd was deafening. Yusuf gestured to the men who held the people back, and they stepped aside, allowing the throng to rush forward. Yusuf stood calmly as the people raced up the steps. The crowd parted as it reached him. Grinning faces flashed by on his left and right: dark and light men, old and young, all driven by greed. Then there was a familiar face. Yusuf turned to follow, but he was already lost in the crowd rushing towards the palace.

Yusuf felt his father's hand on his shoulder. 'We should return to the palace, Malik. It is not safe here.'

Yusuf nodded. He gave the crowd behind him a final searching glance and then shook his head. Surely John was not here. He had imagined it.

John pulled a fold of his keffiyeh over his mouth and nose as he managed to push his way out of the stream of people and took shelter behind one of the columns of the portico. He looked out from behind the column to where Yusuf was now heading down the steps to the square. John had hardly recognized his friend, dressed in brilliant gold, a jewelled sword at his side and a towering turban atop his head. He thought back to when he had first met Yusuf; he had been a skinny boy, bullied by his older brother. Even then, Yusuf had dreamed of greatness. Now he was a king.

John waited for Yusuf and his men to march from the square and then hurried down the palace steps. He headed north, in the same direction Yusuf had taken. John would have liked nothing more than to follow his friend to his palace, to celebrate this day with him. Instead he turned left down a broad street that led to the mamluks' barracks. Their commander was now king, and they would be in the mood to celebrate. John would buy a few drinks, and in short order he would know everything there was to know about Yusuf's rule and the state of his army. Then he would write to Jerusalem. Yusuf was his friend, but Amalric was now his lord. John had taken an oath before God, and he would not betray it.

Part II
The Will of Allah

Saladin was a deeply religious man, but he was not a fanatic, not when I knew him. He respected the Franks, and he believed that the Christians, Muslims, and Jews could share the Holy Land. All of that changed in the desert . . .

The Chronicle of Yahya al-Dimashqi

Chapter 13

Yusuf lay on the floor with his second son, Al-Aziz, on his chest. The boy was a fat-cheeked babe, not yet one year of age. He smiled, and Yusuf grinned back. Yusuf's first son, Al-Afdal, tottered across the room and shoved his brother off Yusuf's chest. The babe began to cry. Yusuf lifted him back to his chest and gave Al-Afdal a hard look. 'Why did you do that?' The young boy's lip trembled. He tottered away, tripped and fell. Shamsa scooped him up and began shushing him.

'You baby him too much,' Yusuf told her. 'He will never learn to be a warrior.'

'Then he shall live longer.'

Yusuf smiled at his wife. Since he became king two years ago, he had spent most of his time in the courts, in council meetings or training his troops. The pain in his gut had grown worse, and he often could not sleep at night. He treasured these rare moments with his family. Al-Aziz had ceased crying. He gurgled. Then he was sick on Yusuf's chest. A nurse took the child and patted its back. A servant girl brought a wet cloth and wiped the vomit from Yusuf's silk caftan. He smiled again. He might be a king, but here in the harem he was definitely not in charge. It was a nice feeling.

'Saladin.' It was Ayub, standing in the doorway. He held out a roll of paper. 'A message from Nur ad-Din.'

Yusuf took the paper and went to the window to read. His brow furrowed.

'What is it, Husband?' Shamsa asked.

'The Frankish king has taken men north to join the Emperor Manuel in a campaign in Cilicia. The Kingdom of Jerusalem is only weakly defended, and Nur ad-Din is planning an invasion. He will march from Damascus in one month. He has ordered me to attack from the south at the same time. Our first object-ive is Kerak.' Yusuf scowled. 'I had hoped the peace with the Franks would last.'

'Then stay,' Shamsa said. 'You are no mere emir to come at Nur ad-Din's beck and call. You paid back the two hundred thousand dinars he gave Shirkuh for the invasion of Egypt. You owe him nothing.'

Ayub glared at her and then turned back to Yusuf. 'You should teach your wife to hold her tongue. Nur ad-Din made our family what it is. We owe him everything.'

Shamsa opened her mouth to retort, but Yusuf raised a hand, cutting her off. 'My father is right. Nur ad-Din is my lord.'

'He is a man obsessed with defeating the Franks. You have said so yourself. You do not need to sacrifice the happiness of your people to his bloodlust.'

Privately, Yusuf agreed. Still, Nur ad-Din was his king. 'It is not your decision to make, Wife. If Nur ad-Din calls on my army, then we shall march.'

'Shall I send messengers to gather the emirs in Cairo?' Ayub asked.

'I shall do it myself.' Yusuf rose and went to the door. He looked back to his children. He would not have time to see them again until after the campaign. He went to Al-Aziz and kissed him on the forehead. 'Allah yasalmak, young prince.' He knelt and kissed Al-Afdal. 'Be good, my son.' Then, he rose and turned to his father. 'Come. There is much to do.'

★

'*In nomine patris, et filii, et spiritus sancti,*' John murmured as he knelt on the stone floor of his cell in the monastery in Mataria. He performed his morning prayers here instead of with the monks, who prayed in Coptic, a tongue he did not understand. John kissed the cross that hung from his neck and then rose and went to the window. Fifty mamluks were riding past the monastery on the way to Cairo. Men had been pouring into the city all week, joining the growing army camped along the Nile.

He went to his bed and flipped over the straw mattress. Monks in the monastery were not allowed private possessions, and although as a visiting priest he was given some dispensations, his mattress had to do for the rest. He reached through the hole he had cut in the cotton covering and felt in the straw for a moment before pulling out a leather-bound notebook and his dagger. He belted the dagger about his waist and carried the notebook to his desk, where he began to sharpen a quill.

John had spent the previous night at his window counting the campfires of the Egyptian army. He added the number of men who had arrived today to his estimates and then dipped the quill in ink and marked the total: eight thousand men. Egypt was preparing for war. John would ride that day for Ascalon to send a message to Amalric. But first he needed to know where the army was headed.

He tucked the notebook into his saddlebag, which he slung over his shoulder. He left his room and walked through dim hallways to the quarters of the abbot, who sat reading at his desk. He looked up, and his eyes moved to John's saddlebag. 'You are leaving us, Father John?' he asked in Arabic. John nodded. 'I hope you found your stay profitable.'

'Thank you for your hospitality, Father Abbot.'

'You return to Jerusalem?'

John shrugged. Once he had delivered his message, he would wait in Ascalon for further orders. He might be called to Jerusalem or sent back to Cairo.

The abbot reached into a drawer in his desk and removed a

stack of letters. 'These are for the Coptic Bishop in Jerusalem. Will you see that they are delivered?'

'Of course.' John put the letters in a pocket of his saddlebag.

'I wish you a safe journey. God be with you.'

'May God grant you peace, Father Abbot.'

John left the monastery on a dusty path that cut through green fields before turning south to follow the Nile. The sun had just risen in the east, but the fishermen were already at work. John watched as a nearby boat pulled up a net where a dozen silver fish thrashed and squirmed. The road was also busy. Farmers called encouragement to the donkeys and mules that pulled their carts. Long lines of camels shuffled alongside the river, their drivers taking advantage of the morning cool to cover the last distance to Cairo. The tall white walls of the city were just visible in the distance.

By the time John reached the Al-Futuh gate the sun had risen, and the day had grown warm. 'Morning, Father,' said one of the guards, a thin man with a gold tooth.

'Morning, Halif.' John had passed through this gate every morning for nearly two years, and he knew most of the guards by name. 'Will you be joining the army when it goes to war?'

'No. I am stuck here on guard duty.'

'My condolences. I hear the army is heading for the Kingdom,' John guessed. 'You shall miss your chance to enjoy the Frankish women.'

Halif shrugged. 'I have three wives; women enough for one man.'

'My condolences again,' John said and continued into the city. So the army was headed for the Kingdom. But where? He meandered along narrow streets towards the north-west corner of the city, where Yusuf's mamluks were quartered in a collection of buildings built around a square where they trained. The square was empty at this early hour. John stopped in the shade of a tree on the far right edge, near some merchants who were setting up stalls to sell fruit and water to the training men. John approached a merchant he knew well. Shihab was a bald man with ropey arms and an enormous potbelly over which hung a crucifix, identifying him as a Copt. 'Salaam,' John greeted him.

'As-salaamu 'alaykum, Ifranji.'

John selected a mango from Shihab's cart and gave him two fals.

'Three fals,' Shihab corrected. John arched an eyebrow. 'I am sorry, friend, but our lord Saladin, in his infinite wisdom, has raised the tax on all goods entering Cairo. The extra fal goes not to me but to him, to fund his war.'

John handed over the extra copper piece. It was a small price to pay for information. 'Do you know where the army is headed?' he asked. 'I have family in Jerusalem. I fear for their safety.'

'They are safe enough,' Shihab replied. He lowered his voice. 'A merchant friend of mine says the army will march on Kerak. It sits near the route from Damascus to Egypt, and Frankish raiders from the castle prey on the caravans. With it in our power, communication between Cairo and Damascus will be secured.' Shihab smiled, revealing the broad gap between his front teeth. 'Trade will prosper. Fortunes will be made.'

John handed him a piece of silver. 'Thank you, friend.' He had just started to walk away when two dozen mamluks entered the square. They wore protective leather vests and paired off to spar. John stopped to watch. He was particularly interested in the two mamluks who faced off only a few yards from him. One of the fighters looked to be about fifteen. He had only the beginnings of a beard, but he already had the broad chest and muscular arms of a man. His sandy-brown hair was light for a Saracen. His opponent was older and had the thick beard of a grown man. He was short and stocky.

The two mamluks were circling one another. Suddenly the younger man sprang forward. He slashed down, and his opponent parried the blow. The young mamluk kicked out, catching the bearded warrior in the gut. He stumbled backwards, and his younger opponent was on him immediately. The bearded warrior parried, but the light-haired mamluk spun and lashed out, catching him on the side. The older fighter backed away, clutching his ribs and holding his sword with one hand. His adversary attacked furiously, hacking down until he knocked his injured opponent's sword from his hand. The young mamluk reared back to strike his now defenceless foe, but his sword arm was caught at the last second by Qaraqush.

'Easy, Ubadah! You have won.'

Qaraqush released him, and Ubadah made the smallest of bows to his injured opponent, who threw down his practice sword and hurried from the square. He was clearly embarrassed, but there was no shame in losing to Ubadah. John had seen Ubadah defeat dozens of older warriors. He was speaking quietly with Qaraqush now, and John edged forward to hear.

'You are a natural swordsman, Ubadah,' Qaraqush said, 'but you must learn patience.'

'I won,' the boy replied.

'This time, yes. But the Franks are clever warriors, they will turn your aggression against you.'

'I do not fear them. None have bested me yet.'

Qaraqush walked over to the practice sword the other mamluk had discarded and picked it up. 'Then perhaps it is time.'

Ubadah laughed. 'Are you jesting, greybeard? I do not wish to hurt you.'

Qaraqush did not reply. He swung the sword from side to side to test its balance and then stood straight, the weapon held casually in his right hand with its tip towards the earth. The mamluks nearby stopped fighting and turned to watch.

Ubadah raised his sword and began to circle Qaraqush. He feinted forward and then jumped back, but the old warrior did not so much as blink. Ubadah feinted several more times. Only Qaraqush's eyes moved as he tracked his opponent. Ubadah circled behind Qaraqush, and this time he attacked in earnest, lunging for the small of Qaraqush's back.

Qaraqush moved quickly, pivoting to his right and swinging his sword up to knock aside the attack. Ubadah spun left and brought his blade arcing towards his opponent, but Qaraqush stepped back so that the blade passed inches from his chest. Then he moved inside Ubadah's guard and punched the boy hard in the shoulder. Ubadah was already off balance from his spin, and the blow toppled him. He rolled away and sprang to his feet, sword at the ready. But Qaraqush had not followed up his attack.

'In a true battle you would now be dead,' the grizzled mamluk said.

Ubadah's forehead creased and his knuckles whitened around the hilt of his sword. He attacked, his sword moving with blinding speed, hacking, lunging, slashing. Few could have withstood such an attack, but Qaraqush was a seasoned warrior. He made small movements of his blade, just enough to steer Ubadah's attacks aside, and gave ground as he waited for his opponent to make a mistake. Then it came. Qaraqush was back-pedalling, and Ubadah lunged at his chest, overextending himself. Qaraqush brought his sword up, knocking Ubadah's blade above his head. The boy brought his sword slashing back down, but Qaraqush sidestepped and slammed his practice blade into Ubadah's side. The boy cried out as he stumbled back holding his ribs. Qaraqush sprang forward and brought his blade down on the boy's forearm.

'*Yaha*!' Ubadah cried as he dropped his sword. The blades were blunted but the blow still stung.

'As I said, you must learn patience,' Qaraqush told him. 'There is no prize for dispatching your opponent quickly. Dead is dead, no matter how long it takes.'

'My Uncle Saladin says I am the best young swordsman he has ever seen,' Ubadah pouted as he gingerly touched his side. The protective leather jerkin would have softened the blow, but John guessed a deep bruise was already forming. 'Better than him, even.'

'You are just good enough to get yourself killed. That is enough for today.'

Qaraqush walked away, and the other mamluks went back to sparring. Ubadah stood red-faced, rubbing his sore wrist. The boy was upset, although John was not sure if it was because of his defeat or because Qaraqush had dressed him down before the other men. But Qaraqush was right. Ubadah was too aggressive. He fought as if he wished to prove something. The songs of poets were filled with tales of such men, of their glorious victories and their early deaths.

Ubadah looked up, and his eyes settled on John. Looking at the boy's face was like looking into a mirror. He had the same arch of the brow as John, the same square jaw, the same thin nose. John turned away and casually asked for a cup of water from one of the merchants. From the corner of his eye he could see that Ubadah was still watching him. Surely the boy did not recognize him. It was nearly seven years since Ubadah had last seen him.

John handed a copper to the merchant and took a cup of water. Ubadah had begun to walk in John's direction. John handed the cup back without drinking and walked away. When he reached the street leading from the square he glanced back. Ubadah had stopped at the edge of the practice arena, but his eyes were still on John. Their gazes met for a moment, then John strode away. The sooner he left Cairo, the better.

He was leaving through the Al-Futuh gate when a guard hailed him. 'John! Stop!'

'What is it, Halif?'

'You are a Frank, yes?'

John nodded. He had never tried to hide his origins. It would only raise more questions. 'I am a priest, come to pray at the holy sites.'

'Wait here.' Halif turned to one of the other guards. 'See that he does not leave.'

Halif disappeared into the gatehouse. He returned a moment later with Ubadah. John felt his stomach tense.

Ubadah scratched at his patchy beard as he peered at John. 'I thought I recognized you, ifranji. You are John.'

John knew that it was too late to lie. 'Ubadah.'

'What are you doing in Cairo?'

'I was here to pray. I was just leaving.'

Ubadah shook his head. 'My uncle will want to see you. Guards, bring him.'

The burning in Yusuf's gut grew worse as he examined a page of the notebook taken from John's saddlebag. It was covered with detailed sketches of the walls of Cairo. He flipped to another page, the first of several containing figures on the number of men in Yusuf's army, the supplies they had and how long they could stay in the field. The next few pages discussed the training regimen and tactics of Yusuf's troops.

'You should execute him publicly,' Ayub said. He was standing in the corner of Yusuf's private audience chamber, watching his son.

Yusuf ignored his father and continued flipping through the book. A series of pages were covered with the designs for the citadel that Yusuf planned to build south of the city. How had John obtained those?

'You have seen what is in that book,' Ayub continued. 'I spoke with a merchant who says the Frank has been around for months asking questions. He was here as a spy, Yusuf.'

'He broke no laws, Father.'

'You cannot afford to appear weak in the eyes of your men, not when we are going to war. What better way to show your strength and to rally the troops than to execute a Frankish spy?'

'John is a man of God.'

'He is a spy!' Ayub was red-faced, angry at his son's intransigence.

Yusuf met his father's eyes. 'He is my friend.'

Ayub sighed. 'You are a king now, my son. You cannot afford friends, least of all Frankish ones.'

Perhaps his father was right. Yusuf looked at the notebook in his hands. Perhaps John was not truly his friend. No. Yusuf closed the book and tossed it aside.

'A great king is generous with his enemies,' he said. 'He shows mercy.'

'You would show mercy to those who have shown us none? Have you forgotten what the Franks did when they took Jerusalem? What they did in Bilbeis? What they did to your mother?' Yusuf flinched. Before he was born the Franks had raped his mother. It was something that was never discussed. 'Have you?'

'John is not like the other Franks.'

'They are all the same. There is no place for them in our lands. They must be driven back into the sea from whence they came.'

'They are savage, so we should be savage in return? That is your counsel? Why, tell me, do we deserve these lands if we are no better than the Franks?'

'Because they are our lands!'

'Yes!' Yusuf replied, his voice rising to meet his father's. 'And we must strive to be worthy of them.' He took a deep breath, and when he spoke again his voice was calm and even. 'Have the prisoner brought here.'

'You must kill him.'

'That is for me to decide, Father. Bring him.'

Yusuf retrieved John's notebook and took a seat on the dais. He flipped through the pages again while he waited. The door opened, and Ayub pushed John into the room.

'You may wait outside, Father.' Yusuf turned his gaze on John, who stood with his hands tied together before him. His friend was perhaps a touch heavier, the lines on his face a bit deeper, but other than that he was unchanged. He had the same square jaw, the same clear blue eyes, which met Yusuf's gaze and did not look away. 'It has been a long time, John.'

'Too long.'

Yusuf held up the notebook. 'Why did you come to Cairo?'

'King Amalric sent me.' John lowered his eyes. 'To—to gather information.'

'To spy, you mean.'

John nodded.

'Ya Allah!' Yusuf cursed. 'How could you, John? I am your friend.'

'And Amalric is my king. I took an oath to serve him, just as you have sworn to serve Nur ad-Din. That is why you prepare to march on Kerak, is it not? Your lord has summoned you, and so you must go. You have no choice. Nor did I.'

'And if your lord commanded you to fight against me, John?'

'I am a priest. It is not my role to fight.'

'Answer my question.'

John met his eyes. 'Whatever you may think, I am still your friend, Yusuf.'

'You do not act the part.'

'Do I not?' There was a touch of anger in John's voice. 'I have already broken my oath to protect you. During the siege of Alexandria the Franks were searching for tunnels into the city. I discovered them first and made certain they remained hidden. I saved your life. Is that the act of an enemy?'

'I did not ask for your help at Alexandria, John.'

'You did not need to.'

Yusuf opened his mouth to retort and then thought better of it. John was right. He took a deep breath and rubbed his temples. 'I am sorry, friend. But you have placed me in a difficult position. My father wants you executed. The emirs feel the same.'

'I was willing to die for you at Butaiha, Yusuf. I still am.'

'No. Your death would please the emirs, but if I can ransom you, the money will please them still more. You will come with me as a hostage. We leave for Kerak in three days.'

'It will be no easy thing to take,' John murmured.

They stood gazing at the castle of Kerak. The thick walls were uneven, lower on the left, where they protected a lower court, and higher on the right, where the keep was situated at the crown of a hill. Even reaching the walls would be difficult. Kerak sat astride a strip of land only forty yards across, and the ground to either side of the strip fell away sharply into deep wadis. The Franks had faced the slopes of the wadis with stone to remove all handholds. The only possible path of attack was along the narrow spur of land that sloped up to the castle. A trench some ten feet deep and thirty feet wide had been cut into the stone of the spur, separating the castle from the land where John and Yusuf stood. The bridge across the trench had been burned by the castle's defenders.

John turned from the fortress to look behind him, where Yusuf's men were forming ranks. 'It is too soon to attack,' he said. 'We have only just arrived. You should allow the catapults to do their work.'

'I do not expect to take the citadel in our first assault, John. I wish to show the defenders my intentions. Sometimes a little bloodshed is all that is needed to force an enemy to capitulate.'

'I have met the lord of Kerak. Humphrey is a hard man. He will not surrender.'

'No, I suspect not.' Yusuf turned at the sound of hoofbeats. John followed his gaze to see Selim approaching.

'The men are ready,' Selim said.

Ubadah arrived just after him. The young man was dressed in mail and had wrapped a scarlet cloth around his helmet.

'Why are you dressed for battle, Ubadah?' Yusuf demanded.

'I want to fight, Uncle. I am ready.'

'You are only fifteen.'

'You were not so old when you saw your first battle.'

Yusuf opened his mouth to reply, but John spoke first. 'He is not ready.'

Ubadah reddened. 'Silence, ifranji! Who are you to speak thus of me?'

A group of emirs stood a dozen yards off, and now they all looked towards John. Yusuf too gave John a dark glance. 'You may fight,' Yusuf said reluctantly, 'but do not leave your uncle Selim's side. Do exactly as he tells you.'

'Yes, Uncle,' Ubadah said, grinning.

Yusuf looked to Selim. 'Keep him safe, Brother, and Allah protect you, as well. You may begin the attack.' Selim and Ubadah spurred their horses back towards the troops, and the emirs followed.

'You should not have sent him,' John told Yusuf. 'I have seen him fight. He is impulsive, rash. He will get himself killed.'

'I would not send him into battle if I did not think him ready. He is my nephew.'

'And he is my son!' John hissed so that only Yusuf could hear.

'He is never to know that,' Yusuf snapped. He shook his head. 'If you had wished to protect him, then you should have held your tongue, John. You gave me no choice but to send him. My men were watching. I could not be seen to favour the word of a Frank over that of my own nephew.'

Selim's horn sounded and the ranks of mamluks advanced, marching on to the narrow strip of land that led to the castle. The sixty foot-soldiers at the head of the column carried a mobile wooden bridge that would be used to span the trench. They were surrounded by another hundred soldiers, each carrying a tall, body-length shield. It was their duty to protect the men carrying the bridge.

Selim and Ubadah came next, riding amidst fifty hand-picked mamluks. Behind them marched two hundred men carrying tall ladders for scaling the wall. Bringing up the rear were another hundred infantry with tall shields, surrounding a dozen men pushing a wheeled battering ram.

The men carrying the bridge reached the steepest part of the slope and began to labour up it. As they climbed, arrows from the castle began to rain down among them. The soldiers around them raised their shields above their heads and held them sideways to protect both themselves and the men carrying the bridge. Here and there a man stumbled and fell as he was hit, but most of the arrows bounced harmlessly off the shields. A catapult within the castle hurled a huge chunk of stone towards the men. It landed just short and shattered on impact, sending splinters of stone into the front ranks of soldiers. Several men fell, crying in agony. The rest marched on. More catapults fired, and chunks of stone began to fall all about the men. Selim blew his horn again, and the men carrying the bridge quickened their pace. Behind them, the mounted mamluks spurred their horses to a trot. At the end of the column the ram bounced and jolted as it rolled over the uneven ground.

The bridge had reached the edge of the trench. Long ropes had been attached to the front of it, and now men began to pull on them, raising the front end up towards the sky as the men in the back walked the rear of the bridge forward. They continued this procedure until the bridge was nearly vertical, its bottom end resting only a few yards from the trench. Then they released the ropes and the bridge fell forward to span the gap. Immediately the troops parted, and the mamluk cavalry galloped across. John lost sight of Ubadah as the mamluks dismounted some thirty yards from the wall. They ran the final distance. A few men fell as arrows rained down amongst them, but most reached the lower portion of the wall, where they began to hurl grappling hooks up over the battlements. Men began to climb, only to fall crashing down when their rope was cut. The next wave of mamluks hit the wall, and ladders went up all along its front.

'There is Ubadah,' Yusuf shouted, pointing.

John spotted his son's scarlet helmet. Ubadah was second up one of the ladders, following a man with a shield. As they reached the top Ubadah speared a Frank off the wall, then another. The mamluk with the shield scrambled over the battlement, only to be cut down. Ubadah was moving after him when a defender placed a notched stick against the top rung of the ladder and began to push it away from the wall. The men below Ubadah scrambled down or jumped off. He dropped his spear and used his hands to guide him as he slid down the ladder, touching the ground just before it tumbled over backwards.

The ram had now reached the walls, and John could hear the boom as its steel-capped head slammed into the wooden gate. It hit the gate a second time, and then the defenders poured a thick, black substance down upon it. It coated the ram and splashed over the men pushing it. A moment later a burning torch was dropped from the wall, and the ram burst into flames. The men who had been pushing it were engulfed as well, and they scattered, screaming desperately. Selim's horn sounded the retreat.

Yusuf's men formed ranks and fell back, the men with tall shields coming last to protect those behind them. The mounted troops had reached their horses and were swinging into the saddle. As they clattered across the bridge, John spotted Ubadah's crimson helmet amongst them. John realized that his hands had been clenched into fists, and he relaxed them. The boy had made it.

Then, as the last of the mamluks approached the bridge, the gates of the citadel opened. A hundred knights on horseback poured out and split into two groups, galloping to either side of the retreating infantrymen. Their goal was clear: they sought to cut off the troops, trapping them on the far side of the trench. If they succeeded, several hundred men would be lost. Suddenly the infantrymen scattered to either side as two dozen mamluk cavalry spurred back across the bridge. Ubadah rode at their head.

''Sblood!' John cursed. 'What is he doing?' The mamluk cavalry divided into two groups, and Ubadah galloped to the right, towards one branch of the onrushing Frankish cavalry.

'He is trying to save the men,' Yusuf said.

'He will get himself killed—' John started forward, but Yusuf grabbed his arm.

'No, John. There is nothing you can do.'

'Let me go!' John jerked his arm away.

'It is too late, friend. Look.'

As Ubadah and his men met the Frankish knights, several mamluks were immediately knocked from their mounts by the knights' lances. The others were soon surrounded. They began to throw their arms down in surrender, but Ubadah's sword continued to flash under the bright sun as he faced three men. Then a Frank slammed the pommel of his sword into the back of Ubadah's head, and he slumped unconscious in the saddle. The other group of mamluks had fared no better, but their charge had accomplished its purpose. The last of the foot-soldiers were crossing the bridge. Beyond them, the Franks were leading their captives into the citadel.

Yusuf put his hand on John's shoulder. 'The boy is a prisoner. He is not dead. And he is brave. That is good.'

'A brave fool,' John muttered.

Yusuf smiled wanly. 'Like his father.'

John looked back to Kerak, where the gate was now closing. 'It is my fault.' Had he not spoken earlier then Yusuf would not have sent the boy into battle. 'I am your hostage, Yusuf. Exchange me for the boy.'

Yusuf frowned. 'I mean to take Kerak, John. Many inside will die. If you go, I will not be able to protect you.'

'Send me.'

Yusuf scratched at his beard. 'Do you think Humphrey will accept the exchange?'

'I am a canon of the church of the Holy Sepulchre, and I know Humphrey. He will accept.'

Yusuf stood at the start of the strip of land that led up to the walls of Kerak and watched as John walked towards the citadel. He was nearing the walls when the gate swung open, and Ubadah emerged. The two men met in the shadow of the walls and exchanged a few words. Then, John entered the castle and the gate closed behind him. Ubadah continued to where Yusuf stood.

'Thank Allah you are safe,' Yusuf said and embraced his nephew. 'What did John say to you?'

'He told me there was no glory in dying young.'

'He is right.'

'He is a Frankish dog,' Ubadah spat.

Yusuf slapped him. 'You have him to thank for your freedom. Now go to your tent and stay there.'

Ubadah trudged away, and Yusuf looked back to the castle. The exchange had taken weeks to arrange, and during that time Yusuf's catapults had taken their toll. The walls were crumbling. It was only a matter of days before Yusuf's men forced their way into the citadel. And when they did, the slaughter would begin. Yusuf had ordered his men to spare any who surrendered, but he knew well how hard it was to restrain men once their blood-lust was stoked. Many amongst the Franks would die, perhaps John with them. The thought upset Yusuf, but not as much as it should. And that fact upset him even more.

In the periphery of his vision he noticed a trail of dust approaching from the south. That would be a messenger from Nur ad-Din. The Syrian king had already led several raids across the Jordan as he worked his way south from Damascus. He would be pleased to hear that Kerak was almost theirs. Yusuf squinted as the trail of dust drew closer. There were a dozen riders approaching. That meant that the messenger was of some importance. Yusuf watched as the men reached the edge of the camp and dismounted.

A short time later, Selim approached on horseback. 'A messenger has come from Nur ad-Din, Brother.'

'I saw him arrive. Why did you not send him to me?'

'The messenger is impertinent. He waits for you to come to him.'

'What is his name?'

'Gumushtagin.'

Yusuf frowned. It had been years since he had heard from the eunuch, but he would never forget the note that Gumushtagin had sent after Yusuf became vizier. *You are Vizier, as I said you would be*, it had read. *The opportunity will come soon for you to aid me in turn.* Had Gumushtagin now come to collect that debt?

'Go and tell Gumushtagin that I await him in my tent. If he wishes to see me, then he will find me there.'

Once inside his tent, Yusuf poured himself a glass of water. He had just begun to drink when Gumushtagin entered.

'As-salaamu 'alaykum, Saladin,' the fat-faced eunuch said in his high voice. 'So good to see you again.'

'Spare me the formalities, Gumushtagin. Why have you come?'

The eunuch tutted. 'I made you ruler of Egypt, Saladin. You should be more grateful.'

'You killed my uncle.' Yusuf did not bother to disguise the hostility in his voice.

'No. Al-Khlata had him murdered and paid for it with Frankish gold. I merely facilitated their relationship.'

Yusuf drew his dagger. 'I should kill you here and now.'

The eunuch smiled. 'That would be a mistake. I left a letter addressed to Nur ad-Din in my suites in Damascus. If you kill me, it will be found, and he will know of your treachery. How do you think he will respond when he learns that you seduced his wife, that the son he dotes upon is your child?'

Yusuf glared at him for a moment and then sheathed his dagger. 'What do you want?'

'Nur ad-Din sent me to tell you his plans. He will arrive in two days. You are to wait for him here, and then the two of you will drive westward to take Ascalon.'

'You rode all this way to tell me this?'

'Of course not. I want you to eliminate Nur ad-Din.'

'You waste your time, Gumushtagin. If you want Nur ad-Din gone, then do it yourself. Kill him like you killed my uncle.'

'Unfortunately, that is not possible. I am closely watched at Nur ad-Din's court. There are many there who do not trust me.'

'With good reason.'

Gumushtagin ignored the jibe. 'If Nur ad-Din were to die in suspicious circumstances, then all eyes would turn to me. That is why I need you. Think! You would no longer have to take orders from Nur ad-Din. You are already a better ruler than him.'

Yusuf took a sip of water. The eunuch was right. Nur ad-Din was too obsessed with war, too blinded by hatred of the Franks – like Yusuf's father. But that did not matter. Nur ad-Din was his lord. Yusuf's hand went back to his dagger. 'You speak treason.'

'It would not be treason if Nur ad-Din attacked first. He fears your growing power. He knew Saladin the emir. He has never met Saladin the king.' Gumushtagin smiled disingenuously. 'Someone may have put it into his head that Saladin the king is dangerous. Why do you think he sent your father to watch over you? If you return to Egypt before he reaches Kerak, he will see it as insubordination, or worse.'

'And why would I do that?'

'If you do not, then Nur ad-Din shall be informed of your treachery. Asimat will die, as will your son.'

'I have other sons now.'

Gumushtagin laughed, a hollow, mirthless sound. 'Come now. You are not so hard as that, Saladin. You have seen a woman stoned, yes? Is that the fate you want for Asimat? Do you want Al-Salih's blood on your hands?'

Yusuf's hands clenched and unclenched at his sides. Finally, he shook his head.

'I thought not. Tomorrow, your army will withdraw to Egypt. And before a year has passed, your son Al-Salih will sit on the throne of Syria.'

'And you will be the power behind that throne,' Yusuf said bitterly.

Gumushtagin shrugged. 'Al-Salih is only a child. He will need someone to look after his interests.' He met Yusuf's eyes. 'Do we have an agreement, Saladin?'

Yusuf nodded. What else could he do?

'Good.' Gumushtagin turned to go, but Yusuf grabbed his arm.

'Be careful what you wish for, Gumushtagin. Once Nur ad-Din is dead, you will have no power over me. The next time we meet, I will kill you. I swear it.'

Chapter 14

Yusuf and his guard entered Cairo through the Al-Futuh gate after a tour of the new walls that Qaraqush was building. Extending the wall to the Nile meant that a besieging army would no longer be able to cut Cairo off from the river. In addition, Yusuf was extending the southern wall to include the rich gardens south and west of the city. In Alexandria, he had witnessed what happened when a city ran short of food. That would not happen here. Once the walls were finished, Cairo would be able to withstand a siege lasting months, even years.

When he reached the palace, Yusuf handed his horse to an attendant and strode inside. He was halfway across the entrance hall when he stopped short. Turan stood waiting at the far end. Yusuf had not seen his older brother for nearly twelve years, not since he had left Turan in charge of Tell Bashir, the fortress in Syria that had been Yusuf's first fief. Turan had always been an imposing man, tall with a broad chest and shoulders, but now his thick build had softened. He had a paunch and heavy jowls. His dark hair showed traces of grey. Yusuf wondered if he, too, looked so old.

Turan grinned. 'Brother! As-salaamu 'alaykum!' He crossed the hall and engulfed Yusuf in a hug, and then kissed him on both cheeks.

'Ahlan wa-Sahlan, Turan,' Yusuf murmured, thrown off balance by his brother's warm greeting. As children, Turan had bullied Yusuf mercilessly until the day Yusuf finally bested his brother in a fight. Even after Turan had agreed to serve as one of Yusuf's emirs, the two had not been close. It seemed that Turan's temperament had softened with time.

'What brings you to Cairo?' Yusuf asked.

Turan's grin faded. He glanced at the mamluk guards stationed in the hall. 'We should speak in private.' Yusuf led Turan to a small chamber where visitors were sent to wait for their audience with the king. 'Nur ad-Din has taken Tell Bashir from us, Brother.'

'What? When?'

'A month ago. A thousand mamluks under Al-Muqaddam arrived and demanded that I hand over the fortress. I had no hope of holding out against such a number. Nor did I think it wise to defy our lord.'

'You did well, Brother. Did Al-Muqaddam say why Nur ad-Din was reclaiming Tell Bashir?'

'No. I went to Aleppo to assure Nur ad-Din of my loyalty. He refused to see me, Brother. Men at court whisper that you are a traitor. They say that Nur ad-Din was furious when you withdrew from Kerak. He has declared publicly that if you do not come to him in Aleppo, he will march on Cairo and sack the city.'

The sudden burning in Yusuf's stomach was so painful that he was forced to place a hand on the wall to keep from doubling over. He took a deep breath. 'And if I do go to Aleppo?'

Turan shook his head. 'Gumushtagin has poisoned our lord against you. I believe that Nur ad-Din means to see you dead, whether you go to him or not.'

'Dark times are upon us, friends.' Yusuf paused and looked around the council chamber at his advisers: his father Ayub, his brothers Selim and Turan, the mamluk emirs Qaraqush and Al-Mashtub, and his private secretaries Imad ad-Din and Al-Fadil. They met atop the tallest tower in Yusuf's palace, a practice that he had borrowed from Nur ad-Din. Here, he could be sure they would not be overheard.

'Turan has brought news from Aleppo,' Yusuf continued. 'Nur ad-Din is preparing to march on Egypt.'

No one spoke, but the pale faces of the men revealed their alarm. Ayub recovered first. 'You must send a message to him immediately. Tell Nur ad-Din that there is no need for him to attack Egypt. Tell him that if he wishes to see you, he need only send for you and you will come as his humble servant.'

Yusuf shook his head. 'Turan says that Nur ad-Din means to see me dead, and my friends in his court confirm this. If I go to him, I shall never return.'

'What will you do?' Selim asked.

'I have no choice. I will fight.'

Ayub scowled. 'But Nur ad-Din is your lord!'

'I am the King of Egypt, Father, and my first duty is to my people. But none of you are kings. If any of you do not wish to fight Nur ad-Din, then I understand. You may leave now.'

There was a pause that seemed agonizingly long to Yusuf. Finally Qaraqush spoke. 'I will stand by you, Yusuf.'

One by one, the others also pledged their loyalty, until only Ayub had not spoken. All eyes turned towards him. He rose and strode to the door.

'Father!' Yusuf cried, but Ayub left the chamber without looking back. His footsteps echoed in the stairwell that led down from the tower. Yusuf hurried after him. 'Father, wait!' He caught up to Ayub at the bottom of the curving stairway and grabbed his arm. 'Where are you going?'

Ayub shook off Yusuf's hand. 'I will not stay and listen while you plot treason.'

'It is not treason to defend my lands.'

'No, but it was treason to refuse to meet Nur ad-Din in Kerak. And it is treason to build walls around Cairo to keep out your rightful lord.'

'You will return to Damascus?' Yusuf asked, unable to keep

the bitterness from his voice. 'You would choose Nur ad-Din over your own son?'

Ayub sighed and bowed his head. He suddenly looked every bit of his more than sixty years. 'I am your father, Yusuf, and if there is anyone who loves you and wishes you well, it is I. I will stay in Cairo and serve you as I am able. But know this: if Nur ad-Din comes here, nothing will prevent me from bowing before him and kissing the ground at his feet. If he ordered me to lop off your head with my sword, I would do it.'

Yusuf turned away so that his father could not see the wetness in his eyes. 'I do not understand why you love him so.'

'He took us in when we had nothing. We owe him everything.'

'*You* owe him everything.' Yusuf turned to face his father. 'I have made my own kingdom.'

'Such talk reeks of treason, my son.'

'Who are you to speak to me of treason? I am your king so long as you live in Egypt. I am your son, too, yet you think nothing of betraying me. Tell me truly, Father: what will happen if I go to Nur ad-Din, as you suggest?'

Ayub lowered his gaze. His silence spoke for him. Yusuf's jaw clenched as he fought back tears of anger and disappointment. His father had taught him to value honour above all else, to put loyalty before family and friends. He should have expected nothing less from him.

Ayub placed a comforting hand on his son's shoulder. 'More than your life is at stake. What do you think will happen if you resist our lord? It will plunge the East into chaos. The Franks will take advantage of our dissension to attack. Everything we have gained over the last thirty years will be lost. But if Nur ad-Din controls Egypt and Syria, then he can take Jerusalem. He can drive out the Franks.'

'And I will die.'

'A sacrifice worth making. I will go with you to Aleppo,

Yusuf. Whatever fate Nur ad-Din decrees for you, I will share it.'

'I cannot.' Yusuf opened his mouth to continue, but then shook his head. He could not tell his father that he had already betrayed their lord, and in a far worse manner than Ayub could have imagined.

'Do not turn your back on Nur ad-Din—' Ayub was pleading now. 'He will not forgive it.' He met his son's eyes. 'Nor will I.'

It took all Yusuf's will to speak without his voice breaking. 'Do what you think right, Father. I shall do the same.'

'Very well.' Ayub kissed Yusuf once on each cheek and then walked away.

Yusuf stood at the window of his bedroom and looked south, beyond the city to where men were working on the new wall by torchlight. He frowned as he thought back to his last conversation with his father. It had been a week ago, but it was never far from his mind. It nagged at him, like a sore tooth. 'He does not love me,' he murmured.

'What?' Shamsa called sleepily from bed. 'Who does not love you?'

'My father. He never has.'

She rose and came to stand beside him. 'Come to bed, my love.'

'Later.'

She rested her head on his shoulder. 'I have seen Ayub with you. He is proud of you. But he has had a hard life. Affection does not come easily to such a man.'

'He said he would kill me if Nur ad-Din commanded it. Does that sound like love, Shamsa?'

'He only says such things because he is frustrated. You are his son, Yusuf, but also his lord. It is not easy for him.'

Yusuf shook his head. 'He meant what he said.'

Shamsa examined his face for a moment. She nodded. 'You

may be right. Your father sees dishonour as a fate worse than death. He would do anything to save you from it.'

They stared out at the low, scudding clouds, lit silver by a crescent moon. 'Come, habîbi,' Shamsa said at last. 'Let us to bed.' She took his arm and was leading him across the room when loud shouting and the unmistakable ring of steel upon steel came from just outside the bedroom. An axe slammed into the door, splintering the wood near the lock. Shamsa paled. '*Assassins!*'

Yusuf retrieved his sword from where it hung beside the bed and drew the blade. He took Shamsa by the arm and led her to his private audience chamber. He had just placed his hand on the far door when it shook as someone tried to force his way in. Yusuf backed away. Shamsa hurried to shut and lock the door through which they had entered. A moment later someone slammed into it from the other side.

'The window!' Yusuf shouted.

It looked out over a flat rooftop that ran along one side of an interior courtyard. Shamsa crawled out first. Yusuf followed, feeling for the thin ledge below the window with his bare feet. He had just lowered Shamsa to the roof below when one of the doors burst open behind him. He tossed his sword down and jumped, rolling as he landed. Above, men dressed in black and wearing masks were crawling out of the window. One of them jumped, and Yusuf impaled the man as he landed. He turned to Shamsa. 'Go and bring the guards.'

She shook her head. 'I will stand by you.'

Yusuf shoved her towards the far side of the roof. '*Go! Now!*'

He turned to see two men on the ledge above. They jumped at the same time, and Yusuf was forced to back away. Behind them, more men were climbing out of the window. Yusuf lunged forward, thrusting his blade at the man on his right. The man parried while the other man swung for Yusuf's head. Yusuf dropped to a crouch to avoid the blade and then kicked out, sweeping the man's legs from beneath him. Yusuf knocked aside an attack from his other assailant and swung his sword back, catching the man in the throat. Then he ran. After a dozen yards the roof ended, a gap some ten feet wide separating it from the roof on the far side. Yusuf accelerated and jumped, just clearing the gap. He glanced back as he ran and saw three of the masked men take the jump. Two made it but one missed, cursing loudly as he fell. More men were gathering on the roof behind them.

Yusuf veered left and jumped down into the courtyard. He rolled and then sprang to his feet. He raced past a rose bush, which tore at his silk robe, and through a door into a long hallway, the marble floor cold under his bare feet. Where were the guards? This hall should have been patrolled. He glanced back to see his pursuers enter the hall behind him. Yusuf raced to the far end of the hallway and pushed open a heavy door. In the entrance hall two-dozen mamluks were headed his way with Shamsa and Selim at their head.

'*Alhamdulillah*!' Shamsa cried as she rushed forward and embraced him.

The first of the masked men burst into the room. When he saw the mamluks, he turned and ran. A dozen of Yusuf's men gave chase. Yusuf looked to his brother. 'Send men to block every exit from the palace. Take them alive if you can.'

'No, no! Please! *Ya Allah*! *Ya Allah*! Have mercy!' The assassin squirmed as Al-Mashtub slowly turned one of the screws of the steel vice that encircled his head. The head crusher was a truly terrible instrument. It had two clamps, one putting pressure on the forehead and back of the skull, the other squeezing the victim's head just above his ears. Al-Mashtub continued turning the screw, putting unbearable pressure on the sides of the man's skull. '*Please*! *Please*!' the assassin moaned. 'Make it stop!'

Yusuf forced himself to watch. It was late, only an hour after the assassins' failed attempt. He was tired and sickened from watching men suffer, but he wanted to know who had hired them. He wanted to know, and yet he feared the truth.

The tortured assassin was now screaming incoherently, one long wail of agony. Then he passed out and the room fell silent. Yusuf turned to another assassin who had been tied to a chair and forced to watch his friend suffer. The man's eyes were wide with fear. 'Let us try again,' Yusuf said. 'Who gave you access to the palace? Who told you where my chambers are?'

The man's lips curled into a sneer. 'I will tell you nothing, Sunni dog.'

The man was brave, but Yusuf knew that even brave men could be made to talk if one applied the correct combination of fear, pain and hope that it all might end. The man had called Yusuf a Sunni dog. He would start there.

'You sought to kill me because I am a Sunni, because I have converted the mosques of Cairo,' Yusuf suggested. The man did not speak. 'No, it is something else. You are loyal to the Fatimids, perhaps? You resent their imprisonment. I could have had them killed, you know. I showed them mercy. I will show you mercy as well, if you tell me what I want to know.' The man shook his head. 'Very well.' Yusuf nodded to Al-Mashtub.

The giant mamluk unscrewed the vice from the first victim's head and pulled it off. It had cracked the sides of the man's skull, and purplish-black blood had pooled under the skin around his temples and below his ears. Al-Mashtub brought the head crusher towards the second assassin, who began to squirm in his chair, thrashing his head from side to side. A mamluk stepped behind the man and put a leather strap around his neck. He pulled up and back so that the strap dug into the flesh under the man's chin, holding his head motionless. Al-Mashtub pressed the vice down over his head.

'*No!*' the man cried. '*Wait!*'

Al-Mashtub tightened one of the screws, just enough so that the man could feel the cold metal pressing against the sides of his head.

'*Please*! *Stop*!' The man's eyes were jerking wildly from side to side. 'It was Najm ad-Din! He is the one who showed us into the palace!'

Yusuf felt as if he had been punched in the gut. He closed his eyes and gripped the back of the chair, waiting until his breathing returned to normal. He leaned close to the assassin's face. 'If you speak false, you shall suffer such pain that you will wish to die, but I will not let you.'

'I do not lie,' the man said. 'It was your father. I swear it.'

'I want details.'

'On his way to Cairo from Damascus, Najm ad-Din stopped in Yemen. There are many loyal to the Fatimids there, men who fled Egypt when the Caliph died. He recruited us, brought us to an apartment in Cairo and told us to wait. Then we did not see him for months. We thought he had changed his plans until last week when he came to us. He told us how to enter the palace and where to find you. He said that if we killed you, he would place one of the Fatimids back on the throne.'

Yusuf looked to Al-Mashtub. 'See that this one dies quickly. Crucify the others outside the northern gate.' He turned to Saqr, who stood at the door. 'Come with me.' Yusuf left the torture chamber and crossed the palace to his father's quarters. He took a deep breath to steady himself, and then he nodded to Saqr, who pushed the door open.

Ayub sat across from the door, bent over a lap desk as he wrote by the light of a single candle. He looked up as Yusuf entered. Ayub's face was drawn, his eyes red. He placed his quill aside, took the piece of paper on which he had been writing, and held it to the candle flame. As it began to burn, he rose and dropped it out of the window behind him. Then he turned to face Yusuf.

'Alhamdulillah. I am pleased to see you are well, my son.'

'Are you, Father?' Yusuf looked to Saqr. 'Leave us.' Saqr departed and drew the door closed behind him. Yusuf turned back to his father. 'Were you writing to Nur ad-Din? Congratulating your lord on my death?'

'I only wished to protect you, Yusuf.'

'By sending assassins to kill me in the night?'

'You would have died with your honour intact.'

'Honour? That is all you care about, Father!'

'Without honour we would be little better than animals,' Ayub replied softly. 'I thought I taught you that much, Yusuf, if nothing else.'

'You taught me that you care more for Nur ad-Din than for your own family. You taught me that nothing I ever did would be good enough to earn your love!'

'That is not true.'

Yusuf opened his mouth to retort, but no words came. Across the room a single tear had fallen from his father's eye to zigzag down his weathered cheek. Yusuf had never seen his father cry. He had not thought him capable of it.

'I am sorry, Yusuf,' he said. 'But loyalty is the most important virtue, even more than love.'

'And what of your loyalty to me? I am your king.'

'And I am your father.' Ayub straightened and some of the old fire returned to his grey eyes. 'Why would you not do as I asked? You have always been too headstrong.'

Yusuf did not reply. He did not know which he desired more: to forgive his father or to order his death. He was suddenly very tired. He wished only to be gone from here. He turned to leave.

'Son!' Ayub called, and Yusuf turned back. 'I—' His father met his eyes. 'I understand what you must do. I only ask that you let me die an honourable death. Do not shame me. And do not let your mother know what I have done.'

'Yes, Father.'

Yusuf was on his knees, prostrate so that his forehead touched the carpet beneath the domed ceiling of the Al-Azhar mosque.

Morning prayers had ended, but Yusuf remained, surrounded by members of his private guard. He whispered the same words again and again. 'Allah forgive me. What I do, I do in your name, for your glory. Allah forgive me. What I do, I do in your name, for your glory—'

He heard soft footsteps on the carpet and felt someone touch his shoulder. He looked up to see Qaraqush. 'It is done,' he said. 'Your father had an accident while hunting. He fell from his horse and broke his neck.'

Yusuf rose. 'He is dead?'

'In a coma. The palace doctors do not expect him to live long.'

Yusuf felt a tightening in his chest. Suddenly it was difficult to breathe. It was like one of his childhood fits when no matter how much he gasped the air would not come. He had not suffered such a spell in years. He closed his eyes, forcing himself to breathe slowly and steadily. The fit passed, but the heaviness in his chest remained.

Yusuf rode at a gallop back to the palace, where he went straight to his quarters. Shamsa was waiting in the antechamber. Yusuf strode past without a word and went to his bedroom. She began to enter after him, but he turned to block her way.

'Leave me be! I am not to be disturbed. I want food and water brought to my chambers, but nothing else. Do you understand?'

'Yes, habîbi.'

Yusuf closed the door and sank to the floor. Tears began to form, but then he thought of something his father had said to him long ago: 'Do not cry, boy. Only women cry.' Yusuf shook the thought from his head. He tried to weep, but no tears would come.

Yusuf sat cross-legged in his bedroom. His hair was unkempt and his robe filthy, but he was oblivious to his appearance. A volume of the *Hamasah* lay open before him. He knew all of the poems by heart. How many afternoons had he spent in the shade of the lime trees behind his childhood home, lost in tales of love and glory? Yusuf smiled, but the smile faded as he thought of his father, his mouth set in a thin line of disapproval as he watched his son read. Yusuf closed the book and set it aside.

The door to the room creaked open. 'I said I was not to be disturbed!' Yusuf snapped.

Shamsa entered. 'It has been two weeks, Yusuf. You have a kingdom to rule.'

'I am not fit to rule,' he muttered.

Shamsa sat across from him. 'You look tired,' she said and reached out to touch his hair, which was now flecked with grey.

Yusuf pushed her hand away. 'Go, Shamsa. I wish to be alone.'

She did not move. 'You did the right thing, Yusuf.'

'I do not wish to speak of it.'

'He tried to have you killed. He had to die.'

Yusuf felt the heaviness settle on his chest again. It was never far away. 'I told you to go.' He rose and went to the window, his back to Shamsa. 'Why will you not leave me in peace?'

She approached and gently touched his shoulder. This time, Yusuf did not push her away. She wrapped her arms around him, embracing him from behind.

'What sort of man am I, Shamsa?'

'A great man.'

'I do not wish to be great.'

'You have no choice. Allah has chosen you.'

'I wish he would choose someone else.' Yusuf stared out of the window for a long time. Finally he turned to face Shamsa. 'He was my father.' Yusuf's lip trembled. He could feel himself losing control. 'I—I wish—' Words failed him, and he buried his face in her shoulder and began to sob. It was the first time he had cried since his father's death. Shamsa held him and gently stroked his hair.

Finally the tears stopped flowing. 'To rule, you must make painful decisions,' Shamsa whispered in his ear. 'It is the price for greatness, Yusuf.'

Yusuf stepped back from her. The weight on his chest had vanished, and now he stood straight. 'Some prices are too high. I should not have killed him. I am a warrior, not an assassin.'

'You are a king.'

'And I shall rule as a virtuous king, or I shall fall.'

She gazed into his eyes for a moment and then nodded. 'Very well, but first you must have a bath.' She wrinkled her nose. 'You are filthy.'

Yusuf looked down at his soiled robes. Was it really two weeks since he had bathed, since he had left his apartments?

'And afterwards you will hold court,' Shamsa continued. 'Turan and Selim are worried. We receive news daily that Nur ad-Din is gathering more troops. The emirs need you to reassure them.'

'Have my councillors gather in the council chamber,' Yusuf told her. 'But first, bring me Ibn Jumay.'

Yusuf had bathed. His hair had been oiled and his beard trimmed. He sat in a clean robe when Ibn Jumay entered his study. The doctor bowed. 'Saladin.'

Yusuf motioned for him to sit. 'Thank you for coming, my friend. You are well?'

'My practice is busy.'

'I hope you have time for one more patient.'

Ibn Jumay shook his head. 'I cannot, Yusuf.'

'I promise you that I will not sacrifice virtue for power. Not again.'

'And what of Nur ad-Din? The rumour in the streets has it that he is marching on Egypt, and he means to have your head.'

'If he wants me dead, then so be it. I merit death for what I have done.'

Ibn Jumay's eyes widened in surprise.

'You taught me that there are more important things than power, than life even. If I die, Nur ad-Din will unify Egypt and Syria. The Franks will be forced to make peace, and if they do not, he will defeat them and drive them from Jerusalem. If I fight, then I will bring nothing but suffering to my own people. Peace will be impossible.' Yusuf took a deep breath. 'I will present myself to Nur ad-Din and submit to his judgement.

'He will have you killed.'

Yusuf nodded. 'I fear I will not have need of your services for long. What do you say, old friend? Will you stand by me in my last days?'

Ibn Jumay bowed. 'It would be my honour.'

Chapter 15

John pulled his cloak tight about him as he stepped into the chill air atop one of the towers of the palace of Jerusalem. Winter had passed but the mornings were still cold. John could see the breath of Cephas – a stooped Syrian Christian with a curly grey beard – as he pottered about the cages of the royal dovecote. He had explained to John that the pigeons could cover more than five hundred miles in a single day and find their way home from as far off as Constantinople.

'Twelve today,' Cephas said as handed John a box filled with capsules, each of which John knew held a tiny scroll of paper.

'Thank you, Cephas.' John carried the box to the palace chancellery. Baldwin was already seated at the table. Ever since John had returned from Kerak last July, Baldwin had been helping him sift through the correspondence that came to the palace. William felt that it was a good way for him to learn statecraft. John handed him six of the capsules and then sat on the opposite side of the table and unrolled a scroll. He squinted as he read the minuscule Arabic script.

It was a detailed report from one of the Kingdom's spies in Damascus. The spy provided the exact number of pack animals the army had gathered; the most accurate predictor of the size of an army. 'Nur ad-Din has raised an army of ten thousand,' John said to Baldwin.

Baldwin looked up from the report he was reading. The

young prince's disease had advanced. He now had small red lesions on his forehead, and his eyelashes and eyebrows had fallen out, giving him a strange appearance. Other than that, he looked like a thinner version of his blond, square-jawed father. 'Such a force could threaten Jerusalem,' the prince noted.

'Jerusalem is not its target. Our source says that Nur ad-Din is headed for Egypt.'

Baldwin frowned. 'That is odd.' The prince held up a scroll. 'I have a report from Cairo here. The Egyptians are making no preparations for war. Indeed, Saladin has recently sent five thousand of his best men out of the country.' He glanced at the parchment he had been reading. 'They appear to be headed to Yemen under the command of his brother, Turan.'

It was John's turn to frown. He took the paper from Baldwin's hand. The prince had not misread it. 'Why would Saladin do such a thing?'

'It is disappointing indeed. My father had hoped that the war between Nur ad-Din and Saladin would be long and bloody. While they battled both Egypt and Syria would have been ours for the taking.' The prince bit at his thumbnail while he thought. 'Perhaps we can still take Damascus while Nur ad-Din is on campaign in Egypt.' He made a note on one of the papers before him and then cursed as he mishandled the quill and a blob of ink marred the page. The numbness in his hands made writing difficult. In anger, he snapped the quill in two. John handed him another, but the prince waved it away. 'It is not the quill that troubles me,' he said peevishly. 'I cannot concentrate today.'

'Why?' John asked, although he could guess the reason well enough.

'She is here.'

John did not need to ask who 'she' was. Baldwin's mother, Agnes de Courtenay, had arrived in Jerusalem the previous day. It was her first visit to the city since John's return from Egypt.

'I wish to see her,' Baldwin said.

John shook his head. 'Your father would not approve.'

'That did not stop you before.'

'You were a child then, and disobedience in a child is easily forgiven. You are thirteen now, Baldwin. I can no longer allow you to flout your father's commands.' That was only part of the truth. He had departed Jerusalem without a word to Agnes, and she was not the sort of woman to suffer such a slight lightly.

Baldwin rose. 'I am a prince, John. I do not need your permission.'

John watched the prince leave and then turned back to the report he had been reading. The curving Arabic letters swam before his eyes. He could not help but think of Agnes, of her green eyes and her high musical laugh. While in Egypt, he had missed her more than he cared to admit. He rose and hurried after Baldwin, catching up with the prince as he exited the palace grounds.

Baldwin grinned. 'I knew you would want to see her.'

'It is my duty to look after you, my lord.'

Baldwin continued grinning, but said nothing. They walked in companionable silence to the Syrian quarter. The door to Agnes's home opened before John even knocked. The same sallow, thin manservant stood in the doorway. He bowed when he saw Baldwin. 'My lord.' He nodded to John. 'Father.'

The servant led them through the tiled entryway and into the courtyard. Agnes met them there. She was nearly forty now, but she had lost none of her beauty. Her tight-fitting blue silk caftan displayed her slim figure to advantage, and the golden hair that fell down below her shoulders showed not a trace of grey.

'My son!' she cried as she embraced Baldwin. Then she held him at arm's length. 'You are so tall! Like your father. And John!'

Agnes approached as if to embrace him, but John bowed and kissed her hand. 'My lady.'

The corners of her eyes crinkled in a way that John knew

meant she was amused. 'So good to see you again, *Father*,' she said. 'You must tell me all about your adventures in Egypt.'

'There is little to tell, my lady.'

'I am sure that is not true.' Agnes went back to Baldwin and put her arm around him. 'You are a man now, my son.' She squeezed his arm. 'And strong. You must be a fierce warrior.'

Baldwin blushed. 'I am adequate.'

'I am sure you are more than that.'

'My hands—'

Agnes pressed her lips together in a thin line. 'I'll hear none of that. The battlefield is no place for excuses.'

'Yes, Mother.'

She smiled, all good cheer again. 'Perhaps you can show me later. I have kept your practice swords. Now come inside. I wish to hear of your studies, your training, and—' she winked '—your loves.'

Baldwin flushed scarlet. 'Mother!'

'Ah, I see that you do have something to tell.'

John followed them inside and sat quietly while Agnes talked with her son, plying him with questions, flattering him, offering advice. The boy had not seen her in three years, yet he fell under her spell immediately. She had that power over men. Her attention was like the sun, and they longed to bask in its warmth.

Finally, Agnes sent Baldwin away to retrieve the wooden practice swords and turned her green eyes on John. 'You have been very quiet, John.'

'I have little to say, my lady.'

She pouted playfully. 'You could say that you have missed me, that you are overjoyed to see me again.'

'I have, and I am.'

'You do not look it. You look as if you are frightened of me.'

'I am that, too.'

She gently touched his arm. 'There is no need to be frightened.'

John could feel the hairs on his arm stand up as she ran her fingers lightly from his elbow to his hand. 'What brings you to Jerusalem, my lady?'

She smiled slyly. 'Would you believe me if I said it was you?'

'No.'

'That is what I missed most about you, John. You are so refreshingly blunt, so unlike the other men in my life. My husband Reginald is a bore.' Her smile faded, and she became serious. 'Baldwin will be of age soon. That is why I am here, to help him become king.'

'Why should he need your help? He is Amalric's son and heir.'

'Amalric does not plan for Baldwin to rule. He believes him to be cursed by God. Baldwin's sister Sibylla is almost of an age to marry. It is her child that will take the throne, not Baldwin.'

John frowned. 'But William—'

'William agrees with Amalric.' Agnes met his eyes. 'We both want what is best for Baldwin, John. William does not. When Amalric is gone, you will have to decide whose side you are on. You could go far, if you would let me help you. You could be patriarch, even.'

'Amalric is younger than I. He will be king for many years yet.'

'Even kings die.' Agnes cocked her head at the sound of Baldwin's footsteps approaching down the hall. 'Say nothing of this to him. The boy does not know.' She clapped her hands with pleasure as Baldwin entered. 'Ah! You have found the swords. Come, John. You must show me what my son has learned.'

MAY 1174: CAIRO

Yusuf paced back and forth before the window in his bedroom, a crumpled scrap of paper in his hand. The message had been sent by pigeon from one of his spies in Damascus. Nur ad-Din's army had left the city two days ago. Yusuf had hoped to stay in Cairo until Shamsa delivered, but he could delay no longer. He would leave tomorrow to meet his fate.

'Please, stop pacing and sit down,' Shamsa said as she patted the bed beside her. She lay propped up by pillows. Her loose silk robe was untied in front, leaving her swollen belly exposed. Yusuf came and sat beside her. He could see movement under the skin of her stomach. This child had been more active than the others. He – Yusuf already thought of him as another son – seemed eager to enter the world.

'What are you thinking of?' Shamsa asked.

'Of you.' He touched her stomach, feeling a strange bulge on the left side – an elbow, or perhaps a head. 'Of the child inside of you. You should leave for Aden soon. Turan has taken the city.'

'I do not wish to go.'

'You must.'

She took his hand. 'You can stay, Yusuf. Fight! Defend your kingdom.'

'And betray my lord?'

'Better that than betray your sons. What will become of them?'

'They will be safe in Yemen. It is far from Nur ad-Din's lands.'

'Yemen.' Shamsa grimaced as if the word left a foul taste in her mouth. 'Here they are princes of Egypt. They will be nothing there.'

'There are more important things than power and wealth.'

'So says a man who has never been poor.'

'Even the poor man treasures honour, Shamsa.'

'That is because it is all he has.' Her eyes took on a faraway look, as if she were watching events from her past. She looked back to him. 'You do not have to fight. There are other ways. When you eliminated the Caliph—'

282

'*No!*' Yusuf resumed his pacing. 'I will not resort to murder. Never again. I am a man of honour, a warrior.'

'A warrior who refuses to fight,' she said sharply. 'There is another word for that, one that your emirs know well.'

He flinched. 'I am no coward. I fight when and where my lord wills it.'

'Nur ad-Din is not coming to recruit you for battle, Yusuf. He wants your head.'

'And he shall have it!' he shouted. Shamsa winced, and her hands went to her belly. All anger drained from Yusuf. 'Forgive me. I should not vent my anger on you. Are you well?'

'It is nothing. The baby is shifting.'

There was a knock on the door. 'Enter!' Yusuf called.

Ubadah stepped into the room. He was sixteen now, and the soft lines of his face had given way to sharper angles. He looked more like John than ever.

'What is it?' Yusuf asked.

'You are needed in the council chamber, Uncle.'

Yusuf frowned. 'At this hour? Who sent you?'

'Selim. He is there with Qaraqush, Al-Mashtub and Imad ad-Din.'

Yusuf opened his mouth to curse his brother's impertinence, but the words died on his lips. His stomach began to churn. Was this a mutiny? Why else would his leading councillors summon *him* to the council chamber? Yusuf knew they did not approve of his refusal to fight. Had they decided to resist Nur ad-Din, even if that meant removing their king? Ubadah's face told him nothing.

'Ubadah, you will stay here. Saqr!' The head of his khaskiya entered immediately. 'I want a dozen men of my private guard here, now.'

Yusuf waited for the guardsmen to gather, then set out across the palace. He paused at the stairs to the council chamber. 'Remain here,' he told Saqr. 'If you hear me cry out, you are to come with swords drawn. Kill everyone. Do you understand?'

'Yes, Malik.'

Yusuf climbed the stairs and pushed open the door to the council chamber. 'What is this?' he demanded.

The men turned to face him. Selim stepped forward and handed him a creased sheet of paper. Yusuf's eyes widened as he read the short note: *Nur ad-Din is dead. He died suddenly, only two days' march from Damascus.* He looked up. 'Is this true?'

'We have received other messages confirming it,' Imad ad-Din said.

Yusuf read the message again. He could scarcely believe it.

Selim place a hand on Yusuf's shoulder. 'You were willing to die for the good of Islam, for the good of our people, Brother. Allah has rewarded your faith. I am sorry I doubted you.'

'Shukran, Brother,' Yusuf said and then scowled as a suspicion rose in his mind. The note said Nur ad-Din had died suddenly. Could it have been murder? Gumushtagin's doing? No. The eunuch had made it clear that he was unable to move against Nur ad-Din without Yusuf's help. Who, then? Yusuf looked at the men before him. 'Do any of you know the cause of Nur ad-Din's death?'

Imad ad-Din shrugged. 'When Allah whispers the command that cannot be ignored, all men must answer.'

'I do not believe this was Allah's doing.' Yusuf looked to Selim. 'Tell me true, Brother. How did our lord die?'

'We cannot be certain.'

'Was it poison?' Yusuf demanded. Selim looked away. That was all the confirmation that Yusuf needed. His fists clenched. 'Which of you did this?' His voice rose to a shout. 'Who killed him?' No one spoke. Yusuf went to Imad ad-Din. 'Was it you?' The scribe shook his head. Yusuf moved on to Al-Mashtub. 'You?'

'No, Malik.'

'You, Qaraqush?' The grizzled mamluk shook his head. Yusuf came back to Selim. 'You urged me again and again to fight. Was it you, Brother?'

'I did not kill him.'

'I think you lie. We are all sons of Allah!' Yusuf roared. 'We do not murder one another!'

Selim straightened and met his brother's gaze. 'You know me better than that, Brother. I, too, am a man of honour.'

Yusuf's anger ebbed from him as quickly as it had come. His fists unclenched, leaving red marks where his nails had dug into his palms. He took a deep breath, and when he continued his voice was calm and all the more frightening for it. 'I believe you, Selim. But know this, all of you. When I find who killed our lord, they will hang. I swear it.'

Chapter 16

John knelt in prayer on the stone floor of the crowded ante-chamber to Amalric's apartments. He looked up as a low moan of pain emanated from the king's bedroom. Three weeks ago Amalric had grown ill. His symptoms had steadily worsened, diarrhoea giving way to vomiting and then delirium. Just now, William had been called in to administer the last rites. John could hear Baldwin weeping from the corner where the young prince prayed. He was not the only one with tears in his eyes. It was not just that the king was dying; his illness could not have come at a worse time for the Kingdom.

Nur ad-Din's death had presented an unprecedented opportunity for the Franks. Aleppo and Damascus were too weak to hold out on their own against Saladin or Nur ad-Din's nephew, Saif ad-Din, who ruled from Mosul. As recently as last month, Amalric had led an army to Damascus, forcing Emir Al-Muqaddam to form an alliance with Jerusalem. John looked across the room to where Raymond of Tripoli knelt near Reynald de Chatillon. The two men had been freed as part of the deal. Aleppo had also sent envoys to forge an alliance. When it was completed, the Kingdom would finally be secure. But now Amalric was dying, and the alliances would die with him.

John was about to return to his prayers when the bedroom door opened. William emerged and came to kneel beside him. 'How is he?' John whispered.

'Amalric is far gone. I do not believe he understood me.'

John bowed his head and resumed his silent prayers. He looked up as the door opened again, and the king's doctor stepped out. Deodatus was a hollow-cheeked man in monk's robes. John had experienced his notion of medicine years ago, when recovering from torture at the hands of Heraclius. John thought Deodatus a fool, but the king trusted him. Deodatus gestured for William to approach. John came, too.

The doctor spoke in an agitated whisper. 'I tried everything I could. I used buckthorn to help purge him of his foul humours. I used up my supply of blackberry syrup, normally an infallible remedy for the flux.' The monk shook his head. 'Nothing availed.'

William looked as if he had been punched in the gut. 'Do you mean—?'

Deodatus nodded and led them into the king's bedchamber, closing the door behind them. Amalric lay pale and unmoving, his eyes staring sightless towards the ceiling. Strands of his hair had fallen out and lay scattered on his pillow. William went to the king and closed his eyes, then removed the royal signet ring. John noticed Amalric's fingernails. He looked to Deodatus. 'Why are his nails yellow? You are certain he died of the flux?'

The monk looked down his nose at John. 'Do not presume to tell me my business! It was the flux. He had all the usual symptoms: vomiting, bloody discharge, fever, confusion.'

John was not so sure. He thought back to his last discussion with Agnes. She had hinted that Amalric would die soon.

'Thank you, Deodatus,' William said. 'I am sure you did everything in your power. Please prepare him to be viewed. His family and retainers will want to see him.'

Deodatus nodded. 'Give me some time with him.'

John followed William out of the room. All eyes turned towards them. William opened his mouth to speak, but John pulled him aside. 'I am not so sure he was not murdered,' John whispered. 'The lady Agnes—'

'It does not matter how he died, John,' William said in a tired voice. 'He is gone now. We are a kingdom without a king. God help us.'

John gestured to the prince. 'What of Baldwin?'

'He is only thirteen. He will not come of age for three years. Until then, a regent shall govern in his stead.'

'Who?'

'The seneschal Miles de Plancy will take over the government until the Haute Cour decides upon a permanent regent.' William took a deep breath and turned from John to the room of kneeling priests and nobles. He raised his voice and called out: 'The King is dead!'

Shock registered on the faces of the men in the room. The news sank in for a moment. Then they murmured more or less in unison, 'Long live the King!'

'What do you think of our new king?' the fat-cheeked priest sitting in the next stall of the choir whispered to John. He nodded in the direction of Baldwin, who sat on a gilt throne at the centre of the sanctuary of the Church of the Holy Sepulchre. For his coronation, Baldwin's face had been covered with creamy white lard to hide the ugly red splotches, and he was dressed in the royal robe of red silk, decorated with gold thread. The seneschal Miles knelt before the king, holding his sceptre. Beside him was the dour chamberlain Gerard de Pugi, who held the king's sword, a mighty blade with a lengthy hilt, the pommel decorated with gems. Beyond them, a crowd of leading nobles and rich merchants sweated in the summer heat.

'You have spent time with him,' the priest continued. His name was Benedict, and John recalled that he was a fourth or fifth son from a noble family in France. 'Will he be able to rule?'

'And why would he not be?' John whispered back.

'The boy has leprosy, God help him.'

John smiled wryly. Baldwin hated nothing more than when people underestimated him because of his illness. 'He will be a capable king,' he responded.

'That is good,' Benedict murmured. 'I hear the mother is already meddling.' He looked towards Agnes, who stood in the front ranks of the crowd beyond the colonnade. 'Rumour has it that she is a woman who does not know her place, that she seeks to rule through her son. And her daughter is said to take after her; she is a headstrong, wilful child. She is beautiful though, *eh*?' Only fourteen, Baldwin's older sister Sibylla was fine-boned and had long auburn hair and large blue eyes. John noticed several lords in the audience casting longing glances in her direction. It was not just because of her beauty. Baldwin's leprosy had rendered him incapable of producing an heir. The future of the line lay with Sibylla. Now that she had left the convent of Saint Lazarus in Bethany, she was the most eligible woman in the Holy Land.

Benedict leaned close and winked. 'I prefer the mother, though. Exquisite.'

John was saved from having to reply by Stephen, the dean of the canons, who glared at Benedict and hissed for him to be quiet.

The introductory portion of the ceremony was concluding. Baldwin rose from his throne and knelt before the patriarch, who prayed quietly as he anointed the king-to-be with holy oil. When he had finished Baldwin stood, and the patriarch raised his voice so that the crowd could hear him. 'Baldwin, son of Amalric, sixth King of Jerusalem, may God grant you the wisdom to rule justly!' The patriarch nodded to the chamberlain, who took the sceptre from Miles and placed it in the king's right hand.

'May God grant you the strength to defend the kingdom he has given you!' the patriarch continued, and the chamberlain took the king's sword and belted it around Baldwin's waist.

'May God grant you the faith to rule in his name!' the patriarch concluded. Heraclius stepped forward holding the signet ring and a silver orb topped with a jewelled cross. The chamberlain slipped the ring on to Baldwin's finger and placed the orb in his left hand.

Baldwin sat while the patriarch retrieved the crown from the altar and passed it to the chamberlain, who stood behind the throne and held the crown over Baldwin's head. '*In nomine patris, et filii, et spiritus sancti,*' the patriarch declared. 'I pronounce you Baldwin IV, King of Jerusalem.'

The chamberlain lowered the crown on to Baldwin's brow, and the audience knelt. Gerard raised his voice: 'Long live the King!'

'Long live the King!' the crowd answered, their voices echoing off the marble-clad walls. Before the echoes had faded, some in the crowd were already leaving for the coronation feast. John had to stay for another half-hour while the patriarch prayed over the king and delivered a brief sermon exhorting Baldwin to rule according to God's will and to fight the infidel Saracens. Finally the ceremony ended and John was able to return to his quarters and remove his suffocating priestly garb. He changed his clothes and then headed to the feast. He had not seen Agnes since Amalric's death. This was his chance.

The celebration was being held at a luxurious home, built by a rich Jewish merchant before the city fell to the Christians. It was now owned by a Syrian. Two storeys tall, it was built around a series of courtyards that took up most of a city block. John was shown into the great hall. Three long tables ran its length, the king's table, set at the far end, perpendicular to them. Baldwin sat at the centre of the table with Agnes and Sibylla to his right, alongside the patriarch, and the heads of the Templars and Hospitallers. The officers of the realm sat to his left, joined by Raymond of Tripoli and Bohemond of Antioch.

John skirted the perimeter of the hall and took up a position in a side passage not far from the king's table. He waited until he caught Agnes's eye and then nodded to her and stepped into the passage. She arrived a moment later.

'Now is not the time, John,' she said. 'What do you want?'

'You killed Amalric.'

Agnes flinched. 'How could you think that of me, John?' There was hurt in her eyes.

'Do not lie. You told me you were in the city to see Baldwin made king. Not four months later, Amalric lies dead.'

'I have not been in the same room with Amalric since he annulled our marriage eleven years ago. How could I have killed him?' She shook her head sadly. 'I shall miss him. He tried so hard to be a good king.'

John was confused. This was not what he had expected. 'Do not pretend to mourn him.'

'But I do mourn him. I loved him, John.'

'Like you loved your other husbands. William told me what happened to them.'

Agnes's mouth set in a thin line. 'Whatever William might think, I did not kill them,' she said coldly. 'And I did not kill Amalric. I was angry with him, John. But that does not make me a murderer.' She met his gaze unflinchingly. Was she telling the truth?

John lowered his eyes. 'Forgive me,' he murmured. 'But Amalric was poisoned. I am sure of it.'

Agnes reached out to gently touch his cheek. 'We are all of us upset, John. Do not go chasing after shadows. Amalric was only a man. The flux does not take rank into account.'

'I saw his body, Agnes. Men do not lose their hair because of the flux. I owe Amalric my life. I could not save his, but I will avenge his death.'

Agnes took his head in her hands and kissed him. 'God help you, John.'

OCTOBER 1174: JERUSALEM

John pulled his heavy cloak tightly about him to ward off the autumn chill as he dodged the puddles forming in the Street of Herbs. Vaulted stonework covered the narrow market passage and kept out most of the rain, but the vertical slits at the base of the roof that allowed light to penetrate also admitted steady streams of water, which pooled on the cobbles below. Many of the shops were closed. John prayed silently that the one he was looking for was not one of them.

After three months of fruitless investigations, John was beginning to think that the doctor Deodatus might have spoken true when he said the king died of the flux. First of all, John could not imagine how the poison had been administered. Everything that the king ate or drank had to pass two tests. First, it was put in a cup made from unicorn's horn, which several cooks and Deodatus swore would render any poison harmless. John was dubious; when he had offered to have Deodatus drink poison from the cup, the doctor had refused. Still, he was not sure how the poison could have passed the second test: the king's food was consumed by at least one of the dozen tasters in Amalric's court.

Nor had he had any luck discovering who might have administered the poison. There were dozens of candidates: the cooks, Deodatus, even a councillor such as Humphrey. There were too many possibilities and too few clues. So John had finally decided to focus his efforts on the poison itself. If he could identify the type of poison and its seller, then perhaps that man could lead him to the poisoner. John was going to speak with one such dealer in the dark arts. A palace cook had told him of a Syrian merchant named Yaqub the Bald, who was rumoured to sell more than spices.

John had almost reached the end of the street when he found Yaqub's stall. A bald man, perhaps a few years younger than John, sat amidst large earthenware pots filled with fragrant spices. The man had dark features, a prominent nose and fingertips stained reddish-orange from handling spices.

'Yaqub?' John asked.

The man nodded. His eyes narrowed as he examined John. 'What can I help you with, Father?'

'I am preparing a special dish. I was told that you are the man to see.'

'Perhaps,' Yaqub said in a guarded tone. One of his hands moved beneath the counter. 'What is it that you wish to prepare?'

John spoke in a low voice. 'Murder.'

The man's forehead creased. 'Leave, now,' he hissed and pulled a curved dagger from beneath the counter.

John did not move. 'Tristan in the palace kitchens said you were the person to see for such things.'

Yaqub held the point of the dagger close to John's chest. 'Tristan is a fool. Go, now!'

John moved fast, grabbing Yaqub's wrist beneath the dagger with one hand while seizing the man's caftan and pulling him into the street with the other. The merchant in the next stall made no move to intervene. John pinned Yaqub down and leaned over him. 'I do not have time for games. *Talk*.'

'What are you doing?' Yaqub cried, his eyes wild. '*Help!*'

John twisted the knife from Yaqub's hand and held it close to the merchant's face. Yaqub quieted immediately. John pulled him to his feet and hauled him down the street and into a side alley open to the sky. It was raining heavily, and soon they were both soaked. John slammed Yaqub's back against the wall of the alley. 'You will tell me what you know,' he said to the merchant, 'one way or another.'

'W-what sort of priest are you?'

'Who I am does not matter. Talk. You deal in poisons, yes?'

'I am a spice merchant,' Yaqub insisted.

John held the dagger near the man's crotch and tapped it against the inside of his thigh. 'Talk. I will not ask again.'

'I-I sell certain herbs,' Yaqub admitted. 'To increase virility or to ensure love. Not to kill.'

'That is not what Tristan says.' John moved the blade closer to the man's privates.

'I swear to you!' Yaqub whimpered. 'Do not hurt me. I did

sell such things once, but it was a bad business. A dangerous business.'

John looked into the man's wide brown eyes. 'I believe you,' he said and released Yaqub. 'A friend of mine died recently, and I suspect he was murdered. I am looking for a drug that would make it seem as if a man had died of the flux. Do you know of such a poison?'

'Was his death sudden?'

'He grew sick over several weeks.'

'And did you notice your friend's fingernails after he died?'

'They were tinged yellow.'

'Al-Zarnikh,' Yaqub said. 'A most deadly poison. Odourless, undetectable. It takes many doses to kill, so tasters are useless.'

'Who sells it?'

'I know of one man, a Syrian merchant, Jalal al-Dimashqi.'

'Where can I find him?'

'He comes to Jerusalem every other month with a caravan from Damascus. He should be here next week.'

John frowned. He wanted answers today.

Yaqub took John's creased forehead as a sign of anger. 'I promise, I speak the truth! I can tell you where to find him. He stays in the Syrian quarter and worships at the Church of Saint Anne. If you ask for him there, someone will show you the way.'

'Thank you.' John held out Yaqub's dagger, handle first. The spice merchant hesitated. Finally he took it. John started to walk away, but turned. 'If you warn this Jalal al-Dimashqi that I am coming for him, it will not go well for you.'

'I will not,' Yaqub promised. 'I bear him no love.'

'Good day, then, Yaqub, and may God grant you fortune.'

John shook water from his cloak as he stepped into the palace. He was late for the meeting of the Haute Cour. Baldwin had been king for three months, and the court had finally assembled to select a permanent regent. The guards at the door to the council chamber nodded in greeting and opened the door just enough to allow John to slip inside. He could not vote, but he was allowed to be present as an adviser to the king. The throne at the far end of the hall was empty. Some forty nobles were gathered before it, some whispering quietly, others in animated discussion. Barons from all over the kingdom had come, and they had separated themselves into two distinct groups. On the left side of the hall stood Agnes's faction, which was expected to support the acting regent, Miles de Plancy. John found him arrogant and high-handed, and he was not alone in his opinion. Miles's refusal to accept advice had alienated many of the leading barons, but Agnes had stuck with him. John guessed his lack of support made him pliable. Amongst Miles's supporters, John noticed the archdeacon Heraclius speaking with Reynald de Chatillon. That was a match made in hell, if ever there was one. They were talking with a third man who John did not recognize.

The other candidate for the regency was Raymond of Tripoli, an intelligent, cultured man who shared John's respect for the Saracens. He stood on the right side of the hall, surrounded by his supporters, including several of the most powerful barons: the constable Humphrey of Toron, Baldwin and Balian of Ibelin, and the young Walter of Brisebarre. John was surprised to also see Reginald of Sidon, Agnes's husband, with them.

John slipped through the crowd to find William, who stood in the shadows of the right-hand wall. 'Where have you been?' the chancellor hissed.

'Looking for answers to Amalric's murder.'

John had told the priest of his suspicions and kept him apprised of his search. William did not disapprove, but nor was he enthusiastic about John's inquiries. After all, if someone had killed the king, then it would be a small thing for him or her to kill John and William. 'Well?' William demanded. 'Did you find anything?'

'Maybe. What have I missed?'

'Baldwin and the seneschal have not yet arrived. I suspect that Miles is delaying because he knows his time is up. Raymond has the support of the most powerful nobles, and he is young King Baldwin's closest male relative. It will be a tight vote, but he should win. Ah, here is the King.'

The men knelt as Baldwin entered, flanked by Miles de Plancy and Agnes. Baldwin sat and motioned for his subjects to rise. Miles stepped forward to speak, his nasal voice filling the chamber. 'Welcome, lords and friends. As you know, I assumed the burden of the regency upon the death of King Amalric, *requiescat in pace*. But my rule was ever only temporary, until the Haute Cour could be summoned to appoint a permanent regent. Today, we shall accomplish that task. Raymond of Tripoli has put forth his name for consideration. And if you feel that I have governed well these past three months, then I humbly ask that you consider confirming me as regent. Are there any other candidates?'

Miles paused to draw breath and then continued. 'Very well, I—'

'Wait!' Agnes said. The seneschal looked to her in surprise. 'I propose Amalric de Lusignan.'

There was shocked silence and then an uproar as the barons began to talk loudly amongst themselves about this new, unexpected candidate. John looked to William. 'Who?'

'That man there.' William pointed across the hall to the young man who had been speaking with Heraclius and Reynald. He was tall and well built, clean-shaven in the French manner, and had shoulder-length brown hair. He would have been handsome but for a snub nose that gave him a slightly piggish appearance. 'He has only recently arrived from France,' William explained. 'Apparently, Agnes has taken a liking to him.'

John scowled. Was that why she had refused to see him since Baldwin became king? He looked from Amalric de Lusignan to the seneschal Miles, who was standing pale and speechless beside the throne. 'And apparently she has tired of Miles de Plancy.'

'No doubt she did not believe he would be named regent,' William noted. 'He has outlived his usefulness.'

'What of this Amalric? Can he win?'

William shrugged. 'Not likely. But Agnes would not have put him forward if she did not think he had a chance. Look at the barons.' The men were arguing animatedly in groups of three and four. 'Men who were sure they would vote for Miles or Raymond are now being forced to decide anew. Most of Miles's supporters will vote as Agnes wishes. Perhaps some of the other barons will switch their votes from Raymond to this Amalric.' William nodded towards Miles, who had recovered his composure. 'We shall see soon enough.'

'Lords and friends,' Miles began, his shaky voice just audible above the crowd of men. 'Lords and friends!' he repeated more loudly. The barons quieted. 'In light of this unexpected candidacy, we all need time to consider our options. The King and I shall retire to allow you to reach a decision.' The seneschal left the hall without waiting for a response. After a moment, Baldwin rose and followed him. Agnes remained behind and crossed the hall to speak with Amalric de Lusignan. He said something, and she laughed. She reached out and picked a piece of lint from his linen tunic. John looked away, disgusted.

'What now?' he asked William.

'I must speak with Raymond.'

William joined Raymond in discussion with Reginald of Sidon. John remained in the shadows along the wall until he noticed Reynald standing alone. He crossed the room. 'Reynald!'

'Father,' Reynald said in a voice so clipped it was almost a grunt.

'What are you doing here?' John demanded. 'You swore an oath to return to France when you were released.'

'Heraclius has absolved me of my oath.'

The archdeacon had overheard the conversation and now

approached. 'Oaths made to the infidel are meaningless,' he said in his soft voice.

'A man's word is his word, regardless of who he gives it to,' John countered.

Reynald snorted. 'Who are you to speak to me of oaths, Saxon? Have you forgotten that you were my man once?'

'Before you tried to have me killed.'

'And who is this?' Amalric de Lusignan asked as he stepped between John and Reynald.

'John of Tatewic,' Reynald said. 'A Saxon.'

'And a canon of the Church of the Holy Sepulchre,' Heraclius added in a tone that made John's title sound like an insult.

'God grant you joy, Father,' Amalric said. His vacant expression reminded John of a camel chewing its cud. What did Agnes see in him? 'I am pleased to meet you.'

'And I you,' John said grudgingly. 'You are a recent arrival in the Holy Land, my lord, so let me offer a piece of advice: choose your friends carefully, and your lovers more carefully still.'

John walked away before any of the men could respond. He went to where William stood talking with Raymond. Something was wrong. William was biting his lip and Raymond's brow was knit.

'Bad news,' William told him. 'The Haute Cour cannot conduct official business without the seneschal or the regent present. Miles is both, and one of Raymond's men saw him leaving the palace at a gallop.'

'The conniving bastard,' Raymond grumbled.

The doors at the back of the hall opened, and all eyes turned. A thin young cleric stepped out and spoke in a trembling voice. 'I-I'm afraid that the seneschal has been called away from Jerusalem on urgent business. The H-Haute Cour is adjourned until he returns.' His last words were drowned out by a roar of disapproval from the barons. The cleric retreated quickly.

'By the devil's black beard,' Raymond cursed. 'I'll gut the bastard!'

'But Miles cannot simply leave,' John said. 'It cannot be legal.'

'He is the regent and the seneschal,' William said. 'Who is to gainsay him?'

John looked to Raymond. 'You can seize the regency. The barons would support you.'

'They would,' Raymond agreed. 'But my regency would lack legitimacy. There would be nothing to stop the barons from removing me in turn, if they grew tired of my rule. There is only one thing to do. We must find Miles and drag him back to Jerusalem.' Raymond studied John for a moment. 'William tells me that you served King Amalric well, John. You speak Frankish, Latin and Arabic. Like me, you have spent time amongst the Saracens. You understand that they are men, not demons. And you were once a soldier?'

'Yes, my lord.'

'I could use a man like you. You are a priest, so Miles and his men will be less likely to have you killed. Will you retrieve him for me?'

'I have business in Jerusalem, my lord.'

Raymond frowned. 'Surely it can wait.'

John thought of the Syrian poison dealer, Jalal al-Dimashqi. He would be in Jerusalem the following week. 'If you are willing to wait a week before I set out, then I am your man.'

'I have waited three months to be named regent. What is another week?' Raymond gripped John's shoulder. 'You will have as many of my men as you need. Find that bastard for me, John, and bring him back here.'

A week later John walked the narrow streets of the Syrian quarter, winding his way towards the Church of Saint Anne. The quarter was filled with the low, resonant sound of nawaqis – wooden boards played with mallets – that the Syrians used to call their faithful to prayer. Jalal's caravan had been due to arrive in Jerusalem that morning. If the poison dealer had come with it, then he would now be headed to church. John stopped for a moment outside Saint Anne's. It was a Roman-style building with arched windows and a small dome at the junction of the nave and the transept. The men entering were all Syrian Christians, indistinguishable from the Saracens except by their faith.

When the flow of men had slowed to a trickle, John stepped inside. He paused to allow his eyes to adjust to the dim light. Dozens of men were kneeling on the floor before him, while a priest prayed in Aramaic. John spied a young man near the door in the black robes of a Syriac priest.

'Excuse me, Father, I am looking for Jalal al-Dimashqi. I understand he prays here?'

'He did.'

'Do you know where I can find him?'

The priest frowned. His head tilted as he examined John. 'You are a friend?'

'Yes,' John lied.

'Then I regret to inform you that Jalal is dead.'

John blinked in surprise. 'What? How?'

'His caravan was raided during the journey from Damascus. It was a terrible business. All but a few were killed. They were decapitated, and their heads impaled on stakes driven into the ground.' The priest shook his head. 'Jalal was so generous to the church. God rest his soul.'

'Amen,' John said and made the sign of the cross. 'Thank you, Father.'

His mind was racing as he made his way back to the palace. It could not be a coincidence. Years ago, while travelling with Yusuf, John had come across a field of heads on stakes. It was the work of Reynald de Chatillon. Could Jalal's death be his doing? John thought back to the feast in Aleppo, to when Reynald had complained bitterly about Amalric's failure to ransom him. Had he killed the king? And if so, how could John prove it now that Jalal was dead?

John headed for the chancellery to discuss his new suspicions with William. He found the priest bent over a parchment. 'What did this Jalal have to say?' William asked without looking up.

'Nothing. He is dead.'

'Do you think—?'

'Yes. I suspect he was murdered by Reynald. This bears his stamp.' John explained about the caravan and the decapitated heads.

'That is upsetting,' William said when John had finished. 'I have just had news from Acre. Miles de Plancy is dead, murdered by Walter of Brisebarre. It seems they quarrelled over the lordship of Oultrejourdain. Miles claimed it through his wife, but Walter felt the lands should have passed to him.' William frowned. 'After what you have told me, I now suspect there is more to his death.'

'What do you mean?'

'Guess who has been named the new lord of Oultrejourdain.'

John felt a hollow feeling in the pit of his stomach. 'Tell me it is not Reynald.'

'It is. He left this afternoon for Kerak. He is to marry Miles's widow, Stephanie, and to become lord of Montreal, Kerak, and the lands beyond the Jordan.'

'A reward for killing Jalal?'

'I suspect so. But who has the power to grant such a reward? It was surely not Baldwin's idea, and I do not believe Raymond capable of such deviousness.'

'Nor do I,' John agreed.

'Agnes, then.'

'No. She swore to me she had nothing to do with Amalric's death.'

'There is only one way to find out for certain who is behind Reynald's sudden rise in fortune.'

John nodded. 'I must pay him a visit in Kerak.'

Chapter 17

'*I am a loyal man—*' Yusuf stood at the window of his study and looked out over the flat rooftops to where the sun was sinking towards the horizon. Behind him, he could hear Imad ad–Din's quill scratch as he transcribed Yusuf's words. '*I am a loyal man,*' Yusuf repeated. '*I have vowed to protect the kingdom that Nur ad–Din left behind. In the interests of his son Al-Salih, I put first and foremost whatever will safeguard and strengthen his rule. In the interests of Islam and its people, I put first and foremost whatever will combine their forces and unite them in one purpose.*'

Yusuf paused and looked to Imad ad–Din, who nodded when he had caught up. '*I believe we can live in harmony with the ifranj, but not if we allow them to turn us against one another. You have signed a treaty with Jerusalem, a treaty aimed against me and against Al-Salih. Nur ad–Din would regard such a treaty as a betrayal. He is not here to take vengeance, and his son is too young to punish you, as you deserve. So I shall act for him. Tomorrow, I leave for Damascus. My army marches not for conquest, not for riches, but for Allah. We march to save the honour of the great city and its people, and to bring them back to the path of righteousness. If you wish to join us on this path, then you will open the gates of your city to us. If you persist in your perfidy, then you shall be punished for your actions. Bismillah, Saladin ibn Ayub, al-malik al-nasir.* Add whatever other honorifics you see fit.'

'Yes, Malik,' Imad ad–Din murmured. He finished writing

and placed his quill back in its inkwell. His forehead furrowed as he re-examined the document. 'Perhaps you might consider a more diplomatic phrasing. Al-Muqaddam is husband to your sister and a great emir, yet you threaten to punish him as if he were a misbehaving child.'

'If my threat is to have its desired effect, then it must be harsh.'

'And do you truly think he will turn the city over to you?' the secretary asked. 'You plan to ride with less than a thousand men.'

'Speed is more important than numbers. Al-Muqaddam is no fool. He knows that Damascus cannot stand on its own, and with Amalric dead and a boy on the throne, his treaty with the Kingdom is meaningless. He will ally with the first powerful force that arrives at his gates. Gumushtagin does not command enough men to take Damascus. That leaves either us or the ruler of Mosul. I met Saif ad-Din once, at the court of his uncle, Nur ad-Din. He struck me as haughty and impetuous, convinced of his greatness and eager to prove it. He will waste little time in raising an army to move on Damascus.'

'And we must arrive first,' Shamsa said as she entered the room in a tight-fitting caftan of saffron yellow silk. It was only five months since she had given birth to her third son, but she had already recovered her slim form. 'You may go, Imad ad-Din,' she said. Yusuf nodded, and the secretary left the room. Shamsa crossed to Yusuf and kissed him. 'I have something to give you before you leave.'

Yusuf slipped his arms around her waist and kissed her again. She pushed him away. 'No, not that. Come.' She led him into his bedroom, where a chest had been set against the wall. 'Open it.'

Yusuf raised the lid to find a vest of jawshan; an armour made of hundreds of small rectangular plates in overlapping rows. Each plate was laced to the others above, below and to the sides of it, making the armour effective at turning aside arrows or sword thrusts. But this vest of jawshan had not been made with defence in mind. The plates were of gold and shimmered as they caught the late afternoon light filtering though the window. 'It is magnificent, but surely you do not mean for me to fight in this?'

'And why not? You will look a true king.'

'A dead king. Gold is soft. It will provide little protection against a steel blade.'

'It is to be worn over your coat of mail.'

Yusuf frowned. 'It will be heavy.'

'If you wish the people of Damascus to bow before you, then you must look the part. Try it on.'

Yusuf pulled the vest over his head and went to stand before a silver mirror. He looked like a warrior from one of the ancient Greek myths he had read as a child. Achilles or Theseus.

Shamsa came to stand beside him. 'There, you see? The people of Damascus will surely be impressed.'

'I wish I could bring you with me, my clever wife. Al-Muqaddam would be no match for your wits.'

'I am sure you will manage without me, Husband.' She put her arms around him and kissed him. 'You will conquer Damascus, and it will be the start of your kingdom in Syria.'

Yusuf pulled away. 'Syria belongs to Al-Salih. I attack Damascus to return it to his power, not to take it from him.'

'Of course, my lord,' she said, but Yusuf could tell that she did not believe him.

'I mean it,' Yusuf said more firmly. 'Al-Salih is my lord. The kingdom I am building is his.'

OCTOBER 1174: THE ROAD TO DAMASCUS

It was a pleasant autumn morning when Yusuf set out from Cairo, riding at the head of seven hundred mamluk cavalry. He was taking only his best men, many of whom had fought beside him since he first became Emir of Tell Bashir more than twenty years ago. Yusuf knew that he could push them hard and they would not break.

On the first day they covered nearly forty miles and camped just south of Bilbeis. Even though they were still in Egypt, Yusuf set a watch to protect their horses from thieves. Over the next four days they continued north, following the easternmost branch of the Nile delta to the town of Seyan on the coast. From there, they turned east, riding alongside the turquoise waters of the Mediterranean to Daron, the furthest outpost of Egypt, just south of the Frankish fortress of Ascalon. With the Kingdom still reeling from the sudden death of Amalric and a new regent only recently installed in Jerusalem, the Franks were in no mood to fight. The lord of Ascalon stayed in his citadel, content to allow Yusuf's army to pass undisturbed.

They rode east into the massive dunes of the Sinai desert. They crossed in a single day and made camp amongst the ruins of Beersheba, where they watered their thirsty horses and refilled their waterskins. Two days later they rounded the southern shores of the Dead Sea, riding within a few miles of the fortress of Kerak, where, according to Yusuf's spies, Reynald de Chatillon was now installed as lord. Yusuf saw nothing of him or his men as his army rode along the eastern shore of the Dead Sea and then followed the Jordan north to where the river widened into Lake Tiberias. It had taken two weeks to reach its shores. They were making excellent time.

The next day they navigated the jagged hills along the lake's eastern shore, riding through a man-made pass that decades ago had been cut through nearly a mile of solid rock at the command of one of the Umayyad sultans. Beyond the pass they rejoined the Jordan and followed it north to Jacob's Ford, where they turned away from the river for the final, most difficult leg of their journey: three days with little or no water as they crossed arid hills and dusty plains on the way to Damascus. On the final day Yusuf's men had to dismount and walk in order to spare their flagging horses. Yusuf breathed a sigh of relief when the Barada River finally came into view, its waters flowing south from Damascus, which was just visible on the horizon.

Yusuf dismounted within sight of the Al-Saghir gate and allowed his horse to drink from the river while he considered his next move. His message to Al-Muqaddam would have reached the emir by pigeon the same night Yusuf's forces were camping south of Bilbeis. That had given the emir ample time to prepare. Bales of hay and sheets of leather had been hung over the wall to absorb the impact of stones hurled from catapults. The late afternoon sun glinted off the helmets of hundreds of soldiers manning the wall. Yusuf did not doubt that hundreds more stood ready to defend the orchards to the west of the city.

'Shall we make camp here, Brother?' Turan asked. Yusuf's brother had returned from Yemen for the campaign. Selim had remained in Cairo to rule in Yusuf's absence.

Yusuf shook his head. 'I plan to spend the night in Damascus.' He placed his foot in the stirrup, swung back into the saddle, and made to canter towards the city. His khaskiya, led by Saqr, started to follow. Yusuf gestured for them to stop. 'I will ride alone.'

'They have archers on the wall,' Saqr protested.

'Yes, and they will be more likely to accept my rule if they see that I am not afraid of their arrows.'

'But Malik—'

Yusuf raised a hand, cutting him off. 'I have known Al-Muqaddam since he was only a mamluk. I gave him my sister in marriage. He will not let his men shoot.'

Yusuf spurred his horse forward, riding across the hard-packed sand beside the river. On the walk above the city gate, he could see men clutching bows. Yusuf was close enough now that a good archer might hit him. Then the gates began to swing inward. Yusuf's grip on the reins tightened. Perhaps he had been wrong to trust Al-Muqaddam's honour, and this was a sortie come forth to slaughter him. But no. A single man rode forth, and the gates closed behind him. Yusuf stopped and allowed him to approach. As the rider came closer, Yusuf recognized him as Al-Muqaddam.

The Emir of Damascus reined in just short of Yusuf. 'Ahlan wa-Sahlan, Saladin,' he said in the clipped voice of a general issuing orders.

'As-salaamu 'alaykum, Emir.'

They examined one another. It had been years since Yusuf last saw Al-Muqaddam, yet the emir looked to have not aged a day. His olive skin was unlined and his neatly trimmed black beard showed no trace of grey. He was a smallish man, and to look at him, one would never guess he was a great warrior. Yusuf knew better. The emir had risen through the mamluk ranks due in equal parts to his tactical acumen and an almost reckless bravery. He wore simple mail instead of elaborate robes. That was a good sign. Al-Muqaddam had not allowed his new-found position to spur his vanity. Yusuf glanced down at his own golden armour. Perhaps it had been a mistake.

Al-Muqaddam spoke first. 'My cooks have prepared a feast in your honour, Saladin. You are welcome to the hospitality of my palace.'

Yusuf raised an eyebrow. 'Your palace? I am afraid not, Al-Muqaddam. You have allied with the ifranj against me and against our lord, Al-Salih. You must leave Damascus.'

The emir's expression did not change. 'Had I not made peace, Damascus would now be in the hands of the Franks.'

'I understand. But so long as you rule Damascus, your peace with the ifranj will stand, and that cannot be.'

'I can hold the city against you.'

'For a time, yes, but you do not have the men to keep out the armies of Egypt forever. And if you fight me, then I shall show no mercy when you fall.'

'I could ally with Saif ad-Din. Together we could defeat you.'

'You might,' Yusuf agreed. 'But what do you know of Saif ad-Din? Can you trust him not to dispose of you and seize Damascus? You know me, Al-Muqaddam. You know that I will deal with you fairly.'

The emir gazed at Damascus for a long time before he spoke again. 'Some men are born to be kings, Saladin.' He gestured to Yusuf's golden armour. 'You are one such. I am only a simple soldier. But I am a proud man, too. If I surrender the city to you, what shall I have in return?'

'You shall have Baalbek. I will not have Zimat's husband landless.'

'Baalbek is not yours to give.'

'It will be.'

'And if Gumushtagin sends the men of Aleppo south to seize it from me?'

'Then my men will fight alongside yours.'

Al-Muqaddam considered for a moment longer and then nodded. 'Very well. If I must have a master, then let it be you, Saladin.'

Yusuf urged his horse alongside Al-Muqaddam's. He leaned over and the two men exchanged the ritual kisses.

'Now come!' Al-Muqaddam said, smiling at last. 'Your sister is eager to see you. And we must feast the arrival of the new lord of Damascus.'

'Al-Malik al-nasir!' the men greeted Yusuf as he entered the domed chamber where the feast was to be held. The leading emirs of Damascus and Egypt stood around the edge of the circular room. Yusuf nodded to Turan and Al-Muqaddam, who sat on either side of the dais opposite the door. The first time he had come to this room, Emir Unur had sat on that dais. Yusuf had seen Nur ad-Din sit there for the first time. Now the position was his. He mounted the dais and sat, motioning for the men to do the same. Servants entered and set before each man dishes of steaming flatbread and jannaniyya, a heavily spiced vegetable stew. Yusuf dipped a piece of bread. 'Bismillah,' he murmured and took a bite, signalling that the other men could now eat.

Al-Muqaddam scooped up some of the stew and chewed thoughtfully before turning to Yusuf. 'Might I ask your plans, Saladin? I trust you will not tarry too long before marching on Baalbek. I am eager to take possession of my new lands.'

'We will leave before the week is out. I am sure Baalbek will surrender quickly enough. I will offer generous terms, and they will gain nothing but suffering by fighting against us.'

'And after that, will you push north?'

All the emirs looked to Yusuf, eager to hear his answer.

'No. I shall return to Cairo with my men. Turan will stay to govern Damascus.'

'Shukran, Brother,' Turan said. 'But you should not be so quick to leave. None would question your decision if you moved against Aleppo. You could be king of Egypt and Syria!'

The greatest king in the world. With Syria and Egypt in his power, he would not have to fear the Franks. He could make peace. But to do so, he would have to take Aleppo, and it was now ruled by Al-Salih. Yusuf had murdered his own father. He would not kill his own son.

'No,' he said at last. 'Al-Salih is Nur ad-Din's heir and our lord. Syria is his.'

'Al-Salih is only a boy,' Turan grumbled. 'It is the regent Gumushtagin who rules.'

'I have made my decision.'

Turan looked as if he wished to protest, but bit back his words. Servants entered with the second course, a roasted lamb that had been marinated in murri, a pungent combination of honey, anise, fennel, walnuts and quinces that was boiled and allowed to ferment.

Yusuf took a bite. 'Your cooks have outdone themselves,' he told Al-Muqaddam.

The emir placed his hand over his heart and bowed. 'They are yours, if you wish to have them, Malik.'

'No. I have taken Damascus. It would be cruel to also deprive you of the pleasure of such delicious food.'

'Shukran. Might I speak freely, Malik?'

'Of course.'

'You should listen to your brother. Aleppo cannot stand alone, and it is no secret that Gumushtagin has no love for you. He will seek allies elsewhere; in Mosul, or worse, Jerusalem. They will be a threat to Damascus.' Several of the emirs murmured their agreement.

Yusuf could understand why they were so eager. Gumushtagin was dangerous and Aleppo was a great prize. They did not know that Al-Salih was his son. But that should not matter. Al-Salih was these men's lord. It was time they learned a lesson.

Yusuf stood and crossed the room to one of Al-Muqaddam's men who had agreed with Turan. 'Are you a man of honour, Emir?'

The man bristled. 'Of course, Malik.'

Yusuf looked to another emir. 'And you?' The man nodded. 'And you, Turan?'

'You know I am, Brother. We are all of us honourable men.'

Yusuf turned to look each man in the eye. 'You call yourselves men of honour, yet you counsel me to make war on our lord.' There were murmurs of protest. '*Silence!* What are we if we do not have honour? Even the most savage Frank is loyal to the death. Are you lesser men than they? Does your loyalty shift like a banner in the wind? Do your serve only when it suits you?' Yusuf met his brother's gaze, and Turan looked away. Yusuf looked about the room. None of the emirs would meet his eye.

'When I swear an oath, I keep it. That is what it means to be a man of honour. Al-Salih is our lord, and it is our duty to defend him. It does not matter that Gumushtagin is regent in Aleppo. He is our lord's servant and thus our ally. It does not matter that he may join others and march against us. Until that day, I will serve Al-Salih loyally. If you are truly men of honour, then you will do the same.'

Yusuf returned to the dais and sat.

There was an uncomfortable silence. Finally Al-Muqaddam spoke. 'I spoke foolishly earlier. Forgive me, Malik.'

'There is nothing to forgive. You voiced your thoughts, and now I have told you mine. We will not attack Aleppo. That is an end to the matter.'

Chapter 18

The mud sucked at John's boots as he led his horse on to the narrow spur of land that sloped up to the citadel of Kerak. It was a miserable winter's day, the low grey clouds spitting rain. John crossed the bridge over the gap in the spur and walked past a row of decapitated heads impaled on spears. The two guards at the gate were hunkered down under their cloaks. They hardly spared him a glance.

'I am come to see Lord Reynald,' John said.

'In the keep.'

John left his horse with a stable boy in the lower court. He took the ramp to the upper court, where rain was pooling in broad puddles. There was no one about. Firelight glowed invitingly in the windows of the keep. John skirted the puddles and climbed the steps to the door. It was locked. He pounded on it, and a moment later it opened.

A heavy-set guard in mail stood in the doorway. 'If you've come to beg, then you'd best leave before I run my sword up your backside.'

John held up his cross. 'I am a canon of the Church of the Holy Sepulchre. I have come on the King's business. I must speak with your lord.'

The guard examined him for a moment before waving him inside into a draughty entrance hall. Another guard – an adolescent in loose, ill-fitting mail – stood beside the door.

'I will inform Lord Reynald of your arrival,' the heavy-set guard said. 'You have a name, priest?'

'John of Tatewic.'

The guard grunted. 'An Englishman.' He left, his footsteps echoing in the tall stone chamber.

John removed his dripping cloak. Beneath, he wore his chasuble and stole over a coat of mail. A mace was belted to his waist. He handed the cloak to the young guard. 'Find a fireplace and hang this up to dry.'

The boy hesitated and then nodded and started to leave. He met the other guard in the doorway.

'Where are you going?' the heavy-set guard demanded.

'H-he told me to hang his cloak.'

The guard cuffed the boy on the side of the head. He took the cloak and tossed it on the floor. 'Get back to your post, porridge brains. Priest, you come with me. Leave your mace with the boy.'

John followed the guard up a stairwell and down a chilly hallway lined with loopholes. The guard stopped before a set of double doors. He knocked and pushed them open. John stepped into a thickly carpeted room, kept warm by a fire burning in the hearth beside the door. Reynald sat alone at table, bent over a roasted leg of lamb. He carved off a piece and speared it with his fork. Only then did he look up.

'Saxon.' He gestured to one of the seats at the table. 'Sit.'

John did so. The guard stood uncomfortably close behind him.

'What is your business, Saxon?' Reynald demanded. 'I presume you have not come for the pleasure of my company.'

'Raymond sent me. You have been raiding the caravans that travel from Damascus to Cairo. It is a violation of our treaty with Egypt and Damascus.'

'I couldn't give a piss for your precious treaty.'

'Raymond does not share your feelings. We are in no position to go to war with Egypt.'

'Raymond is a coward.'

'He has been elected regent. If you wish to keep your lands, you will do as he says.'

Reynald bristled. 'I have these lands by the King! I earned them!'

'By murdering the merchant Jalal?'

Reynald frowned and made a show of turning back to his lamb. 'I know nothing of what you speak.'

'I recognize your handiwork, Reynald; the heads on spears.'

'So what if it was me? One less Mohammedan to worry about.'

'Jalal was a Syrian Christian. And a dealer in poison. One of his poisons was used to kill King Amalric.'

Reynald's eyes widened and he dropped his knife and fork. He seemed genuinely surprised.

'You had cause to hate Amalric,' John pointed out. 'He failed to ransom you, and he gave your kingdom to Bohemond.'

'What are you suggesting, Saxon?'

'I think you poisoned Amalric. You learned I was investigating his death, and you killed Jalal to cover your tracks.'

Reynald burst out laughing. 'That is ridiculous!'

'Someone poisoned him, Reynald. If not you, then who?'

Reynald was suddenly angry. He grabbed his carving knife and pointed it at John. 'I could have you killed for such an accusation. I am a man of honour! Amalric was my king.'

John met Reynald's eyes without blinking. 'And you killed the one man who knew who murdered him.' Reynald was still holding the knife, but John decided to push him further. 'In Baldwin's eyes, that makes you look guilty,' he lied. In truth, Baldwin knew nothing of John's inquiry. 'The King wants to see you beheaded.'

Reynald lowered the knife. 'I knew nothing about any poison,' he muttered. 'I was only doing Heraclius a favour.'

'Heraclius?'

'He asked me to raid the caravan. Told me it was carrying

spice from the East, that I could sell it for a fortune. He did not say anything about poison.'

John's forehead creased. 'But Heraclius does not have the authority to grant you Kerak. Who did?'

'Baldwin.'

'Why? The King has no love for you.'

Reynald shrugged. 'Perhaps because I am a man of action, unlike Raymond.'

John's mind was racing. Reynald had killed Jalal at Heraclius's bidding. Baldwin had then made Reynald lord of Kerak and Oultrejourdain. Why? What was the link between Heraclius and Baldwin?

'If you are finished, Saxon,' Reynald said, 'then you can go. Oudin, here, will show you out.'

John spent the night at an inn in the town of Kerak. He was surprised to find that the townspeople were pleased with their new lord. The town was thriving. Merchants bought the goods that Reynald stole in his raids on the caravans, and then sold them for a profit. The people felt more secure, too. Reynald meted out strict justice, hanging thieves and personally beheading any Saracens who came too close.

Early the next morning he left for Jerusalem. The rain had stopped, but the roads were still muddy. It would be slow going, so he decided to take the shorter route home; through Saracen lands along the eastern side of the Dead Sea. He doubted that he would run into any trouble. Few travelled in the winter rainy season; the roads were poor and the ravines subject to deadly floods. John saw no one as he rode north along the hilly shore of the sea.

He spent that first night beside a stream that fed into the Dead Sea. He made camp away from the road, well upstream in order to avoid being surprised by other travellers. The wood he found was wet, and he was unable to start a fire. He spent a restless night shivering as he huddled against the side of his horse. The next morning he awoke bleary-eyed and stiff. All his old injuries ached: his left shoulder, which had dislocated on the rack; his right shoulder, where he had taken an arrow; his side, where he still bore a long scar from a sword thrust that should have killed him. He managed to start a fire, but the rain returned and extinguished it. Cursing, he climbed into the saddle and continued north, huddled under his cloak.

The rain drowned out all sound and limited visibility, which was why John did not notice the men on horseback until they were almost upon him. There were three of them, dressed in the loose caftans of Saracens, their keffiyehs drawn down over their faces. When John first saw them, they were only one hundred yards behind him. He accelerated to a trot, but the men kept pace. John spurred his horse to a canter, but glancing over his shoulder he saw that the men were gaining ground. There could be no doubt. They were pursuing him.

John cursed his stupidity. He preferred to travel alone rather than with the Frankish sergeants with whom he had so little in common, but he could have used an escort now. '*Yalla*!' he shouted and flicked the reins, urging his horse to a gallop. It kicked up mud as he turned into a ravine that twisted into the hills bordering the Dead Sea. The winding trail prevented him from seeing his pursuers, but he could hear their hoofbeats coming steadily closer.

The ravine turned sharply and widened into a shallow wash. In the centre was a stream bordered with tall brush. John slid from the saddle and guided his horse into the cold water. He walked north a dozen paces in order to hide his tracks and then left the steam and led his horse up a game trail that wound through thick brush. He tied his horse off amongst the bushes, out of sight.

John crept back to near the stream, which was now noticeably wider. The rain was pouring down in sheets, and as he peered through the leafy branches of a bush, he could just make out his pursuers. They had reined in beside the stream a dozen yards away and were searching for some sign of him. Finally they drew their swords, and one crossed to John's side of the river and began to ride along the bank. The other two searched for tracks in the mud on the far side.

John stepped back into the brush as the rider on his side of the stream approached. The man passed by and then stopped. '*Here*!' he called in French. 'Tracks!' These were no Saracens. John cursed silently as the man rode up the game trail that he had taken earlier. The other men crossed the stream and followed him. John waited a moment and then took his mace from his belt and headed up the trail after them.

The lead rider had stopped beside John's horse. 'Where did the Saxon bastard go?' he growled.

John crept up behind the rearmost rider and grabbed him. The man shouted as he was dragged from his saddle. His scream was cut short when John smashed his face in with his mace. He transferred the mace to his left hand and took the dead man's sword in his right.

The other riders had turned on hearing the cries of their fallen comrade. 'Kill the bastard!' the nearer man shouted.

John used the blade of his sword to slap the flank of the fallen rider's horse. The beast reared up, blocking the two riders' path, and John took the opportunity to run in the opposite direction. After ten feet he stopped in ankle-deep water. The stream was rising fast, flooding the wash. If John did not get to higher ground soon, he would drown. He stepped from the trail and waited, crouching behind a bush. The first man trotted past. As the second came by, John swung his sword, catching the man in the gut. The suit of mail that the man wore beneath his caftan stopped the blow, but it still knocked him from the saddle. The man scrambled to his feet, sword in hand.

John charged. The man held his ground and swung for John's head. John parried, and brought his sword slicing down towards the man's knees. The man managed to block the blow, but his sword was down, leaving him exposed. John swung for his face with his mace. The man lurched backwards, but John caught him in the throat, crushing his windpipe. He fell without a sound.

The hairs on the back of John's neck rose, and he ducked instinctively, just before the third rider's sword flashed over his head. John did not wait for the man to attack again. He sprinted for the brush located alongside the trail. Brambles and thorns tore at his clothes and scratched his face, but he pressed on. The brush was too thick for his foe to follow on horseback. Behind him, John could hear the man roaring with anger. 'Damn you! Come back here and fight, Saxon!'

John stopped. Of course: they were Reynald's men. The lord of Kerak must have decided that John knew too much. John could hear the sound of someone crashing through the brush behind him. He moved on until he came to a small clearing, half of which was already covered in ankle-deep water. John turned and waited. His pursuer stopped when he saw him. The man held a shield in one hand and a sword in the other.

'You are Reynald's man, aren't you?' John demanded.

In response the man reached up with his sword hand and unwrapped his keffiyeh. It was Oudin, the guard from Kerak. His lip curled back in a snarl and he charged, swinging back-handed for John's head. John blocked with his sword and countered with his mace. Oudin took the blow on his shield and thrust for John's gut. John managed to twist out of the way of the blade, but Oudin brought up his shield, smashing John in the face. John tasted blood from a split lip. He stumbled backwards and slipped, landing on his back in the mud. He saw a sword arcing towards his face and parried before kicking out, catching Oudin in the side of the knee. John felt his enemy's leg give way. Oudin fell on his hands and knees.

John rolled towards him and swung his mace for the back of Oudin's head. The Frank pushed himself up to his knees at the last moment, and the mace sank into the mud. Oudin chopped down on John's arm. John felt a flash of blinding pain and dropped the mace. Oudin's sword had cut through the mail over John's forearm, leaving a deep gash.

Oudin raised his sword again, but John struck first, driving his blade into his enemy's right shoulder. Oudin dropped his sword. With a roar, he swung his shield, hitting John in the side of the head. Everything went black for a moment. When John came to, he was lying on his back with Oudin kneeling on his chest. The water had risen so that it almost covered John's face. Oudin had cast his shield aside and was groping in the rising water for his sword. John grabbed his enemy's caftan. He pulled Oudin down and head-butted him, feeling a satisfying crunch as Oudin's nose broke. He then brought his knee up into his enemy's groin. Oudin grunted in pain, and John shoved him off his chest. He searched in the mud for his mace, but before he could find it Oudin slammed into him from the side. The two men grappled in the muddy water, each struggling to get a hold of the other. Oudin's hands found John's throat and began to squeeze. John choked, unable to breath. He managed to grab Oudin's head with both hands and dug his thumbs into the man's eyes. Still Oudin refused to let go of John's throat. John shoved his thumbs deeper. He could feel hot blood running from Oudin's eyes. The Frank pulled away, screaming.

Oudin tried to scramble away, but John crawled after him and seized his leg. He moved on top of Oudin and grabbed his hair, forcing the Frank's face down into the muddy water. Oudin thrashed wildly, but John kept his face pressed into the muck. Finally the Frank went still.

John sat back. 'That's one more reason for me to kill you, Reynald,' he muttered. And then pain flooded through him. His lip was split and his throat had been bruised so that it hurt to breathe. His right arm was bleeding heavily. He groped in the mud until he found a sword, and used it to cut a strip of fabric from Oudin's caftan. He tied the cloth tightly around his arm to slow the bleeding. Then he pushed himself to his feet. The water was up to his calves now. He almost fainted, but recovered and headed into the brush, slipping and stumbling on the slick, muddy ground. God was with him, and he managed to find his horse. He dragged himself into the saddle and urged the animal further along the game trail. Having managed to ride out of danger, he finally stopped to look back. The stream had become a raging torrent, expanding rapidly to fill the ravine. John saw the horse of one of his attackers flash by, swept away in the current. He watched until past noon, when the rain stopped and the waters subsided. Then he rode for Jerusalem.

FEBRUARY 1175: JERUSALEM

'Father? *Father!*'

John jerked awake and nearly fell from the saddle. He blinked against bright sunlight. His horse was standing before Jerusalem's eastern gate. He had ridden day and night without stopping, afraid that if he dismounted he would pass out and never rise again. He must have ridden the last few miles unconscious, slumped in the saddle.

One of the gate's guards was holding the reins of his horse. 'Are you well, Father?' he asked, staring at John wide-eyed.

John looked down at himself. He was caked in dried mud from head to toe. He knew his face was bloody and his lip split and horribly swollen. There was an ugly gash on his right forearm, and the mail around it was crusted with blood. When he had tied the cloth around his arm to stop the bleeding he must have tied it too tight, for his right hand was tinged blue. He looked like he had been dragged to hell and back, but there would be time to bathe and dress his wounds when he had finished with Heraclius.

'I am well enough,' he told the guard. He took back the reins and urged his horse through the gate. He rode straight to the Church of the Holy Sepulchre and entered through the eastern portal. He almost collapsed when he dismounted, but caught himself on his saddle. An acolyte approached with mouth agape. John handed him the reins and stumbled through the cloisters to the refectory, where several canons were eating breakfast. Silence descended as all eyes turned to John. He passed through without stopping and stepped out into a courtyard, which he crossed to the door of what used to be the royal palace and now housed the archdeacon's residence. Two knights of the Holy Sepulchre framed the door.

'Where do you think you are going?' the guard on the right demanded as he barred John's way. 'Get back to the streets, you rabble.'

John showed him his cross. 'I am John of Tatewic, a canon of the church. I have come to see the Archdeacon.'

'The Archdeacon is not receiving.'

John gave the man a withering look. He reached for the mace at his belt, only to find it was not there. 'I have ridden far and I am in no mood to argue. I must see the Archdeacon.'

The guard bristled. 'I said, he is not receiving.'

John's hands balled into fists. The other guard put a hand on his companion's shoulder. 'I will deal with this one, Gersant. Follow me, Father.'

The guard led John inside and upstairs to the archdeacon's private apartments. He knocked, but before there was a response John pushed the door open and stormed inside. A blond man with heavy jowls and red cheeks sat dining at a small table beside the window. He looked at John in surprise, then alarm.

'What is this?' John demanded. 'Where is the Archdeacon?'

The fat man blinked. 'I am the Archdeacon.'

'Where is Heraclius?'

'He has been made Archbishop of Caesarea.'

John frowned. Heraclius an archbishop? So he, too, had been rewarded for his role in Amalric's death. John turned and stumbled from the room. He crossed the street and entered the hospital without a word to the guards at the door. The doctors looked at him with dismay. John strode to a table holding various medicines.

'Wait!' one of the doctors called. He was a beardless young man in a monk's cowl. 'You cannot—'

John glared at the doctor, and the monk backed away. John removed his filthy cloak and alb, and struggled out of his mail, pulling it off over his head. The flesh around the gash on his arm was angry and red. He took a bottle of pure alcohol from the table and poured some over the wound. He gritted his teeth at the stinging pain.

He looked to the doctor who had tried to stop him. 'Can you stitch this wound closed?'

'I can, but I think it best if—'

'Do it.'

The doctor hesitated for a moment and then retrieved a needle and thread. John stood with jaw clenched while the man stitched. 'Thank you.' John took a jar of sulphur paste from the table and smeared it over the wound. 'Now bandage it.'

'Yes, Father.'

The doctor was just finishing when William entered. 'John! What has happened to you? The Archdeacon told me you barged into his quarters looking like death itself. I see he was not exaggerating.'

'Reynald's men ambushed me during my return from Kerak.'

'You are certain it was his men?'

John nodded.

'Leave us,' William told the doctor. He lowered his voice so as not to be overheard. 'So Reynald killed Amalric?'

'No. They used him. Heraclius was involved, too. He poisoned the King, or he will know who did. I am going to Caesarea to speak with him.'

'I do not think that wise, John.'

'They must pay for what they have done, William. It is not just Amalric that I wish to avenge. The bastards tried to kill me.'

'Exactly. Our enemies are alert to you. You must be cautious.'

'So we do nothing?'

'We wait. Heraclius will come to Jerusalem eventually. We will deal with him then. In the meantime there is much to occupy us. Saladin has brought Syria and Egypt together. If the Saracens are united, the Kingdom cannot stand.'

'I do not believe Saladin means to make war with us. He wants peace.'

'Perhaps. But what happens when Saladin is gone? Our only hope for lasting peace is strength, John. We must drive the Saracens apart, convince Aleppo to turn against Saladin. Then we can face him from a position of strength.'

John frowned. 'We would do better to hope the peace with Saladin holds. The regent of Aleppo, Gumushtagin, is not a man to be trusted.'

'Raymond believes we have no choice, and I agree. I am leaving for Aleppo in order to negotiate. You will remain here to advise Raymond.' William placed a hand on John's shoulder. 'I know Saladin is your friend, John, but if we want peace then we must restore the balance of power. We must make war against Saladin.'

Chapter 19

Yusuf spurred his horse to a canter as Damascus came into sight. He had left Selim behind to gather the army and had ridden from Cairo with only one hundred men when he received Turan's news. Aleppo had betrayed him, signing alliances with Jerusalem and the ruler of Mosul, Saif ad-Din. When combined, the three armies would number nearly twenty thousand men. And they were coming for Damascus. Despite the danger, Yusuf was glad. Now, finally, he would be able to deal with Gumushtagin. He had been willing to let the eunuch live in peace so long as he served Al-Salih faithfully, but his ill-conceived alliances had made the boy a pawn in the hands of the Franks and Saif ad-Din. Sooner or later, Aleppo would be absorbed by one of those stronger powers. Yusuf would not let that happen.

Near the gate he rode past some two hundred Bedouin; reinforcements riding from the south to join the camp that sprawled along the Barada River. Yusuf spotted the standards of Al-Muqaddam and Al-Mashtub flying over two of the emir's luxurious pavilions, which stood amidst the ordered rows of mamluk tents. Interspersed amongst them were the dusty, goat-skin dwellings of the Bedouin. A dozen men had organized a game of polo on the sandy banks of the Barada. One struck the kura – a ball of willow root – with a loud crack. It hurtled over the ground, nearly hitting a fat mamluk cook who was headed to the river to fill two buckets. The mamluk began to curse the players and then stopped and knelt as Yusuf approached in his distinctive gold armour. The polo players bowed from their saddles. Yusuf nodded back.

He was almost at the Al-Saghir gate when Turan rode out to greet him. 'Ahlan wa-Sahlan, Yusuf! Thank Allah you have come so quickly. I received troubling news this morning from our spies in Aleppo.'

'We will talk in the palace,' Yusuf said and turned back to his men. 'Qaraqush, make camp alongside the river.'

'Yes, Malik.'

'That is not necessary,' Turan said. 'Your men are welcome in the palace.'

'The palace will make them soft. They will make camp here. After we talk, I will join them.'

'As you wish, Brother.'

Turan led the way to his study in the palace. 'When will Selim arrive with the Egyptian army?' he asked Yusuf.

'It will take time to gather and provision the men, but he should set out before month's end. He will be in Damascus before May is through.'

'We need every man he can bring. I have gathered nearly five thousand warriors, but I fear it will not be enough.' Turan retrieved a scrap of paper from his desk and handed it to Yusuf.

'*Saif ad-Din has arrived in Aleppo with seven thousand men,*' Yusuf read. '*He leaves tomorrow with the army of Aleppo at his side. He wished to march directly on Damascus, but Gumushtagin has insisted that they retake Homs and Hama first.*' The two cities had voluntarily turned themselves over to Yusuf the previous year. Their emirs had complained that Gumushtagin was a poor ruler who taxed them too much and did too little to protect their lands from the raids of the Franks and Bedouin. Yusuf had lowered taxes and sent Al-Mashtub to Homs with five hundred men and orders to secure the countryside.

'With Gumushtagin's men, Saif ad-Din has more than ten thousand warriors,' Turan said. 'If they attack Homs first, that will buy us time. We can wait for Selim to arrive with the army of Egypt. That will even the odds. We can weather any siege they bring against us.'

Yusuf's brow furrowed. Ever since Alexandria, he dreaded the prospect of being under siege. 'We will not stay in Damascus and wait for them. We would still be too few once Saif ad-Din joins forces with the Franks. And we will have lost Homs and Hama. I will not let that happen. We will attack now. I will leave tomorrow morning. You will stay to wait for Selim.'

'I should ride with you,' Turan protested. 'The men of Damascus are mine to command.'

Yusuf placed a hand on his brother's shoulder. 'I ride to fight a force twice the size of mine, Turan. If I am defeated, then I need you to lead the armies of Egypt to avenge me.'

Turan looked as if he were about to protest, but instead he nodded. 'At least wait until next week, when more Bedouin will have arrived.'

'There is no time to wait. We will ride now and trust in Allah.'

APRIL 1176: TELL AL–SULTAN

Yusuf held his arms over his head and arched his back. He had spent the previous two weeks in the saddle as his army criss-crossed Syria in search of the enemy, riding to Shaizar, then Kafartab, Maarat, Artah, Aleppo, Hama, and now back to Aleppo. It was like trying to catch smoke. Again and again they were told by passing Bedouin or local farmers that Saif ad-Din's army was just over the next ridge, but when they arrived they found nothing but cold cooking fires and fields littered with horse droppings. Saif ad-Din was avoiding them, biding his time until he could join forces with the Franks.

Yusuf winced at a pain in the small of his back. The days in the saddle were not as easy as they had been when he was younger. He placed one hand on his back, while with the other he shaded his eyes against the afternoon sun. He watched as his men watered their horses at the wells of Jibab al-Turkman, the last source of water until they reached Aleppo, fifteen miles distant. There were a dozen wells scattered over the quarter-mile stretch of broad plain and a mile to the west there was a low ridge. At each well a camel trudged slowly in a circle, powering a wheel that brought up brimming buckets and dumped them into a pipe, which could be redirected to send the water to different portions of the surrounding fields and orchards. Currently the water was pouring into long troughs, where the horses of Yusuf's army buried their muzzles and drank. Meanwhile the men sat in the shade, some sharpening their swords, others eating or sleeping. Only Yusuf's private guard stood ready. The five hundred mamluks of his khaskiya were still in the saddle. They had formed a protective square around the grove where he stood.

Yusuf spotted Qaraqush nearby, speaking with the sheikh of the tribes who farmed the fields of Jibab al-Turkman. The mamluk general finished talking and walked over to Yusuf. 'The sheikh says they saw a field of fire to the north last night.'

'Campfires?'

Qaraqush nodded. 'Saif ad-Din is close.'

Yusuf glanced at the shadows cast by the palms. They were slowly vanishing as the sun moved overhead. 'We will move on at noon. The horses can drink again once we reach Aleppo.'

Qaraqush began to walk away but froze, his eyes on the ridge to the north-west. Yusuf followed his gaze and saw the flash of sunlight off metal. There it was again, and again. An army was cresting the ridge, and Yusuf's men were spread out over the floor of the valley, in no position to fight.

'Have the men mount up, now!' Yusuf shouted to Qaraqush. 'We will withdraw—' he looked about and spotted a flat-topped mound near the horizon '—east. We will regroup at that hill. I will cover the retreat with my khaskiya.'

'But my lord—!' Qaraqush began. He was stopped with a hard stare from Yusuf. 'Yes, Malik.' The mamluk general strode away, yelling for the men to mount up and ride.

Yusuf called for his horse and then turned to Saqr. 'The khaskiya will come with me. We will ride west and form a rearguard.' Saqr's brow furrowed, but that was the extent of his disapproval. He began shouting orders to the men of Yusuf's private guard, and they quickly formed a column.

Yusuf swung into the saddle. Qaraqush was galloping from well to well, shouting and waving his sword. Men were running everywhere, getting in one another's way as they searched for their horses. The camels and mules of the baggage train were still being loaded. If they lost them, then the campaign would be over. They would have to return to Damascus to gather fresh supplies.

Yusuf looked to the ridge, which was now covered with thousands of warriors, their helmets glinting in the sunlight.

'What are they waiting for?' Saqr asked.

'Perhaps they were as surprised to see us as we were to see them. Inshallah, they will continue to wait.'

Yusuf led his personal guard through an orange grove and then across a field of brilliant green wheat that brushed his horse's chest. They reached the edge of the irrigated land, and the wheat gave way to hard, dry ground. 'We will hold here!' Yusuf shouted.

His men spread out in a line one hundred yards across and five rows deep. With so few men they had no chance of stopping a charge, but they could perhaps delay it long enough to give the rest of the army a chance to regroup. Yusuf took his curved bow from his saddle and strung it. He then tucked the bamboo shaft of his light spear under his right leg, where it would be ready when he needed it. On the ridge a single rider was galloping along the enemy lines, waving a sword above his head.

'They will come soon!' Yusuf shouted to his men. 'Arrows when they come in range, then spears. We will feint forward and then retreat!' Yusuf took his bow from his shoulder and nocked an arrow while his message was relayed down the line. His horse nickered and flicked its ears. It could sense his tension.

There was a loud cry from atop the ridge, then another, and then a wall of noise as ten thousand men shouted at once. A wave of riders poured down from the ridge. Yusuf picked out a target and stretched his bow taught. To either side he could hear the twang of bowstrings as his men began to shoot. Yusuf let out his breath and then released. His arrow joined dozens of others, all black against the blue sky. Before his arrow reached its apex Yusuf had already nocked another and let fly. He shot again and again as all around him his men's bowstrings sang. Dozens of enemy riders fell to be trampled by their comrades, but thousands more galloped on, closing rapidly. Yusuf slid his bow into his saddle and slipped his small, circular shield on to his left forearm. He looked back to the wells. His men were now all in the saddle, and the first of the camels were loaded and lumbering away.

Yusuf raised his voice. 'We must hold them until the army is safely away. Now, men! Make those sons of whores eat dust!'

He spurred forward and his men fell in behind him. They surged across the plain like a spear tip driving towards the centre of the oncoming army. The men in the enemy ranks were close enough now for Yusuf to make out their faces. He picked out an older man with a greying beard and then rose in the stirrups and hurled his spear. It caught the man in the chest, knocking him from the saddle. Yusuf drew his sword just before he reached the enemy line. An enemy warrior thrust a spear towards his chest, and Yusuf veered away and raised his shield. The spear glanced off of it, but the blow was enough to knock him back in the saddle. He straightened and lashed out at the next rider, catching him in the throat and filling the air with a spray of blood. There were enemy warriors all around now, and

Yusuf's horse slowed as it weaved between oncoming attackers. He deflected blows with his shield and hacked to the left and right, while his men followed close behind to finish off those he missed. Out of the corner of his eye, he could see the enemy flanks turning inward to encircle them. They had stood their ground long enough. 'Back, men!' he shouted. '*Retreat!*'

Yusuf reined in, and he and his men wheeled their horses as if one. His guard allowed him to ride to their centre, and then they dug in their spurs and galloped away across the hard ground. Yusuf could hear the thunder of hooves behind him as the enemy gave chase. Arrows soon began to fall around Yusuf and his men. One hit Saqr in the shoulder, but the mamluk rode on as if unaware, crouching above the saddle, his head forward beside his horse's neck.

They galloped back across the green fields around the wells and out on to the dusty plain beyond. In the distance Yusuf could see the mound where his army was gathering. Beneath him, his horse was beginning to labour, its breath coming in explosive bursts. Yusuf glanced over his shoulder. The enemy riders were so close they had begun hurling spears. One of his men was struck in the back and fell from the saddle. Yusuf flicked the reins. '*Yalla! Yalla!*' he cried, urging a last burst of speed from his tiring mount. Ahead, his men had formed a battle line before the mound. They drew back their bows and a cloud of arrows filled the sky, arcing over Yusuf and his men to fall amongst the enemy. Yusuf heard cries of pain. He looked back and saw that his pursuers were falling back.

He slowed his horse and trotted to the line. Qaraqush came out to meet him. 'Subhan'allah!' the grizzled mamluk said. 'You live.' He noticed the arrow protruding from Saqr's shoulder. 'Bring a doctor!'

Saqr waved away his concern. 'It barely penetrated the armour.'

Qaraqush turned back to Yusuf and handed him a waterskin.

'When you charged into their lines, I thought you were a dead man. But we needed the time you bought us.'

Yusuf rinsed the dust from his mouth and spat. 'Had they attacked sooner, they would have routed us.'

'We were lucky. Allah favours us.'

Yusuf looked back to where Saif ad-Din's army was occupying the wells and beginning to water their horses. He grinned. 'He does, Qaraqush. We have found them at last!'

Yusuf stared up at the star-strewn sky. He located the constellations Al-Hirba' and Al-A'sad: the Chameleon and the Lion. It had been a long time since he traced their shapes, but tonight he could not sleep. He had awoken with his heart racing after a particularly vivid dream. He could not remember its particulars, only that it had involved Asimat. It had been years since he saw her last. If he defeated Saif ad-Din's army tomorrow, then he would see her again soon, in Aleppo. If he lost, he might well never see her again. He would lose Damascus, and Cairo would be next.

A gentle breeze blew from the west, bringing with it the sound of a distant drum beating a rapid tattoo beneath the merry notes of a flute. He could see the enemy campfires from where his tent had been pitched atop the tall mound called Tell al-Sultan. His own camp was quiet, the campfires long since extinguished. Those who could manage sleep were in their tents. Others sat awake, sharpening their swords and checking their armour ahead of tomorrow's battle. Some, like Yusuf, stared up at the heavens and wondered if they would soon be joining their forefathers there, in paradise.

'Uncle?'

Yusuf turned to see Ubadah approaching. He was a man now, and Yusuf had given him lands and a new name: Taqi ad-Din, 'Strong of Faith'. He hoped it would remind his headstrong nephew of his duty. This was Ubadah's first campaign, and Yusuf had placed him in charge of over a thousand men.

He stopped beside Yusuf and looked out towards the enemy camp. Yusuf saw that he held a twig, which he rolled back and forth between his forefinger and thumb. The boy was nervous.

'I often have trouble sleeping before a battle,' Yusuf told him.

Ubadah nodded. 'My eagerness to fight has robbed me of my sleep,' he boasted. Then after a moment he asked in a quieter voice, 'How many men will we face?'

'More than ten thousand.'

'And we have only half so many.' Ubadah licked his lips nervously.

'Does the wolf run from the sheep, simply because he is outnumbered?'

'Sheep do not carry swords, Uncle.'

'Even if they did, they would still be sheep.' Yusuf clapped his nephew on the back. 'And we are wolves!'

Ubadah nodded, but he continued to roll the twig back and forth. Then he tossed it aside and turned to face his uncle. 'Why did you lead the rearguard today? You could have sent me.'

Yusuf smiled. His nephew was so eager to prove himself. He, too, had been like that once. 'There will be opportunity enough for you to win glory tomorrow. Today I had to act fast, and my khaskiya was ready to ride when the rest of the army was not.'

'But you could have died.'

'A good leader must be willing to risk his life for his men.' Yusuf placed a hand on his nephew's shoulder. 'Get some sleep, Ubadah. Tomorrow will be a long day.'

'Yes, Uncle.'

Ubadah walked away, and Yusuf returned to his tent. He eventually drifted into a restless sleep, only to be woken what seemed moments later by Saqr. 'It is nearly dawn,' the commander of Yusuf's khaskiya told him. Yusuf performed his prayers, and then Saqr helped him into his armour. He wore leather leggings and a padded vest, over which he pulled on a mail shirt that hung to just below his waist, and over that his suit of golden jawshan, which laced up at the side. Last of all, Saqr attached a mail collar that would protect Yusuf's neck and then handed him a pointed steel helmet with a crossbar that ran down before his nose. Saqr wrapped a piece of white cloth around the helmet to keep the sun from turning the metal into an oven.

Yusuf stepped outside into the grainy light of early dawn. He found Qaraqush, Al-Maqaddam and Ubadah waiting for him.

'A good morning, Malik,' Al-Maqaddam said.

'Did you hear their camp last night?' Qaraqush asked. 'Sounded like a tavern.'

'Let us hope they are feeling the effects of their merrymaking,' Yusuf said, and proceeded to give his instructions for the battle, keeping them short and simple. He had found that the more complex the plans a commander laid out, the more likely they were to go astray. 'We will form the battle line and march at sunrise. Taqi ad-Din, you will command the left, Al-Maqaddam the right. Qaraqush, you will be in the centre. I will keep my guard of five hundred men in reserve. We advance at the sound of my horn and charge at its second sounding. Once battle is joined, you must each hold the line. When I detect a weakness in their ranks, I will strike. At the trumpet's third blast, you will all advance together and drive them from the field. Understood?' The men nodded. 'Good. Allah yasalmak.'

The emirs left to organize their men. Yusuf stood outside his tent and breakfasted on a bowl of boiled wheat as he watched his men form the line: eight men deep and stretching across the plain for two ghalvas – over a quarter of a mile. The men busied themselves stringing their bows and checking their armour. In the distance the enemy line was forming on the plain east of the wells. The men and their horses were tiny at this distance. Yusuf turned to study the sky behind him. It was coloured soft pink and there was a bright spot on the horizon where the sun would soon rise. He handed his bowl to a servant and turned to Saqr. 'My horse.'

Yusuf rode down from the mound and through the ranks of

the reserve force. He nodded in greeting to those he knew well: Liaqat and Manzur, who had been young men when Yusuf first met them, and were now hardened warriors with streaks of grey in their long beards; Uwais, a deadly archer; and Nazam, the bald-headed warrior who Yusuf had fought once long ago upon his arrival at Tell Bashir.

Yusuf reached the front of the reserve force. Ahead, the line of the army stretched far to either side, the men's helmets glinting orange-red as the sun crept above the horizon behind them. It was time. Yusuf raised his voice and shouted, '*For Islam!*'

'*For Islam!*' the men behind him roared back, echoed by the mamluks all along the line.

Yusuf turned to Saqr. 'Signal the advance.'

Saqr held a curved ram's horn to his lips and blew. The piercing sound drowned out the nicker of horses and the jingle of tack. The front line rode ahead at a walk. Yusuf led the reserve force into the dust they kicked up. A series of horn blasts sounded from across the field, and through the dust ahead Yusuf could see that the enemy army was on the move. Those at the centre of their line wore mail and those at the edges were dressed in the leather or quilted armour favoured by the Bedouin. The horn sounded again, and the enemy line accelerated, their horses moving at a trot. The gap between the two lines was closing fast. A few men amongst the enemy let loose arrows, and the shafts shattered on the hard ground ahead of Yusuf's army.

'Signal the charge!' Yusuf called to Saqr, who immediately sounded the horn. The line spurred their mounts to a trot and then a canter, quickly pulling away from Yusuf's reserve force. The opposing army had continued to gain speed. The drumming of their horses' hooves sounded like thunder. They shot arrows as they rode, and Yusuf's men shot back, aiming directly into the line of advancing horsemen. Yusuf reined in and raised his bow to signal the men behind him to begin shooting. He nocked an arrow and aimed high, shooting over his men. His arrow joined dozens of others arcing towards the enemy line. He saw a man in the front ranks of the enemy fall from the saddle with an arrow in the gut. He was lost in the dust, trampled by the horses behind him. The armies raced closer and closer and then slammed together. It was difficult for Yusuf to make out what was happening in the deadly fighting that followed. There were screams of pain, terror and rage. Swords flashed in the light of the morning sun. A horse whinnied loudly. A spray of blood filled the air as one of Yusuf's men was nearly decapitated.

Gradually it became clear that Yusuf's men were falling back under the weight of the enemy's greater numbers. He could hear Qaraqush's deep voice raised over the din of the battle. 'Hold the line, men! Damn you, hold the line!' The enemy advance slowed and then stopped.

As Yusuf scanned the line of battle from right to left he quickly recognized Saif ad-Din's strategy. His army had thrown its greatest numbers against Yusuf's right flank, but Al-Muqaddam and the men of Damascus were holding. On the left, Ubadah faced what looked to be a weaker force. But Yusuf knew better than to charge there. Saif ad-Din had kept several thousand men in reserve, and already they were drifting that way. Saif ad-Din had shown his hand too early. He was hoping to lure Yusuf into a charge on the left. His men would retreat to draw Yusuf's mamluks after them, and then Saif ad-Din would send his men pouring in to cut them off. It was a classic strategy, of the sort one learned in books.

Yusuf turned towards the reserve force and raised his voice. 'We will strike the middle of their line and split their forces in two. Then we will turn left, striking their reserve force in the flank.' Saif ad-Din would find himself caught in his own trap, pinched between Yusuf and Ubadah's men.

Yusuf opened his mouth to signal the charge but the words died on his lips. Ubadah was leading the left flank forward. Saif ad-Din's men fled before them, and then, as Yusuf had foreseen,

335

the reserve force swept in, cutting Ubadah's men off from the rest of the army. The enemy warriors, who had been retreating only moments before, turned to fight. Ubadah's men were surrounded, and Yusuf's left flank was completely exposed.

'*Yaha!*' he cursed. 'The young fool!' He held his sword aloft and raised his voice. 'To the left, men! Follow me!' He spurred his horse to a gallop, and his men thundered after him. The left flank was only two hundred yards away, but it seemed to take an eternity to cover the distance. Ahead, some of Saif ad-Din's men had turned from Ubadah's forces and were striking the exposed flank of Yusuf's line. The centre began to give ground under the pressure. '*Yalla! Yalla!*' Yusuf cried, urging his horse to greater speed.

Saif ad-Din's men were just ahead now. One of them turned, and his eyes opened wide in shock just before the curved blade of Yusuf's sword caught him in the face. Yusuf galloped past without glancing back to see the man fall. He slashed another warrior across the back. Behind him, the rest of the reserve force was cutting through the enemy. Yusuf pushed on into a crowd of riders. He parried a thrust and countered, dropping a man. Out of the corner of his eye, he saw a sword slicing towards his face, but it was blocked at the last second by Saqr's blade. Yusuf chopped the man down. Suddenly something slammed into the back of his helmet, and he slumped in the saddle as the world dimmed around him. He jerked back to consciousness just in time to knock aside a thrust aimed at his heart. Saqr slashed the attacker across the face, and Yusuf turned his horse to face the man who had struck him from behind. But his attacker was dead, having been dispatched by one of his khaskiya. More of Saif ad-Din's men lay dead around him, and the rest were beginning to flee. The flank was secure, but Ubadah and his men were still surrounded and fighting an increasingly desperate battle.

'*Saqr!* Signal for the line to advance.' Saqr blew the horn, and Yusuf waved his sword over his head. '*For Islam!*'

'*For Saladin!*' his men shouted back.

The line surged forward, Yusuf and his men now on the left flank. They drove into the men surrounding Ubadah's force. The enemy now found themselves caught between Ubadah and Yusuf's men. They held for a moment and then panicked and fled, led by Saif ad-Din himself, his banner waving above him as he galloped from the field. Yusuf turned right to attack the centre of Saif ad-Din's line, but they too were in full retreat. Yusuf continued riding until he reached the end of the line, where Saif ad-Din had initially committed most of his men. They were still fighting, and Yusuf and his men encircled them from behind. A horn began to blow repeatedly, calling them from the field, but it was too late. Some two thousand of Saif ad-Din's men were surrounded, unable to retreat. They began to throw down their weapons and surrender.

Yusuf sheathed his sword and removed his helmet. There was a large dent on the back. Had the blow struck only a little lower, he would be dead.

'*Subhan'allah!*' Ubadah shouted as he rode up alongside Yusuf. 'We are victorious!'

'We were lucky,' Yusuf snapped. 'Your foolishness nearly lost us the battle.'

The grin fell from Ubadah's face. 'You said a leader must not be afraid to lead his men into battle.'

'I told you to hold the line! An emir must obey the commands of his lord. Hundreds of my men died because of you. Men with families.'

'I—'

Yusuf did not wish to hear the excuses. He turned his horse and rode away. He had no doubt that Ubadah was brave, but he feared it was a reckless bravery that would some day get him killed.

As he rode towards the deserted enemy camp, Qaraqush came up alongside him. 'A great victory, Malik!' The mamluk general grinned. 'Did you see them run?'

Yusuf could not bring himself to share Qaraqush's enthusiasm. He had a dull headache and felt nauseous. He touched the back of his head and found an egg-sized bump.

'Are you well, Malik?'

'Well enough,' Yusuf replied tersely. 'Move our camp to the wells and see that the horses are watered.'

'And the prisoners? We have captured hundreds.'

'Release them.' Yusuf noticed the look of surprise on Qaraqush's face. 'Harsh measures will only make them hate us all the more. Mercy will rob them of the desire to fight. It will make peace that much easier to achieve.'

'Yes, Malik.'

Qaraqush spurred away, and Yusuf rode on to the enemy camp. Some of his men were already there, searching through the tents and baggage that had been left behind. The booty would be distributed amongst Yusuf's men. He saw a mamluk laughing as he picked at a lute that he had found. Another man emerged from a tent, his long brown beard stained violet. 'Wine!' he roared and then fell silent as he noticed Yusuf.

'You saw how their army fought?' Yusuf demanded.

'Yes, Malik.'

'That is how men drunk on wine fight. See that it is poured out, all of it.'

The mamluk bowed and went into the tent. Yusuf watched while he rolled out a barrel and removed the stopper so that the wine poured out to stain the dry ground red. He looked up at the sound of a strange bird call. The mamluk Uwais was emerging from another tent with a cage that held two parrots. Another man followed with a cage containing nightingales.

'What do we do with these, Malik?' Uwais asked.

'Have them sent back to Saif ad-Din with this message: tell him to play with his birds and leave war to men.'

Chapter 20

John rode under a banner displaying Raymond's arms, a golden cross on a field of red. Before him, a long line of Frankish soldiers followed a path that wound its way along cliffs above the Mediterranean Sea. They had marched from Acre just over a week ago and had left Tripoli and Lattakieh behind. John rode at the centre of the column, along with Raymond, Humphrey and William. The regent rode up alongside John.

'We will reach Antioch the day after next,' Raymond said. 'After that we will head inland to rendezvous with the armies of Aleppo and Mosul. Then we will turn south to confront Saladin.'

John nodded but said nothing. Raymond searched his face for a moment. 'You know Saladin well, John. What sort of man is he?'

John thought for a while. 'When he was a boy, he suffered fits that robbed him of his breath and left him helpless. His father despised him and considered him unfit to be a warrior. His older brother Turan bullied him. Saladin was a skinny boy. He weighed maybe half as much as Turan. He bided his time and learned to fight. When Saladin was twelve and his brother sixteen, Saladin beat Turan to within an inch of his life. Turan never troubled him again.'

'A determined man.'

John nodded. 'When he was aged fourteen he was made

Emir of Tell Bashir. He arrived to find the men there still loyal to the previous emir, who had ordered them to turn the fortress over to the Seljuks. The money Saladin had brought to buy their loyalty had been stolen by bandits. Those same bandits nearly killed Saladin, leaving him with no horse and no men. He arrived at Tell Bashir penniless after a two-day trek through the desert. Within two weeks he had driven off the bandits and earned the loyalty of the men of Tell Bashir.' John met Raymond's eyes. 'Saladin is not the strongest of men, nor the bravest, nor even the wisest, but he has greater resolve than any man I have ever known.'

'And what are his weaknesses?'

John's forehead creased in thought. 'Saladin is a religious man. He does not drink, and he has no interest in games of chance.' John paused. He thought of Yusuf's affair with Asimat and then of the night that Yusuf had spared him, despite John's relationship with his sister. 'But he is perhaps too loyal to his friends. And he has been made a fool by love.'

'As have we all.'

They rode on in silence while the waves crashed against the rocky shore below and the seagulls shrieked and wheeled over-head. Ahead, the road led down to a broad coastal plain, where sandy beaches gave way to emerald-green fields. Even after all these years John found himself surprised by the beauty of the Holy Land. If only it were not riven by war, it could be a para-dise; a kingdom of heaven on earth, as a preacher in England had once described it to him.

John spotted half a dozen riders approaching on the plain. They paused briefly when they reached the front of the army. Then they moved on at a gallop. They pulled up just short of John and Raymond. John blinked in surprise as the lead rider brushed the dust of the road from his face.

'Bohemond!' Raymond exclaimed. 'What are you doing here?'

Bohemond, the prince of Antioch, was supposed to have

waited to meet them there. He was breathing heavily after his ride, and it took him a moment to gather himself. 'I bring evil news,' he said at last between deep breaths. 'The armies of Aleppo and Mosul have been crushed. Aleppo will surely fall soon. Saladin is master of Syria.'

'Are you certain?' Raymond asked. 'They outnumbered Saladin's army nearly two to one.'

'I received the news from one of Saif ad-Din's emirs, who was separated from the army and fled to my lands. The Bedouin and caravans from Aleppo support his account. No allies will be waiting for us in Artah. If we wish to face Saladin, we will do it alone.'

Raymond looked to William.

'If we engage Saladin, we might prevent him from taking Aleppo, but if we lose . . .'

Raymond's brow knit. William did not need to tell him what would happen. If they were defeated, the entire Kingdom would be laid bare before Saladin's armies. The regent looked to John. 'Can Saladin be trusted? If we make peace, will he keep it?'

John nodded. 'He will honour any agreement he makes.'

'Very well. You and William will go to him and sue for peace.'

'Peace will be hard to come by,' William warned. 'Saladin has the upper hand. He will want to press his advantage.'

'Perhaps, but he will also need time to consolidate his gains. He will accept peace with us so that he can turn his attentions to Aleppo.'

The constable Humphrey frowned. 'And after that, he will move on us. He controls Egypt and Syria. We are in a vice. He will crush us, sooner or later.'

John shook his head. 'Saladin does not hate us the way that Nur ad-Din did. I believe a lasting peace is possible.'

'We will pray that is so,' Raymond said. 'In the meantime, I will take the army back to Jerusalem and prepare for the worst.'

John stopped his mount in the shade of a pistachio tree atop a steep hill. In the distance stood the white walls of Aleppo. The city was surrounded by Yusuf's army. Their tents stretched to within half a mile of where John now sat.

William reined in beside John and whistled in appreciation as he caught sight of the Saracen camp. 'A mighty force. How many men do you think Saladin has?'

'Fifteen thousand, at least. He must have received reinforcements from Cairo.'

'Such a force might take Jerusalem. We must not fail, John.'

William led the way down the far side of the hill. John followed, and their escort of twelve knights trailed after him. They were still some distance from the enemy camp when fifty mamluks rode out to meet them. William called for their escort to halt. 'Raise the white flag,' he told John.

They waited while the Saracens galloped up and formed a ring around them. The mamluks rode with bows in hand. If they decided to attack, then it would be a short fight. One of them rode forward from the ranks. It was John's son, Ubadah.

'What is your business here?' Ubadah demanded.

'As-salaamu 'alaykum,' William replied. He continued in Arabic. 'We come at King Baldwin's bidding to speak with your lord, Saladin.'

Ubadah fingered the hilt of his sword. 'You have trespassed on Muslim lands.'

'We are peaceful emissaries. Our past treaties with your lord, and with Nur ad-Din before him, give us permission to cross his lands in order to conduct negotiations.'

'Saladin is leading an army. He has no time for negotiations with Frankish dogs.'

'Nevertheless,' John said, 'perhaps you would do us the honour of informing him of our presence, Ubadah ibn Khaldun.'

Ubadah's eyes widened in surprise at having been recognized, then narrowed as he examined John more closely. 'I am called Taqi ad-Din now, John. Who is your companion?'

'William of Tyre. We are happy to wait here until Saladin decides if he will see us.'

'That will not be necessary.' Ubadah turned to one of his men. 'Take the knights to camp and see that they are fed and their horses watered.' He looked back to John and William. 'You come with me.'

Ubadah led them into camp. John knew that Yusuf's army had arrived outside the city nearly two months previously, having driven Saif ad-Din east across the Euphrates. But Yusuf's men seemed to have made little progress. The walls of Aleppo showed no sign of damage from catapults or mangonels. Mamluks lounged about, talking or playing games of chance.

John followed Ubadah to the top of a ridge that overlooked the city. Yusuf's enormous tent had been pitched there. Ubadah led them into a smaller tent in its shade. 'Wait here.'

'A most unpleasant young man,' William muttered when Ubadah had gone. 'You know him?'

John nodded.

'Thank God for that. I thought for a moment he was going to order his men to kill us.' William removed his cloak and shook the dust from it, then laid it on the ground and knelt. 'Let us pray for the success of our negotiations.'

John knelt beside him, and they bowed their heads. When Ubadah returned, he frowned to see them praying. 'The Malik will see you now,' he said. He led them to Yusuf's tent and motioned them inside.

Yusuf sat on a campstool. He was dressed in spectacular golden armour and flanked on his right by Qaraqush, Al-Mashtub and Al-Muqqadam. Ubadah joined them. John recognized Imad ad-Din amongst the scribes who stood to Yusuf's left. Yusuf studied John for a moment, but showed no sign of recognition. John and William approached and bowed.

'Ahlan wa-Sahlan,' Yusuf told them. Then he added in French, 'God grant you joy and health.'

'And may he grant you the same,' William replied in Arabic. 'We are honoured to be allowed into your presence, great King. Thank you for seeing us.'

'And what is it that you want?' Yusuf asked.

'Peace between our great kingdoms.'

'Peace?' Ubadah scoffed. 'The eagle does not make peace with the hare.'

Yusuf gestured for him to be silent. 'I am a man of peace, William, but I fear the regent Raymond is not. Did he not sign a treaty with my enemy Gumushtagin? Did he not gather an army to fight against me?'

'But he did not fight you, Malik. And that army has been disbanded.'

'And what of the treaty with Gumushtagin? The friend of my enemy is my enemy.'

'Jerusalem is no friend to Gumushtagin. Our treaty was with Al-Salih, the rightful ruler of Aleppo.'

'It was a treaty negotiated by Gumushtagin,' Yusuf insisted, 'a treaty that called for a joint attack on my lands.'

'We wish no harm to your kingdom,' William assured him. 'We have come to make peace.'

'Do not trust them, Malik,' Al-Maqaddam interjected. 'They have turned their back on the treaty they made with Gumushtagin. How are we to know they will not do the same to any treaty they sign with us?'

Yusuf raised his eyebrows. 'A fair question.'

'Raymond never breaks his word,' William insisted. 'As you know, our treaty with Al-Salih called for us to join forces with the armies of Aleppo and Mosul. Those armies were destroyed at Tell al-Sultan. We cannot join with armies that do not exist.'

A smile played at the corner of Yusuf's mouth. 'A clever answer, William.'

The priest bowed.

'It does not matter,' Ubadah insisted. 'We have no reason to make peace. Why negotiate with Jerusalem when we could take it?'

'I think you will find that Jerusalem is not an easy prize,' William countered. 'Our armies are strong, as are the walls of Jerusalem and our other cities. And we have the support of the Roman Emperor in Constantinople.'

Qaraqush snorted. 'Then why have you come begging for peace?'

'Because peace benefits both our peoples.' William looked to Yusuf. 'I am not concerned with battles and glory but with the lives of my flock, just as you, Saladin, are concerned with the lives of your people. War will only bring them death and suffering. Peace will let them prosper.'

Ubadah shook his head. 'There can be no peace until your kind are driven from our lands.'

Yusuf raised his hand. 'Enough, Ubadah. You must respect our guests.'

'He is right, Malik,' Al-Muqaddam said. 'We should strike while we have the advantage.'

The other emirs nodded their agreement. Yusuf rubbed his beard and opened his mouth to speak, but John spoke first. 'May I speak with you in private, Malik?' He met Yusuf's eyes. 'Please, friend.'

Yusuf nodded. 'Leave us.'

John waited until the men had filed out. 'Make peace, Yusuf.'

'My men are against it.'

'They are men of war. That is all they know.'

'And they know it well, John. Qaraqush believes we can defeat the Kingdom.'

'At what cost? Remember when we spoke of peace after Alexandria? It is possible at last. You are lord of Syria and Egypt. You have no reason to fear the Kingdom, and we would be fools to attack you.' John waited, but Yusuf said nothing. 'Make peace,' John urged again. 'I do not wish to fight you, Brother.'

'Has it come to that, John?' Yusuf sounded tired. 'I am forced to besiege my son. Must I also do combat with my closest friend? Will you, too, take arms against me?'

'Not against you. For Baldwin. He is my king. If you invade the Kingdom, I will fight to defend him.'

'I see.' Yusuf rested his chin on his hand. He sighed. 'To tell the truth, I grow tired of war, John. I miss my family. And I have no desire to fight you or your king. I fear such a war would only destroy us both. I will give you your peace, but only for five years. More, I cannot do. The war against the ifranj has cost my people thousands of lives and countless pieces of gold, but it is a necessary evil. Nur ad-Din taught me this: it is only the desire to drive out the Franks that bound his kingdom together. Now that same force binds my kingdom. Peace and prosperity can create new bonds, but it will take time.'

'I understand. Five years is a good start. Thank you, Brother.'

'The men grow tired of waiting, Malik,' Qaraqush said.

Yusuf nodded but did not reply. They stood on the ridge outside his tent and looked towards Aleppo. Summer had brought a stifling heat that rose from the ground and caused the city to shift and waver like a mirage. The siege had lasted for more than two months now – two months with no fresh supplies – and yet the people still held out.

'We should attack, Malik,' Qaraqush urged again. 'Gumushtagin lost much of his army at Tell al-Sultan. With the reinforcements from Egypt, we have enough men to take the city by storm.'

Yusuf shook his head. 'I have not come here to cross swords with Al-Salih's men.'

'The men will not be content to roast under the hot summer sun forever, Malik.'

'It shall not be forever, friend. Aleppo must already be running short on supplies. Eventually the people will turn on Gumushtagin.'

Qaraqush frowned. 'Yes, Malik.'

'In the meantime, send men to capture the fortresses north and east of Aleppo: Manjib, Buza'a and Azaz. That will keep the men occupied.'

'Yes, Malik,' Qaraqush repeated in a brighter tone.

Yusuf returned to his tent. Imad ad-Din was waiting inside with an armful of papers. 'Correspondence from Damascus and Cairo, Malik.'

'Can it wait?

'Yes.'

'Good.' Yusuf passed through the curtain that led to his bedchamber. He unbuckled the belt that held his sword and dagger and tossed it aside. He removed his helmet and untied his vest of golden armour. He pulled his mail coat over his head and removed his sweat-soaked padded vest last of all. He sighed in relief. 'Water,' he called as he pulled on his mail-lined tunic and donned his mail cap and keffiyeh. Yusuf frowned. Where were his servants? He took a seat amongst the cushions on the floor and raised his voice. '*Water*!'

A servant entered carrying a tray with a pitcher of water and a glass. He froze after passing through the curtain. 'Bring it here,' Yusuf commanded. As the servant stepped towards him, Yusuf heard the distinctive chink of mail armour. '*Hashashin*!' he shouted. '*Guards*!'

The Hashashin threw the tray aside and brandished a knife. 'In the name of the Prophet!' he roared.

Yusuf started to scramble to his feet, but the Hashashin kicked him in the chest, knocking him sprawling on his back. Yusuf reached for his sword belt, but the Hashashin stepped on his arm and then knelt and brought his knife down towards Yusuf's chest. Yusuf raised a forearm and managed to deflect the Hashashin's arm, but the knife continued downward, towards his face. Yusuf jerked his head sideways just before the blade struck him on the side of the head.

'*Yaha*!' the Hashashin cursed. The mail cap beneath Yusuf's keffiyeh had saved his life. The Hashashin was raising his dagger to strike again when Saqr tackled him from behind. Saqr grabbed him by the hair and slammed his face into the carpeted ground and then drew a dagger and slit the Hashashin's throat.

'Are you injured, Malik?' Saqr asked.

Yusuf sat up gingerly. He winced as he touched the side of his head where the dagger had struck. A painful bruise was already forming, but there was no blood. 'I live. Alhamdulillah.'

Saqr bowed his head. 'I was not here, Malik. I failed you.'

'You saved my life. Where are the guards who were supposed to guard my tent?'

'They are dead.'

'Surely this one man did not kill all of them. We must find the other Hashashin before they flee.' Yusuf rose and strode from the tent. The five men who had guarded the entrance lay dead. There was no one else in sight. '*Guards!*' he shouted. 'Damn them! Where are they? Saqr, I—'

Someone slammed into Yusuf from behind, knocking him down and landing on top of him. He felt a blade dig into his back, but it was stopped by the mail lining that reinforced his tunic. The blade struck again, and this time Yusuf felt a sharp pain as the tip penetrated the mail and dug into his back. He managed to roll over and found himself staring up at one of the Hashashin. Looking past his attacker, Yusuf could see Saqr engaged with another man. The Hashashin straddling Yusuf stabbed down again, but this time Yusuf caught his arm. With his free hand the man drew another knife from his belt and was preparing to attack when an arrow lodged in his neck. He fell to the side, blood gurgling in his throat. Yusuf looked up to see Ubadah running towards him, bow in hand.

Yusuf took one of the dead Hashashin's daggers and rose to his feet to help Saqr. The Hashashin he was facing backed away. 'You will learn nothing from me,' he spat. 'Your days are numbered, Saladin!' The man raised his dagger high.

'Do not let him kill himself!' Yusuf shouted. The Hashashin

began to bring the blade arcing down towards his gut when an arrow sank into his shoulder. He dropped the knife and Saqr tackled him. He knelt on the Hashashin's chest and pressed his hand to the man's throat, pinning him to the ground.

'I heard you call, Uncle,' Ubadah said breathlessly. He looked at the bodies of the dead guards. 'What happened?'

'Hashashin.' Yusuf knelt beside the man that Saqr held. 'Who sent you? Gumushtagin?' The Hashashin spat at Yusuf, who wiped the spittle away and turned to Ubadah. 'Find Al-Mashtub. Tell him I have a prisoner, and I need answers.'

By the time Al-Mashtub arrived carrying a small trunk, the Hashashin had been taken inside Yusuf's tent and tied down to a table so that he could not move. Al-Mashtub set the trunk down beside the table and drew a knife from his belt.

'I am not afraid,' the Hashashin said. He was a young man with a sparse black beard and a prominent nose. 'I will tell you nothing.'

Al-Mashtub's only reply was to begin cutting through the man's tunic with his knife. He pulled the fabric aside to reveal the mail shirt beneath. He then lifted the bottom of the shirt, exposing the Hashashin's stomach. He opened the trunk and took out a small cage holding a dirty grey rat and then a bronze pot with a wide opening that narrowed to a thin neck before widening again to a broad base. He set the pot on the table and then opened the cage and grabbed the rat by the tail. The Hashashin's eyes widened as Al-Mashtub dangled the rat over the table and then dropped it into the pot. 'What are you doing?'

'I suggest you talk,' Al-Mashtub replied.

'Who sent you?' Yusuf demanded. 'Who paid to have me killed?'

The Hashashin shook his head, refusing to talk. Al-Mashtub lifted the pot with both hands and then quickly upended it, placed the opening on the Hashashin's exposed stomach. He turned to Ubadah. 'Hold it there.'

Yusuf could hear the claws of the rat scrabbling against the inside of the bronze pot. Sweat was beginning to bead on the Hashashin's forehead, and his eyes were wide. 'Who sent you?' Yusuf asked again, but still the man refused to speak.

Al-Mashtub took a shallow dish from the chest. The bottom of the dish had a lip that fitted over the base of the upturned pot. Next the mamluk took out a tinderbox and removed a scrap of char paper, which he placed in the bottom of the dish. He held up a piece of flint and the fire steel on which he would strike it. Al-Mashtub met the Hashashin's eyes. 'Do you know what will happen once I light this fire? The pot will grow hotter and hotter, cooking the rat inside alive. There is only one way for it to escape. It will burrow down, through your gut.'

The Hashashin was trembling in fear, but he clenched his jaw shut and said nothing.

Al-Mashtub struck the flint against the steel. A few sparks landed on the char paper. They smoked for a moment, but the fire did not take. He prepared to strike again. The sound of the rat scratching against the inside of the pot was louder now.

'*Gumushtagin!*' the Hashashin cried out.

'I knew it,' Yusuf said. 'I will have his head.'

'That will not stop us,' the Hashashin said. 'Gumushtagin only paid us for what we would have done regardless. My lord Rashid ad-Din Sinan has sworn that you will die.'

'The Old Man of the Mountain,' Ubadah whispered.

Yusuf had heard of Sinan, of course. He ruled over sixty thousand fanatically faithful Hashashin from his mountain stronghold in Masyaf, some twenty-five miles west of Hama. 'I am no enemy of Sinan's,' Yusuf said. 'Why does he want me dead?'

'You are Sunni.' The Hashashin spat. 'You ended the Fatimid Caliphate. You had the Caliph poisoned.' Ubadah's eyes widened at this.

'How do you know that?' Yusuf asked.

'Nothing you do escapes Sinan. He has men everywhere.'

'In my camp?' The man nodded. 'If you name them, I will let you live.'

'Never!'

'I thought not. Al-Mashtub, see that he does not suffer.'

The mamluk slit the Hashashin's throat with a single stroke. Yusuf left the tent and Ubadah followed. 'You heard what he said, Uncle. There are more Hashashin in our camp. And it is said that when Sinan orders a man dead, his men will not stop until that man lies in the grave.'

'They will stop when they are dead, every last one of them,' Yusuf replied. 'It is time this siege ended. Once I am finished with Aleppo, we will march on Masyaf.'

The towers that framed Aleppo's Qinnarin Gate loomed high above Yusuf and his private guard as they rode into their shadow. Yusuf had been happy to slowly starve the city into submission, hoping to spare his future people bloodshed. But now he did not wish to sit in his tent for another two months, a target for the Hashashin. He had decided to speak to the people of Aleppo himself. He could see men atop the gate, some in caftans, others in mail. There were even a few veiled women. Yusuf reined in his horse only fifty feet from the wall, close enough that the people could hear him but far enough that his armour would stop any arrows, should one of the soldiers dare to shoot.

'People of Aleppo!' he shouted. 'I come to you as a friend. You see my army all around your walls, but they are not here to fight you. I have not come to conquer Aleppo.' He paused to let the words take effect. He and Imad ad-Din had worked on this speech late into the previous night, and it was carefully crafted, pauses and all. 'I am a loyal servant of Al-Salih, as are my men. I do not wish to take his kingdom, or to take Aleppo from him. I only wish to see the city flourish as it did under Nur ad-Din. I wish to see it safe from any who would take it from its rightful lord. But I cannot protect Al-Salih while his regent is sending Hashashin to murder me, while he is calling on the armies of Mosul and Jerusalem, inviting them into Al-Salih's kingdom in order to fight me. These are not the acts of a man loyal to Al-Salih. These are the acts of a man who serves only himself.'

Yusuf paused again. The people were listening quietly. That was a good sign. He took a deep breath and continued. 'I lived in Aleppo for many years while I served at the court of Nur ad-Din. I consider it my home, and I do not wish to destroy its walls or harm its people. I ask for only one thing: Gumushtagin. Deliver him to me, and there will be peace between us. But if you stand with him, then you stand against me. If you do not send him to me, then I will attack in earnest. You have until sunset tomorrow to decide.'

Yusuf rode back to his tent, where his advisers waited for him. Al-Maqaddam spoke first. 'Do you think they will surrender Gumushtagin?'

'Inshallah,' Yusuf said. 'But we must be prepared for them to resist. Qaraqush, you will be in charge of sapping the walls. Al-Maqaddam, you will build the mangonels. Ubadah, you will lead an attack tomorrow night. We will see if the people of Aleppo are willing to die for Gumushtagin.'

Saqr entered the tent. 'Malik, a messenger has come from the city.'

'So soon,' Al-Maqaddam responded.

'A good sign. Show him here,' Yusuf ordered.

'*Her*, Malik,' Saqr corrected. 'The messenger is a woman.'

A moment later, Saqr held the tent flap aside for a veiled woman who wore a violet silk caftan trimmed with silver. Her long chestnut hair flowed down her back from beneath a niqab that covered all but her eyes. Yusuf felt a burning in his stomach as he met those dark eyes.

'The lady Asimat,' Saqr declared. 'Mother of Al-Salih.'

'Leave us,' Yusuf said to his men.

When the men had filed out, Asimat removed her veil. Her

skin was still milky white and smooth, her face long and thin with a small nose and full lips. She had a fragile beauty, but Yusuf knew that she had a will of steel. When they had been lovers, she had been willing to betray her husband Nur ad-Din to put Yusuf on the throne. He had refused and put an end to their relationship. Asimat had not understood. She had scorned him for what she saw as weakness.

'It has been a long time, Yusuf,' she said.

Yusuf ignored her use of his informal name. He did not want these negotiations to become personal. 'You have come to negotiate on behalf of Gumushtagin?'

'On behalf of Al-Salih.'

'You know my terms. I want Gumushtagin delivered to me, and a treaty between Aleppo and Damascus. If either is attacked, the other will come to its defence.'

Asimat seemed to be considering his proposal, but when she spoke her response surprised him. 'I said once that you were too honourable to be great. I was wrong.'

'I am a man of honour,' he said stiffly.

'Is that why you have led your army against Aleppo, against your lord Al-Salih?'

'I move against Gumushtagin, not Al-Salih.'

Asimat dismissed his protest with a wave of her hand. 'Gumushtagin is nothing. The palace guard seized him this afternoon, just after your speech. Al-Salih rules in Aleppo now.'

'Alhamdulillah. I rejoice to hear it.'

'Do you? I understand the Caliph in Baghdad has invested you with the government of all Syria.'

'As regent for Al-Salih. I will not make war against our son.'

'He is hardly your son,' she snapped. 'He has known no father but Nur ad-Din.'

That blow hurt, but Yusuf did not let it show. 'Nevertheless, I will not move against him. Everything I have done has been to secure his kingdom. What do you suppose would have happened had I not defeated Saif ad-Din? Do you think he would have allowed Al-Salih to keep Aleppo?'

Asimat did not reply. She walked to the table at the centre of the tent and poured herself a cup of water. She sipped at it. Then she sat down amidst the silk cushions on the thickly carpeted ground. She met his eyes. 'You do not care for my son, Yusuf. Do not lie and tell me otherwise.'

Yusuf sat across from her. 'I have told you. What I have done, I have done for him.'

'No. Surely you knew what would happen when you refused to fight Nur ad-Din. Gumushtagin revealed our secret to him. You would have let our son die!'

'I was willing to die, too.'

She looked at him coldly. 'I was not. It was I who had Nur ad-Din killed.' Yusuf recoiled at this. 'Do not look at me like that. I loved Nur ad-Din. It is you who are responsible for his death, not I.'

'I was prepared to let him kill me,' he repeated.

'Your life is your own to give,' she hissed, 'but not mine, and not that of our son!' She took a deep breath and looked away, collecting herself. When she spoke again, her voice was quiet. 'The night that Nur ad-Din learned of our affair, he beat me. He promised to have me stoned, but not before he brought me your head on a plate. And he swore that Al-Salih would be tortured and crucified.' She looked to Yusuf, her dark eyes burning with rage and sadness. He looked away. He did not know what to say. 'So do not dare tell me that you are loyal to Al-Salih! And do not speak to me of your honour. What sort of honour is it that sacrifices the lives of women and children?'

Her dark eyes dug into him as she waited for him to speak. 'What do you want of me, Asimat?' he asked.

'Our son Al-Salih will remain the ruler of Aleppo. In addition, he will have Azaz and the other towns near Aleppo.'

'It will be done.'

'That is not enough. You will marry me and officially adopt

354

Al-Salih as your son.' Yusuf blinked in surprise. 'Your word is not enough for me, Yusuf, not anymore. Al-Salih must be your son. That is the only way he will be safe.'

Yusuf studied her as he considered her proposal. She was still beautiful, shockingly so. 'There was a time when I would have given anything to marry you,' he said softly. 'Allah works in strange ways.'

'Do you accept?'

'Yes. Once Gumushtagin is delivered to my camp in irons, I will marry you.'

Yusuf stood across from Asimat on the grassy field at the centre of the citadel in Aleppo. They were both dressed in white. During the previous day's henna ceremony, twisting patterns in dark brown had been traced on the little finger of Yusuf's right hand. Asimat's hands and feet had been decorated and her dark eyes – the only part of her face not covered by her veil – were outlined with kohl. Imad ad-Din stood between them. He was giving the marriage *khutba*, a brief sermon rejoicing at the marriage and calling Allah's blessing on the bride and groom. The hundreds of guests waited patiently, the leading emirs of Aleppo mingling with the commanders of Yusuf's army. Al-Salih stood in the front ranks of the crowd. He was dressed in luxurious robes of silk and gold and his sparse adolescent beard had been filled out with kohl. Shamsa stood with the veiled women. She had arrived the previous day, along with Yusuf's sons.

Shamsa and Asimat both had wills of iron, and Yusuf had feared that sparks would fly when they met. But Shamsa had surprised him. When she arrived she asked to meet Asimat alone. They spent the night in a locked and guarded room. The next morning Shamsa had told him that she approved of the marriage. 'Asimat does not love you,' she had informed him, 'and she wants no sons by you. She is no threat to me. And she is clever. She will make an excellent wife.'

'I call on all of you to witness this marriage,' Imad ad-Din declared as he finished the khutba. He turned to Yusuf. 'Saladin Yusuf ibn Ayub, King of Syria and Egypt, will you take this woman, Asimat bint Mu'in ad-Din Unur?'

'I will.' Yusuf stepped to a table that sat between him and Asimat and signed the marriage contract. It specified the *mahr*, or bride gift – fifty thousand dinar and the towns of Menbij and Bizaa – and it officially declared Al-Salih to be Yusuf's adopted son.

Imad ad-Din turned to Asimat. 'Will you accept this man, Saladin?'

'I will,' she said loudly. She too signed the marriage contract.

'May Allah bless your union,' Imad ad-Din declared.

The crowd roared its approval. Yusuf went to Al-Salih first and kissed the boy on both cheeks. 'I am your father now,' he said, 'but you remain my lord.' He knelt before Al-Salih.

The boy's face twisted into a scowl. He turned his back on Yusuf and walked away. Yusuf rose. He could understand Al-Salih's anger. To him, Yusuf was a stranger and a rival. It was bad enough that he had been forced to sign a treaty with him; it was a further insult that Yusuf had married his mother. The boy no doubt hated him. Yusuf hoped that would change in time.

It was time for the marriage feast. The men would meet in the great hall of the palace, while the women would celebrate with food and dance in the harem. But first there was one more task. Yusuf turned to Qaraqush. 'Bring him.'

Qaraqush nodded to a mamluk, who hurried away. A moment later the crowd parted as Gumushtagin was pulled forward, shackles around his wrists and neck. He had been brought to Yusuf's camp shortly after the meeting with Asimat, but Yusuf had refused to see him. He had entered Aleppo and ordered Gumushtagin thrown in the palace dungeon. After four weeks Gumushtagin looked a broken man, walking with his head down and his shoulders stooped. He was pushed forward to stand before Yusuf.

'I swore that I would kill you if we ever met again,' Yusuf told him. 'I am a man of my word.' He took the sword that Qaraqush handed him. The guards pulled on the chain that led from Gumushtagin's neck, forcing him to kneel.

The eunuch straightened, and a trace of his old arrogance returned as he met Yusuf's eyes. 'The Hashashin never fail. You can kill me, but you will join me soon enough. I will—'

Gumushtagin's eyes widened as Yusuf drove the point of his sword into his gut. The eunuch fell forward on to his hands and knees, moaning in pain and spitting blood. Yusuf raised his sword and brought it down on the back of Gumushtagin's neck. He wiped the blade on the eunuch's tunic and handed it back to Qaraqush. Then he raised his voice to address the crowd. 'Come. We have much to celebrate.'

Chapter 21

A fat bee buzzed through the air and landed on the sleeve of John's tunic. Its antennae wavered and then it flew off, back towards the herbs and flowers at the centre of the small cloister of the Church of the Holy Sepulchre. In the belfry tower on the far side of the church the bells began to toll, calling the faithful to Sunday Morning Mass. John stepped back into the deep shadows of the colonnade that surrounded the cloister. The stone was cold beneath his bare feet.

A vicar on his way to the sanctuary entered the cloister and passed John without noticing him. Two canons followed. John's stomach tensed and he tightened his grip on the dagger in his hand. He was waiting for Heraclius. William had forbidden John to go to Caesarea, but now Heraclius had come to him. The archbishop was in town, staying in the patriarch's palace. He would pass through the cloister on his way to Mass.

John heard the approach of booted feet. Four knights of the Holy Sepulchre stepped into the cloister, trailed by the patriarch and Heraclius. John let them pass and then followed, moving silently on his bare feet. He need not have taken the precaution of removing his sandals, for the bells were still ringing, their tolling drowning out all other sound. He crept after Heraclius into a shadowy hallway. On the right-hand wall was a narrow staircase; the night stair, which gave the canons easy access to the sanctuary for late night prayers. The guards marched up the stair in single file, followed by the patriarch. Heraclius had just put a foot on the bottom stair when John grabbed him from behind, clamped a hand over his mouth and slammed the butt of his dagger into Heraclius's temple. The archbishop went limp, and John slung him over his shoulder and carried him from the room.

He hurried as he crossed the paved courtyard of the central cloister and slipped into the canon's dormitory. He passed the vicars' beds – pallets of straw, separated by wooden screens – and took a narrow staircase down to a long underground hallway with rooms opening off on either side. He stepped into a small square chamber, the only furniture a trunk and a chair lit by light filtering through a window high on the far wall. John placed Heraclius in the chair. He shut the door and then took rope from the trunk and tied Heraclius down at the wrists and ankles. John retrieved a bucket of water from the corner of the room and poured it on the archbishop's head.

'*Strewth*!' Heraclius spluttered as he started awake. He looked about at the bare-walled room, then to John. 'John? Where am I?' He tried to rise, only to find that he was tied down. 'Release me at once!'

John turned his back on Heraclius and went to the chest. He rooted about inside, pulling out a series of horrifying torture implements – knotted whips, spikes, hooks – before tossing them back in the chest.

'Do you hear me?' Heraclius screamed. 'Release me! *Guards*! *Guards*! *Help*!'

'No one will hear you,' John told him. 'They are all at Mass.' He found what he was looking for: a pear of anguish. He took the device out and turned to face Heraclius.

The archbishop blanched. 'What are you doing?' There was panic in his voice. 'If you dare touch me, I'll have you burned. Release me at once. Release me!'

'I have a few questions first.'

'Who are you to question me?' Heraclius demanded, but his voice shook. 'I am an archbishop. I answer only to the Patriarch and to God.'

John brought the pear closer. He had taken the wicked device from the palace dungeon. It was the same one the priest had once used on him. 'You will answer to me, Heraclius. I am sure of it. If you answer truthfully, you shall go free. If not—' John twisted the wing nut on top of the pear so that it expanded slightly. 'Did you kill King Amalric?'

'That is preposterous!'

'Reynald told me that he killed the poison dealer Jalal at your bidding. The poison Jalal prepared was used to murder Amalric. The King was not dead a year before you were made archbishop of Caesarea.' John leaned close, so that his face was only inches from Heraclius's. 'It all points to you as the murderer.'

'I do not know what you are talking about.'

'Wrong answer.'

John grabbed Heraclius's chin and tried to force his mouth open, but the archbishop clenched his jaw shut. John pinched his nose closed. Heraclius's face shaded red, and finally he opened his mouth to breath. John tried to shove the pear inside, but failed as Heraclius jerked his head to the side. John dropped the pear and drew his dagger. He held it close to Heraclius's face. The archbishop went still.

'If you continue to struggle, I will have your nose, Heraclius. And if you do not answer true, you will suffer the pear of anguish. If you will not take it in your mouth, then there are other places I can introduce it. Do you understand?'

Heraclius nodded. He was wide-eyed with fear.

'Good. We shall begin again. Did you kill Amalric?'

'No.'

John pressed the flat of his dagger against the side of Heraclius's nose. 'I told you the price of lying, Heraclius.'

'No! Please! I speak the truth!'

'You had Reynald kill the poison merchant. Why?'

'Because—' Heraclius swallowed. 'Because I purchased the poison. But I did not use it! I swear it!'

'Who did? Who did you give it to?'

'Agnes.'

John stepped back as if he had been struck. Agnes. She had lied to him. John felt the blood begin to pound in his temples. He stepped back and sheathed his dagger. He placed the pear of anguish back in the small trunk, which he shut and placed under his arm. He went to the door.

'Wait!' Heraclius screamed. 'You said you would free me.'

'Mass will be over soon. If you yell loudly enough, I am sure one of the canons will find you before the day is through.'

John deposited the trunk in his cell and went straight to the palace. Once Heraclius was found, there would be a price to pay. He had to speak with the king first. The guards posted at the door to the king's apartments barred his way. 'The King is occupied.'

John pulled an old scrap of paper from his pocket. It was a list of things William had asked him to purchase at market last week. 'I have important news from our spies in Damascus,' he lied. 'I must see the King.'

The guards made a show of examining the scrap of paper, but John knew that neither of them could read. After a moment they waved him inside. The curtains were drawn, and the king's receiving room was dim but for the light cast by a low fire in the hearth. John closed the door quietly and stopped in the doorway to allow his eyes to adjust. The king sat in a chair close to the fire. His malady left him cold, even in the heat of summer. Agnes sat across from him, her back to the door. Baldwin's sister Sibylla stood by the curtained window. She was sixteen, and John had heard that since leaving the convent of Saint Lazarus to live in the palace, she had been caught in bed with no less than three men. It was said she was now forced to wear a chastity belt, and that only Agnes held the key. Sibylla was plucking the petals from a pink rose. No one had noticed John's presence.

'He is a good match,' Agnes was saying. 'The son of the Marquis of Montferrat. He will bring us powerful allies.'

'He is a Provençal who cannot speak French properly,' Sibylla protested. 'I will not understand a word he is saying.'

'Then you can put your Latin to good use. Guilhem is fluent.'

'He is *old*, Mother.'

'Hardly. He is thirty-six. And you need an older man to take charge of you. Besides, it is not your decision to make.' Agnes looked to Baldwin. 'What do you say?'

'Sibylla will marry Guilhem.'

'I shan't!' Sibylla pouted. She threw down the rose and almost ran into John as she stormed from the room.

Baldwin frowned, and Agnes placed a hand on his knee. 'It is what is best for her,' she said.

Baldwin nodded and then straightened in his chair as he noticed John. 'John, you have a message for me?'

John stepped forward so that he could see both Baldwin and Agnes. 'I must speak with you, sire. Alone.'

Agnes laughed. 'You *must* speak with him? You forget your place, John.'

John ignored her light tone. 'It is about Amalric. I know who killed him.'

'He died of the flux,' Baldwin protested.

'He did not.' John's eyes were locked on Agnes.

'Tell us what you have to say, John,' she said. 'My son has no secrets from me.'

Baldwin nodded.

'Very well.' John spoke to the king, but he kept his eyes on Agnes. 'Your mother is a liar and a traitor, sire. She murdered your father.'

Agnes did not so much as blink. 'Careful, John. A baseless accusation like that could cost you your head.'

'It is not baseless. I have just come from speaking with Archbishop Heraclius. He admitted to purchasing the poison that was used to kill Amalric. He delivered it into your hands, Agnes. You murdered the King.'

'You are mistaken, John.'

'I am not!' John shouted, his anger mounting in the face of her calm denial. 'You had Reynald kill the poison dealer. He was made lord of Kerak as a reward. Did you also have him send the men who tried to murder me?'

'I am only the mother of the King, John. I have no power over Reynald.'

'You lie!'

'Please, John!' Baldwin intervened. 'I am certain my mother had nothing to do with Amalric's death.'

'Do not trust her word, sire. She is a liar. She should be cast in irons and thrown in the dungeon.'

'How dare you!' Agnes rose and looked down her nose at John. 'You call me a liar? You are a priest who has betrayed his vow of chastity. You were a crusader who joined the Saracen army. You are the liar, John. If anyone here should be suspected of killing Amalric, it is you.'

'You duplicitous bitch!' John stormed from the room. He crossed the palace to the chancellery, hoping to find William there, but the room was empty. John locked the door and sat at the broad desk, his head in his hands. There was a knock at the door. No doubt guards had come for him. He had assaulted an archbishop and accused the king's mother of murder, and he could only guess at what his punishment would be. The knock repeated, louder. John went to the door and opened it.

It was Agnes. Her eyes were moist, as if John's accusations had actually hurt her. As if she could be hurt. She touched his arm. 'Do not be angry with me, John.'

He shrugged her hand off. 'How could you do it, Agnes?'

'I did not kill him. You must believe me.' Her green eyes met his. 'I miss you, John.'

'What of Amalric de Lusignan? I hear he warms your bed now.'

'He is an oaf, disagreeable but useful,' Agnes said, and John turned away in disgust. 'I am a woman, John. I need men to act for me in the world. But I have nothing to gain by loving you. Think on that.'

John hesitated for a moment and then shook his head. 'I will not fall for your lies. Not again. I will see you punished for what you have done.'

'You have no proof.'

'I do not need it. I will undergo ordeal by fire to prove that what I say is true.'

'You will not pass the trial, John. You will be executed for daring to accuse me publically.'

'It does not matter. All the world will know the truth.'

Agnes shook her head sadly. 'Stop this madness before it is too late, John. You do not want to know the truth.'

The bells of Saint Sepulchre were tolling the call to None – the afternoon prayer – when John left the palace. The king had gone to the baths in the Hospitaller quarter, and John was headed there to tell Baldwin of his decision to undergo ordeal by fire. He would be forced to carry a red-hot iron rod for nine paces. Afterwards, his hand would be bandaged, and three days later a priest would examine it. If God had miraculously healed his hand, then that would prove that he had right on his side. If his hand were still red and blistered, then John would be killed.

John entered the baths and strode through the warm and cold rooms. Four guards stood outside the hot room. John began to push past, but one of them grabbed his arm. 'What are you doing?' John demanded. 'Let me pass.'

'Sorry, Father. You are to be arrested. King's orders.'

John raised his voice so that Baldwin could hear him in the room beyond. 'Tell the King that I must speak to him about his father. Tell him I can prove how he died.'

The guards exchanged a glance, and one of them stepped into the room. He returned a moment later. 'The King will see you.'

Inside the hot room steam hissed through cracks in the tiled floor. A blazing torch near the door barely illuminated a series of shadowy alcoves built into the far wall. In one of them sat Baldwin, naked. His torso and arms were covered with sores and patches of thick, white skin. He studied John for a long time. Sweat began to bead on John's forehead. More sweat ran down his spine and his priest's tunic began to cling. The door swung closed behind him.

'What do you want, John?' Baldwin asked. 'To make more baseless accusations against my mother? I spoke with Heraclius. He denies knowing anything about Amalric's murder.'

'He lies. He told me himself about the poison.'

'When you tortured him, you mean?'

'I barely touched him.'

'He has a bump the size of an egg on his head. He demands that you hang like a common criminal. I have convinced the Patriarch to spare your life, but you will lose your monthly prebend. I ordered my men to arrest you for your own good. If the Patriarch's men catch you on the street, nothing I say will spare you a beating, or worse.' The king sighed. 'You are making yourself powerful enemies, John. And to what end?'

'What I say is true, sire. I am willing to undergo ordeal by fire to prove it.'

'I cannot allow that.'

'You cannot prevent me. Our laws—'

'Damn our laws! I am your king, John! You will do as I say!'

'Amalric was also my king. I have a duty to him, too. If you will not hear me, then I will go to Raymond. He is the regent. He can oversee the ordeal.' John turned to go.

'Wait!'

He turned back to see that Baldwin's eyes were shining in the torchlight. The king blinked back tears. 'My mother did not kill Amalric.' When he spoke again, his voice was so low that John barely heard him. 'I did.'

John felt suddenly short of breath. The heat in the room was suffocating. John shook his head. He could not believe it. He had known Baldwin since he was a child. 'Why?'

'Because he would never have let me become king.' Baldwin took a deep breath. 'I spent every waking moment trying to prove to him that I was worthy of the crown, yet he could never see me as anything but a monster.'

John recalled the conversation where Agnes had said just that. 'You heard her, the day Agnes told me you would never succeed your father?'

Baldwin nodded. 'I was furious. I confronted my mother. She told me what I must do. You know the rest.'

John turned and headed for the door.

'Where are you going?' Baldwin demanded.

'I am leaving your service. I am a man of honour, sire, and though you are my king, justice must be done. I will undergo the ordeal to prove your guilt. Your father deserves as much.'

John pulled the door open and strode from the room, pushing past the guards at the door. He had not gone far when he heard Baldwin calling for his guards. They caught up with John in the cold room and dragged him back to face the king.

'I cannot let you go,' Baldwin told him when the guards had left. 'No one must know the truth.'

'What then? Will you kill me like you killed your father?'

Baldwin winced. 'I pray not. Sit, John.' The king patted the bench beside him. John did not move. '*Sit!*' Baldwin said more forcefully, and John reluctantly crossed the chamber to sit beside the king. 'I know what I did was wrong, John. I do not expect you to forgive me. But you of all people should understand. You, too, committed a crime against your family.'

John flinched. How did Baldwin know that John had killed his brother?

'It is not our past that defines us, John,' Baldwin continued, 'but what we do in the present. My father was a mighty warrior, but he was also a drunkard and a womanizer. His judgement was often clouded by passion. And he feared and despised the Saracens. He was willing to make peace with them, but only because he had to. Thanks to you, I know our enemy as he never did. I speak their tongue. I respect their faith. I believe we can live in peace with them. But I need your help, John. There are few at court who share my vision, and even fewer who I can trust. Agnes knows my secret, and she will reveal it if I do not do as she demands. That is why I rely on her counsel, why I have distanced myself from Raymond and William.'

John shook his head. 'You do not have to obey her, sire. She cannot accuse you without compromising herself.'

'No. With the poison dealer dead, there is nothing to link my father's death to Agnes. She has the power to destroy me.'

'But you are her son!'

'I once believed that mattered.' Baldwin's laugh was hollow. 'Agnes is not afraid to sacrifice those she loves for power. You of all people should know that, John. Sibylla will be married soon, and if she gives birth to a son, I will be dispensable. In fact, it might better suit my mother's purposes were I to die. Sibylla's child would then be king, and a regent would rule for years. Agnes would select that regent.'

'Reynald.'

Baldwin nodded. 'Or another of her puppets, should Reynald prove insufficiently pliable. So you see, I cannot oppose my mother directly. But I do intend to fight her. I need allies I can trust.' Baldwin met John's eyes. 'I will have you executed if I must, John, but I would rather have your service. Will you help me?'

After a moment's hesitation, John nodded. 'But only because I believe that despite your crime, you are a good man, sire. I pray you do not prove me wrong.'

'I will not, John. You have my word.'

Chapter 22

'Allah yasalmak,' Yusuf said to the pimple-faced mamluk before him. He kissed the young man on both cheeks. The mamluk mounted his horse, saluted, and rode away.

'Poor bastard,' Qaraqush murmured.

'He volunteered to deliver the message.'

'Poor dumb bastard.'

They watched as the mamluk rode through the tents that dotted the field where the army was camped. He passed the sentries and rode through a breach that Yusuf's men had opened in the low wall that encircled the base of the rocky hill atop which stood the Hashashin fortress of Masyaf. It was a forbidding sight. Two massive keeps stood behind high limestone walls that rose directly from the rock of the hillside.

The mamluk messenger stopped before the gatehouse and began to read from a sheet of paper. His words did not reach Yusuf, but he knew what the messenger was saying, for he had written the message himself.

Hear the words of Saladin, ruler of Egypt and Syria, defender of the faith. For too long you have sown seeds of chaos amongst the children of Allah. You have played kingdoms against one another. You have murdered our leaders. You tried to murder me. There must be an end to it. I will kill your men, tear down your walls, burn your homes, enslave your women. Even your memory will

369

be wiped from the face of the earth. You have only one hope.
Surrender now. If you do—

The messenger had reached approximately this point when an arrow struck him in the chest. Three more arrows hit home and he slumped from the saddle.

'So much for diplomacy,' Qaraqush said.

Yusuf frowned. He had not believed the Hashashin would surrender, but he had hoped they would spare the messenger. He looked to Al-Mashtub. 'What have you discovered from the townspeople?'

The huge mamluk shrugged. 'The Hashashin have put the fear of God into them. Most refuse to say a single word, even after I threaten to rip off their ears. I have found one man who has been inside the citadel and is willing to talk, but he has conditions.'

Yusuf raised an eyebrow. 'What are they?'

'He wants five hundred dinar.'

'Done.'

'There is more. Until the siege is over he wishes to stay with our army in a tent guarded at all times by four men. Lime and ashes are to be spread for twenty paces in all directions around the tent, to detect footsteps. No one is to set foot in this space without his permission. When the siege is done, he will travel with the army to Cairo, where he will be given two permanent guards.'

The requests were odd, but they would not be difficult to fulfil. 'Show him to my tent. Qaraqush, you will interview him with me.'

Yusuf entered his sprawling red tent and poured water for himself and Qaraqush. A moment later Al-Mashtub led in a thin man with a patchy beard and a pronounced overbite. The man knelt on the thick carpet and prostrated himself.

'What is your name?' Yusuf asked.

'Sabir, Malik.'

'Get up, Sabir. Tell me what you know, and you shall have your gold. But I warn you: if you speak false, I will have your head.'

The man rose. 'I will tell you everything, Malik, but you must guarantee my safety. The Ismaili will kill me if I tell you what I know.'

'You need not fear them. You will be safe enough in my camp.'

'No man is safe from the Ismaili. There are ways out of the fortress; tunnels in the rock. They will send men to assassinate me. You, too! You must take precautions, as I have done.'

'I will consider it. Tell me of Masyaf.'

'You cannot starve them out. They have ample food and cisterns dug into the rock that provide water for months. And the castle is all but impossible to take by force.'

'All castles can be taken.'

'Perhaps. I have visited Masyaf many times, and I have never seen a stronger fortress. Each step you take in conquering it will be bought with much bloodshed. Your army of thousands will be reduced to nothing.'

Yusuf set his water aside. 'You have told me precious little of use. If you have no information, then our deal is off.'

Sabir's eyes widened. 'I have information, Malik. I swear it!'

'Tell me what my men will face when they breach the gate.'

'The gate you see is but the first of many. Beyond it, you enter a vaulted, U-shaped hall. It is a deathtrap. Slits in the walls allow men in the castle to fire arrows and stab with spears. They will pour boiling oil and hot sand down on you through grates in the ceiling. If you can fight your way to the end of the hall, you will then be faced with a narrow staircase that ends at a mighty gate framed by enormous guard towers. Your men will have to hack through with axes. All this time, the defenders will rain arrows and burning sand down upon you.'

'Go on.'

'Past the gate, your men will find themselves in a chamber

with doors on three sides. The doors to the left and right lead to towers. Each level of the towers must be taken in turn, for if they are not, then your men will be vulnerable to attack from behind. The far door leads further into the citadel. A murder hole in the ceiling over the door allows the defenders to pour yet more hot sand on your men. Beyond that door is a similar room. A door to the right leads into the citadel proper. Once there, your fight will have only just begun. There are two keeps you will have to take. The first sits at the southern end of the complex and defends the eastern approach to the main citadel. Once you take it, you will have to fight your way through a series of courtyards and halls to the main citadel's eastern gate.'

'Why not attack the citadel's western gate?' Yusuf asked.

'Because that is suicide. The only way to reach it is through a tunnel sixty paces long. Pipes in the wall allow the tunnel to be flooded.'

Sabir stopped speaking. Yusuf and Qaraqush exchanged glances. 'Sounds like it will be hell to take,' the mamluk general said.

Yusuf felt the familiar burning in his gut. 'Al-Mashtub, see that Sabir is paid, then take him to a tent and post guards there.' Al-Mashtub led the man out, and Yusuf turned to Qaraqush. 'We will situate the catapults on the south-eastern side of the citadel. We need to bring down the southern keep.'

'Even then, we will lose thousands of men in an assault.'

'It is a price worth paying. There will be no security in my kingdom so long as the Hashashin live. And I do not wish to spend the remainder of my days worrying about a knife in my back.' Yusuf scratched his beard as he considered his options. 'Have some of the catapults launch fire at the citadel. Perhaps we can burn it down. And have diggers undermine the eastern wall.' Yusuf raised his voice. 'Saqr!'

The head of Yusuf's bodyguard entered. 'Yes, Malik?'

'Have extra guards posted around my tent and sprinkle the

ground with lime and ash, as at Sabir's tent. No one but you is to enter without my permission.'

That evening Yusuf ate a simple meal of rice and lentils while Imad ad-Din updated him on the correspondence from Damascus, Cairo and Aleppo. It was late when they finally finished. Before retiring to bed, Yusuf stepped outside. At twenty paces his tent was ringed by torches tied to posts. Armoured guards stood by each of the thirty torches. The ground between the tent and the guards was covered in ash and lime. No one could walk there without leaving footprints. Four guards walked the perimeter of Yusuf's tent, their eyes scanning the ground for any trace of an intruder. Saqr stood beside the entrance.

'All is well?' Yusuf asked him.

'You are safer here than in your palace in Cairo.'

Yusuf went inside and passed through the curtain that separated off his sleeping quarters. He blew out the lamp and lay on his cot. At regular intervals he could hear the footsteps of the guards as they passed outside his tent. He was listening to their footsteps when he fell asleep.

He awoke with a start some time later. There was shouting outside the tent. He stepped outside to see mamluks running here and there. He looked to Saqr. 'What is happening?'

'The informer Sabir has been murdered by one of the Hashashin. The men are looking for his killer.'

'Only one man? His was guarded by four mamluks.'

'They are all dead. The Hashashin was seen fleeing.'

Yusuf frowned. 'Inform me at once if he is found.'

He re-entered his tent and pushed through the curtain to his sleeping quarters. He froze. Someone was sitting at the foot of his cot. The man wore the saffron yellow caftan of one of Yusuf's men over his mail, but this was no mamluk. Yusuf reached for the sword propped against the tent wall.

'Do not do that,' the man said quietly. 'And do not call for help, either.' He had a flat voice with no trace of emotion in it. Yusuf saw that the man held a dagger in his hand. It was wet with blood. 'It would be a pity to kill you, Saladin. Come. Sit.'

Yusuf sat at the head of the bed. 'Who are you?'

'You know who I am.'

Yusuf squinted in the darkness and made out a black beard with a few streaks of grey, a beak of a nose and dark eyes. 'Rashid ad-Din Sinan,' he said, and the man nodded. The Old Man of the Mountain, head of the Hashashin. 'Why have you come?'

'To talk.'

'Why not just kill me as you tried to do before?'

'Circumstances have changed. The position of my people is fragile. We are caught between the Sunnis to the east and the Franks across the mountains to the west. We have had to play one off against the other to survive. But this policy cannot last forever. You are now lord of Syria and Egypt. You can guarantee us security. But if I kill you, then nothing will change. We will continue to balance on the tip of a sword, the Christians on one side and the Sunnis on the other.'

'I, too, am a Sunni. I thought that is why you wanted me dead.'

'I am a reasonable man. The Fatimid Caliphate is gone, and killing you will not bring it back. I must do what I can to protect the few Ismaili who remain.'

'So you seek a truce. What are your terms?'

'First, you will withdraw your men and swear never again to move against us. Second, you will raze the Templar and Hospitaller fortresses that border our lands. They force us to pay tribute, and until such time as they are crushed, you will send an annual payment equivalent to the moneys they demand of us.'

'And what do I get in return?'

'Your life.'

Yusuf shook his head. 'That is not enough.'

Sinan smiled, and Yusuf could see his white teeth in the dark. 'I was told you are a bold man, Saladin.'

'You must swear to spare not only me but also the lives of my family and my men. If so much as a single mamluk dies at the hands of one of the Hashashin, then I will return to tear Masyaf down stone by stone.'

Sinan considered this. 'No,' he said at last. Yusuf opened his mouth to protest, but Sinan raised a hand to stop him. 'Your family and your emirs will be safe, but I cannot promise to respect the lives of all your men. Our lands are small, Saladin. We must find ways to supplement our meagre income. Murder can be most profitable. But I swear to restrict it to common men.'

'Very well,' Yusuf said reluctantly. 'I will send a man tomorrow to finalize the terms of our treaty.'

'Your word is enough.'

'You have it.'

Sinan rose, and Yusuf began to do so as well. The assassin motioned for him to sit. 'Please, wait until I have gone.'

'But I must order my guards to escort you back to Masyaf.'

'That will not be necessary.' He pulled back a flap of the screen that led to the main chamber of the tent and then turned back to Yusuf. 'You will not regret having us as allies. If there are any that you wish dead . . .' He let the words hang in the air.

'I do not deal in murder.'

'You will.' Sinan disappeared though the screen.

Yusuf rose and followed him to the next room. No one was there. Yusuf stepped out of the tent, but again there was no sign of Sinan. Saqr still stood beside the entrance.

'Did you see him?' Yusuf asked.

'Who?'

One of the guards who circled the tent was approaching, and Yusuf turned to him. 'A man was here. Dark hair and a long beard. Did you see him?'

'No, Malik.'

Yusuf circled the tent and found a slash in the side where Sinan must have exited. His eyes went to the ash- and lime-covered ground. There were no footprints. How was that possible? He came back to where Saqr stood and peered into the darkness beyond the torches.

'Are you well, Malik?' Saqr asked.

'Have Qaraqush and Al-Maqaddam come to my tent.'

Qaraqush arrived first. He was still blinking sleep from his eyes. 'I was dreaming I was in paradise surrounded by virgins. Why in the name of—' He stopped short when he saw the expression on Yusuf's face.

Al-Mashtub arrived a moment later. 'We were unable to find Sabir's killer.'

'Sinan,' Yusuf said.

'Sinan was here?' Qaraqush demanded.

Yusuf nodded. 'We will strike camp first thing tomorrow.'

Qaraqush blinked, speechless. Al-Mashtub recovered first. 'Why, Malik?'

'Our business here is finished. The Hashashin will trouble us no more. We will return to Cairo. It has been too long since we were home.'

Chapter 23

'You cannot make Reynald regent, sire,' John said. He stopped pacing the king's private chamber and turned to face Baldwin, who, as usual, was huddled before the fire. 'You cannot.'

'I have no choice, John.'

Baldwin had come of age and assumed the throne the week before, but his illness had left him too weak to leave the palace except on rare occasions. The Haute Cour had called for a new regent to be elected. Agnes had already forced Baldwin to send Raymond back to Tripoli, and now she was pushing for Reynald to take his post.

'He hates the Saracens, sire. He will bring war, a war that we cannot win. Particularly not after Myriokephalon.'

Baldwin frowned. 'Do not remind me.' Six months ago, the army of Emperor Manuel had been caught in a pass and routed by the Turks near the fortress of Myriokephalon. The Kingdom could no longer hope for any help from Constantinople. They were on their own.

'Anyone but Reynald, sire.'

'I have no choice,' the king repeated. 'I am expendable now that Sibylla is with child. I cannot defy Agnes.'

John met his eyes. 'But I can.'

Baldwin shook his head. 'She will not listen to you, John.'

'I must try.'

John crossed the palace to Agnes's apartments. Before he reached the door, Reynald emerged. He walked down the narrow corridor towards John.

'Out of my way, Saxon.' John did not move aside to let him pass. 'I will be regent soon. I can have you hanged for your insolence.'

'I have the backing of the King,' John replied.

'The King is a leper. He will be dead soon enough. You would do well to remember that.' Reynald pushed past John and strode away.

John reached Agnes's chambers and knocked. She opened the door herself. 'John. I thought I heard your voice. Come in.'

John waited until she had closed the door. 'What have you done?' he demanded.

Her perfect eyebrows arched in surprise. 'What do you mean?'

'Reynald is not fit to be regent.'

'He is a man that the Saracens fear. With him as regent, they will think twice before attacking.'

'He is a savage who kills for sport. Reynald did not honour the treaty while lord of Kerak. If he fails to honour it as regent, he will start a war we cannot win.'

She smiled. 'I am no fool, John. I do not need a priest to give me lessons in politics.'

John took a step towards her. 'Please, Agnes. Do not make him regent.'

'It is already done. It will be announced tomorrow.'

John shook his head in disgust.

'Do not look at me like that, John. I know you despise me, but what I have done, I have done for Baldwin, for the Kingdom.'

'Why do you care what I think of you?'

She shrugged. 'Because you understand. Because you too would do anything for Baldwin. Because you loved me once. And I loved you.' She reached out to touch his face.

John caught her hand. 'You never loved me.' He went to the door and then turned back. Her eyes were shining. 'You had best keep Reynald on a short leash. Peace is our only hope.'

AUGUST 1177: JERUSALEM

'Why did he have to show up now?' Baldwin complained as he entered his chamber with John and William in tow. 'The man is a damned nuisance.'

They had just returned from a feast held in honour of Philip of Alsace, who had arrived in Jerusalem on crusade only the day before. As Count of Flanders, a rich province north-east of Paris, Philip was one of the most powerful lords in Europe. He had come on crusade at the head of two hundred knights. His arrival could not have come at a worse time.

'It is all I could do to keep Reynald in check these last few months, and now this. Philip has spoken of invading Egypt. Egypt!' Baldwin sank into his chair beside the fire. The flickering light played on his features. Baldwin had always been mature beyond his years, but over the past few months the skin over his forehead had thickened, deepening the creases in his brow and making him look much older than his sixteen years.

'Egypt is not why he is here,' William noted as he sat across from the king.

'I know,' Baldwin said darkly. 'He is here for my sister.'

Sibylla had not been married four months when her husband Guilhem died of malaria, leaving her pregnant. Her child would rule as king or queen, and her husband would be king until that child came of age. She was once again the most sought-after prize in the Kingdom.

'Philip would not be a bad ally,' John noted. 'He is your kinsman, and they say he is a great warrior. He has men, money and influence in France and England.'

William snorted. 'Influence will not bring us the men we

need to defeat Saladin. We need blood ties to either France or England. And Flanders is far from the Holy Land. It would be better to marry her to a local lord.'

'She should not marry at all,' Baldwin said. 'Her husband has not been in the grave for two months. She should mourn for a year at least.'

'What does your mother say?' John asked.

'On this, at least, we are in agreement. But Sibylla is beside the point. What matters is that Philip has come on crusade, and Reynald supports him. That means war with Saladin, a war that I fear we cannot win.'

'Perhaps Saladin will not attack,' William offered. 'If Philip strikes in the north, against the lands of Al-Salih—'

'Al-Salih is his lord,' John said. 'Saladin will fight to defend him.'

'By Christ's wounds,' Baldwin cursed. 'Damn Philip!'

The three of them lapsed into silence. Baldwin huddled in his chair while William poked the fire. Even with Philip's knights, the Kingdom did not have nearly enough men to fight Saladin's armies. Philip and Reynald's crusade would doom them all. Reynald! John looked to the king. 'Perhaps Philip's arrival is a blessing in disguise, sire.'

'How so?'

'Philip is your cousin, yes?'

The king nodded. 'We share a grandfather. Philip's father married King Fulk's daughter while on crusade.'

'Which makes Philip the closest male relative you have, closer even than Raymond, and much, much closer than Reynald.'

Baldwin sat up straight. 'Which makes him an ideal regent. Very clever, John. William, go and draw up the forms of investiture for a new regent. John, fetch Philip here. My mother is to know nothing of this.'

John knocked on the door of Philip's chamber in the palace. There was no response. 'Count Philip!' John called. He knocked louder. Finally the door opened a crack to reveal a girl of no more than sixteen, a sheet held up to cover her nakedness. She was thin, with delicate features and saucer-like eyes. John recognized her as a palace servant, charged with washing and changing the linen.

'Lord Philip is occupied,' the girl said shyly.

'Tell him that King Baldwin wishes to speak with him.'

The girl looked over her shoulder, and John could hear a low voice coming from the room. She turned back to John. 'He— he will wait on the King shortly.'

'Baldwin wishes to speak with him now,' John insisted. 'Tell him it is about Sibylla.'

The door opened wide. Philip stood beside the girl. He was tall, broad-shouldered and clean-shaven with long brown hair and dark-green eyes. He was completely naked.

'Why did you not say so?' Philip slapped the servant girl's buttocks. 'Off with you now, Alda.'

'My name is Celsa, my lord.'

'Of course it is.' Philip kissed her hand. 'Run along now, Celsa.' He gently pushed her out of the door. She stood in the hallway barefoot, still wrapped in the bed sheet. She hesitated. Then she hurried away, her cheeks scarlet. John shook his head.

Philip had stepped back into his room and was sitting on the bed as he pulled on fitted linen hose. 'I was told by Lady Agnes that I would not have an audience with the King until tomorrow.'

'She was mistaken.'

Philip pulled a tunic of blue velvet over his head and cinched it about his waist with a leather belt. He slipped his feet into pointed leather shoes and stood to smooth back his long hair. 'Take me to him.'

Baldwin's chambers were in the same wing as Philip's, no more than fifty paces away, but John led them on a circuitous path that took them down into the kitchen and then up the servants' stairs and into the king's chambers though a back door. Baldwin sat waiting in his chair by the fire.

Philip bowed. 'Cousin.'

Baldwin looked past him to John. 'Were you seen?'

'No, sire.'

Baldwin turned to Philip. 'Sit.' He gestured to the chair across from him.

Philip sat and crossed his legs casually, his elbow resting on the arm of the chair. 'You wished to speak with me of your sister, Sibylla?'

'Unfortunately, I cannot offer her to you.'

Philip's relaxed posture vanished. He gripped the arms of the chair. 'But your man said—'

'I know what John said. He asked you here to speak of Sibylla, and we are speaking of her. Her husband died less than two months ago. It is too soon for her to marry again.'

'Then we have nothing to discuss.' Philip started to rise, but John put a hand on his shoulder and forced him back down.

Baldwin leaned forward. 'On the contrary, we have a great deal to discuss. You have come to the Kingdom to go on crusade. I am asking you not to.'

'But that is preposterous! I have brought hundreds of men at great cost.'

'And you could not have come at a worse time. The Kingdom is in no position to go to war. Our peace with the Saracens is all that protects us.'

'That is not what Reynald de Chatillon says.'

'Reynald is a fool.'

Philip's eyes narrowed. 'He is your regent.'

'Yes, and now we have reached the crux of the matter. John, bring our guest some wine.'

John went to a table by the window and returned with two cups that had already been poured. Philip took a sip, nodded in satisfaction, and took a long drink. Baldwin examined his cup before setting it aside. 'I wish to offer you the regency, Philip.'

'What?' Philip blinked in surprise.

'You would serve as co-ruler until I die. Afterwards, you will rule alone until my heir comes of age.'

'But what of my lands in Flanders?'

'I am offering you a kingdom, Philip. If you accept, you will be given Jaffa and Ascalon. That will solidify your standing here in the Holy Land.'

Philip sat speechless, staring at his cup of wine. Finally he looked up. 'And the barons of the Kingdom will accept this?'

'They can hardly refuse. You are a powerful lord and my closest male relative. And I am their king. If I tell them to support you, they will do so.'

'And in return?'

'You will abandon your crusade.' Philip opened his mouth to protest, and Baldwin raised a hand to silence him. 'You may fight, only not now. Wait until the advantage lies with us.'

Philip took another drink of wine. He shook his head. 'Why offer me the regency? You have only just met me.'

'I have told you my reasons.'

'Surely the Saracens are not so great a threat as you suggest. Reynald tells me the Kingdom still has thousands of sergeants and hundreds of knights. Jerusalem itself was conquered with fewer men.'

'The Saracens were not united then as they are now.'

'And if I refuse?'

'Then you must leave Jerusalem. You will not use my lands to launch your attack.'

'I could still attack from Tripoli or Antioch.'

'You could.'

Philip ran a hand through his hair as he considered the situation. 'I swore an oath, Baldwin. I have come to fight, and many of your men have already pledged their support. The Templars and Hospitallers are with me. Reynald has offered a hundred knights. I do not need your permission to go to war.'

'No, you do not. But I urge you to do as I ask. You are new

to these lands, Philip. I have lived here all my life. I know what the costs of an attack on the Saracens would be.'

Philip moved to take another sip of wine, realized his cup was empty, and set it aside. 'When must I decide?'

'Now.'

'Then my answer is no.'

'I beg you to reconsider.' Baldwin leaned forward and grasped Philip's wrist.

The count looked down at Baldwin's sore-covered hand and flinched. He pulled his hand away. 'My home is in Flanders, not here. I have come to fight for God. Afterwards I will return home.' He rose.

The calm that Baldwin had maintained now broke. 'But you are dooming the Kingdom!'

'No, Cousin, I am saving it. You said yourself that the Kingdom is weak and the Saracens strong. You need me to redress the balance. I will march north and I will not stop until I have taken Aleppo.'

Baldwin studied his cousin for a moment; then his shoulders slumped and he looked away to the fire. 'You will leave Jerusalem before week's end,' he told Philip. 'John, take him away.'

OCTOBER 1177: CAIRO

Yusuf's forehead creased as he stared at the scrap of paper in his hand. He squinted as he re-examined the minuscule script used in the pigeon post. He shook his head in disbelief. He had read it correctly.

'The peace has been broken, Brother,' Selim said. 'An army from the Kingdom has laid siege to Hama.'

Yusuf set the paper aside and looked to the men standing before him in the audience chamber. They were his most trusted councillors: Selim, Imad ad-Din, al-Fadil, Ubadah and

Qaraqush. 'Has Baldwin taken leave of his senses?' Yusuf asked of no one in particular. 'He must know he cannot win.'

'It is not Baldwin who leads the attack,' Imad ad-Din responded, 'but a crusader from the West; Philip, the Count of Flanders, wherever that may be.'

'I do not give two straws where he is from,' Yusuf snapped. 'We had a treaty with Jerusalem.'

'The treaty does allow for a suspension of the peace in the event of a crusade,' Imad ad-Din pointed out.

Ubadah stepped forward. 'It does matter who or why, Uncle. This is our chance! This Philip has taken most of the knights of the Kingdom with him to the north.'

Selim nodded. 'Jerusalem is practically undefended. Allah has given us a clear path to the Holy Sanctuary. You will be the conqueror of Jerusalem, the saviour of our people!'

Yusuf rose and went to the window. He could see the white walls of the new citadel rising on the hills south of the city. The citadel was to be the new seat of his government, the heart of a flourishing kingdom. It was only one of many projects he had begun. He had dug new wells in Cairo and begun a bridge across the Nile at Giza. Further north, his men were at work on dams in the Nile delta. The port of Alexandria was being dredged. He had built new madrasas for learning in cities across Syria and expanded the courts to ensure swift justice. And he had posted men to secure the caravan routes from bandits so that trade could flourish. Peace had been good to his people, much better than the years of victories bought with blood and taxes. War would threaten all of it.

Yet what choice did he have? The Franks had attacked, and it was his duty as king to defend his lands. 'The damned fools,' he muttered. If they wanted war, then he would bring it to them. When he was done, the Franks would never spurn peace again. His decision made, Yusuf straightened and spoke with authority. 'Qaraqush, gather the army, and send to my brother in Damascus for more men. We will set out at once for the

Kingdom and meet Turan's men at Ascalon. Allah willing, Jerusalem will be ours before the new year. If the Franks do not then beg for peace, I shall drive them into the sea.'

John entered the chancellery with a box containing the pigeon post under his arm. He sat down and began to sort through the messages. He looked first at missives from Tripoli and Antioch. They all related the same news. The army under Philip was making little progress in its siege of Hama. John continued to scan the messages until he came to one from Ascalon. He left at once for the king's quarters.

He arrived to find Baldwin in a meeting with Reynald, Agnes and Amalric de Lusignan. The king sat huddled by the fire while the three others stood around him. They were discussing possible husbands for Sibylla. John took up a position in the corner and waited for an opportunity to present his news.

'Guy de Lusignan,' Agnes said emphatically.

Baldwin frowned. 'No, Mother. For the hundredth time, no. I do not pretend to think I will live to an old age. After I die, the man who marries Sibylla will be king of Jerusalem until my sister's son comes of age. He should be a great lord.' Baldwin glanced at Amalric, who was Guy's brother. 'Guy is a nobody. And he is a Frenchman, new to our lands.'

'That is why he is perfect,' Agnes replied. 'He can bring the support of the French king and also of Henry II of England, who is his lord.'

'Henry chased him from his lands, Mother. That is why he is in Jerusalem.'

'Sire!' Amalric protested. 'We left France to fight for Christ in—'

Baldwin held up a hand. 'Save your talk for my mother's bed, Amalric.'

'How dare you!' She raised her hand to slap him.

Baldwin caught her wrist. 'I am the King, Mother. How dare you?'

They locked gazes.

John cleared his throat. 'Excuse me, sire. I have important news.'

Baldwin waved him forward. 'Speak.'

'Saladin is on the march from Cairo. He will reach Ascalon in a matter of days.'

Agnes paled. 'All our men are in the north. We must recall them.'

'There is no time,' Baldwin said. 'By the time the army returns, Saladin will have taken Jerusalem.'

Agnes looked to Reynald. 'Why did you insist on supporting Philip? You have doomed us all.'

Reynald flushed red. He turned to John. 'How many men does Saladin have?'

'As many as thirty thousand,' John replied.

'We cannot defeat such a number.' Reynald swallowed. 'The court should withdraw to Acre.'

'And let Saladin take Jerusalem?' Baldwin asked. 'No. Saladin will have to take Gaza and Ascalon on his way north. Ascalon is strong. If we can stop him there, then we can save Jerusalem.' Baldwin looked to Reynald. 'How many men can we gather?'

'Perhaps eight thousand sergeants, but most of our knights went north with Philip. There are no more than five hundred available.'

'Have the constable assemble them as quickly as possible.'

'Humphrey is gravely ill, sire,' John said.

'Then you do it.'

'But sire!' Reynald protested. 'I am your regent. It is my duty to command your army, and I must insist that we withdraw to the north. Riding to confront Saladin is mad. If we fail to reach Ascalon before him, then we will have to face him in the field. He will outnumber us nearly three to one. We will be slaughtered.'

'Then we shall have to reach Ascalon first.'

'No. I insist that we—'

'Reynald!' Agnes's sharp voice cut the regent short. 'We have followed your advice and look where that has led us. We will do as the King says.'

Baldwin turned to John. 'Send out the call for men. We leave tomorrow.'

Chapter 24

A crow's harsh cry carried from the branches of a dead tree, startling John awake. He had nodded off in the saddle, lulled to sleep by the even gait of his mount. The army had left Jerusalem the day before. They had reached the coast and ridden south late into the night until Baldwin finally allowed the men a few hours of sleep. The march had resumed early, when the birds were still sleeping and the only sounds were the jangle of tack and the crash of the surf. Now it was getting light and the crows were waking. They were the inevitable companions of every army. They picked over the scraps of food the army left behind during its march. After the battle they would feast upon the bodies of the dead. John watched as one of the infantrymen scooped up a pebble and threw it at the crow in the dead tree, sending the bird flying off, cawing in protest.

John shivered as a chill wind blew off the sea. The long column marched along the coast under low, scudding clouds. At their head the Patriarch of Jerusalem and the knights of the Holy Sepulchre carried the True Cross: a small fragment of the original, embedded in a huge cross of gold. Just behind the cross rode John, Baldwin, Reynald and the other great lords, followed by nearly four hundred knights. Eight thousand sergeants brought up the rear. It was a sizeable force, but less than half as large as Yusuf's army.

Baldwin slowed his mount to draw alongside John. The king wore mail under a white surcoat adorned with the Jerusalem cross: a single large cross of gold with four smaller crosses around it. Despite the weight of his armour, he rode straight-backed. His helmet had a long nosepiece and wide cheek pieces, which together hid most of the sores on his face. He looked nothing like the sickly man who had spent most of the past year huddled before the fire in his chamber.

'That armour suits you better than priestly robes, John,' he said.

John had set aside his alb, chasuble and stole for mail and a surcoat. Instead of the cross around his neck, he wore a sword at his side. It was normally forbidden for priests to shed blood, but under the circumstances no one had protested. The Kingdom needed every soldier it could find.

Baldwin spoke again in a lower voice. 'I do not trust Reynald. Keep an eye on him for me. If he so much as takes a piss, I want to know the colour.'

'He will not welcome my presence, sire.'

'Tell him you are there on my orders. Say that I feel he needs a spiritual adviser, and that I have chosen you.'

'Very well.'

John rode ahead to join Reynald. The regent had been talking with Odo Saint Amand, the bull-necked grand master of the Templars. The two fell silent at John's approach.

'What do you want, Saxon?' Reynald demanded.

'Baldwin has asked me to ride with you. I am to be your spiritual adviser.'

Reynald snorted. 'Tell Baldwin he can—'

'Good day, Reynald,' Baldwin said as he joined them. The regent flushed red. 'Tell me,' the king continued, 'will we reach Ascalon soon?'

'This afternoon, sire. But if Saladin has arrived first, we are dead men. Perhaps it would be best to stop some distance off and send scouts ahead.'

'We do not have time to be cautious. We will ride on and pray to God that we reach Ascalon first.'

'I have no talent for prayer,' Reynald muttered.

'That is why I have instructed John to remain by your side every waking moment. He is a priest. He shall pray for you.'

They rode on as the afternoon sun burned off the clouds and the gulls began to circle overhead, filling the air with their harsh cries. Finally they saw Ascalon, at first only a smudge on the distant horizon. It was an ancient city, already great when the Romans conquered it. It was said to be the place where Delilah had cut off Samson's hair. Now it was a fortress town, its thick walls protecting the frontier with Egypt. As the city grew closer John began to make out some details: walls dotted at regular intervals with square towers; tall buildings of white stone; a church fronted with twin, massive towers. He squinted. The cross still flew above the city gates.

Baldwin grinned. 'God is with us! We have arrived in time!'

'You may have spoken too soon, sire,' John said. He pointed beyond the city to the horizon, where a tall cloud of dust was rising. 'Saladin's army.'

'There is still time to retreat,' Reynald said.

Baldwin shook his head. 'We must reach the city first.' He raised his voice. 'Forward, men! As fast as your legs can carry you!' He urged his mount to a trot. The knights followed, and the sergeants jogged to keep up.

All eyes were fixed on the ever-growing cloud of dust on the horizon. Ahead, the city was no more than half a mile off. John could clearly see the walls, which were thick and fronted with a broad moat on the land side. On the ocean side, waves crashed against their base. He looked back to the horizon. He could now make out figures, thousands of men on horseback, stretching inland across the plain for as far as he could see.

'We will not make it, sire!' Reynald said. 'The sergeants are moving too slowly.'

'We must buy them more time. Knights, follow me! We will hold them off. For the Kingdom!'

Baldwin urged his horse to a canter, and John followed. The rest of the knights thundered in their wake. Behind, the careful ranks of the army dissolved as the sergeants ran for the city gates. The knights continued south with Baldwin at their head, his sword held aloft. Ahead, the Saracens were surging towards them; a solid wave of warriors covering the plain. Baldwin spurred his horse to a gallop.

Reynald pulled alongside John. '*He is mad!*' the regent shouted over the rumble of hooves.

John ignored him and spurred after the king. The Saracens were no more than two hundred yards off, close enough that John could make out the banners flying above them. He spotted the eagle of Saladin. Then the Saracen advance stopped. They began to form ranks in order to meet the Frankish charge. Baldwin reined in just outside bow range. John pulled up beside him. He glanced over his shoulder. The sergeants were pouring through the city's northern gate.

'The men are safe, sire.'

'Let us not press our luck. Ride fast, men!' Baldwin shouted. 'We may yet escape with our lives!' He wheeled his horse and spurred towards Ascalon.

John followed at a gallop. He heard a roar from the Saracen ranks behind and then the thunder of thousands of hooves. Leaning forward in the saddle he flicked the reins, urging his mount to greater speed. An arrow hissed past and shattered on the hard ground. '*Faster!*' he shouted in his horse's ear. Ahead, the southern gate of Ascalon had opened. Arrows were falling thick about them now. One struck Baldwin in the back, but the king seemed not to notice. And then they were clattering across the drawbridge and through the city gate. As the last of the knights entered behind them, the drawbridge went up, sealing the city off.

Baldwin ignored the cheers of the people crowding close to

greet him. He dismounted and took the stairs to the top of the gate. John followed.

'Are you injured, sire?' he asked, gesturing to Baldwin's back.

Baldwin craned his neck to see the arrow. 'I did not even know I was hit. It did not penetrate my jerkin.' He looked back out past the wall. Saracen riders were spreading out to surround the city. To the south, thousands more continued to pour over the horizon.

Baldwin looked to John and grinned. 'They are too late! Ascalon is ours!'

'Fifty-three towers,' Qaraqush reported. He had just returned from an inspection of the city's defences. 'The wall is thirty feet high. On the far side it is protected by the sea. Ascalon will be a tough nut to crack.'

Yusuf said nothing. He was standing outside his tent with his hands clasped behind his back, his eyes fixed on the city. The walls were crowded with men whose helmets gleamed in the setting sun. The flag of Jerusalem flew from the top of each tower.

'How long to take the city?' Turan asked.

Qaraqush shrugged. 'We will have to starve them out—three months, if then.'

'We do not have three months!' Turan paced in frustration. 'Winter will be upon us soon, and the Frankish army will return from the north. *Akh laa*! If only we had arrived a day earlier. We would already have the town in hand.'

'It does not matter,' Yusuf said. 'We do not need Ascalon.'

'But we cannot leave an enemy in our rear,' Qaraqush protested. 'It is unheard of. They will attack us when we make camp.'

'Not if they are locked away inside Ascalon. The Franks think they have entered a mighty citadel, but we shall transform it into a prison. Turan, you will stay here with ten thousand men, more than enough to keep the Franks trapped. Ubadah will go to Gaza with a thousand men, to ensure that their garrison cannot escape. I will ride for Jerusalem.'

Qaraqush and Turan were silent for a moment. Then the grizzled old mamluk grinned. 'There will be no one to stop you.'

'Exactly. By the time the Franks return from the north, the city will be ours, and they will be forced to besiege us.'

The following morning Yusuf led the army away from Ascalon, leaving Turan's troops ringing the city. Yusuf and his men angled inland, towards Ramlah and the road to Jerusalem. Every small settlement they passed had been abandoned. Yusuf gave orders to take what provisions could be found and put the rest to the torch. He sent detachments to take the towns of Lydaa, Arsuf and Mirabel, while he marched on with a reduced army of some thirteen thousand men. Before the sun had set they made camp beside a river less than a day's march from Jerusalem. With Saqr in tow, Yusuf toured the camp, occasionally stopping at a campfire to speak with the men. They were in a festive mood; they spoke of what they would do when they took the city. Some spoke of women or riches, but most said they would go to the Al-Aqsa mosque to pray. Yusuf promised that he would join them.

At one of the last fires he found a dozen men sitting silently, sharpening their blades as they stared at the embers. Yusuf recognized Liaqat and Nazam. With them sat Qadir, a mamluk who had already distinguished himself in Shirkuh's service when Yusuf was only a boy. Qadir was still an imposing man with biceps as thick as Yusuf's thighs, but he now had a paunch and his beard was streaked with grey.

Yusuf stepped into the circle of firelight and the men began to rise. He motioned for them to remain seated and took a place before the fire. He drew his eagle-hilt dagger and asked for a whetstone. Nazam handed one to him. Yusuf began to sharpen the blade.

'Is it true that the Franks have left Jerusalem unguarded?' Nazam asked.

Yusuf nodded.

'How could they be so foolish?'

'They had little choice. They do not have enough men to meet us in the field. They no doubt hoped I would pause to lay siege to Ascalon.'

Yusuf was surprised to see wetness in Qadir's eyes. 'Al-Quds,' the huge mamluk said. 'Your uncle told me long ago that we would conquer it together. I wish Shirkuh were here to see you, Màlik.' He shook his head sadly before he met Yusuf's eyes. 'Do you remember the day we first met?'

'I do.' Qadir had called him a little bugger. He had humiliated Yusuf before the rest of Shirkuh's men. But Yusuf had deserved it. He had not known the first thing about how to lead men.

'What a fool I was,' Qadir said.

'Not as great a fool as I. But the years have made us wiser.' Yusuf smiled. 'Although in your case, Qadir, no prettier.'

The mamluk chuckled and waved a fist in mock anger. 'Do not make me teach you a lesson, little bugger.'

'Maybe some other time.' Yusuf rose. 'Get your rest, men. There will be a long march tomorrow before we reach Jerusalem.'

Yusuf returned to his tent, where he lay in the dark, unable to sleep. He had wanted peace but war had found him. Tomorrow he would take Jerusalem. It was the culmination of nearly eighty years of struggle by his people. But Yusuf knew it was a beginning, not an end. The Franks would try to retake the city. Yusuf had not taken Ascalon or Gaza, so he would be surrounded with no open road to Egypt. He would have to hold Jerusalem with the men he had. The walls would need to be fortified. And he would have to deal with the populace. After the carnage that had occurred when the Christians took Jerusalem, Yusuf knew his men would want blood, but there was no sense in creating martyrs who might provoke another crusade. He would allow the Christians to leave. Perhaps afterwards he could negotiate peace. Then he could remake the city. He would drive the monks from the Dome of the Rock and rid the Temple Mount of the Templars. The Al-Aqsa would become a mosque once more, and he would go there to pray. *Inshallah*, he added silently. *Inshallah*.

NOVEMBER 1177: ASCALON

John hurried up the steps to the top of the wall and strode to where Baldwin and Reynald stood looking out at the enemy campfires, which seemed as innumerable as the stars. Closer to the walls, thousands of mamluks were massed before the nearest gate, ready in case the Franks tried to sneak out. They were less than a hundred yards off, but John could barely see them. It was a dark night, cloudy with no moon.

'The tide is out,' John told Baldwin. 'It is time, sire.'

'Are you sure of this?' Reynald asked. 'The lands beyond the sea wall are dangerous, a morass where sucking sand can swallow a horse whole.'

'We have no choice,' the king replied.

They rode across the city to where the army had gathered before the west gate. Most of the time the ocean crashed against the bottom of the gate, but the tide had receded, exposing the ground beyond it. They would have to go far out amongst the receding waters to avoid being seen by the Saracens. A local boy, who often visited the tidal flats to hunt for clams, had volunteered to guide them. He stood in front of the gate, biting his thumbnail.

'We haven't much time,' he said as Baldwin and John rode up to him. 'When the tide returns, it will come like a horse at gallop.'

Baldwin nodded to the men at the gate. 'Open it.'

The gate swung open and the boy led them out on a winding path across the dark tidal flat. Soon the ocean was washing against the ankles of John's horse. When he looked back, the walls of Ascalon had been swallowed up by the darkness. Suddenly there was loud shouting. '*Help! Help me!*' A knight had strayed just a short distance from the path picked out by the guide. His horse was mired in sucking sands, and the more it struggled, the deeper it sank. '*Help!*' the knight shouted again.

'You, sergeant,' Baldwin called quietly to a nearby foot-soldier. 'Silence him.'

The sergeant drew back his bow and let fly. The arrow hit the knight in the chest, and he cried out in shock. The second arrow lodged in his throat. Baldwin rode on. John watched for a moment as the knight slowly sank into the sands. 'God have mercy on his soul,' he murmured, and spurred after the king.

The waves were now slapping against the knees of John's horse. 'The tide is coming,' their guide called softly. 'We must hurry.' He began to jog, lifting his knees high. They angled back towards shore, but the water continued to rise around them. Then the land sloped up sharply. A moment later they were leaving the sea behind and riding on to the sandy shore. John looked south, but saw no sign of the Saracens.

'Praise God!' Baldwin said. He tossed their guide a pouch heavy with gold coins and then turned to John. 'Come! We ride for Jerusalem!'

NOVEMBER 1177: MONTGISARD

The morning dawned cold with a driving rain, and Yusuf wrapped his fur cloak tight about him as the army set out for Jerusalem. The rain muddied the ground and filled the ravines with turbulent brown water. By noon the sun had burned off the clouds and dried Yusuf's cloak, but the ground remained a morass of sucking mud. They did not reach Ramlah until mid afternoon.

The city had been deserted and everything of value carted away. Yusuf's men watered their horses and then put the city to the torch. They left it burning, sending roiling black smoke into the sky as they continued on towards Jerusalem. The road passed through low hills and then out on to a broad plain, which sat in the shadow of a tall peak named Tell al-Safiya, or Montgisard, as the Franks called it. The plain was bisected by a steep-sided ravine some twenty feet deep. It was flooded with fast-moving water from the rains. Yusuf's men had to dismount to lead their horses down the sides. At the bottom the turbulent water reached to the horses' chests, making their footings treacherous.

Yusuf dismounted and took a small meal of bread and water while his army crossed. He was finishing the bread when Saqr pointed to the horizon.

'Someone is approaching, Malik.'

Yusuf squinted but saw nothing. 'Can you tell how many?'

'It is hard to say. The ground is wet, so they kick up no dust. There could be dozens, or thousands.'

Yusuf made to call for Qaraqush, but the mamluk general was already approaching. He dismounted and nodded towards the horizon. 'We have visitors. Men returning from Arsuf or Lydaa, perhaps?'

'Perhaps.' Yusuf could now see sunlight flashing off steel in the distance. 'They are close.' He looked to the ravine. A third of his men had reached the far side. That left only eight thousand mamluks with Yusuf. And whoever these new arrivals were, they would arrive long before the rest of the army had crossed. 'Qaraqush, have those who have crossed return to this side. And send scouts to find out who is approaching.'

Yusuf paced as he waited for the scouts to return. He could now see tiny figures in the distance. There seemed to be thousands. Flags flew over them, but he could make nothing out.

'The scouts are returning,' Saqr said. Yusuf spotted a dozen mamluks in saffron yellow racing across the plain. 'They are driving their horses as if shîtân himself were at their heels.'

'The Franks,' Yusuf whispered. He called for Qaraqush. 'Have the men form ranks. Prepare for battle. *Quickly!*'

Qaraqush rode away waving his sword and shouting orders. The scouts galloped across the plain and pulled up before Yusuf. When they spoke, they only confirmed what he already knew.

'It is the Frankish army, Malik. They are here!'

'God is with us!' Baldwin cried. 'We have surprised them!'

John sat in the saddle beside the king and the other Christian leaders. They were atop a hill with the Frankish army behind them. The knights were in the front ranks, grouped in the middle. Thousands of foot-soldiers spread out to either side of them. They had marched through the night, taking the coastal road in order to avoid the enemy scouts. The morning's rain had profited them, dampening the dust that would have revealed their approach and slowing the Saracens. Now, they had caught them. Before John, the ground sloped down to a broad plain, where the Saracen army stood. The enemy was in chaos as men scrambled to form ranks. Thousands of warriors were stuck on the far side of the ravine that bisected the plain.

'Reynald!' Baldwin called. 'Are the men ready to charge?'

'Aye, sire. The knights will ride first to break their ranks. The sergeants will clean up the mess.'

Baldwin nodded and then turned to John. 'Help me from my horse.' The king could ride well enough, but his leprosy had weakened his legs, making it difficult for him to dismount. John helped him down. The king drew his sword and knelt with the blade pointing towards the earth. He bowed his head so that his brow touched the pommel.

'O God!' he prayed loudly. 'What I ask now, I ask not in my name but in the name of all the faithful, and in the name of your son, who died on the cross in Jerusalem. That same city is now under threat from the infidels. Give us strength, O Lord, that we may defend it. Guide our swords that we may strike down our enemies. Look with favour on the armies of God. In your name, Amen!'

The men began to cheer. Baldwin rose, and as John helped him back into the saddle the king grasped his arm and leaned close. 'Godspeed, John. Stay close to Reynald.'

John nodded and mounted his horse. He drew his sword and rode alongside Reynald, who scowled at him before pulling on his helmet. John pulled on his own helmet and readied his kite-shaped shield.

'Godspeed!' Baldwin called in his direction and raised his sword. 'For Christ! For the Kingdom!'

His cry was echoed by all the men down the line. '*The Kingdom*! *The Kingdom*!' The knights charged, and the sergeants poured after them.

John galloped down on to the plain. Ahead, the Saracen line was still forming. The Egyptian lancers had been caught on the far side of the ravine, meaning there would be no one to blunt the Christian charge.

Reynald spurred to the head of his men, and John kicked his horse's flanks to keep pace. They rode for the centre of the Saracen line. The men there were dressed in the saffron yellow of Yusuf's personal mamluks, and above them flew Yusuf's standard: a golden eagle on a field of white. The Saracens had bows in their hands, and John saw strings being drawn taught. They let fly. Several arrows hit the ground before John, and then one struck him in the chest. It penetrated his mail but was stopped by the padded vest beneath. Another hit him with the same result. John ignored them. His eyes were fixed on the Saracen line only fifty yards away. Forty. Thirty. John could see the men's bearded faces. The mamluks were shouldering their bows and readying their bamboo spears. John gripped his sword tight. Then he hit the line.

A Saracen spear shattered on his shield, and John swung out, catching his attacker in the throat. John's charger slammed its shoulder into a Saracen mount, and the Arabian stumbled and fell. John slashed to the right and left as he followed Reynald into the Saracen ranks. Behind him, he could hear yells of anger and pain as the rest of the knights hit the line. John caught sight of Yusuf just ahead. Then the Saracen line broke. The men facing John turned and fled, pushed back by the impact of the Frankish charge.

'For the Kingdom!' Reynald roared. 'Kill every last one of the bastards!' He spurred after the enemy, but the Saracens pulled away on their fleeter horses. Suddenly they stopped and turned. John spotted Yusuf at their centre, waving his sword overhead and shouting to his right. John looked in that direction and his eyes widened. The Saracens had not been retreating. They had been laying a trap.

'Reynald!' he shouted. He grabbed the regent's reins and pulled back, stopping him. 'We've gone too far!'

'Release me!' Reynald snarled and knocked John's hand away. 'We've almost won!'

'Look around you!' The Frankish knights had punched through the centre of the Saracen line, but to the left and right the enemy flanks were now closing in on them. They would be surrounded in moments.

'Christ's beard,' Reynald cursed. 'Back, men! Back!'

He turned his horse, but it was too late. A roar went up from the enclosing Saracens: '*Allah! Allah! Allah!*'

'I'll see you in hell, Saxon,' Reynald muttered. He spurred his horse straight towards the onrushing Saracens.

''Sblood!' John cursed and galloped after him. Ahead, Reynald had disappeared into the crowd of Saracens. John charged after him, swinging his sword in wide arcs. He felt blows raining down on him from all sides, swords and spears glancing off his mail. There were no other knights in sight. The Franks had been swept up in the flood of mamluks, and each knight was now an island facing dozens of circling men.

John glimpsed Reynald through the crowd of mamluks and forced his horse alongside the regent's. His surcoat was soaked in blood, though John could not tell if it was his or a Saracen's. 'To me!' Reynald cried. 'Men of Jerusalem, to me!'

A knight joined them, then another and another. Soon they had more than two-dozen men alongside. John and Reynald found themselves at the centre of the Christians and momentarily free from the fight. Reynald took a horn from his saddle.

'What are you doing?' John demanded.

'We have lost.' Reynald raised the horn to signal the retreat, but lowered it as there was a roar behind them. John looked to see the sergeants, with Baldwin at their head, slam into the Saracen line. The king drove into the Saracen ranks, hacking furiously at the enemy. Foot-soldiers came after him, spearing the Saracens off their horses. Reynald hesitated for a moment and then brought the horn back to his lips.

John knocked it from his hands. 'The King has charged. We must ride to join him.'

Reynald looked from John to Baldwin and then raised his voice. 'Retreat! Retreat, men! Re—'

John smashed the pommel of his sword into Reynald's face, knocking the regent from his horse. He waved his sword overhead. 'For Jerusalem! For Baldwin! Follow me!'

Yusuf watched as the victory that had seemed certain only moments before turned into defeat. His line of mamluks gave ground as the Frankish sergeants led by Baldwin cut into them. The Frankish knights had regrouped and were driving through Yusuf's men and towards the king. They joined up around him and pressed forward. Yusuf's men began to leave the field in ever greater numbers.

Yusuf looked to Saqr. 'Sound the retreat.'

'Are you certain, Malik?'

'Do it!'

Saqr raised a curved ram's horn and blew three times. Before the last of the piercing notes had faded men began to pull back, the line dissolving as mamluks rode for their lives. The Franks rushed after them. The knights led by Baldwin drove straight towards Yusuf.

'Come, men!' Yusuf shouted to the members of his khaskiya. 'Let us save ourselves.'

He turned and galloped away from the Christians. Ahead, at the edge of the ravine, hundreds of riderless horses were milling about. Yusuf's men had abandoned them in order to scramble down the steep side. Yusuf reached the edge and leaned back in the saddle as he urged his horse into the ravine, zigzagging down the slope. He reached the bottom and urged his mount into the water. The animal struggled against the swift current. '*Yalla! Yalla!*' Yusuf shouted in encouragement. But the horse stumbled on a hidden rock and fell.

Yusuf managed to free his feet from the stirrups just before he disappeared under the muddy water. He hit the riverbed and was tumbled head over heels by the swift current. Finally he managed to gain a footing and stand, breaking the surface. The water came up to his chest, but he was able to hold his ground by leaning into the current. He spotted his khaskiya some fifty yards upstream. He would never reach them while in the water. He began to make his way to the far side of the ravine. He lost his footing for a moment and drifted downstream. A mamluk on horseback was just ahead of him, and the current slammed Yusuf into the side of the horse. The rider grasped Yusuf's arm and held him there for a moment, but then Yusuf was forced under. He passed between the horse's legs and broke the surface again. He continued to struggle across and finally reached the far side of the ravine. He scrambled up the slope and collapsed, gasping for breath. He was covered in dark-brown mud and his head was ringing. His helmet was lost in the water. After a moment he forced himself to stand.

His army was no more. On the far side of the ravine the field was littered with dead and the Franks were cutting down any who remained. On Yusuf's side, scattered groups of men scurried from the field, heading for the hills to the south. A group of Frankish knights had crossed the ravine and begun to ride down the Saracens. Small skirmishes broke out here and there as groups of mamluks banded together to make a stand. Their bravery was foolish. The Frankish sergeants were starting to cross the ravine. Once they reached the far side, any mamluks remaining would be slaughtered.

Yusuf started south, towards the hills. He tried to run, but his right leg buckled. Gritting his teeth against the pain, he reached down and felt his knee. It was swollen and throbbing. He must have twisted it in the ravine. He looked up at the sound of approaching hoofbeats. A knight was riding towards him, sword in hand.

A sudden wave of fury swept over Yusuf. He had wanted peace. The Franks had forced him to fight, and, somehow, he had lost. But he would not lose his life on this Godforsaken field, and this Frank, at least, would pay for the humiliation he had suffered. Yusuf drew his sword. 'For Islam!' he shouted and limped towards the knight. The Frank spurred to a gallop and brought his sword slicing down. Yusuf managed to parry, but the weight of the blow knocked him to his knees. As he rose the knight wheeled his horse and came charging back. Yusuf parried another blow. But this time his sword went flying from his hands and he was knocked flat on his back. He rose to see that the knight had already turned. Yusuf looked about desperately. On the ground beside him was a dead mamluk, still gripping a bamboo spear. Yusuf prised the spear from his dead fingers and rose to see the knight bearing down. He stood directly in the horse's path and braced himself. At the last moment he plunged the spear into the charger's chest and dived to the side. The horse fell, throwing its rider. The Frank lay still for a moment before pushing himself to his feet and stumbling towards his sword.

Yusuf retrieved his own blade and turned to see the Frank staggering towards him. He wore a helmet that hid his face, but

Yusuf could see enough of his sparse beard to know his opponent was a young man. The Frank attacked with a roar, hacking down at Yusuf's head. Yusuf turned the sword aside with his own blade and swung backhanded. The Frank surprised him by charging, slamming his shoulder into Yusuf's chest before his blow could land. Yusuf stumbled backwards. He raised his sword just in time to parry a thrust that would have skewered him. The knight pressed the attack, and Yusuf gave ground. His knee ached, making him slow and clumsy. He stumbled, and the knight lunged to finish him. Yusuf just managed to sidestep the blow. He swung his sword up in a wide arc and hit his foe in the side of the helmet. There was a loud ring, and the knight fell to the ground, unmoving.

Yusuf raised his sword to finish him. Then he heard a familiar voice. 'Yusuf, wait!'

'*Wait!*' John called again. He dismounted and took a step towards Yusuf. John removed his helmet and Yusuf's eyes widened.

'John? What—?'

'Serving my king.' John gestured to the prone figure that lay between them.

'This is Baldwin?'

John nodded. Yusuf met his eyes. 'This war could be over now. Let me kill him.'

'I cannot.'

Yusuf hesitated for a moment and then raised his sword.

'Yusuf!' John took two steps forward. Yusuf paused, his sword held high. 'Leave him be!'

Yusuf hesitated a moment longer and then swung down. John was already in motion. His blade met Yusuf's steel only a handspan above the king's prone figure. The two friends locked gazes.

'You choose him over me?' Yusuf demanded.

'I choose to do my duty.'

Yusuf's lips pressed into a thin line. 'I am your friend, John. Your brother in all but blood.'

'He is my king.'

'If Baldwin dies, the Kingdom will be in chaos. I can take Jerusalem. I can bring peace, to your people and mine.'

John shook his head. 'I cannot let you kill him.'

John saw the knuckles of Yusuf's hand whiten as he gripped his sword tighter. Then he swung for John's head. John blocked the blow. Yusuf drove him back a few feet, slicing at his chest again and again. But Yusuf's injured leg made his steps slow, and John turned each blow aside with ease. Finally he stepped back and lowered his sword. 'I will not fight you, Yusuf.'

Yusuf's only response was to attack with renewed vigour. He slashed at John's side, and when John blocked the blow, he spun and swung for his head. John ducked, and for a moment Yusuf was completely exposed. John could have killed him, but he again stepped away.

'Fight me!'

'Never, Brother.'

'I am not your brother. You have betrayed me to fight with the Franks.'

'I did not betray you. I was captured by the Franks because I saved your life.'

'You could have come back to us, but you chose not to. You betrayed me, just like you betrayed my sister. You used her and left her.'

John's grip tightened on his sword. He felt the blood begin to pound in his temples. 'I loved her,' he said quietly. 'I would have stayed with her.'

'You made her into a whore!'

A roar boiled up from deep within John. He charged, hacking down at Yusuf's head. Yusuf sidestepped and swung for John's side, but John was already spinning away, just out of reach of Yusuf's sword. He attacked again, thrusting for Yusuf's chest. Yusuf parried, and John swung backhanded for Yusuf's throat.

Yusuf ducked and lunged. John just managed to twist out of the way of the blow, but Yusuf's blade still glanced off his side. The sudden pain in his ribs only made him angrier. He roared again and, gripping his sword with two hands, brought it slicing towards Yusuf's unprotected side. Yusuf recovered from his lunge just in time to block the blow. Their swords met and locked together, bringing them close. Yusuf head-butted John, snapping his head back. John responded by kicking Yusuf hard in his injured leg. With a cry Yusuf fell to his knees. John slammed the flat of his blade down on his wrist, and Yusuf dropped his sword.

John kicked the weapon away. He was breathing hard and his pulse was still pounding in his temples. Yusuf looked up at him and closed his eyes. He was prepared to die. John raised his sword, but froze. A memory had risen unbidden in his mind: Yusuf standing over him while John knelt, waiting for his friend to kill him. Yusuf had spared him then.

John lowered his sword. 'Go.'

Yusuf opened his eyes. They shone with tears. 'Kill me,' he pleaded. 'Do you not see? I have lost everything. I have been humiliated. Kill me.'

John tossed his sword aside and then gripped Yusuf under his arms and pulled him to his feet. 'It is only one battle, friend. Live to fight another.' He shoved Yusuf away, towards the hills to the south. 'Go!'

Yusuf hesitated for a moment and then limped away. John watched until he was sure his friend would reach the hills safely before turning and kneeling beside the king. Baldwin's face was masked in blood. John carefully removed his dented helmet. There was an angry wound above the right temple, but it did not look fatal.

Baldwin's eyes fluttered open. 'John?'

'I am here, sire.'

'What happened?'

'You have won the day. The enemy is fled.'

Baldwin reached up and touched the wound on his head. He winced. 'How did I come to be here?'

'You were knocked unconscious.'

Baldwin blinked, then nodded, remembering. 'I thought he would kill me—You saved my life, John.'

'I did my duty, sire.'

'I will not forget it. I owe my life, and this victory, to you.'

Chapter 25

John and Baldwin walked past scores of fallen Saracens as they crossed the plain towards where the first Christian tents had been erected. Most of the Franks were still running down the enemy, but a few hundred had begun to set up camp. Cooks were starting fires while other men gathered booty from their fallen enemies and piled it in camp, to be divided later. The men knelt as Baldwin passed on the way to his tent.

'Hail, Baldwin!' someone shouted.

'Long live the King!' another cried. 'Long live the saviour of Jerusalem!'

John followed Baldwin into the tent. Reynald was already there, giving orders as to how the camp should be set up. His nose was swollen and crusted with blood. 'Sire!' he cried. 'Thank God you are well.' Then he saw John and scowled. 'Guards! Seize that man!'

Two of Reynald's men grabbed John's arms.

'Stop!' Baldwin roared. 'Release him.'

'He struck me, sire,' Reynald protested. 'He broke my nose.'

Baldwin looked to John, who shrugged. 'He was trying to signal the retreat.'

'Is this true, Reynald?'

Reynald ignored the question. 'I am the regent. This man assaulted me. He should be placed in irons.'

'John saved my life.' Baldwin drew himself up straight and

409

looked down his nose at Reynald. 'If anyone should be placed in irons, it is you, Reynald. Had I followed your advice, Jerusalem would now be in the hands of the Saracens.'

'But sire—'

'Silence! I'll not hear any more of your excuses. You are my regent no longer. You may go.'

Reynald did not move. His face shaded red and his hands balled into fists.

'I said, go,' Baldwin repeated. 'Or shall I have the guards show you out?'

Reynald gave a perfunctory bow and stormed from the tent, followed by his men. Baldwin went to a stool and sat, slumping forward with his elbows on his knees. John suddenly remembered how ill the king was. 'A doctor!' he shouted. 'Bring the King's doctor!'

'I am well, John,' Baldwin replied. 'Only bring me some water.'

John poured a glass and handed it to the king. 'What now?' he asked. 'Who shall you appoint as regent?'

'No one. I shall rule alone.'

'Your mother will not like it, sire.'

'She will have no choice.' Baldwin grinned. 'You heard the men; I am the saviour of Jerusalem, John. She dare not oppose me now.'

Night had fallen but Yusuf stumbled on in the dark, tripping frequently over rocks, thorny shrubs tearing at his tunic. He glanced up at the stars to orient himself, then continued, walking south along the floor of a wadi, his boots sucking in the mud. His knee ached and he longed for sleep. But the night was chill, and if he stopped he would suffer from the cold. Worse, the Franks might find him.

He had escaped from the field of battle and retreated into the hills. As he walked south he had seen the occasional corpse of one of his men, but he had met no one living. He did not know how far the Franks would pursue his men, and he did not plan to find out. He would keep on the move for as long as he could. A hundred miles of desert lay between him and Farama, the easternmost outpost in Egypt, but he would find a way to cross it. He had to.

The moon rose to bathe the landscape in silvery light, and Yusuf moved more surely now that he could see his footing. But he was tired, so very tired. The sky was just beginning to lighten when he collapsed, unable to go any further. He fell asleep instantly, despite the cold that tinged his lips blue and left him shivering.

He awoke blinking against bright sunlight. He rose stiffly and gingerly put weight on his injured knee. He was in a hollow between two hills, the bases of which were lined with low, scrubby trees. Not twenty feet away a camel stood chewing its cud. It had a harness on its back to carry supplies, but whatever its cargo had been, it was gone now. Yusuf guessed that the camel had escaped from the baggage train during the battle. The lead rope that hung from its head had become tangled in the branches of one of the trees. The camel tugged on the rope for a moment but could not break free. It ceased struggling and resumed chewing its cud.

Yusuf edged towards the beast. 'Easy, friend,' he said softly. 'Easy.'

The camel regarded him impassively. Yusuf patted its neck while he untangled the rope. When he had freed it from the branches he led the camel a few feet away. '*La-that!*' Yusuf commanded, and the camel knelt. Yusuf swung on to its back, the lead rope still in his hand. '*Fauq!*' The camel lifted its back legs, then its front. Yusuf flicked the lead rope. '*Yalla!*' he called, and the camel moved off.

By noon he had left the hills behind and entered amongst the towering dunes of the Sinai desert. It was autumn, and the brutal, ovenlike heat of the Sinai was gone. But the desert was still hot, and sweat was soon dripping from Yusuf's forehead.

He tore a piece of fabric from the hem of his tunic and wrapped it around his head to keep off the sun. He could do nothing about his lack of water. He had had no food or drink for more than a day. By the time the sun set his mouth was sticky and dry, and he had developed a dull headache. That night he huddled next to the camel for warmth.

He rode under a bright sun the following day. Each time he reached the crest of one of the towering dunes, he hoped to see some sign of his men. He saw nothing. The pain in his head was worse now. It felt like a nail being driven ever deeper into his brain. His throat was parched and his lips were cracked. It became difficult to focus on the path ahead, and he began to nod off, sleeping while sitting upright. Near evening, while climbing a steep dune, he slumped from the camel's back, waking with a start as he hit the sand. He found himself rolling down the slope. He spread his arms and legs and slid to a stop. The camel was thirty yards off. It looked back at him for a moment before it trotted away.

'Wait!' Yusuf shouted hoarsely. The words were hard to force through his dry throat. '*Waqqaf*!'

The camel disappeared over the shoulder of the dune. Yusuf rose and stumbled after it. When he reached the crest there was no sign of the beast. He followed its tracks. It was difficult walking in the shifting sand. His knee ached. He was dizzy with thirst and exhaustion. Eventually he lost the camel's tracks. He staggered on until sunset, when his legs buckled. He slumped down on the warm sand and fell asleep.

'Yusuf!'

He awoke with a start. It was nearly dark, and a figure stood before him in the twilight. It was a thin man, straight-backed and with short, greying hair. Yusuf blinked and sat up straight. 'Father?'

The man nodded. 'You disappoint me, Son.'

'I am sorry, Father.' Yusuf felt a sudden overwhelming shame for having ordered his father's death. 'Forgive me.'

Ayub waved away his plea. 'My death is not important.'

Yusuf frowned, trying to marshal his fuzzy thoughts. 'Why have you come back?'

'You have betrayed the faith, Yusuf. You have strayed from the path set out for you by Allah.'

'It is not my fault. Turan—'

'His incompetence is no excuse. You put too much faith in your friends and family, my son. If they fail, you must push them aside. Nothing must stand in the way of driving out the Franks. That is all that matters. There can be no peace with the Franks. They are a pestilence. They must be eliminated.'

A pestilence. Yusuf thought of John. Not all Franks were evil.

'Even your friend has betrayed you to save his own,' his father said as if in reply to Yusuf's thoughts. 'You cannot trust the Franks. You must drive them into the sea. Allah has spared you for this purpose, my son. Do not fail him.'

Yusuf nodded. 'I understand, Father.'

Ayub turned and walked away.

'Wait! Father!' Yusuf rose and stumbled after him. He gained on his father. He reached out to touch him, then collided with him. Yusuf felt himself falling backwards, but strong hands caught him and lowered him gently to the sand.

'Father,' he whispered.

'It is I, Malik. Qaraqush.'

Yusuf blinked. The grizzled mamluk was leaning over him. 'Are you well, Saladin?'

'Allah,' Yusuf breathed, his voice rasping in his dry throat.

Qaraqush turned away. 'Water!' he called. A moment later he held a waterskin to Yusuf's lips. Yusuf drank greedily, the cool water a blessed relief. 'Are you well, Malik?' Qaraqush asked again.

Yusuf nodded, and when he spoke his voice was firm. 'I have seen the will of Allah.'

Yusuf rode up to the gates of Cairo at the head of two-dozen mamluks. Qaraqush had told him that after the battle these were all the men he had managed to gather. Thousands had been killed by the Franks or lost in the desert as they struggled back to Egypt. Yusuf's mighty army had vanished like the morning dew under the hot sun.

When the guards at the gate saw Yusuf, they paled. The mouth of one of the men opened, but he was unable to speak.

'What is it, man?' Qaraqush demanded. 'You look as if you had seen a ghost.'

'You live, Malik,' the guard managed. He knelt.

'Allah has spared me,' Yusuf told him.

The word spread quickly. As he rode through the streets, people came running. They called his name. '*Saladin! Saladin! Malik! Malik!*' By the time he reached the palace a crowd surrounded him. They parted, allowing Yusuf to enter. He found Selim waiting and Ubadah at his side. They wore the indigo robes of men in mourning.

Selim grinned broadly. 'I cannot believe it!' There were tears in his eyes as he embraced Yusuf. 'It has been days since the last men returned from the battle. We had thought you dead.'

'He nearly was,' Qaraqush said. 'I found him wandering in the desert. He would not have lasted another day under the sun.'

Selim clapped Yusuf on the back. 'We will have a feast to celebrate your return.'

Yusuf shook his head. 'No. There is work to be done. You must rebuild our army. Spend whatever it takes. I want a force stronger than the one I marched on Jerusalem. You have five years.'

Selim started to protest but then saw the look in his brother's eyes and nodded.

'Now, I wish to see my family,' Yusuf told them.

He went to the harem. Shamsa was waiting with tears in her eyes. She rushed forward to embrace Yusuf and buried her head against his shoulder.

'I thought I had lost you!' she sobbed.

Yusuf returned her embrace stiffly. 'I was spared.'

'Spared?'

'I was lost in the desert, but Allah spared me for a purpose. I will drive the Franks into the sea.'

Shamsa pulled away. 'At what cost, Yusuf? The people—'

'The people must be prepared to suffer to achieve the will of Allah,' Yusuf said firmly. 'As am I.'

'Is it Allah's will, or yours, Husband?'

'My will is His. I have seen what I must do, Shamsa. I will not be swayed.'

There was a moment of silence as Shamsa examined Yusuf anxiously, trying to understand the change that had come over him. Finally she spoke. 'You will attack the Kingdom again?'

'In time. But to conquer them, we will need more men than Egypt alone can provide. Mosul and Aleppo must be made to join my kingdom.'

'Aleppo?' Shamsa's eyes widened. 'What of Asimat? She is your wife. Al-Salih is your adopted son.'

Yusuf met her eyes. 'Allah has spoken to me, Wife. I will do what needs to be done.'

Historical Note

The story of Saladin Yusuf ibn Ayub's rise to become king of Egypt is well documented from both the Christian and Muslim sides. The Egyptian vizier Shawar was every bit as savvy as I depict him, and he paid for his double-dealing with his life. Yusuf's uncle Shirkuh did become vizier only to die suddenly – from overeating, the chroniclers claim. Yusuf followed him as vizier. Later he became king and put down the Nubian rebellion by burning their barracks. Nur ad-Din was wary of Yusuf's growing power. He sent Yusuf's father to curb the young king, and while Yusuf's decision to murder Ayub is my addition, it is true that Yusuf had a public argument with his father only days before Ayub died in a hunting accident. Nur ad-Din was preparing for war with Egypt when he died suddenly. Yusuf did take Damascus and marry Nur ad-Din's widow, Asimat, afterwards. In 1177 Yusuf invaded the Kingdom and came within miles of Jerusalem before being routed by King Baldwin at Montgisard.

John's story is also based in fact. The court of Jerusalem was just as riven by intrigue and infighting as I depict it. Agnes of Courtenay had many husbands, and many lovers, if the chronicle of William of Tyre is to be believed. History has often portrayed her as a meddling harpy, and while my account is not exactly flattering, I did strive to add some humanity to a woman who was forcibly divorced from her husband and then kept from her young children. The real Amalric did have a mild stutter and was prone to fits of uncontrollable laughter. He died suddenly, purportedly of the flux (dysentery), at a particularly inopportune time for the Kingdom. The plot to murder him is my own invention, but it is true that after his death, Reynald became lord of Oultrejourdain, Heraclius was named Archbishop of Caesarea and Agnes rose to a position of influence at the court. And there is nothing fictional about the poison that I have Baldwin use. *Al-Zarnikh* – or arsenic, as we call it – was well known in the Arab world and does cause symptoms similar to the flux, while also leading to loss of hair and yellowing of the fingernails.

The history of these years is so rich that I could not include everything. I combined the Egyptian campaigns of 1164 and 1167 into one. Yusuf actually defeated the combined armies of Mosul and Aleppo twice (first at the Horns of Hama in 1175 and second at Tell al–Sultan in 1176); he besieged Aleppo twice; and he was attacked by the Hashashin twice. In each case, I combined the events in order to avoid repetitiveness. In one notable case, I manipulated dates in order to streamline the story. Reynald de Chatillon was actually freed in late 1175, over a year after the date I indicate, as part of the agreement that brought the Kingdom on to the side of Gumushtagin. He was made lord of Oultrejourdain a short time later, much as I describe.

These changes aside, I have endeavoured to remain true to the chronology of events and the texture of the times. Even the most incredible elements of *Kingdom* are based in fact. A terrible sandstorm really did strike Shirkuh's army as it was crossing the Sinai, although I shifted the date of the storm from 1167 to 1168. The catacombs that John explores outside Alexandria still exist. The Kom el-Shoqafa, or Mound of Shards, was built by the Romans and filled with the dead over a period of four centuries. The bottom levels are now flooded and have never been fully explored. The Nizari Ismailis were also very real, as was their fortress stronghold of Masyaf. They disliked the name Hashashin, which, depending on the source consulted, was derived from *asasiyun* (faithful to the foundations of the faith) or *hishishi* (rabble), or perhaps meant 'users of hashish'. They preferred to call their assassins *fidais*, meaning 'devotees'.

Although it was seldom invoked, the law did allow men like John to appeal convictions before the High Court by fighting each of those who had voted against them. Most trials by combat were fought with staffs, not swords, but they were still violent affairs in which combatants were occasionally beaten to death. The trial by fire that John decides to undergo towards the end of the book was one of several forms of trial by ordeal, and actually one of the least dangerous. Trial by water, in which the defendant was cast into a pool of water and found innocent if he or she sank, sometimes led to drowning. The life of a canon was much as I depict it, although John is made a canon unusually quickly in my story – typically, laymen first spent at least eighteen months as an acolyte. Canons often lived in town, frequently with mistresses, and allowed their vicars to take their place at the canonical prayers. They were rarely present in church, save for Penny Masses, and when they were forced to lead Mass, they often shortened the service by reading a line here and there from the prayer book, confident that their parishioners spoke no Latin and would not know any better.

The world of medieval Syria and Egypt is a fascinating one. And its conflicts live on. The Crusades still evoke powerful memories: memories in the West of armour-clad knights on a mission to reclaim the Holy Land; memories in the East of savages from beyond the sea. *Kingdom* is of course a work of fiction, but I hope that it nevertheless demonstrates that, then – as today – there were good and bad men, truth and falsehood, on both sides of the conflict.

Book Three of the Saladin Trilogy
available soon in hardback

Holy War

JACK HIGHT

Saladin has been defeated and Baldwin rules once more, with
the Saxon knight John of Tatewic at his side. Yet all is not
well in the Kingdom of Jerusalem. Baldwin is dying, and rival
factions divide the kingdom as they plot for the throne.
Meanwhile, Saladin has gathered an army, the likes of which
the Holy Land has never seen. In June 1187, he marches
on the Kingdom at the head of twenty-four thousand men.
He has sworn to take Jerusalem, or die trying.

As the two armies march towards their climactic
confrontation, a new threat is rising. In England, Richard has
taken up the cross. He is the greatest warrior of his age, an
enemy unlike any Saladin has faced. And the Lionheart
is coming . . .

Now read on . . .

www.jackhight.com

Chapter 1

Yusuf tugged his warm panther-skin cloak more tightly about him. The chill wind from the north brought with it a stinging rain and the distant sound of masons' hammers. The winter weather had not stopped construction on the citadel rising on the hills south of Cairo. Nor would it prevent Yusuf's monthly inspection of his troops. The pennants that rose above the ranks of Yusuf's army hung wet and limp, but the men beneath them sat straight in their saddles, despite the rain that soaked their caftans and beaded on their well-oiled mail.

'You have done well,' Yusuf told his younger brother. It had been Selim's task to rebuild the army after the disaster at Montgisard. Four years earlier, Yusuf's army had marched within a few miles of Jerusalem before being surprised and routed by the Christians. Yusuf had lost thousands of men. Afterwards he had given his brother five years to rebuild the army. Selim had done it in four. The army before them was fifteen thousand men strong, larger than it had been before Montgisard. 'You have earned yourself a new name, brother: Saif ad-Din.'

'"Sword of Islam." It is a good name.' Selim bowed in the saddle. 'Shukran Allah.'

Yusuf spurred forward to inspect the ranks. He rode first past the *mushtarawat*, four thousand men strong, all mounted on horseback. They wore saffron yellow caftans over their mail to distinguish them as his personal troops. Each man carried a light bamboo spear in one hand and a small round shield in the other. Curved bows were slung over their backs, and swords hung from their sides. The rain pinged off their steel helmets. They were Yusuf's most fearsome warriors and some of his oldest friends. He nodded as he passed Husam, with his gold tooth, and Nazam, a bald-headed, lean man, quick as a snake. Yusuf acknowledged several other men, but it was the absences that struck him. The peerless archers Liaqat and Uwais, and the giant Qadir had all fallen at Montgisard.

Beyond his yellow-clad warriors were his brother's mamluks and those of the emir Qaraqush. Some of them wore *jawshan* vests composed of hundreds of tiny steel plates sewn together. Others wore mail or padded cotton lined with steel plates. Next came the five thousand men of the light cavalry, all in padded vests and with only bows and light spears for arms. Last of all, Yusuf rode through the ranks of the infantry. The five thousand men carried tall shields and long spears, which would allow them to turn aside charging cavalry.

When he had ridden past the final row, Yusuf turned his horse and cantered to the front of his army. It was a mighty force but still not enough for Yusuf's purposes, even if combined with the men of Damascus and the Bedouin warriors who would flock to his banner if Egypt went to war. To take and hold Jerusalem, he needed to unify all of Syria, including Aleppo and Al-Jazirah, the rich lands between the Tigris and Euphrates. His defeat at Montgisard had shown him that.

Yusuf turned to Qaraqush. 'Are there any cases for me to hear?'

The stout emir with the grizzled beard nodded. 'Prisoners!' he shouted, and the guards herded forward three men. Yusuf was disappointed to see that one of them was his cousin, Nasir ad-Din. It was not the first time that the young man had been brought before him. Nasir ad-Din had been only a boy of seven when his father Shirkuh died. He had been raised at the palace in Cairo and had become fast friends with Yusuf's nephew Ubadah. Yusuf had given his cousin Homs to rule, hoping that commanding others might teach him discipline, as it had Yusuf, but Nasir ad-Din had not yet set foot in his lands. He preferred to stay in Cairo while he enjoyed the revenues from Homs. Qaraqush pointed to him. 'Nasir ad-Din was found drunk in the barracks with two women. One of them was married.'

Nasir ad-Din was as thin as a stalk of wheat and, like a stalk of wheat, he was trembling in the wind, though more likely from fear or shame than the cold. His eyes were fixed on the ground at Yusuf's feet.

'Look at me, cousin,' Yusuf commanded. 'Explain yourself.'

'I—I meant no harm,' Nasir ad-Din began. He spoke haltingly at first, and then the words came out in a rush. 'Three of my men reached their eighteenth year this last month. They were freed and became full mamluks. A leader must share his men's joys as well as their pains. My father taught me that. I took them to Chandra's to celebrate. I fear I became quite drunk.'

'And the married woman? Who was she?'

'She never told me her name, Malik. She never told me she was married, either. I swear it! I—'

'Enough.' There was a time when Yusuf might have forgiven his cousin's indiscretions. After all, he too had once slept with another man's wife. But Yusuf had been another man then, before Montgisard, before the desert. 'You have disgraced yourself and our family with your drunkenness and lewd actions. There are few crimes more heinous than to sleep with another man's wife, and to do so in public, in the barracks amongst your men . . .' Yusuf shook his head. 'You are an emir and a member of my family. You should be setting an example for your men, not leading them into dissolution. You will suffer ten blows from the lash and you will pay a hundred dinars to the man you have wronged. As of tomorrow, you are banished from Cairo. Go to your lands in Homs and learn to rule justly and wisely. I pray, for your sake, that I do not hear further ill tidings of you.'

Nasir ad-Din opened his mouth to protest, then thought better of it. 'Yes, Malik.'

The next man to be brought forward was bald, with a fat face. His sodden caftan was plastered over a round belly. 'Shaad is a cook,' Qaraqush declared. 'He has been found guilty of thievery.'

'Malik, I never!' the man protested. 'I have been a cook for twenty years and more. I served your uncle, Shirkuh. I—'

Yusuf drew his sword and the cook fell silent. 'What did he steal?'

'Each month, he kept some of the money intended to buy food for the troops.'

Shaad fell to his knees on the muddy ground. 'It was only the once, Malik. I swear it. Have mercy!'

Yusuf dismounted. 'You have grown fat on food that was intended for your fellow soldiers. You shall lose your post and suffer a thief's punishment.' He gestured to the guards who grabbed the cook from behind. One of them stretched out his right arm. Another took a strip of cloth and tied it tightly just below the elbow, to staunch the flow of blood that was to come. As Yusuf raised his sword, the cook thrashed and squirmed. 'I will have your hand,' Yusuf told him. 'Hold still if you want a clean cut.' Shaad ceased resisting and Yusuf brought his sword down. The cook fainted and the guards dragged him away, leaving his severed hand behind on the parade ground. Yusuf's gut burned but he hardly noticed. It was always burning, of late.

Yusuf returned to the saddle as the final prisoner was brought forward. The man was very handsome, with a trimmed black beard and golden eyes. 'What did this one do?'

'Rape, Malik. A glass merchant's daughter.'

'There are witnesses?'

Qaraqush gestured for four men in silk caftans to approach.

With them came a woman, wearing a niqab that hid all but her eyes. 'Four men, as required by law, Malik.'

The prisoner met Yusuf's eye without flinching. 'It was no rape. She wanted it, Malik.'

'He lies!' one of the men in silk shouted. 'Look what he did to my daughter, Malik.' The woman removed her niqab. Her cheek was bruised, her lip split and bloodied. 'He has ruined her. What sort of bride price will I find for her now?'

'The mamluk will be stoned to death as decreed by law,' Yusuf declared. 'You shall be compensated for your loss. A hundred dinars.'

The condemned mamluk was shouting in protest as Yusuf turned his horse and rode for Cairo with his guard trailing behind him. He was cold and wet and in a black mood, as he often was after dispensing justice. He wanted nothing more than a hot bath and a warm meal, but that was not to be. No sooner had he shed his cloak in the palace entrance hall than Al-Fadil limped towards him. The tiny, hunch-backed secretary had been suffering from gout of late.

'The birds have brought news,' Al-Fadil said. Yusuf frowned. 'It is important, Malik.'

'Walk with me,' Yusuf told him and continued towards his chambers.

'I have a letter from the Barka. The Almohad sultan is said to be preparing his fleet to move on Tripoli, on the African coast.' Yusuf's forehead creased. He had sent Ubadah to conquer the coast west of Egypt over a year ago, but his nephew's victories had brought nothing but trouble. 'Reduce the size of the garrison. *Inshallah*, the sultan will take Tripoli from us. It has cost me more to keep the city than it pays in tribute.'

'Very good, Malik.' Al-Fadil took another scrap of paper from one of the pockets that lined his silk robes. 'News from Alexandria. Two more ships have launched to join your new fleet.' Yusuf could only nod. He stopped for a moment and clutched the wall, sweat beading on his brow as pain twisted in his gut like a knife. 'Are you well, Malik?' Al-Fadil asked in alarm.

'A passing indisposition,' Yusuf managed. He straightened and continued down the hall. He could not think of Alexandria without thinking of Turan. Yusuf had sent his older brother to govern the city after the Montgisard campaign. In only a few months in Alexandria, Turan had run up debts of more than two hundred thousand gold dinars, before he had died of what was officially declared as excessive use of hashish. Yusuf knew better. It had been justice, but the memory of his brother's death still pained him.

When they reached Yusuf's study, Al-Fadil handed him another scrap of paper. 'I thought it best that you read this in private.'

Yusuf scanned the message, written in the minuscule script used for the pigeon post. Al-Salih was dead. The young man had been the ruler of Aleppo, and Yusuf's son, the product of his affair with Asimat when she was still the wife of his lord, Nur ad-Din. Yusuf dropped the paper and went to stand at the window, his knuckles whitening as he gripped the ledge. 'The message does not say how he died.'

'It appears he was murdered, Malik.'

'And who rules in Aleppo now?'

'The boy's cousin, Imad ad-Din. He was given the city by his brother, Izz ad-Din, who rules in Mosul.'

Yusuf turned to face Al-Fadil. 'That cannot be allowed to stand. I cannot take Jerusalem if I must also defend Damascus from Izz ad-Din and his brother. You will begin setting aside coin for a campaign. We will march in spring, when the winter rains have ended. Go now and tell my brother Saif ad-Din to begin gathering arms and provisions.'

'Very good, Malik.' Al-Fadil moved to the door, where he paused. 'One more thing: I have received news that your wife Asimat is on her way here from Aleppo.'

Yusuf had not seen her in years. After they married, Asimat

had stayed in Aleppo with their son. He did not wish to face her now, but he could hardly refuse. 'You will inform me when she arrives.'

Al-Fadil bowed and left. Yusuf returned to the window. He thought of those nights long ago in Aleppo, when he had climbed through the window of Asimat's chambers to be with her. They had risked everything. They had made a child together. And now that child was dead.

The door behind Yusuf creaked open, and he turned to see Shamsa enter. His first wife was no longer quite the beauty she had been when he met her. Motherhood had left her with round cheeks and a small belly. But her skin was still flawless and creamy brown. And he still saw that enticing mixture of challenge and invitation in her dark eyes. She smiled, showing straight white teeth. Then her smile faded. 'You are not well, *habibi*.'

'I am fine.'

She came to him and wrapped her arms around his waist. 'You work yourself too hard. Come. We must get you out of these wet clothes.' She began to untie the lacing that secured his vest of golden *jawshan* armour.

Yusuf gently pushed her away. 'There is work to be done, wife. We will have war in the north.' He sat and placed a portable desk on his lap. He reached for a quill, but Shamsa plucked it from his hand.

'Surely that can wait until after you have had a bath. The roads will not be passable for some months.'

Yusuf picked up another quill. He did not want to bathe. He wanted to lose himself in work, to drive away his thoughts of Turan and Al-Salih and the man he had ordered stoned today. 'And we must be ready to ride when they are. I cannot allow Imad ad-Din time to build his strength in Aleppo.' Yusuf picked up a sheet of paper. His brow furrowed in concentration as he began composing a message to Al-Muqaddam, his governor in Damascus.

Shamsa watched him for a moment. 'You are not alone, *habibi*,' she said softly. 'You should share your burdens with me.'

'No.' Yusuf feared she would not call him her beloved if she knew all he had done. 'I am the king, Shamsa. They are not your burdens to bear.'

FEBRUARY 1182: CAIRO

Yusuf stood motionless, his face an expressionless mask as he waited in the entrance hall of the palace. Asimat would arrive any moment. Yusuf could feel sweat trickling down his spine. He had dressed in his kingly garb: robes of heavy gold thread, a tall white turban and a jewelled sword at his side. Selim and Shamsa stood just behind him, along with his children. Al-Afdal and his brother Al-Aziz were ten and nine now, almost old enough to be given lands of their own. They both fidgeted, unable to contain their boyish energy. Az-Zahir, who was two years Al-Aziz's junior, stood motionless, a mirror image of his father. The younger children – Ishaq, Mas'ud, Yaqub and Da'ud – were off to the side with their nurses and Yusuf's six daughters. Yusuf noticed the budding breasts of his oldest daughter, the child of a slave girl. He would have to find her a husband soon enough.

The doors to the hall opened and Yusuf squinted against the bright sunshine. Asimat came striding forward out of the light, followed by an entourage of guards and courtiers. They knelt while Asimat continued towards Yusuf. She seemed to have aged immensely in the five years since he last saw her. Her skin was still milky white and smooth, but now her cheeks were hollow and there were dark circles under her eyes. Her long black hair was touched with grey.

'Wife,' Yusuf greeted her.

'Malik.' She bowed. Her gaze moved from him to Shamsa,

and then to the children. She blinked away tears. 'I wish to speak with you, alone.'

'Of course. I will show you to your quarters. Selim, see that her retinue is taken care of.'

They did not speak as Yusuf led her across the palace to the harem. 'These will be yours,' Yusuf said as they entered a comfortable suite of rooms, the floors covered with thick goat-hair carpets and the walls decorated with silks. The windows looked out on a courtyard filled with fragrant rosebushes.

Asimat hardly spared a glance for her new home. 'It will do.' She met his eyes. 'You do not seem happy to see me, husband.'

'Why have you come? You could have stayed in Aleppo.'

'With the men who murdered my son? He did not die a natural death. He was poisoned.'

'I know.'

Her eyes widened. 'You know?' She seized his arm. 'Who did it? Tell me.'

'Izz ad-Din.'

'But he is Al-Salih's cousin!'

'He is an ambitious man. Now he rules from Mosul and his brother sits on the throne of Aleppo. With Al-Salih dead, they are the heirs to Nur ad-Din's kingdom. They will look to Damascus next.'

'Izz ad-Din,' Asimat murmured. 'I should have known.' All strength seemed to go from her, and she sank into a pile of cushions on the floor. She sat with her head cradled in her hands for a moment, then met Yusuf's eyes. 'I am the one who found him. He was alone in his chamber when he died. His cup of wine had fallen from his hand. His face was blue as if he had been strangled, but there was no sign of struggle. I should have been there. I should have protected him.'

Yusuf knelt beside her and took her hands in his. 'You did all you could.'

'No. There is one last thing I must do for my son. I must give him vengeance.' She clutched his hands. 'If you ever loved me,

Yusuf, then avenge me. Avenge our son. Take Aleppo. Kill Izz ad-Din and Imad ad-Din. Kill those who took my child from me.'

Yusuf looked away, unable to bear the sight of her grief. His stomach was burning again and he tasted bile in the back of his throat. 'Those who killed Al-Salih will suffer,' he told her. 'You have my word.'

Yusuf's shadow flickered on the wall before him as he knelt in prayer on the carpeted floor of the Al-Azhar mosque. He had come straight from his meeting with Asimat and had remained through the afternoon, evening and night prayers. Now the mosque was empty save for a dozen men of his private guard who stood around him at a discreet distance, their forms lost in the dark shadows beyond the tiny circle of candlelight in which Yusuf knelt. Another shadow detached itself from the wall between two of his men, and a man in a hooded cloak moved towards Yusuf. He had taken only a few steps when he froze, Saqr's dagger at his throat.

'Shall I kill him, Malik?' Saqr asked. Yusuf had made the young man the head of his private guard after he saved his life during the siege of Alexandria, years ago, and he had never had cause to regret the decision. The men called Saqr 'Saladin's shadow', because he was always at Yusuf's side.

'Please! I only wish to speak with Saladin.'

Yusuf rose to face the intruder. He was middle-aged, with a thick beard and the glint of mail armour beneath his caftan. After a moment Yusuf recognized his pale grey, hooded eyes. It was one of the guards who had come with Asimat from Aleppo. 'Say what you will,' he told the man.

'What I have to say is for your ears only, Malik. The Old Man sent me.'

'Search him.'

Saqr felt the man's robes. 'He is unarmed.'

'Come,' Yusuf told the man. He led him away from the

candles and into a shadowy alcove. 'Who are you?' he demanded in a hushed voice.

'Who I am does not matter. The deed has been done as you asked.'

'The boy did not suffer? His mother said—'

'The poison is painless, I assure you.'

Yusuf closed his eyes, fighting back nausea. He took a deep breath. 'Tell Sinan that he shall have his reward. I shall make certain that the Templars and Hospitallers no longer exact tribute from your people.'

'He will be pleased.'

Yusuf nodded and turned to go.

'One more thing,' the man called after him. 'If you should fail us . . . the blades of the Hashashin cut both ways, Malik,'

Read more ...

Jack Hight

SIEGE

It will be Christendom's last stand ...

The year is 1453. For more than a thousand years the mighty walls of
Constantinople have protected the capital of the Eastern Roman
Empire, the furthest outpost of Christianity. But now endless ranks of
Turkish warriors cover the plains before them, their massive cannons
trained on the ramparts. It is the most fearsome force the world has
ever seen. No European army will help: the last crusaders were cut to
pieces by the Turks on the plains of Kosovo. Constantinople is on its
own. And treachery is in the air.

From the intrigues within the Emperor's household to the Sultan's
harem and the savage fights on the battlements, *Siege* is a full-blooded
historical adventure novel.

'This is an ambitious book, written on an ambitious scale, offering a
fascinating picture of momentous events' *Daily Mail*

Read more . . .

Jack Hight

EAGLE

Book One of the Saladin Trilogy – A warrior is born

When the Crusader army is routed beneath the walls of Damascus, a young Saxon named John is capture and enslaved. He is bought by a Kurdish boy, Yusuf, for the price of a pair of sandals.

Timid Yusuf will grow up to become the warrior Saladin; John will teach his young master the art of war. And so begins the story of two enemies brought together by fate, and of a friendship that will change the face of the Holy Land.

'This is an ambitious book . . . a fascinating picture of momentous events' *Daily Mail*

'Excellent . . . a trip to a distant and dangerous era' Barry Forshaw

*Order your copy now by calling Bookpoint on 01235 827716 or
visit your local bookshop quoting* ISBN 978-1-84854-299-0
www.johnmurray.co.uk

From Byron, Austen and Darwin
to some of the most acclaimed and original
contemporary writing, John Murray takes pride in
bringing you powerful, prizewinning, absorbing
and provocative books that will entertain you
today and become the classics of tomorrow.

We put a lot of time and passion into what we
publish and how we publish it, and we'd like to
hear what you think.

Be part of John Murray – share your views with us at:

www.johnmurray.co.uk

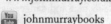 johnmurraybooks

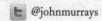 @johnmurrays

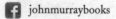 johnmurraybooks